Murder in Good M

When a tudor dance course a
for the violent death of a c
disappearance, Detective Cl
complex murder case on his hands.

From encounters with a varied bunch of informants – fina
businessmen, a radical woman criminologist and an ex-nark – he pieces together an intricate tale of rejection, obsession and chilling revenge …

Fringe Ending

Detective Chief Inspector Baxter investigates a deadly crime on the fringe of the university community in Cambridge when elderly Rupert Parsingham, great-grandson of a famous Victorian botanist, is murdered. Suspects include a scientist, a jewel thief and a playwright with bitter memories of the university city, and Baxter needs his daughter Emma's intervention to finally track down the killer.

'Margaret Moore elegantly packs in a wealth of wit and mind-stretching wickedness'

JOHN COLEMAN, ***Sunday Times***

By the same author

FORESTS OF THE NIGHT
DANGEROUS CONCEITS

MARGARET MOORE

Murder in Good Measure

Fringe Ending

Diamond Books
An Imprint of HarperCollins*Publishers*
77–85 Fulham Palace Road
Hammersmith, London W6 8JB

This Diamond Crime Two-In-One edition
published 1994

ISBN 0261 66258 9

Cover photography by Monique Le Luhandre

Printed in Great Britain

Murder in Good Measure

CHAPTER 1

Tum-tum-tee-tee-tum-tee-tee-tum-tum. The fingers danced across the *Financial Times* to their own tune. A tune which had nothing to do with the muzak filtering through an international departure lounge in London Airport that sticky August afternoon.

The barman looked without seeming to look at the drumming fingers with their well-groomed nails and the well-groomed face above them. It was the tanned, sharp-featured face of a blond man in his mid-twenties. A face that would have looked more at home in a VIP lounge than the Simla Bar, with its maple laminate and wickerwork and old-style fans. Fitments selected, so Len Wardle supposed, to con the customers into believing they were all sahibs now.

As he polished glasses, Len wondered how many of the current patrons shared the designer's passion for the defunct British Raj. Not the bespectacled Japanese girl who was dribbling orange juice over a paperback edition of *The World's Wickedest Women*. Not the gaggle of sober-suited Africans, weighed down by the proceedings of an ecological symposium. Not even the blond man, whose right hand drummed on as his left smoothed his copy of the *Financial Times*.

Len cursed himself for forgetting the name that went with that sharp-featured face. A well-known face, he felt sure, though not yet a famous one.

He cursed himself again for caring that he couldn't remember. Once it might have done him some good. Not any longer. As a Pan-Am air hostess scuttled past, he thought of his daughter Melanie doling out the duty-free somewhere over the Atlantic.

Of Melanie standing over him in the Orthopædics Ward at St Thomas's after his last spot of trouble five years ago and telling him she didn't want a coppers' nark for a father. She'd been right, Len conceded, fingering the scar on his jawline. With an effort of will he redirected his attention from the blond man to the sports programme on the miniature television screen on the shelf below the bar counter.

'Bitter lemon, please.' Len put a name to that voice straight away. But a flicker of Olly Brentwood's left eyelid warned him not to say it. So Olly was on a job. A job with its end in sight, to judge by the reek of mouth deodorant and the exaggerated care with which he carried his drink across the bar.

Olly stayed sober in business hours as a rule, but he had been known to celebrate in anticipation of a final pay cheque, with expensive consequences. Which was why the Brentwood Detection Agency now operated from a shabby fourth-floor bedsitter in Earls Court, and no longer advertised its services through the Yellow Pages.

Olly was good all the same. Beat the all-singing, all-dancing outfits hands down when it came to long-haul assignments requiring more sense and stickability than electronic gadgetry. He'd plenty of satisfied clients, one of whom had evidently passed the word to the fair man reading the *Financial Times*. Len watched in the bar mirror as Olly sat down at the reader's table.

The drumming fingers fell silent. The fair man flashed a wide, reflex smile that rang bells in Len's memory. Over the last two or three years David Sharrock, or Mr Sunnyscene, as the tabloid City editors dubbed him, had swum, scubadived and waterskied smilingly through several dozen photo-opportunities in the furtherance of his leisure enterprises. More recently, his smile had featured in a set of Government advertisements alerting business readers to the challenges of the anticipated Single European Market.

Len had vaguer recollections of something else. Like many another bratpacker, Sharrock had form. A juvenile police record of some sort. Len tried in vain to dredge up the details. Frustrated, he transferred his attention to the line-up of runners in the three o'clock at Newmarket now displayed on his television screen. More particularly to an Arab filly by the name of Oriental Ffizz.

Out of old habit he glanced occasionally at Sharrock and

Brentwood, failing to interpret their spoken exchanges but registering a transfer of envelopes. Brentwood left first, turning right as if heading for the terminal entrance. He moved hurriedly, swaying a little, no longer concerned to preserve the illusion of sobriety.

Sharrock glanced in his direction, not smiling now. Then his eyes met Len's and fell. He pulled out a wallet, made a business of consulting a set of travel documents, checked the time on his wristwatch. His fingers restarted their drumming, as if on their own initiative, but were quickly stilled.

Their owner read the *Financial Times* for five more minutes. Then he got up and walked unhurriedly towards the Customs enclosure.

Sixty-odd miles away, Oriental Ffizz was posing for photographs, having joined the ranks of the insiders.

Three weeks later, Len got out of the lift on the seventh floor and carried the holdalls the last ten yards to Janet's front door. Thanks to Melanie's friend who had lent them her Kos apartment for nix and to Oriental Ffizz who had contributed £500 to their spending money, it had been one of their better holidays.

In fundamentals, the mixture had been as in the seven years before, and none the worse for that. The good-humoured spats over Len's beachboob watching and Janet's window-shopping, the shared hassles with foreign currency and foreign menus, his annual proposal of marriage and her annual rejection. Such were the rituals which celebrated their relationship and safeguarded it.

'Oh my God.' Janet had gone ahead to open the door of her flat. 'Forgot to cancel, didn't I?'

Leaving her to dispose of the pile of junk mail and newspapers accumulated on the hall carpet, Len retrieved the most recent *Standard* from the letterbox and carried it through to the lounge. *Inquest on Earl's Court fire victim*, he read as Janet got out the tea-things in the kitchen.

'Poor Olly Brentwood's copped it.'

'Moira put a notice in the paper, did she?' Janet opened the hatch. 'Surprises me, everything considered.'

'Not Moira, it was some bloody reporter. Old Olly's ended up a news item. Funny in a way, for a bloke in a low-profile business.'

'What happened?'

'Set himself alight, or someone else did. Open verdict.'

'Ugh. Who'd have it in for poor old Olly? Never gave anyone any aggro barring Moira, and that was when he couldn't see straight. Can't have been for cash, either. From what Moira said, he hadn't two ha'pence to rub together.'

But he'd seen the sweepings under a few pricey carpets, Len reflected. 'Did it himself most likely, if he'd had a skinful. Dropped a match or a fag-end. Pad was a real tip last time I went round. Papers all over the place. Fire hazard if ever you saw one. Ninety-nine to one it was an accident, but they can't say if they've no proof, can they?'

'When did it happen?'

'Twenty-fifth. Day before we went to Greece.' The day Oriental Ffizz won at Newmarket. The day David Sharrock and Olly Brentwood exchanged envelopes at Heathrow. The videotape began to unroll in Len's memory. It stuck at an unsolved puzzle, the tune on the invisible piano.

'Poor Moira. She didn't want to split, but I don't see's she'd any option. Not with the kid to consider.' Janet said it in the throaty little voice that always excited him.

When he went out to the kitchen she was heating the teapot. He kissed her hair on top of her head where it needed restreaking.

'You and me's never going to split, are we, girl?'

'Never's a long time.' She swirled the hot water round the pot and emptied it down the sink, before spooning in the Brooke Bond.

He pulled her against him, unresisting, and unfastened the top button of her shirt. 'Tea in bed, then?' It was the last of the holiday rituals.

Afterwards, Len showered first and made a start on the backlog of newspapers. But he couldn't settle. Rooting round the lounge for a tape or a disc to match his mood, he noticed a new addition to the shelf of toys belonging to Janet's grandchildren. A miniature keyboard.

He plugged it in and strummed, moving his fingers in the same sequence and rhythm as Sharrock's, but far more slowly. The melody was familiar, a day-before-yesterday hit. But he couldn't for the life of him put a name to it. He played the first few bars again, a little faster, and again, at something approaching Sharrock's speed. Tum-tum-tee-tee-tum-tee-tee-tum-tum.

Then Janet opened the bathroom door and joined in.

'*Midnight. Not a sound on the pavement* . . . Great show, *Cats*.'

'One of the best.'

'You too, love, you too.' Showering him with talc, she whisked off to dress.

Len reopened the current *Standard* at the racing page. Tried to concentrate on the selections for tomorrow's meeting at Goodwood. Tried to block out the tune of *Memories* and the image of Sharrock's dancing fingers.

CHAPTER 2

'My trouble and strife. And she's all yours, mate.' Louis Mercier handed over the phone.

'Decided, Dick?' Jo Mercier asked in a snap-crackle-pop voice. Her Camden Lock shop had been open for two hours this February morning, Richard Baxter reminded himself, although his morning and his host's had only just begun.

Baxter's eyes ran lovingly over the curving top-rails and slender uprights of the three Georgian canterburies Jo had left at the flat for his consideration.

'The satinwood'll be perfect.'

'Sure? Rather thought you'd plump for the banded mahogany.'

'Maybe if the sun had been shining . . . But more often than not it isn't. Satinwood's a warming colour for dull weather. Thanks a mill, Jo. I'm really grateful.'

'So to prove it you'll stay to lunch? OK, food's not what you wish to contemplate just now, but there's this incredible new salad I've discovered. Best hangover cure in creation. Ask Lou.'

'Take your word, Jo. Love to add to the testimonials, but—'

'But me no buts. It's Friday. Sarah's weekending away, you say. So what's the rush? Another date?' Her voice took on a coy tone.

'Spring-cleaning assignment. Want to clear some of my clutter before she gets back on Tuesday, and I'm on duty tomorrow.'

'Lucky old Sarah.' A distant tinkle. 'Oh shit, a customer. 'Bye, darling.'

''Bye.' Baxter replaced the receiver and turned to his host. 'Be on my way, then, Lou.'

'Something for the road? Hair of the dog? More coffee?'

'The latter. Help myself.' Baxter wandered back, mug in hand, to join Mercier at the penthouse window and share his view of Tower Bridge and the grey, empty river. He didn't see himself coming back to London or the Metropolitan Police, but after reunions like last night's he hankered a little after both. And after the companionship of old friends. 'Never thought to see you a Dockney, my son,' he said.

Mercier laughed. 'Toytown-on-Thames gets you down, does it? And you a Brummie. Plenty of my mates in the Met, Londoners born and bred like me, feel it worse. Rape of the Port, rape of the City, rape of the East End. Who wants to be faced with that lot at the end of a day's work, they say. So off they skedaddle to the suburbs, first chance comes along.'

'How come you and Jo bucked the trend, then?'

'Bloody-mindedness, if you like. Why should the square-eyed whizzkids have all the best views of the river? Our river. First Merciers hereabouts were Huguenots. My dad was a lighterman, Jan's a totter. Docklanders and proud of the place. Brought us up to be proud of it. Besides, it's the proper setting for this lot.' He gestured at the several dozen naïve ship paintings on the walls behind them.

Baxter nodded. 'They deserve it.' Canalettos were more

to his taste, but the rough vigour of these seamen's pictures was truer to the spirit of the once-busy river.

'What are you collecting yourself these days?'

'*Collector's Guides*, mostly. Which is where the canterbury comes in. Sarah'll have more shelf space for her *Lancets* when she gets back from Hare Holt.'

'Hare Holt? That's the Lakes' stately home, isn't it? Friends of yours?' Lou sounded suddenly very wide awake.

'Lord, no. Place is run as a cultural centre. Sarah's going to a weekend course there—Tudor dance. Frances Lake and she belong to the same historical dance society. Why the interest?'

'No special reason. If you'd mentioned a Rothschild or Hambro pad you'd have got the same reaction. Square Mile names, and I'm an honorary Square Miler these days remember.'

'Ah yes. How goes your City of London secondment?' Lou had probably said something on the subject last night at supper, but Richard's recollections of the table-talk were more than a little hazy.

'Better than I'd hoped. Jo thought I was crazy to take it on. Said I'd be bored silly sifting through accounts or fooling around with fancy surveillance equipment. Hasn't worked out like that. Liaison post, they call it. Most of the time, I do what I do best. Nosing around pubs, salerooms. Lots of these City bratpackers want to get into antiques. Fast. Don't know their Aubussons from their anti-bloody-macassars and can't be bothered to do their own homework.'

'Which is where Uncle Lou comes in?'

''S right. I tell you, Dick, you'd never believe what some little buggers'll cough up in exchange for a word in season at a viewing day. Sometimes they'll even squeal for free—to do the other bloke down. Biggest tip ever came my way landed on my desk ten days ago. From an anonymous admirer.' A sudden pause.

'You can't stop there, Lou.'

'Sorry, old son. Not that I don't trust you, but I've got this superstitious streak, you see. If the thing works out, it could mean promotion when I transfer back to the Met.'

'Not before time.'

Mercier nodded. 'Jo wants to sell her share in the Camden Lock shop—start her own little business in Docklands. It'll cost her a bob or two and I'd like to help out financially. But I've this crazy notion there's Someone Up There or Down There waiting to see if I deserve a break, waiting to slap me down if I open my big mouth too soon.'

'I take it we're talking corruption in high places?'

'You're talking to yourself, Richard.'

'Shit hitting the fan in one of our more prestigious financial institutions?'

Lou moved away from the window and subsided into an armchair, from which he smiled sweetly upwards, arms folded above his head. 'Let's talk about you. What's decentralization done for the Mid-Anglian Constabulary?'

'Put two miles between me and Victor Highcroft, now I've moved down the road to Holtchester District.'

'Improvement?'

'Decidedly. Clay Warren—my uniformed Super—and I talk the same language, whereas Highcroft—'

'Communicates in Evangelical Systemspeak, or did during his sojourn at Star Street.'

'That's it. He means well, and he's not stupid. But he's far more enthused by whatever fancy new system he's designing than run-of-the mill CID work. A think-tanker by temperament, I'd say. As a line manager he's an unmitigated disaster.'

'You could have had his job if you'd tried for it.'

'Maybe.'

'Will you have a go when he packs it in.'

'Maybe.'

Lou laughed. 'No comment? Tit for tat?'

'No . . . Honestly. I just haven't given it a thought.'

'Give the Met a thought, then. Be good to have you back. OK, you nearly burnt out last time. But you weren't alone. And you're older now—better able to pace yourself.'

'No, Lou. You and Jo have found your rightful habitat. Sarah and I have found ours.' Baxter picked up the canterbury, impatient, even on this bleak February morning, for Kings Covert—the old house, the garden, the little orchard and the half-made terrace. And for Sarah's company when she came home on Tuesday.

'Let's compromise,' Frances Lake said firmly. 'Let's do what I suggest.'

Sarah Baxter joined in the acquiescent laughter. It was a tribute to the speaker, she reflected, that the laughter was friendly. Like the other members of the Holtchester Historical Dance Society committee, now assembled in the winter parlour of Hare Holt Manor, Sarah admired her hostess enough to put up with her occasional bullying.

The programme for the Tudor dance course had finally been settled. The last, faintly ridiculous, bone of contention had been period costume. In view of the lack of laundry and dry-cleaning facilities, it was now agreed that Tudor dress would be worn only on Saturday and Monday evenings. The Saturday evening programme would consist almost entirely of songs and dances by selected skilled exponents, known to possess a change of costume. The Torch Branle, a simple, sociable and photogenic dance, would be the sole item in which everyone would be encouraged to participate.

Sarah checked her watch as the meeting broke up. Three-thirty. Plenty of time for a second cup of tea before taking up her post at the registration desk. As the other committee members gathered round the huge fireplace, she carried her cup to the window-seat for a better view of the grounds. She had come to Hare Holt, she reminded herself, to escape the concerns of her part-time medical practice and the good works that gobbled up most of her spare time. To escape the twentieth century.

The view from the mullioned window was not, after all, any more relaxing than the caffeine in Sarah's Earl Grey tea. Much had been achieved since her last visit two years before. The South Front and the East and West Wings of the E-shaped Elizabethan manor were now complemented by formal gardens in late Tudor idiom. Their overall effect was dramatic rather than restful.

Box hedges, topped with topiary effigies of men, animals

and ships, separated square and oblong knot gardens, their geometric patterns defined, this February afternoon, by variously coloured sands and gravels. Some of the plots had stone artefacts as centrepieces. From where she sat, Sarah could see three heraldic beasts of uncertain species perched on pillars, two sundials and a Diana fountain spouting water from its stone nipples.

'I do hope we haven't packed too much in,' said a voice in her ear.

She realized just in time that her hostess was referring to the course programme rather than the horticultural reconstructions.

'No, no, I'm sure we haven't.' Sarah noted with slight surprise the anxiety of Frances's handsome face beneath its well-disciplined coronet of grey-blue hair. Over the last few years the house and grounds had been the venue for an astonishing assortment of cultural activities, well publicized in the local media.

'I'm afraid I spoke out of turn in committee.' Frances perched beside Sarah on the window-seat. 'I know it's Haviland's show, but the HHDS haven't run a residential course before, and as a member I'm keen everything should go well. Haviland's a poppet, but he's not exactly God's gift to administration, is he?'

'Good teachers seldom are,' Sarah observed, catching a glimpse of the spare, gesticulating figure of the Course Director. Haviland Prynne, by profession a Cambridge mathematics don, was an enthusiastic exponent of the European tradition of courtly dance, with a special affection for the Renaissance period.

'Quite. Don't think I don't appreciate Haviland,' Frances said hastily. 'It's largely for his sake I'm concerned the weekend should succeed. But also, to be honest, for the sake of Hare Holt. I'd like to see it become an annual event.'

'Yes, I imagine it's reassuring to have a nucleus of groups who use the house on a regular basis. People you can trust to behave responsibly.'

'Reassuring both socially and economically,' Frances said bluntly. 'Robin and I aren't getting any younger. Hare Holt does well out of summer visitors at present, but expenses are heavy. We want to build up a regular winter income, to make sure the house is a going concern before we hand over the reins.'

'An impressive inheritance,' Sarah murmured, thanking her stars that no one had ever saddled her with a vast heap of four-hundred-year-old masonry. Her own eighteenth-century house, little more than a cottage, which she and Richard had chosen seven years before after much deliberation, was a joy to them both.

'Oh, our children don't want the place for themselves, you know. Too much for Derwent to manage, on top of his responsibilities at the bank. And Fenland winters don't suit Gabriella. Idea is to set up a trust with local community representation. A centre for English Renaissance studies is what we have in mind. Nothing too academic, though. We'd like to convert the stables into craft workshops. Build Real Tennis courts. And we'd hope to retain family tenancy of the East Wing, for Robin and me and the grandchildren's holidays.'

'Glorious place for children to grow up in.'

'Yes.' Frances bit her lip. 'Which brings me to what I especially wanted to talk to you about, Sarah. Why I'm so glad you're not commuting.'

Kings Covert was only fifteen miles away, but Sarah, with her husband's approval, avoided night driving in winter months outside the line of duty. 'Oh?' she prompted.

'It's Marina—my granddaughter. She's just six. Don't think you've met her?'

Sarah shook her head.

'Been staying down here these last few days, because her mother's in Queen Charlotte's. New arrival's expected any day now, but Gaby's had two recent miscarriages. Bio-chemical problem I don't quite understand. Anyhow, they insisted on hospitalizing her six weeks early.

'We'd have carried off Marina down here straight away, but everyone felt it was important for her to maintain regular contact with her mother. Derwent took time off from the bank when he could and looked after her in London with the help of a really excellent au pair. Swedish girl. Then Kirsten left a few weeks ago for no very good reason, and work was piling up on Derwent's desk. He did the sensible thing and brought Marina down here.'

"So what's the problem?'

'The child's just not herself, Sarah. Withdrawn. Can't concentrate. Shows no interest in cooking or modelling or any of her usual activities. Same story from the village school, and her class teacher's a delightful woman.'

'Don't you think she's just worried about her mother?'

'That's what Robin thinks. He gets on to her wavelength more easily than I do, oddly enough. She'd a nightmare in the early hours one morning, and I did my nut trying to get her back to sleep. Then Robin took over—settled her in five minutes.'

'Does Marina know about the dance course?'

'Oh yes. Haviland kindly said she could join in, and I hope she will. She really brightened up when I took her to the Cambridge dress hire shop to choose a costume. Trouble is, I'll have so much else to attend to this weekend I shan't be able to give her the attention she needs. Robin and Derwent should be here all day tomorrow, as it's Saturday, but I did wonder, Sarah, whether you could keep an eye out for her this evening. I know it's a dreadful imposition . . .'

'Nonsense, I'd be delighted. Perhaps Marina and I should get acquainted before the hordes descend. Where is she now?'

'In the kitchen with Pat. D'you know Patricia Gorridge? Officially, our bursar stroke housekeeper. Unofficially, all kinds of everything. Knows far more about local history than Robin or I ever will.'

'My ex-patient.' Sarah recalled that without her professional advice to Mrs Gorridge, then torn by the irreconcilable demands of a tough DHSS job in Holtchester and a housebound mother in Fen Holton, Hare Holt might have been denied its paragon.

They found Patricia, a short, sturdy figure in white overalls, kneading dough in the New Kitchen, which dated, so Sarah had read in the guidebook, from the house's Edwardian modernization. Marina, a fine-boned child, with nut-brown hair woven into looped braids, was filling small wooden bowls with pot-pourri.

'On your own, Pat?' Frances Lake asked. 'Where's Audrey?'

'Laid up with 'flu. Her husband's just off the phone.'

'Oh *no*!' Frances's worry-lines deepened. 'You can't possibly cope with the catering single-handed. I'll organize a dogsbody rota from among the course members.'

'If I can help in any way . . .' Sarah began.

Patricia smiled. 'Thanks, Dr Baxter. If five or six people could spare an hour or two, we should manage. No need to involve everyone. Mrs Dryden brought a freezerful of pies over this afternoon, and she'll be back with the pottage very shortly.'

'Pottage? As in mess of?' Sarah asked.

'Thick soup. Modified Tudor recipe,' Frances cut in. 'We're having one or two period dishes at every meal. Deborah Dryden's idea—and a good one, don't you think?'

Sarah murmured endorsement, praying that the cook had reduced the proportions of sugar, spice and animal fat beloved of their ancestors.

'Deb's become something of an expert on Renaissance cookery,' Frances went on. 'So nice for her to have found her own niche. Coulter's devoted, I'm sure, but he's also rather—well—overwhelming. Deb made some lovely things for our charity feast.'

'And Mrs Gorridge is an expert bread-maker, I see.' Sarah watched the housekeeper's firm fingers slapping the dough. 'Any special sort?'

'It's for manchets, for tomorrow's breakfast,' Patricia said. 'As eaten by Queen Elizabeth, so Mrs Dryden tells me. I've a feeling they may lie heavily on modern stomachs, so I've asked my son to pick up some wholemeal loaves from Marks and Spencer's. Would you mind if Nigel stayed for supper, Mrs Lake?'

'Of course not.'

'He's between contracts—got time on his hands. I wouldn't say he's domesticated, but he's capable of clearing dishes and stacking the dishwasher. And he's promised to give me a lift home afterwards. My scooter's been acting up, and there's rain forecast.'

'Fine—fine, Pat.' Frances Lake's eyes strayed to the several dozen virgin candles now fixed in holders and lined up on the kitchen shelves. 'I see we're well provided for the Torch Branle. Deb and Haviland have contributed, I believe. Do we know which candlesticks are whose?'

'The dozen brass ones belong to Mr Prynne and one of his friends. He says he can tell them apart.'

'No doubt. Haviland's obsessional as they come.'

'The pewter ones are all yours or Mrs Dryden's. Marina's marked the bases of yours with nail polish.'

'Making yourself useful, are you, chicken?' Frances crossed the kitchen to caress her granddaughter. 'Going to take that pot-pourri up to the bedrooms now?'

'Come with me, Grandma?' Sarah was startled by the look of panic on the child's face, the hand clutching at her grandmother's cardigan.

'Sorry, darling, I just haven't time. Perhaps Dr Baxter . . .'

Sarah picked up her cue. 'Love to. It's ages since I was last at Hare Holt, Marina. I really need someone to show me round.'

Marina looked her in the eye for several seconds. 'All right,' she said at last.

CHAPTER 3

'How many are we?' Haviland Prynne shouted above the babble in the screens passage.

Sarah totted up the ticks on her checklist. 'Fifty-nine. One cancellation, so we've eight still to come. Not bad going.'

'Not good either, considering we're within half an hour of supper.' Haviland fiddled with the yellow Course Director badge on his black sweater. 'Unpunctuality is a bloody nuisance.'

Lowering his head, he charged through the open doors of the great hall, where the newly enrolled participants were drinking sherry. Frances Lake's grey-blue head bobbed up every few minutes as she wove among the throng, introducing pink-badged visitors to white-badged members of the HHDS. She moved quickly but gracefully, almost as though she were dancing a hay.

'Poor Haviland.' Lucy Talbot, Sarah's companion at the registration desk, looked up from the badges she had been colouring with Marina's wax crayons.

'Poor us.'

The course director had left it to the other committee members to cope with the last-minute shortfall in visitors' badges and several dozen other minor hitches. While Frances Lake, as hostess, concentrated her energies on the sherry party, and Deborah Dryden laboured with the Gorridges in the kitchen, Lucy Talbot had helped Sarah cope with registrands' queries and amuse Marina.

The child, at Lucy's instigation, had embarked on the creation of a picture-story book, a project which might, Sarah hoped, extend throughout the duration of the course. The heroes of the tale were white mice, kissing cousins, so it was to be surmised, of the artist's London pets: their enemy a marmalade cat, sharp of tooth and long of whisker, who had no real-life counterpart its creator would admit to. In the course of an hour, Marina, deeply absorbed, had illustrated four episodes in full crayon colour. At Lucy's suggestion, because the mechanics of writing were still beyond her, she had dictated the accompanying narratives to whichever adult was free to act as amanuensis.

'Shall we hide your book away for today?' Sarah suggested, noting signs of boredom in the last dictation. 'Would you like to give it to your Mummy when it's finished —a surprise present?'

'To Gramps,' the child said firmly. And five minutes later, when Robin Lake appeared in the screens, she hurled herself upon him without a backward glance. The expression on the merchant banker's bearded face as he picked her up was both loving and attentive. A man, Sarah had concluded from her few earlier encounters, who would dispense money prudently and refuse it kindly.

'Tell you something, Lucy,' she volunteered as they began to tidy the registration table. 'We've known each other for six months, but it wasn't until I saw you in action this afternoon that I could really believe you were married to a Bishop.'

Lucy laughed, the laughter lighting one of those faces that looked wonderful at thirty-something and would look wonderful at fifty. A face that might have been a Florentine angel's had its frame of springy hair been tawny instead of black. 'How do I usually strike you?'

'As a free spirit.'

The younger woman flushed.

'Sorry. I didn't mean to be offensive.'

'You weren't. Someone else said the same thing recently. At the risk of sounding pi, I quoted the collect for peace at him.'

Sarah looked blank.

'The one about God's service being perfect freedom.'

'It must be lovely to have a faith like that. I do envy you, Lucy.'

'Not something I can take credit for. I was born into a believing household, and I've never doubted, probably because I shy away from life's hard questions. And even if I've always had that deep-level freedom, I do miss the ordinary kind. There was a travel agent's near our London vicarage. Every time I saw ads for last-minute bargains I wished Jon and I could drop everything and run.'

'But you feel freer in Fenport?'

'Yes. It's my home town, you see, and my mother still lives there. She's marvellous about babysitting. Besides, the children are nine and eleven now. We have such fun exploring the Fens together. Nature reserves, windmills, farm museums. I just wish Jon could come with us more often.'

'He's a heavy workload?'

'Horrendous. The Dean says it'll settle down, and I do hope he's right. The Dean's been a lifesaver. A grandfather in God to all of us. And there's so much going on in the cathedral, too. The people who work there—both paid staff and volunteers—are so friendly. Almost an extended family. I'm really awfully lucky. You were right, though. As a Bishop's wife I'm a fraud. I've tried hard to bone up on doctrinal issues and synod politics. No joy. Anything beyond fund-raising and arranging flowers defeats me. I sometimes think I should have married a verger.'

'Lucy! Someone I'd like you to meet.' Frances's pink-tipped fingers beckoned. In the same instant, noises off signalled the arrival of more latecomers.

'Do go!' Sarah urged, wondering, as her companion obeyed, about her marriage to the Church of England's most recent and possibly most photogenic Bishop. Jonathan Talbot's decision to attend the course had surprised and delighted his hostess. Frances had, however, raised a few HHDS hackles by using his name and that of the property magnate, Coulter Dryden, in a pre-course publicity hand-out.

Talbot had visited the registration desk only to deposit his and Lucy's luggage. Long-standing engagements would force his absence this evening and tomorrow morning, he had explained, with the apologetic grimace Sarah recalled from brief encounters at Age Concern meetings.

Leaving the sherry party early to check that all was well in the kitchen, Sarah nearly collided with the bulky figure of Deborah Dryden in the screens passage. Stepping backward, Deborah caught her heel on something underfoot. Sarah bent to retrieve a headsquare.

'Whose . . .?'

'Karen East's.' Sarah folded the square, which was decorated with a garish miscellany of wildfowl and looked as though it had been washed more than once in the wrong detergent, and hung it on the peg above a lovat tweed coat. 'Karen was one of the very late arrivals. I suggested they left their things here until after supper. What is it, Deb? Feeling wonky?'

Deborah was standing with her back to the wall opposite the row of coathooks, her eyes fixed on the headsquare, colour draining from the unrouged areas of her heavy face, the fingers of both fat, ringed hands digging into her cashmere-covered solar plexus.

'Here. Sit down for a sec.' Sarah guided her to a chair, pushed the permed taupe head gently forwards. Within seconds she felt resistance.

'So sorry—don't know what came over me, Sarah. Not like me to pass out. On my feet too long in the kitchen, I suppose.'

'Expect you're right.'

'This East girl. Name doesn't mean anything to me. Is she a new member?' Deborah asked.

'No. A pink-badger. Londoner, I seem to remember.'

A colourless creature, Sarah had at first supposed, from Karen's drab clothes and gawky, self-effacing manner. A girl unhappy with her image but too cowardly to change it. But the voice with which Karen East had announced herself hadn't quite fitted. A deep, attractive, self-confident voice, a voice that might at any moment give way to giggles.

Dismissing her restless patient with orders to stay off her feet for the remainder of the evening, Sarah also dismissed thoughts of Karen and hurried to offer assistance in the kitchen.

Patricia Gorridge, who was straining vegetables, introduced her son, Nigel, who looked to be in his mid-twenties. The Gorridges were physically similar. The same stocky build, pale red hair and broad faces. But there was a marked difference between the two in current mood, if not in temperament. The housekeeper, obviously hot, was not in the least flustered. Steel clashed on steel as her son loaded the first course on to a trolley and propelled it at high speed over the uneven floortiles. Why such urgency, Sarah wondered. It was hard to believe Nigel was hell-bent on getting Deborah's pottage to table in prime condition.

'Are you happy working here, Mrs Gorridge?' she asked Patricia as they transferred the second course to serving-dishes.

'For the time being. A job near the village made life easier when my mother was alive—'

'So you've lost her? I'm sorry.'

'No need, thanks. She was glad to go. Mrs Lake was good about giving me time off when I needed it, so I feel I should stay on until the end of the summer.'

'She'll be sad to see you leave. You're quite an expert, aren't you, on the history of the house? But perhaps you'd prefer a post with more scope?'

'It's not that. Much as I like the Lakes, Dr Baxter, I don't altogether approve of what they're doing here. And more particularly what they're going to do. I don't want to be part of it.'

'But surely, if you made your views known . . .'

Patricia laughed, not unkindly. 'As a member of the local community? Waste of breath, I'm afraid. Mrs Lake prefers the idea of democratic process to the reality.'

Recalling Frances's performance in committee, Sarah found it hard to disagree.

'She'd like to be on Christian-name terms with me, for instance,' Patricia went on. 'I suppose you think it's small-minded to refuse, but I hate shams. Shall I tell you what sticks in my throat most of all?'

Sarah nodded, curiosity overcoming her growing sense of disloyalty to Frances.

'Know those stone letters on the parapet—DL?'

'Denys Leveson's initials. Yes. Self-made Elizabethans were no slouches at self-advertisement, were they?'

'And DL fits Derwent Lake. That's why Mrs Lake persuaded her husband into buying this place. I'm prepared to bet any son of Derwent's will have the same initials.'

'And you object to the dynastic principle? Aren't you taking this a bit too seriously? When I heard Frances tell the story she made a joke of it.'

'She would. It's the attempt to turn the clock all that way back I object to. Occasional weekends like this are fine. But why make the place into a Renaissance museum? What of the hundreds of people who lived and worked on this estate in the years between? People who've as much right to be remembered as Denys Leveson or Derwent Lake.'

'I still think you should say your say.'

'Perhaps I shall. But not this weekend.'

For a moment Patricia's steady voice faltered. Sarah realized that she had misread the housekeeper's mood. That her ex-patient had something more urgent and more personal on her mind than the ambitions of her employers. As Nigel clattered back, grim-faced, with the dirty soup-plates, Sarah wondered whether he was the focus of his mother's anxiety.

As he prepared to do his rounds with the main course, Sarah allowed herself to be persuaded into the dining-room, where she found a seat on Coulter Dryden's left. Deborah, apparently quite recovered, sat on her husband's right. The Drydens, like many couples, must have grown more alike during the passage of time. Not just in their expansive gestures, or in the intonation of their Cambridgeshire voices, but even in their appearance. Whereas Coulter's face might always have had a squashed-tomato look, the features beneath Deborah's subcutaneous fat must once have been delicate.

Sarah wondered about that long and childless marriage which had received its fair share of media attention. There was ample evidence this evening of the couple's continuing attachment. Deborah punctuated Coulter's critique of the National Health Service with appreciative if often ill-timed giggles. Coulter joined others at the table in singing the praises of his wife's cooking.

Sarah couldn't readily imagine herself married to a property magnate, but if such a fate had been forced upon her, a younger Coulter Dryden might have proved a more congenial mate than many of the species. Like his wife, he took an open pleasure in his wealth and in public recognition of his contributions, not inconsiderable, to charitable causes. He took open pleasure too in his business ventures, or, as Sarah's husband had once pointed out to her, in a judicious sample thereof.

For Dryden Construction, whose every estate was replicated in miniature in some corner of its chairman's Holtlchester home, was the tip of Dryden Enterprises, a large and potentially lethal iceberg.

'Sorry, love.' Sarah realized that Coulter's attention, like her own, had been distracted from his wife's last remark. What interested her more than Deborah's reprise was the evident source of her husband's distraction—the back views of Karen East and Lucy Talbot at the second of the three refectory tables. Of Karen leaning back, laughing that deep laugh of hers. Of her right hand reaching across as if to touch Lucy's left, and as quickly recoiling.

The moment passed. Deborah seemed to have seen nothing. As she helped Nigel Gorridge clear dishes at the end of the meal, Sarah paused by Lucy's seat. 'D'you think you could help me lay the tables for breakfast while the tour of the house is going on? Unless you want to do the tour yourself, of course?'

'No, I've been over the place twice already.' For the second time that evening the Bishop's wife seemed faintly embarrassed. 'Do you mind if I show Karen up to her room first, though? Won't take a tick. She's got a bit of a headache —wants to have an early night.'

Karen East smiled bravely.

As Sarah wiped tables in the empty dining-room she could hear Robin Lake's voice echoing through the hall next door.

> Go to the ant, thou sluggard;
> Consider her ways, and be wise
>
> A false balance is an abomination to the Lord:
> But a just weight is his delight

Not content with initialling the parapet of his mansion, the first owner had followed the custom of other upwardly mobile Elizabethans by advertising his moral worth in a series of Biblical texts, painted on the interior walls of the great hall.

'Everything *is* going to be all right, isn't it?'

Sarah looked up, dishcloth in hand, to see Frances Lake.

'Of course it is. Why shouldn't it, for heaven's sake?' she said warmly. 'Want to talk?' She sat down and Frances followed suit.

'It's just . . . this house means so much to Robin and me. Robin especially. You can hear it in his voice when he's talking about that old pirate Leveson, can't you? You'd never believe I practically had to go down on my knees to persuade him to buy.'

'How long have you been here?'

'Nearly four years. Robin had already decided he'd retire early from the bank chairmanship, and he didn't want to get embroiled with other directorships. Modern finance is a young man's game, he says. We wanted something we could enjoy doing together, and the idea of restoring an old property appealed to us.'

'And you've enjoyed doing it, haven't you?'

'Oh yes.' Frances's thin face lit up. 'Robin and I aren't great verbalizers where emotion is concerned. I've often regretted that. Felt shut out. But since he's been at home more—since we've been working and planning together at Hare Holt—it hasn't mattered so much. We've had the feeling of closeness. Do you understand?'

Sarah nodded. She understood, too, Patricia Gorridge's objections to the Lakes' plans, but this didn't seem the moment to voice them. 'What's worrying you, Frances? What are you afraid of?' she asked.

'The future—my family's future.' Her hostess forced a smile. 'Making mountains out of molehills, I expect. Robin's been a bit off-colour these last few weeks. Brushes it off—won't see his doctor. Then there's been the business about Marina.'

'From what I've seen of her, I don't think there's a lot wrong. If I change my mind before the end of the weekend—if I think you should seek specialist advice, I'll tell you. OK?'

'I'd be so grateful. There's something else. Treat this as confidential, won't you, Sarah?'

'Of course.'

'Derwent rang up just before supper to say he wouldn't be down this weekend. Didn't give any real reason, just that he'd paperwork to catch up on. But he'd been drinking, and he hardly touches alcohol as a rule.'

'He must be anxious about your daughter-in-law.'

'He swore she was fine, and I can't think he would lie about that. I'm very fond of Gaby, even though we're so different in background and temperament. Gaby's Italian, you know. She and Derwent have a good marriage. Physically, as well as in other ways. They're very . . . demonstrative. It must have been hard for Derwent to give all that up when Gaby was hospitalized—'

'And for your daughter-in-law.'

'Not the same thing, surely? Once or twice when I rang up, Derwent was a long time answering. I used to wonder if he and Kirsten, the au pair, had something going. She's a big, busty blonde—attractive in all the obvious ways.'

'Would it matter terribly? She's left his employment, you said?'

'But that's another thing. Derwent said he didn't know why she'd gone. But I'd this horrible feeling he was lying. And he's always been so honest. The thought struck me this evening that they might have made love—that Marina might have seen them.'

'Have you discussed this possibility with your husband?'

'I couldn't. I just couldn't. Robin's such an honourable man. It would hurt him dreadfully to think that Derwent—'

A squeaky door-hinge interrupted.

'Leave this till later, shall we?' Sarah murmured as a middle-aged man in a black leather trenchcoat strode into the dining-room.

'Gideon! Lovely to see you. Gideon Poynter, Sarah. Our photographer.' Frances advanced upon him.

'Unclean, unclean!' Poynter extended heavily ringed and grease-stained fingers. His manner, Sarah thought, deserved a Bermuda bronze complexion and apricot mane. But no doubt pasty features and thinning grey locks were less conspicuous behind a candid camera. 'Tyre trouble', he elaborated. 'Student minibus that Annie Urquhart insisted on bundling us into at Cambridge. Penny-bloody-wise.'

'Toby!' Frances transferred her attention to a younger, less flamboyant young man in a dripping Barbour. 'Where's Annie—and Father Yardley?'

'Gone straight upstairs to change and shower. Separately, I hasten to add. Speaking of which—'

'Our bathroom's free,' Sarah put in. 'The one between the Talbots' room and mine. No reason why we should hog it throughout the weekend. You don't mind, do you?' she asked Lucy Talbot who had now reported for dining-room duty. 'You can get access from my room—here's the key. Number 17, first floor, West Wing.'

'Come down to the kitchen when you're ready,' Frances added as the newcomers departed. 'We'll heat you up something in the micro.'

'Poynter's quite a big name, isn't he?' Sarah said when the latest arrivals had departed. 'How did you nobble him, Fran?'

'I didn't. His people live locally, but Gideon's London based, and it never occurred to me that he'd consider the assignment. When I approached Toby French to write a piece for us, I assumed he'd bring a photographer colleague from the *Holtchester Echo*. But apparently Toby sounded Gideon out when he ran into him at a Cambridge wedding recently and got a positive response straight away. Gideon felt sure he could get a commission from a Sunday mag colour supplement. National publicity—just what we need.'

'Poynter works for one of the tabloids, doesn't he?' Sarah asked.

'The *Clarion*. And apparently the stuff he does for them is rather crude, but Toby assures me the quality Sundays won't buy anything distasteful.'

Sarah, unconvinced, maintained a diplomatic silence.

'Sarah Baxter!' The high, donnish voice carried across the winter parlour which now functioned as a course common-room and was presently occupied by those who had chickened out of the first informal dance session. 'How'd you get yourself involved in these shenanigans?'

'I *like* courtly dancing,' Sarah retorted, wishing, not for the first time that Dr Annie Urquhart, Reader in Criminology at the University of Cambridge, would outgrow her adolescent pleasure in provocation.

'Where's Richard?' Annie disentangled her still-damp fringe from the purple hexagonal glasses that dominated her small face.

'Flat out in front of the telly, I'd guess. There was a farewell do last night for one of his former colleagues in the Met. And he's back on duty tomorrow.'

'So he won't be coming here? Shame.' Annie's professional path crossed Richard's occasionally, with explosive consequences. She was, he had told Sarah, the only criminologist of his acquaintance he enjoyed arguing with.

'Not a shame from our point of view. Farewell booze-ups aren't my thing, fancy dress isn't Richard's. What brings you here, Annie?'

'Lust,' said Toby French, taking possession of the criminologist's left hand.

'I'm half way through a sabbatical,' Annie elaborated, unembarrassed. 'First half-term Valparaiso, second Stockholm. With just six days to play around with in between, I wasn't going to spare Toby a long weekend for some damnfool dancing project.'

Sarah turned to the journalist. 'You must have been tempted to cop out of this assignment.'

'Probably should, if it'd been a straight HHDS job, but then I heard the Bishop of Fenport was expected. Been trying for an interview with him for months now, for a book I'm writing.'

'*Pillars of the State* he's calling it,' Annie volunteered. 'God have mercy on the state, say I, if the Right Reverend Jonathan is typical of its support system.'

'Annie has a blind spot where organized religion is concerned,' Toby explained.

'It's not that, Sarah.' Annie retrieved her left hand. 'Far as I'm concerned, Jon Talbot scores low by his own grading system. Isn't there something in the Good Book about setting one's hand to the plough and not looking back? Remember Tekbridge?'

'Vaguely.' The young offenders' rehabilitation scheme had made national headlines and the cleric's name.

'Richard will fill you in. Talbot started it in Cambridge, you know. Eleven years ago—year I went up to Newnham. Rarely known a project grow as fast—before or since. It impressed a lot of people, starry-eyed undergraduates among them.'

'Yourself included, love.'

'When did I deny it? I'd never have dreamt of specializing in criminology if it hadn't been for Tekbridge. Hit a high when they took me on to the evaluation programme after I graduated. And the scheme came out well on evaluation. Better than any similar rehab project in the UK. Then two years later—phut! Talbot makes off for some cosy sinecure in South Ken. And two years after that Tekbridge falls apart.'

'Do you blame Talbot for that?' Sarah asked.

'Absolutely. The man's not stupid. He ran the outfit as a one-man show, a vehicle for his talents. Made no provision for a future change of leadership. Gave no indication he was contemplating backing out. Offered no good reason when he did—just some platitudinous claptrap about family considerations.'

'Easy on, love,' Toby admonished. 'Jet-lag gets her like this,' he told Sarah.

Annie scowled, then laughed. 'OK, I'm spaced out. Let's go to bed, shall we?'

But Toby's eyes were on the chattering dancers, now filtering back into the parlour. 'You go on up, sweetie. Won't be long—honest. If you'll excuse me, Sarah, I'll try for a quick word with the bishopess.'

'Oh yes? If you can't get at the pillar, go for the poison ivy!' Annie snarled.

'Now you *are* being unfair!' Sarah leapt to her friend's defence. Yet as she watched Lucy, with her springing walk and her dark springing hair, Lucy, who had blushed twice that evening for no obvious reason, she asked herself whether their six months' acquaintanceship could count as friendship. Whether Lucy, for all her friendliness, had any real friends.

CHAPTER 4

Sarah, showered and ready for bed, stared down at her dressing-table. A mass-produced item, in teak veneer, dating no doubt from Hare Holt's boarding-school period. What struck her, however, was not its unworthiness of the setting, or Marina's pot-pourri which took pride of place on its top surface, but its shallow central drawer. She had tried in vain to close that drawer after stowing away her cosmetics shortly after her arrival.

Someone else had succeeded.

She opened the drawer with difficulty, but found nothing missing. She examined the interiors of the two deeper side drawers, and the matching wardrobe, with the same result. Was everything a shade too tidy? Had the contents been touched? She wasn't an obsessional. She couldn't be sure.

Creaming her face, she considered alerting her hosts. Reluctant to add to Frances's worries, she changed her mind. She did, however, set the latch on the Yale lock before going to bed.

In the early hours of Saturday morning she woke, lay awake, half-decided to use the payphone on the landing to ring her husband, found Gideon Poynter in possession of the instrument, and returned to bed and sleep.

Breakfast was self-service. As Sarah washed down her manchet with coffee in the company of other late arrivals at the breakfast-table she saw Annie Urquhart bearing down on her.

'Have any trouble last night, Sarah?' the criminologist asked, slopping coffee over her saucer and within inches of her neighbour's green cords.

'What sort of trouble?'

'Any of your gear nicked—mucked about with?'

Sarah reported her observations, and her unwillingness to trouble her hosts with them.

'You're as bad as Toby. Didn't want to know when I told him someone had been through my papers. When I eventually convinced him, he said it wasn't worth making an issue of.'

'If someone has had something taken, no doubt they'll complain,' Sarah reasoned.

'Until such time, you propose to sing dumb? Don't think the Chief Inspector would approve.'

It was absurd to be jealous of Annie's relationship with Richard, but jealousy was always a little absurd. Sarah counted ten and finished her meal in silence, wondering how Elizabeth I would have dealt with such provocation. As she helped clear away, she discharged her nagging guilt by cornering Lucy Talbot.

Lucy, more of a principal boy than a Renaissance angel in this morning's black-and-cyclamen leotards, frowned and set down the tray she had been carrying.

'Didn't notice a thing myself—but I'm scatty about my possessions, Sarah. Not the noticing kind. Jon may just have had something taken, though.'

'Then perhaps we should have a word?'

'Sorry—he left early for Cambridge. Back before eleven, I expect. He's an appointment with Toby French. But anyhow, I'm sure he won't want to make a mountain out of a molehill.'

'What happened exactly?'

'Not a lot. Saw Jon riffling through his briefcase before he left. Asked him if he'd lost something. He said he couldn't find a paper he'd intended to bring—must have left it at home. The possibility of theft obviously didn't occur to him—or me.'

'An important paper?'

'I didn't ask. He didn't say. Oh, don't put on your diagnostic look, Sarah!'

'Sorry, I didn't mean to—really.'

'And I didn't mean to snap. It's just that Jon's been

strung up recently. Not surprising, having just taken on his first bishopric. Seems so unfair, with the kids and me taking to Fenport like ducks to water. I try hard not to aggravate him, not to ask unnecessary questions. But that puts me under strain, too.'

'I can imagine, Lucy. I've been there.' Sarah touched the younger woman's arm and thanked whatever gods there might be for Richard's deliverance from the Met. 'I shan't raise the matter myself, but I'd like your husband to know that others of us suspect our rooms have been gone over. He may feel, in those circumstances, that the Lakes should be alerted.'

'I'll tell him. Promise.'

Tuning-up was in progress as they passed the great hall on their way to the kitchen. Lucy left almost immediately to join the dancers. Sarah waited to help Marina weigh sugar and almonds while Deborah Dryden answered Patricia Gorridge's summons to the kitchen telephone. The housekeeper explained, *sotto voce*, that incoming calls were being re-routed at such times as the course office was unmanned.

Pink and visibly distressed, Deborah grimaced as she hung up the receiver. 'Holtchester police, would you believe, Sarah? They asked for Coulter, but he's off to a meeting in London, and I'm sure that's why—'

'Why what? Nothing wrong, I hope?'

'Not really . . . At least, I think not—I hope not.' Deborah was unbuttoning her overall. 'It was our neighbour in Holtchester, Mrs Kawolski, who rang the police station. Know her?'

The others shook their heads.

'Coulter and I don't see much of her—I think she socializes mainly in the Polish community. Nice woman, but a bit of a fusspot and heavily into Neighbourhood Watch. She always offers to keep an eye on our place when we're away, and we're away on business quite a lot, of course.'

The Drydens, Sarah had gleaned from Holtchester gossip, rarely spent a night apart. 'Mrs K made a tour of inspection this morning, it seems, and saw a light in our basement.'

'Light? Nothing else?

'She *thought* she saw someone moving, but she didn't stay long enough to get a proper look, silly woman. It was Coulter, you see. Must have been. He said he'd some papers to pick up on his way to Town. Mrs K didn't see his car, but he may well have left it at the end of the road. He's quite exercise-conscious, you know. The police are trying to contact him on his car phone, but they want me to check up on the house in the meantime.'

Sarah recognized the note of panic in Deborah's voice. 'Would you like me to tag along?'

'Sweet of you, but I wouldn't hear of it.' The offer seemed only to have added to the panic. 'Coulter would hate to think he'd caused a fuss,' Deborah continued unconvincingly. The architect of Dryden Enterprises had a public reputation as a stirrer.

Sarah contented herself with taking over Deborah's culinary activities. She and Marina, Deborah explained, were about to make marzipan.

'Marchpane,' Marina corrected.

'I'll cope. Off you go—and good luck, Deb. Do ring up for moral support if you don't get things sorted out quickly. Promise?'

Deborah having promised and departed, Sarah and Marina devoted themselves to the business of colouring and pounding almond paste, in which they were interrupted several times by the telephone. The third call was from Sarah's husband.

'Having fun, darling?' Richard sounded sober and wide awake.

'Mm-hm.' Sarah disposed of a mouthful of marzipan trimmings. 'How and where are you?'

'Fragile and in my office.'

'Nice booze-up?'

'Can't remember. Nice canterbury for sure. Satinwood.'

'Good. Busy day ahead?'

'Lousy day. Bill Armstrong and I are bidden to HQ where Highcroft's holding a seminar on his latest brainchild. Multifactorial evaluation package for neighbourhood watch programmes, would you believe?'

'That's funny.'

'As you very well know, darling, the Super's never funny by design. And rarely by accident.'

'Funny peculiar, you clown. In view of the business at the Drydens'. You've heard?'

'Drydens, Bill?' Sarah heard him say. 'Seems there's something somewhere in the in-tray.'

'Then I'll leave you to excavate. 'Bye, darling. Duty calls.'

Sarah hung up just in time to dissuade Marina from popping a third marzipan ball into her sticky mouth. Patricia Gorridge was stowing the last of the breakfast things into the dishwasher.

'Is your son with us again today?' Sarah asked her.

'No. An old client sent out an SOS he couldn't afford to refuse. Computer systems seem to go down at awkward times. Like human systems, I suppose, Dr Baxter. But my scooter's back in action and so is Audrey—upstairs emptying wastebins. Luckily, her 'flu was of the twenty-four hour variety. So I expect we'll muddle through.' Muddling wasn't Patricia's way, Sarah decided, as she watched her stack plates with maximal economy of time and effort.

'I've been sent to relieve you, Sarah.' She looked up from the sugary worktop to see Robin Lake tying himself into a butcher's apron.

'I'm really quite happy to be here.'

'But it's absurd to come to a dance course and not do any dancing. That goes for you, too, Patricia.'

'As I've told you before, Mr Lake, I've never been a dancer. My mother used to say I was born with two left feet.'

'You haven't that excuse, Sarah. Besides, they're doing the pavan, and my wife tells me it's one of your favourites.'

'Well . . . How about you, Marina? Fancy a change of scene?'

The child made a face. 'Gramps doesn't know how to make marchpane, do you, Gramps? Want me to show you?'

'Nothing better. Sweetmaking is my idea of heaven, Sarah. I'm sure I'd have run away from prep school if the housemaster's wife hadn't let us make fudge on Saturday nights.'

'If you're quite sure.' Sarah removed her apron and rinsed her hands before hurrying out of the kitchen and into the corridor. As she turned right into the screens passage she was greeted by a peal of giggles. Gideon Poynter was bent double in helpless mirth, clutching the payphone by the registration table.

Sarah opened the hall door and entered the soundworld of tenor voice, sackbut, hautboy and drum.

Belle qui tiens ma vie
Captive dans tes yeulx . . .

Beauty, holding my life
Imprisoned in your eyes . . .

At first, as she watched the dancers, she was irritated by the mismatch between their twentieth-century leisurewear, hairstyles and spectacles, and the austere beauty of Arbeau's choreography. Partners danced side by side, holding hands. Two singles and a double forward, two singles and a double forward: the same movements backwards. Marina would have been bored rigid in no time. Her idealistic phase was yet to come: she would have been untouched by the high romance of the song.

As the first verse ended, Sarah invited Toby French, the sole spectator, to dance.

'At your own risk. As the rawest beginner, I didn't dare offer.'

'I'll risk it. Where's Annie?'

'Working—or pretending to. We've had a spat.'

'Nothing serious, I hope?'

'No. We thrive on them. It's that sort of relationship. Whoops—sorry!'

'We've been talking too much. I'll shut up—give you a chance to concentrate on the music.'

Sarah glanced round her and saw that the simple, repetitive rhythms and melody were hypnotizing others beside herself. Even the women who had been forced by logistics to dance together seemed to have suspended their disbelief in reality. Ideal partners, recalled or imagined, took over from their flesh-and-blood surrogates. Lips curved in dreamy smiles. The room was awash with heady adolescent emotion recollected in adult tranquillity. Sarah wallowed with the rest.

Then she caught a glimpse of Karen East who was partnering Lucy. No smile there, no dream. The young woman's expression was intent. Hungry, even. Lucy hung back a little, her face hidden by her neighbours.

I am dying, angel
I am dying in your embrace.

As the tenor sang, the image of an even older dance, the mediæval Dance of Death, flickered in Sarah's imagination, its skeletal procession obscuring her twentieth-century companions and the exuberant Elizabethan panelling behind them. She shivered, missed her step.

Toby kicked her ankle. 'Sorry.'

'It's all right.' *Oh please, let everything go all right*, Sarah prayed to her god of tight corners. But she felt in her bones now that something might go very badly wrong.

CHAPTER 5

'*No*, darling!'

When Sarah next looked into the kitchen, Frances Lake was making a grab for the vegetable knife with which Marina was attempting to open a packet of biscuits.

'Over-reaction—sorry.' The apology seemed intended as much for the onlookers as for her granddaughter. 'It's just that Derwent caught his right hand in a chainsaw when he was about her age.'

'Daddy doesn't do my plaits properly,' Marina volunteered. 'Not as well as Granny. And Granny doesn't do them as well as Kirsten.'

'How can I make myself useful?' Sarah asked, conscious of Frances's discomfort.

'Just see that Patricia takes a breather. Marina and I are just going to serve up coffee. She and her grandfather finished the marchpane before he left.'

'Left?'

'Isn't it a bore? First the Bishop and Coulter. Then Robin. He had to go up to Town at short notice, worse luck.'

'I wanted Gramps to take me, so I could see Mummy, but he wouldn't,' Marina complained. 'Why wouldn't he, Granny?'

'Because he won't have time to go to the hospital today. We'll go soon, you and I. Promise. Now we must get this coffee out to all those thirsty dancers. No, not another chocolate biscuit, darling.'

'I can see you don't need advice,' Sarah said to Patricia Gorridge, who was already pouring coffee for two at the kitchen table.

'I've learnt to conserve my energies.' Patricia picked up Marina's picture-story book, which had acquired some recent additions.

'Good, aren't they?'

Patricia leafed through the book before replying. 'The drawing is good for a six-year-old,' she conceded. 'But I'd find the story content worrying if I were her grandmother.'

'Cat threatens mice. Standard children's fantasy, wouldn't you say? Tom and Jerry stuff.'

'But Jerry gave Tom a run for his money. Lucy's mice go to bed, get up, make tea. Their cage door stays locked.'

Sarah studied the drawings and the dictated narrative. 'Why didn't I notice that? Perceptive of you.'

'Not really. And I may be way off the mark. It's a quarter-century since I dropped out of teacher-training. A little outdated psychology is a dangerous thing.'

'Believe you're right, though. Marina's an anxious little girl just now. But wouldn't you say that's normal for a six-year-old whose mother's in hospital?'

'I bow to your clinical experience, Dr Baxter.' Patricia opened the local freesheet with the air of one who had offloaded her responsibilities.

Sarah finished her coffee with little pleasure, and, having been assured by Patricia that catering help was forthcoming from other sources, departed for the winter parlour where most of the course members were taking their coffee-break. Lucy Talbot detached herself from the group nearest the log fire.

'Owe you an apology, Sarah. Clean forgot to pass on your message about our intruder to Jon when he got back, and now he's incommunicado with Toby French.'

'Never mind. Enjoying yourself?'

Lucy coloured slightly. 'Oh yes. The Arbeau pavan's dreamy, isn't it? But the *pavaniglias* and *passo e mezzi* will be more fun. Coming back to the hall?'

'Thought I'd take the lazy option for the rest of the morning. Father Yardley should be worth hearing on Dowland.' Yardley, a pale, plump man with drooping eyelids, was already assembling audio equipment in a corner of the parlour. His illustrated talk on the Elizabethan composer was to be one of several items provided for those who wished to skip occasional dancing sessions.

'That man.' Lucy shivered. 'It's wrong of me, but I just can't take him.'

'Known him long?'

'Only since I married. But Jon and he met years earlier. They're at opposite poles theologically, but Jon had High Church leanings as a teenager. Yardley led a school retreat he attended when he was fifteen or so. For a few months Jon even toyed with the idea of joining his monastic community.'

'Lucky for you he didn't.'

'Yes. The community broke up for some reason. Personality clashes, I think. Yardley had been appointed to his lectureship before Jon took up his curacy in Cambridge. That was just after we married—before Tekbridge. Jon felt sorry for Yardley. Invited him to our house a couple of times. Brr! That's when I learnt what people mean by icy disapproval. Directed at me, not my husband. It was a great relief when he stopped accepting the invitations. Jon says he's a sad, sick man, but I can't help feeling he could be dangerous.'

'Not to me, I'm sure,' Sarah said robustly, as she prepared to join the priest's audience.

In the light of Lucy's assessment, it came as no surprise that the musicologist dwelt lovingly on the gloomier aspects of John Dowland's life and compositions. *In darkness let me dwell* received a generous share of his attention. So too the composer's reworking of the galliard ascribed to the doomed Earl of Essex. *Fine knacks for ladies* and the tragicomic Frog galliard got short shrift.

Gideon Poynter, somewhat to Sarah's surprise, was among those present. The photographer lay on a window-seat throughout the proceedings, an open newspaper covering his face. Asleep perhaps, but hardly fast asleep; for when the lunch bell rang he was first out of the room. When Sarah passed through the screens passage, he was in possession of the payphone.

On her way to her room for a quick wash, Sarah knocked on the Drydens' door. Deborah emerged, wearing a plum towelling tracksuit and smelling strongly of *Je Reviens*. Her husband's favourite, she had once confided in the cloakroom at Browne Community College, where the Historical Dance Society practised.

'Everything all right at home?' Sarah asked.

'Oh, absolutely all right. The police got through to Coulter on his car phone before we reached Holtchester, as it happened. He confirmed that he'd called in for some papers. He was a bit worried about his brakes, so he left his car in the Green Hill garage and walked over. I gave the house the once-over to keep the police happy. Everything as it should be.'

When Sarah joined the others in the dining-room Deborah was eating and swapping recipes with her usual good humour. Lunch, which was served buffet-fashion, looked in essentials like a twentieth-century meal, but Frances had distributed menus, illustrated by her granddaughter, on which salad was spelt as *sallat*. The reader was informed in a footnote that the strapwork pastry on Deborah's spicy apple pies was copied from a Tudor woodcut.

The dances taught on Saturday afternoon were taken from Fabritio Caroso's *Nobiltà di Dama*. The Italian master, Sarah knew, was a favourite of Haviland Prynne's, who was clearly determined his pupils should do justice to the choreography. She felt rather sorry for those, like Jonathan Talbot, who lacked previous acquaintance with flourishes, cadences and limping hops.

Under his wife's guidance, the Bishop made a fair showing in the sixteen variations of the *pavaniglia* before crying halt. Prynne seized his chance to appropriate Lucy, a star pupil, as co-demonstrator of the *passo e mezzi* which were to follow.

Karen East, Sarah noted, was not among the dancers, but Gideon Poynter, who had changed into cricketing gear, rather surprisingly was. When one of the other men took Marina off her grandmother's hands, he offered himself as a partner to Frances.

'Now what do you suppose that's in aid of?' Annie Urquhart, heavily sweatered and scarfed, had materialized at Sarah's side.

'Knowing as little of Gideon as I do, I couldn't say. Maybe he wants to be one of the crowd. Maybe he's a thing about older women.'

'Maybe he's gone scavenging.'

'Scavenging?'

'For the latest on whatever scandal brought him here. Muckrakers don't change their spots, Sarah. And that's our Gideon.'

'Must you, Annie? We're here to enjoy ourselves, for goodness' sake. Where's Toby, by the way?'

'Gone to the village to buy booze for this evening. Wanted me to go walkies with him. Radiator in our bedroom's packed up, so anywhere else would be warmer, but the prospect of Fen Holton in a drizzle didn't appeal.'

'Try indoor exercise, then. My grasp of this dance is uncertain. But I'm prepared to give it a whirl if you will.'

After a brief hesitation, Annie allowed herself to be led through the figures. Before long, she was fully engaged, responding to the challenge with the myopic concentration of the workaholic. It was Sarah and not she who registered Toby French's return to the hall. He must, she supposed, have cadged a lift to or from the village.

The reporter paid no attention to either of them, but made straight for Jonathan Talbot. Almost immediately, they left the room together.

Rain lashed against her bedroom window as Sarah drew the curtains to change for supper. The radiator, though functional, was too small to counteract the dank chill of the high-ceilinged room. The warming effects of a bath wore off as she repaired a split seam in the Tudor costume she had rescued from her attic.

It was a black and gold affair with double ruff and French hood, which her daughter Emma had run up four years ago from Oxfam bargains in the intervals of swotting for A-levels. She had worn it when she played Maria in a school production of *Twelfth Night*. Now general dogsbody for a radical touring company, she had urged Sarah to wear and tear it with abandon. Emma's trad Shakespeare days were long past, she had added in a tone which suggested her mother was entering her second cultural childhood.

If so, I'm jolly well going to enjoy it, Sarah told herself, but it wasn't until she re-entered the dining-room that genuine cheerfulness broke through. By what means she couldn't guess. Frances had bullied almost all the course participants and hangers-on to beg, borrow or steal Tudor or neo-Tudor costumes. Some, like Father Yardley's and Toby French's, had been crudely tailored from fading curtains. Others were more or less accurate replicas of outfits worn by the sitters of Nicholas Hilliard and his contemporaries.

Frances herself, in curly red wig, figure-of-eight ruff and pearl-studded gown, was barely recognizable as a magnificent middle-period Elizabeth Tudor. The woman she was talking to was, however, even more striking. Two ropes of pearls overhung without obscuring a white square-necked dress brocaded with black and brown ogival bands and pomegranates. A gold caul studded with pearls almost covered her dark hair.

'Who's that beauty?' Sarah asked Frances at the first opportunity.

Frances laughed. 'The East girl—dear Lucy's lame duck. Had me fooled, too. Outfit's on loan from a friend who's a theatrical wardrobe mistress, it seems.'

'Is she anyone special?' The costume had an Italian look —or was in Spanish?

'Elenora of Toledo. Haven't you seen her portrait in the Wallace collection? They say she was buried in that dress.'

How appropriate, Sarah thought. Pomegranates—Persephone's fruit. The fruit of the dead. A train of thought too morbid for Marina's ears, she decided.

'Let's set an example by sitting down,' Frances proposed. 'Will you join us, Lucy? Jonathan', she bellowed above the buzz of exclamatory compliments—'isn't Lucy gorgeous? The Unknown Girl from the Tate. My idea. We just had to have one. Lucy thought the hire charge was sinfully extravagant, but I had a private word with the Bishop.'

Sarah admired the coral, gold and white confection, but regretted the red-gold wig into which Lucy had stuffed her black hair. Marina, pirouetting in French hood and simple, square-necked gown, innocent of stomacher and farthingale, was a child out of Holbein.

'Sit!' her grandmother hissed at last. And surprisingly Marina complied, taking the empty place between Frances and Sarah and opposite the Talbots.

'Black mark, Bishop.' Frances pointed an accusing finger at his everyday canonicals. 'Not abandoning us again, I hope?'

'Sincerest apologies. As you know, I'd unbreakable engagements for last night and this morning, but I'd absolutely no intention of leaving the house again, as Lucy will confirm.'

She did so. Grudgingly, Sarah thought.

'Fact is, a college contemporary I ran into on King's Parade this morning passed on the word that our old tutor is terminally ill. A rare man, Henry Claverhouse. Infinitely patient, yet wonderfully stimulating. I'd hate not to see him again.'

'But surely a day or two's delay wouldn't matter?' Frances objected.

'Just what I said. The Torch Branle's so lovely. Please, Jon.' There was urgency—desperation, even, in Lucy's voice.

'Sorry, love. Sorry, Frances. From what I heard, Claverhouse hasn't long to go. But tomorrow and Monday I'm all yours. Promise.'

'And you'll dress up on Monday evening?' Marina checked. 'What as?'

'The explorer Frobisher.'

'In a dreary buff outfit. I much preferred him in red as Drake. But no.' Lucy made a face. 'Mean trick, after talking me into this fancy gear.'

'With a sword?' Marina persisted.

The Bishop grinned. 'A swordbelt and a pistol.'

'Gramps is the Earl of Leicester, and he's got a sword and he's going to teach me a sword dance tomorrow. Will he be back tomorrow, Granny?'

'Tonight, if his meeting's over in time.'

'Silly old meetings. Why does he have to go to meetings on Saturdays?' Marina grumbled.

'You must ask him tomorrow.'

Leek pottage was served, and for several minutes Marina gave it her full attention. At Frances's instigation, Sarah and the Talbots pooled their scrappy knowledge of Elizabethan exploration. What were other people talking about, Sarah asked herself later that evening. And found no answers. All she could hear over the general buzz were fingers tapping and a low voice humming somewhere behind her and to her left.

But Marina, as she stiffened, looked neither to right nor left. Replacing her soupspoon with deliberate care, she froze, eyes fixed on the space between the Talbots' shoulders.

Almost, it seemed, as if an unnecessary sound or movement might betray her.

'Bed.' She said it so softly the first time that Frances didn't hear.

'Bed. Can I go to bed, please, Granny?'

'Whatever's wrong, darling? Feel sick?'

'No.' The child shuddered, pressing against her.

'Is it something scarey?'

A nod.

Frances bent her wigged head to the child's. 'Come on, sweetie. Tell Granny? Tell Sarah?'

'I can't!' The words came out in a loud wail. 'Daddy made me promise I wouldn't tell anyone—ever.'

'*Daddy?*' Frances Lake's eyes signalled her alarm to Sarah, as she hugged the child, sobbing now. The conversation level fell and rose almost immediately as the other diners pretended not to notice. 'We'll have to go back to the flat, I'm afraid. Would you and Lucy hold the fort here, please? I'll send Robin over as soon as he comes in. And could you possibly pop round to our quarters later, Sarah? I'd very much appreciate your advice.'

'Of course.'

To Sarah's relief, the Talbots made few conversational demands during the rest of the meal. She brooded on Marina's distress, and its possible causes. Had the child, as her grandmother had guessed, seen her father making love to the au pair? Perhaps. Other and darker questions suggested themselves. Questions which only Derwent Lake could answer—must answer. Questions overlaid, irritatingly, irrelevantly, by the sound-track of those fingers tapping and that low voice humming. Karen East's voice.

Belle qui tiens ma cœur
Captive dans tes yeulx . . .

Marina hadn't learnt the Arbeau pavan, Sarah reminded herself firmly. Absurd to suppose the tune could have induced her terror. If Karen East was anyone's problem she was Lucy Talbot's. Or one of them. The faces of the Bishop and his wife were shut and silent.

Elsewhere the meal seemed to be proceeding cheerfully. The spiced wine which Coulter Dryden had contributed was imbibed freely. The donor, a substantial Henry VIII, returned half way through the main course to join his wife. Deborah looked almost elegant this evening in a sleeveless black gown over a waistless underdress.

More wine went the rounds after supper, when almost everyone gathered in the great hall, now lit only by wall-fixed candelabra, to hear an instrumental programme and watch three complex *baletti* danced by Haviland Prynne and his most advanced students.

'This what we can expect from you and Deb next year, Sarah?' Coulter Dryden had materialized in the gloom on her left.

'Not from me, certainly,' she said more sharply than she had intended. 'I don't think I started young enough. Besides, I haven't much time to practise.'

'Keeping the Chief Inspector happy hard work, then?'

Sarah flinched as the feather in Dryden's cap brushed her cheek.

'No offence. Our policemen are wonderful, far as I'm concerned. Said as much to the Chief Constable only last week. Good man, Montgomery, eh?'

Only her sense of responsibility as deputy hostess glued Sarah to her seat as Dryden slapped her knee.

'It's these bloody amateurs that try the patience. You'll have heard about our neighbour's whistle-blowing effort this morning?'

'Deborah mentioned it in the kitchen.' As Dryden pushed his gross face close to hers, Sarah was surprised to read anxiety in his piggy eyes. Anxiety about what? That Deborah had been indiscreet? Had let slip some business secret? She considered passing on the news of last night's bedroom intrusions, but decided against it. Coulter Dryden was more than able to defend his own interests.

When Coulter lumbered off at the end of the first set of dances it was to join Elenora of Toledo.

The Torch Branle, Prynne announced, would be danced lengthways up the hall by sixteen couples at a time, each equipped with a pair of candles. Half the dancers would drop out at the end of each sequence, and the other half would seek new partners. The dance was simplicity itself—two quick demonstrations would be more than adequate.

When these were done Prynne consulted with Gideon Poynter, a preposterous Earl of Surrey in abbreviated doublet and padded codpiece. Poynter had evidently taken his day's quota of photographs. With a valedictory twirl of his short cloak, he departed.

The candles in the individual candlesticks were lit and those in the candelabra extinguished. The transformation was extraordinary. As Sarah watched the first dancers, their candles held shoulder-high, their faces modelled in bold chiaroscuro, she felt herself a child again at the pantomime, sucked into the world of illusion. Left-right-left-kick, right-left-right-kick. The monotony of the sequence exerted a hypnotic effect.

An Oxbridge voice restored her to the present.

'Isn't the Bishop about? I'd hoped for a few words this evening.' Father Yardley, attired, as far as Sarah could see, in his usual grubby cassock, was addressing Lucy Talbot.

'He's with the Claverhouses in Cambridge. Mayn't be back much before midnight, I'm afraid. Can I be of any help?' Lucy sounded ever so slightly tipsy.

'*You?* No, I really don't think so, Mrs Talbot. Church business.'

'And I, of course, am a mere clergy wife,' Lucy muttered as he departed. Then, without warning, she burst into tears.

'Hey, there.' Sarah offered tissues. 'Not going to let that miserable old so-and-so get under your skin, are you? Want to pop outside for a minute?'

'It wasn't Father Yardley—not really,' Lucy said when they were alone in the screens. 'Fact is, I wasn't quite honest about our marriage yesterday.'

'No reason why you should be.'

'I don't think anything's drastically wrong. It's just there are things Jon and I need to talk over. We both know it.

That's why I was able to bully him into coming. This weekend away from the children was to be our big chance. You'll think me uncharitable, Sarah—grudging a visit to a dying man. But I don't believe it was all that urgent, you see. I believe Jon was running away from what we need to say to each other. And I'm so frightened he'll go on running.'

'Sounds to me as though you should give him an ultimatum,' Sarah said.

'Yes, I suppose you're right.' Lucy managed a watery smile over the paper handkerchief.

'Do you need a backer?'

'No. Thanks, Sarah, but no. Let's go in, shall we? It's such a pretty dance.'

Robin Lake, who had returned unnoticed by Sarah, was now among the dancers. He made a poised, if slightly superannuated Leicester, his Little George medallion gleaming discreetly against a salmon-pink satin doublet.

'How's Marina?' Sarah asked when he invited her to dance at the next change of partners.

'Sleeping off whatever upset her, thanks. My wife says she's no idea what got her going. Any suggestions?'

'Children go through vulnerable phases,' Sarah evaded. 'I promised to pop round for a chat with Frances on the subject. Perhaps now that you're back to keep an eye on things—'

'—such as fire hazards?' Robin's laugh sounded a little forced. 'I'm sure Fran would be grateful, and so would I, Sarah.'

His eyes had been raking the dance floor as they spoke, and when he left her it was without hesitation. Sarah watched, mildly curious, then more than a little surprised.

There was no reason why her host shouldn't seek out the wife of an old acquaintance—for all she knew, of an old business associate. But, as they made their preliminary reverence, her brass and his pewter candlestick held high, Robin Lake and Deborah Dryden had the look of a couple who sought and expected comfort from each other.

What Karen East sought from Lucy Talbot, Sarah was less certain. Attention or something more? They were at the moment the only two women dancing together. They danced well and looked well in their jewelled brocades. For those reasons alone, they would have attracted attention. Karen was grimacing as though to make Lucy laugh, and Lucy, although she giggled intermittently in response, looked tense and embarrassed. Would Karen be on the agenda, Sarah wondered, when the Talbots came clean with each other?

None of your business, she told herself as she went upstairs to change.

An hour and a half later, Frances and Sarah were lounging in the Lakes' comfortable but characterless sitting-room. Released from the obligation to furnish in the Tudor idiom a room which was out of bounds to tourists, its owners had failed to impose a style of their own.

For the last twenty minutes the two women had been watching a televised snooker match. A boringly one-sided snooker match.

'Please do go if you want to, Sarah,' Frances said for the third time.

'I'll wait until Robin comes back.'

'But you won't tell him what Marina said Derwent said—'

'Not if you don't want me to.'

'He'd go crazy, you see, if he thought Der—anyone—had—frightened her in some way.'

'We don't know yet if anyone has.' Sarah had considered and rejected the idea of arranging an immediate physical examination.

'But you said yourself it's a possibility we must take seriously.'

'I believe it is.'

'And you'll come up to London with Marina and me first thing Monday to tackle Derwent? No matter what?'

'If you're still sure you want me with you. Tomorrow morning, if you prefer.'

'No. She'd hate missing the mime *branles* I taught her. Besides, Derwent may be away for the weekend.' Frances had tried several times in Sarah's hearing to reach her son by phone. 'If you think he's evading, you'll speak out, won't you, Sarah?' she went on. 'Promise?'

'Promise.'

'Thanks again. Mind you, I'm sure there's a perfectly inno-' A buzzer rang. 'Damn. The intercom—excuse me. It's Father Yardley—for you.' She handed Sarah the receiver.

'Yes, yes—I see. I'll come at once. Must run, Frances. There's been some sort of accident.'

'Oh God. Not Robin?'

'Lucy Talbot.'

'Serious?'

'Afraid so. Better stay here in case Marina wakes, hadn't you? Ring you first chance I get.'

Father Yardley stood, head bowed, outside the Talbots' bedroom. The face he raised was expressionless. Sarah wondered if he had been praying. 'The door was ajar. I closed it,' he said.

Sarah pushed past him and knelt beside the body lying face down on the floor. Blood trickled from below the feathered cap and gold caul into the battered embroidered ruff. The pink Lucy had worn behind her ear lay some yards to the left. A bloodied pewter candlestick had rolled into the far right-hand corner of the room.

'Poor girl.' Sarah reached out to touch her. 'Did you see or hear what happened?' she called out over her shoulder.

The priest kept his distance at the doorway.

'She was an occasion for sin,' he said.

CHAPTER 6

Sarah knew as soon as she touched the flaccid right hand that she was too late. Half an hour too late, perhaps. She knew too that the hand wasn't Lucy's. Some instinct warned her not to share that knowledge with Yardley.

'Will you ring the police, please?' she called across her shoulder. 'Then find someone downstairs to let them in—

Mr Lake for preference. Best if you didn't say anything to the others, I think.'

'Discretion is as highly regarded in my profession as yours, Dr Baxter.'

'Sorry. Didn't mean to underline the obvious. But please do ring. And I'd be glad if you'd post yourself in the corridor again afterwards to ward off intruders.'

But not, Sarah resolved, to look at the face of the dead. She waited until the priest had closed the door behind him before rolling the body on to its back to begin her examination.

At first she took the bruised face for Karen East's. But this Karen stared up at her through one blue eye and one brown. She looked for the second contact lens and found it inside the ruff. The wisps of hair straying on to the temples were fairer than Karen's mousey mop, which must, she now realized, have been artificial. Pulling off the headdress and the red-gold wig below it, she exposed the head and face of a blond young man. A man who had made a name for himself in some field she couldn't immediately think of.

She stood up, conscious that she could do nothing for the victim but stand over him. The police surgeon would say she had already done too much. A minute or two later, she heard approaching footsteps. A knock. Expecting Lake or Yardley, she switched off the bedroom light before opening the door.

'Toby!'

'Sarah! I was looking for the Bishop. Not ill, is he?'

'He's not here.'

'Oh hell. I've something to return to him.' He waved a long envelope. 'If I could just leave it on the dressing-table . . .'

'Sorry. Room's out of bounds until the police come. Something's happened.'

'Police? Someone's *died*, you mean? Oh Christ! An accident?'

'Go away, Toby. Please go away.' She shut the door on him and switched on the light.

*

'David Alexander Sharrock.' Superintendent Clayton Warren read aloud from the driving licence that had been retrieved from the boot of Karen East's Mini. 'Run-of-the-mill name for a maverick.'

'Mr Sunnyscene, the media boys called him,' Richard Baxter observed. The policemen stood in the corridor outside the bedroom now occupied by scenes-of-crime personnel.

'God knows what they'll call him tomorrow, or whenever Highcroft releases the sordid details.'

'Does it have to be Highcroft?'

'Oh, come on, Dick. You know and I know that the CC plays these things by the book. And in his book big businessmen who cop it in Mid-Anglia rate the services of a detective-superintendent. To which rank it has pleased the powers that be to promote Victor Highcroft. I could hold off for half-an-hour if you want a preliminary shufti in there . . .'

'And have my beloved leader chew me up for mucking up his scene? No, thanks.' Sarah's activities had already created problems. Baxter fumbled for an antacid as Warren radioed his preliminary report to Police Headquarters. That achieved, the Superintendent announced his intention of touring the grounds, while the Detective Chief Inspector made his way to the winter parlour. There he found most if not all of the house's residents, some still in Renaissance finery, some—like Sarah—in casual day clothes, some already in dressing-gowns.

Having dispatched Haviland Prynne under escort to retrieve his course register, Baxter snatched a brief exchange with his wife. She looked strained and tired.

'Not much of an escapist weekend, eh, love? Are you all right?'

'Fine. Don't start worrying about *me*, for Heaven's sake.'

'OK. Who d'you want me to worry about, then?'

'Lucy Talbot for starters. Whoever killed that man almost certainly took him for Lucy. And now she's disappeared—against her will, perhaps?' Sarah shivered.

'Point taken. Promise. And when Prynne gets back, we'll know who else is missing.'

'Hello, Dick. Long time no see, etcetera. What the hell's going on?' Annie Urquhart, reeking of musty perfume, and wearing only, it appeared, a multicoloured bathrobe and furlined boots, had pushed herself between them. 'There I was having a quiet soak when one of your fuzzy friends started banging on the bathroom door. "Incident" was all I could get out of him. If I'd been Sarah here, that might have made sense. As I'm me, it doesn't. So spit it out, Dick. What sort of incident? Who was involved?'

As Baxter drew breath to answer, her face crumpled. 'Oh Christ, it's not Toby. You're not going to tell me something's happened to Toby?' She began to whimper like a toddler.

'Pull yourself together, Annie. I'm here with a job to do, and officially I've no authority to tell you anything.' Of Sarah's discretion he was confident. 'If you'd looked across this crowded room with your specs on you'd have seen Toby or his doppelgänger. Here for the *Echo*, I presume?'

'That and research for a book. Toby's nothing if not thorough. He's been interviewing the Bishop of Fenport off and on all day. Hoped to catch him when he got back from Cambridge. Which he hasn't yet, I take it?' She squinted shortsightedly around the assembly. 'Unless, of course, Talbot's the victim of your "incident"?'

'No comment. Now, listen. This course list Prynne's digging up may not cover hangers-on like Toby and yourself. Anyone else in that category?'

'Gideon Poynter, the photographer. But he sneaked off two or three hours ago.'

'Sneaked?'

'Well, he left Toby to make his excuses to the Lakes. Wouldn't have said anything to anyone, I dare say, if I hadn't caught him ordering a hire car before supper. He told Toby to say he'd another job to fit in and he'd be back for the next fancy-dress session on Monday.'

'Sounds plausible,' Baxter observed.

'I doubt if it's the whole truth, though. Gideon's been on edge all weekend—on the blower every other minute. As though he was expecting something newsworthy to happen.'

'But left before it did? Thanks, Annie. I'm afraid you'll be interviewed formally in the course of the night. And now, if you'll excuse me. As professionals, you'll both appreciate that I have to be seen to be professional in the present context. Detective-Superintendent Highcroft will be here shortly to take charge of the case.'

Sarah contented herself with a quick grimace out of Annie's line of vision. Baxter moved off to confer with the returning Prynne. A roll-call revealed that of the registered conference members only Frances Lake, Karen East, Coulter Dryden, the Bishop of Fenport and his wife were absent.

'An errand of mercy—in the Bishop's case,' Ambrose Yardley put in. 'Sickbed visit to an old Cambridge friend, name of Henry Claverhouse. Madingley Road address, I seem to recall.'

Baxter thanked him. 'What about family and staff?' he asked Prynne quietly.

'Mr Lake is here, as you see. Mrs Lake is with her granddaughter in the family's private quarters. Mr Derwent Lake was expected for the weekend, but it seems he was held up in London by business.'

'The family business—the bank?'

Prynne fiddled with the points of his doublet. 'I assumed so, but I'm not the best person to ask. Mrs Lake is the only member of the family I could claim as a friend.'

'Staff, then?'

'I saw Mrs Gorridge, the housekeeper, leave shortly after supper with Audrey, the domestic help.'

'Audrey who?'

'No idea, I'm afraid. Never met her before today. Perhaps Mr Lake . . .?'

'Yes, thanks. We'll pursue that later.' Baxter left the course director to report to the slight, anxious-looking man who had appeared with Clayton Warren in the doorway. Detective-Superintendent Victor Highcroft's thin lips were compressed in the expression that emphasized his facial resemblance to a Dover sole. They quivered briefly as Baxter joined him in the corridor.

'Messy business, Richard.'

'Murder is, don't you find? Shall we go upstairs, sir?'

'Went straight to the Scene on arrival. Trevor Bly's a sound SOC man. No sense in getting under his people's feet, especially as there's no doubt about the weapon.'

'The candlestick? That what Dr Green thinks?' Over their eight years' acquaintance, Baxter had come to attach considerable weight to the police surgeon's judgement.

'Oh, you know Green. Cagey as ever. Injuries consistent with blows to the back of the skull with a candlestick. But we've got the bloody candlestick, haven't we? Bloody in the literal sence, I hasten to add. Don't know what state your eyesight's in, Richard, but I'm not in need of a path report to tell me what I saw with my own eyes.'

'Sarah saw it too, sir. In which connection, I should like to say that if you find my wife's presence here prejudicial in my serving under you on this case—'

'I've drawn the problem to the Chief Constable's attention. I shall—we shall both—be bound by his ruling. Understood?'

'Of course, sir.' Baxter's antacid tablet began to take effect. He belched softly and smiled, not only from physical relief. Among the group of policemen in Highcroft's wake he had spotted a chunky figure with a split-melon smile. 'Glad to see DI Armstrong's to be with us.'

'Ah yes. You've worked together on murders before.'

'A few.'

'I've dipped into some of your case files. I'm not denying you get results. As to your methods—'

Warren cleared his throat.

'This is of course neither the time nor the place for a counselling session.'

Bill Armstrong, now within earshot, raised his eyes to the intricately moulded ceiling.

'I should, however, like to reiterate my view that every major investigation should be approached as a Learning Experience.'

'Yes, sir.'

'By which I do not mean trial-and-error learning.'

'No, sir.'

'Procedures must be clearly defined and closely monitored.'

'Yes, sir.'

'As a means to these ends the mobile incident room should be in place in the car park and fully operational at eight a.m. tomorrow.'

He's time-wasting, Baxter thought. He's scared rigid. 'Any immediate instructions, sir?'

'When I've made a general announcement I propose to interview Dr Baxter—like you to sit in on that one, Armstrong. Meantime, Richard, you might initiate the usual—the usual formalities. Over the network. No need to leave the premises.' Highcroft licked his thin lips.

'Usual formalities to include a media statement, I take it? Do we realease the victim's name?'

'Not until we've traced the next-of-kin. London address. Have to liaise with the Met on that one, I suppose.'

'Can't see any alternative, sir. Time is of the essence, I imagine?'

'Absolutely. The Chief Constable has high expectations in that regard. Unrealistic expectations, if I may say so in confidence.'

'And Mrs Talbot? All-stations alert?'

'I suppose so.' Highcroft sighed. 'But don't let the media in on her disappearance. Not yet.'

'And the room searches, sir? Like me to liaise with Scenes of Crime?'

'Won't be necessary. The candlestick was grasped with a gloved hand, I understand. That being so, I've no great hopes of the physical evidence to be secured on site, although I agree with Superintendent Warren here that all rooms should be searched before anyone is allowed to go to bed. I've instructed Bly to report any significant findings direct to me until the computer system becomes operational.'

'Yes, sir.'

'This is essentially a people problem.'

'Yes, sir.'

'If I can't be of any further assistance, Vic—' Warren murmured.

Highcroft brightened visibly. 'No need to detain you, Clay. Let you know my staffing requirements first thing tomorrow.' It was only when the uniformed superintendent had departed that Highcroft returned to the parlour to make his short public announcement. Baxter lingered at the open door to observe reactions.

'You will have been wondering why you have been asked to assemble here, ladies and gentlemen. There has been an incident—a fatal incident, which for the time being we are treating as murder. The victim, a course participant, went by the name of Karen East.'

The hearers' faces registered a predictable sequence of emotions. Shock, mild distress, and then perplexity as the implications of the ambiguous phraseology sank in. It was from the corridor behind him that Baxter picked up the faint but authentic signal of grief. He swung round to see Coulter Dryden, still robed in the black fur and brown velvet of Henry VIII.

'You all right, sir?' Dryden's WPC escort staggered as he slumped against her. Baxter hauled him upright.

'Prints man found him in the deceased's room. Asleep in a chair. Quite chilled, he was.'

'How d'you feel now, Mr Dryden?' Baxter touched the cold cheek, which had a faint purplish tinge.

'Aw ri.'

'Better thaw out gently, all the same. Don't sit too near the fire, will you? Could you organize a hot drink, Officer?'

The girl nodded and disappeared. Dryden, clutching at Baxter's arm now, allowed himself to be led to an X-chair.

'We've met before, haven't we?' he said.

'Detective Chief Inspector Baxter.'

'Sarah's husband? Richard? Been at my house, haven't you?'

'Yes, but—'

'Bishness is bishness? Know how to mind my Ps and Qs, for God's sake. Not asking any favours. It's just—it's just that I didn't take in what that mingy-mouthed bugger was saying just now. And I wanna get it straight. I just wanna get it straight, that's all.'

'Like me to take over, Chief Inspector?' Deborah Dryden spoke with an authority he wouldn't have supposed her capable of, her white overall enhancing the paramedical image. 'Coulter's apt to overdo on punch, I'm afraid. And Tudor dancing's thirstmaking, as Sarah will have told you. But your hands are like ice, darling! Where on earth have you been all this time?

The why of Dryden's recent whereabouts teased Baxter as he retreated to the screens passage which offered quiet to use his radiophone and a table-top where he could rest his notepad.

It being a Saturday night, communicative efforts proved more than usually frustrating. He wasn't surprised to find, on his return to the winter parlour, that Sarah had already been interviewed and dispatched to the Lakes' flat to release Frances from babysitting duties. Superintendent Highcroft, he was informed, required his presence in the buttery.

This was, to Baxter's eyes, a more agreeable setting than the more heavily restored public rooms. Here, the smoke-darkened panelling was relieved only by a well-maintained display of pewterware on the huge dresser. Robin Lake's salmon-and-gold costume stood out in contrast to the prevailing gloom. The detachable sleeves of the doublet had been removed to expose a lawn shirt, its cuffs unfastened. Framed by a white net ruff, the banker's face looked greyish.

'Half an hour?' Highcroft prompted as Baxter slipped on to the bench beside him. 'The candle dance went on for a full half-hour?'

'As near as makes no difference. People didn't want to stop, you see. The dancers changed over every five minutes or so and a new pair of instrumentalists took over half way through.'

'You danced yourself?'

'Three times.'

'And the names of your partners?'

'Dr Baxter, Mrs Dryden and another lady. Cynthia

something-or-other. Can't remember her surname. She was wearing a brown-and-yellow costume.' The response was slow, effortful.

'You knew Karen East?'

'Very slightly. Someone introduced us at breakfast—Mr Prynne, I believe.'

'How'd she strike you?'

A fractional pause. 'A nice, ordinary young woman. Very ordinary. The Tudor costume made a difference, of course.'

'Any contact with her this evening?'

'Contact?' Lake repeated dully. 'I didn't speak to her, if that's what you mean. Last time I saw her, she was dancing with Mrs Talbot.'

'Were they in the hall when the dance finished?

'I—I couldn't be sure. I don't think they were there when the electricity was switched on, but that was some minutes later.' Lake sagged suddenly, then straightened, pressing his right fist against his forehead.

'Sorry. Haven't come to terms with this horrible thing that's happened. Poor Karen. And poor Lucy Talbot. My wife would be terribly distressed if anything happened to her. You're taking steps?'

'A search has been initiated, sir. Tell us what you did after the dance, please.'

'Tidied the hall with the help of a few others. Straightened chairs. Picked up the odd scrap of litter. Collected the candlesticks and took them into the kitchen. I'd missed supper, so I heated up some pie in the microwave and ate it while Mrs Dryden made a start on washing and polishing the candlesticks. We both wanted to save Mrs Gorridge and Audrey the trouble in the morning. When I'd finished eating I gave Mrs Dryden a hand. It was a slow job.'

'Anyone else muck in?'

'To begin with. Then they drifted off to a drinks party in the winter parlour. People had stocked up at the village off-licence earlier in the day.'

'But you didn't join then?'

'No. I was feeling a bit whacked, to be honest. Not up to party tricks.'

'What then?'

'Nothing much. When we'd finished cleaning the candlesticks, Deb—Mrs Dryden—made tea. We sat and chatted about this and that. That's where I was when Father Yardley came down to tell us the terrible news. I went out to the car park to wait for the police.'

'Why did you do that?' Baxter took up the questioning as Highcroft answered a call on his personal radio.

'To make sure your people were let in without delay, Chief Inspector. To make sure no one left the house. And, to be frank, because I felt the need of fresh air.'

'Feel the need of fresh air earlier in the evening too?' Baxter asked.

Lake coloured slightly. 'Sorry, I don't quite—'

Baxter got up and moved round the table. 'Would you mind standing up, sir?'

He complied.

'Damp mud on your shoes, Mr Lake. Dry mud on your breeches—and a tear. Looks like a rose thorn, doesn't it? With a scrap of dead leaf attached. I don't seem to remember any rose-bushes on the direct route from the house to the car park. We've a long night ahead, some of us. Will you think again, please?'

Lake sat down heavily. 'When I got back from London, my wife told me she was worried about our granddaughter. Apparently the child went into a panic about something or other at supper. She's had nightmares recently—I was worried too. Last thing I wanted to do was to dress up in this bloody rigout and go dancing. Frances felt strongly that one of us should put in an appearance, so I gave in. But I went the long way round from our flat to the hall—out into the grounds and all round the house, matter of fact.'

'Why was that, sir?'

'To steady my nerves. Often do, when I feel frazzled.'

'Any special reason why you should feel frazzled today, sir? Apart from your anxieties about your granddaughter? Business, for instance? Is it usual for you to go to Town on a Saturday?'

Lake's face closed. 'Less unusual than it was. It's no

secret that competition among City finance houses is fiercer than ever these days.'

'You don't propose to draw aside the corporate veil, I take it?' Baxter followed up.

'Certainly not. What went on in the bank today has no bearing whatsoever on this appalling tragedy. And now, gentlemen, if there's nothing else?'

'Any comments?' Highcroft asked when the door had closed behind him.

'Only the obvious one,' Armstrong offered. 'Mrs Dryden and he may have been up to more than he let on.'

'Which might account for his evident anxiety,' Baxter conceded. 'But my guess is he has business worries. He over-reacted to the suggestion.'

'Hmm.' Highcroft added hieroglyphics to a diagram he had been constructing on a sheet of graph paper. 'We may have to pick up both points later. Bly's news is of more immediate concern.'

'Prints?' Armstrong asked.

'Something more disturbing. There were cuts on Sharrock's left-hand glove. Shallow cuts. As though he'd been testing the blade of a knife.'

'Which is now in someone else's possession?'

'Right. This must obviously increase our concern for all absent parties, Mrs Talbot especially. Something else came through just before you joined us, Richard. David Sharrock has form.'

'The blue-eyed boy of British industry? Tell me more.'

'Nothing too exciting. It was nearly eight years ago. Bank and credit card frauds in London and Cambridge. Most of his victims were undergraduates.'

'Did he do time?'

'Probation. During which he was taken on by a rehab outfit called Tekbridge.'

'Tekbridge, you said?'

'Should the name ring a bell? Never been into rehab myself, to be honest.'

Armstrong repressed a snigger.

'This particular outfit was headed by Jonathan Talbot.'

'Good God! We're going to have a lot of questions for the Bishop when he shows up.'

If the Bishop showed up.

CHAPTER 7

It was an odd experience for Baxter to hear Armstrong's recapitulation of the interview with Sarah. Highcroft listened with evident attention, adding occasional embellishments to his multicoloured diagram which looked to the Chief Inspector less of a visual aid than a visual hindrance.

'A very creditable performance.'

It was several seconds before Baxter realized the assessment was of Sarah's evidence rather than Armstrong's shorthand. He grunted non-committally.

'Which makes her failure to report Friday night's intrusion all the more extraordinary. Any policeman's wife—'

'Sarah doesn't usually define herself in those terms. As she explained to you, she had other priorities.'

'Concern for her hostess? Yes, well. Spilt milk. What emerges most startlingly from her story is the familiarity between Sharrock and the Bishop's wife.'

'Lucy's a kindly soul, Sarah reckons. A soft touch for lame ducks.'

'And an occasion for sin, according to our reverend friend.'

'That could mean almost anything.'

'What it means to me, Richard, is that we need to locate the lady soonest. Armstrong, I want you to go to HQ to get the search operation under way.'

'What about the Bishop?' Baxter put in. 'Should we check if he's still in Cambridge?'

'Take that one on board, too, Armstrong.' Highcroft's bluster evaporated with the Inspector's departure. 'Prynne next for us, would you say, Dick?'

'French, for preference.'

'Very well.' Highcroft radioed the request to the uniformed sergeant in the parlour. The reporter appeared a few minutes later, an absurd figure in his overlarge and cobbled costume.

'You know Chief Inspector Baxter, I expect?'

French nodded. 'I've worn a crime correspondent's hat among others in my *Echo* days.'

'Deputy Feature Editor now, isn't it?' In Armstrong's absence, Baxter resigned himself to the role of official notetaker.

French nodded again. 'White, male and twenty-seven.'

'Really, Mr French—' Highcroft protested.

'Sorry. These questions seem irrelevant, that's all. A woman has been killed, as I understand it.'

'A person known as Karen East has been killed.'

French's eyes widened. 'You're saying she was a transvestite—or a transsexual?'

'For the time being we're saying what we've just said,' Highcroft snapped. 'What we'd like from you is an account of your activities today—more especially this evening.'

'From supper-time? I ate, I watched the demonstration dances in the hall. I joined in the candle dance.'

'For how long?'

'Until ten, when the music stopped, but with a couple of sitting-out breaks. There were rules about changing partners, but people didn't stick to them.'

'Can you give us a list of your partners?'

'Oh God. They were none of them people I'd met before, so it's not easy. But I'll try.' He named five names, and hesitated over a sixth. 'I'll confirm that when you let me go to my room where my notes are.'

'Notes?'

'For this feature Poynter and I are doing. That's why we're here.'

'But Poynter isn't,' Baxter put in. 'Left somewhat unexpectedly, Dr Urquhart says.'

'Just before the candle dance.'

Highcroft retrieved the questioning. 'Why was that?'

'Said he'd another assignment to fit in.'

'What sort of assignment?'

'No idea—we're not buddies. It's a fluke he's on this job with me.'

'On one of your jobs here?'

'Annie told you I was interviewing the Bishop, did she?'

'Merely interviewing, Mr French?'

'What does that imply?' Toby reddened.

'According to Dr Baxter, you are or were anxious to return something to the Bishop. Something you'd *borrowed*?' Highcroft's narrow mouth expanded briefly.

'Something I was given.' Toby's colour deepened.

'Which I must request you to hand over.'

'Look, this is Mr Talbot's personal property. It has nothing whatsoever to do—'

'Sure, Mr French? A dead body was found in the Talbots' room. The Bishop and his wife are missing.'

'You're not inferring—'

'I'm inferring nothing.' Highcroft's temper snapped. 'Come on, French. You're well aware of the penalties for withholding evidence.'

With evident reluctance, the reporter handed over an unsealed envelope, with the words *Scandals of the Suburbs* scrawled across it in a bold hand. The contents, as Baxter discovered when Highcroft had read his fill, were heavier going than the title had suggested. The deficiencies of outer-city housing estates and their social effects were itemized in graphs and tables and six pages of solid text.

'You've read this, Mr French?' Highcroft looked stunned, his multicoloured diagram momentarily neglected.

'I have. Shouldn't, I suppose, but Mr Talbot had mentioned the paper—a report he's recently presented to a General Synod working party—in one of our talks earlier today. Said he'd meant to bring it here to show me, but he seemed to have left it at home.'

'But he hadn't, had he, Mr French? When was it that the document fell into your hands?'

'After supper this evening. After the Bishop had left for Cambridge.'

'You were *given* the envelope, you said. By whom?'

'Sorry, Superintendent. Never reveal my sources. You know the convention.'

'I know that silly-ass games are out of place in a murder inquiry. You're obstructing, Mr French.'

'Sorry again.' The face above the overlarge ruff was no longer absurd.

'If I could have a word, sir.' Baxter whispered a suggestion in his senior's ear. Highcroft frowned, shook his head, and consulted his visual aid before acting on it.

'The Chief Inspector thinks it might make a difference if you knew the deceased was killed wearing Mrs Talbot's fancy-dress, including Mrs Talbot's wig. This is not yet for publication, you understand.'

'You mean Lucy Talbot could have been the intended victim? May herself be dead or in danger?'

'Precisely. I ask you again, Mr French. Who gave you that letter?'

The reporter shook his head. 'It's irrelevant. I'm one hundred per cent sure it's irrelevant. And there's another thing. I'm sure Mr Talbot wouldn't kill his wife. What I saw and heard of him today convinced me that he's a decent bloke. An honest, decent bloke.'

'Interesting. But I want facts from you, Mr French, not opinions.' Highcroft glared across the table.

Toby glared back.

Baxter handed his superior a scrap of paper on which he had written the words 'give him time' followed by a diplomatic question-mark.

Highcroft sighed, and changed tack. 'What did you do after the candle dance?' he asked.

'Went up to the bedroom to see Annie. Told her there'd been a development which meant I wanted to see the Bishop again this evening. She was working, didn't want to be interrupted, she said. So I went back to the winter parlour.'

'And stayed there how long?'

'Until a quarter to eleven or thereabouts, when I went up to the Talbots' room to check if the Bishop was back. Dr Baxter will confirm. Then back to my own room to tell Annie something was up. She wasn't there. Clothes all over the place, so I checked the bathroom we'd been using. Heard her inside yodelling her head off. No sense in spoiling things, so I left her to it. Back to the winter parlour.'

'See anyone upstairs apart from Dr Baxter?'

'Met Father Yardley on my way down.'

'Bloody journalists,' the Superintendent complained when Toby had departed without revealing the donor of the envelope. 'Your softly, softly approach hasn't done us much good with this one.'

'But it yet may.' Baxter flexed his writing hand.

'In the meantime, we'd better see Yardley.'

In profile, as Baxter had first glimpsed him, the face above the priest's cassock had an austere distinction. Frontally revealed at close quarters, it had the shape and texture, though not the warm colour, of a peanut.

'Father Ambrose Yardley,' Highcroft read from Prynne's checklist. 'Are you in Catholic orders?'

'Church of England. Anglo-Catholic.'

'You told Dr Baxter that you found the body?'

'I did.'

'Did you know the person who went by the name of Karen East?'

'By sight. Never spoke to the woman.' Baxter wondered if he had imagined a stress on the word *woman*.

'Did you see her in the candle dance?'

'From a distance. I was playing tenor sackbut. Dancing itself holds little interest for me.'

'In that case, why are you here?'

'As a favour to Mrs Lake. She and her husband have made generous donations to several Renaissance music groups with which I'm associated.'

'Nevertheless, you saw something of Karen on the dance floor this evening. What do you remember?'

'Very little. Her beautiful costume.'

'And her partners?'

'Mostly, as I recall, she danced with Mrs Talbot.'

'Strike you as unusual, women dancing together?'

Yardley shrugged. 'Not particularly. The sex ratio here is unbalanced.'

'Did Karen and Mrs Talbot stay until the end of the dance?'

'I didn't notice.'

'You yourself went on playing?'

'That's right.'

'And then?'

'Went up to my room.'

Highcroft consulted the checklist. 'West Wing, I see. Same corridor as the Talbots?'

'But at the other end.'

'Go on.'

'Drank orange juice I'd brought with me. Caught up with some academic work—essay-marking.'

'Hear anything outside your room while you were working?'

'Occasional footsteps, voices, but I've learnt to shut out distractions when I'm working or praying. At ten forty-five I said Compline. My usual practice. At eleven-fifteen I went along to the Talbots' room.'

'Why?'

'I wanted to see the Bishop on Church business.'

'An unorthodox time to talk business.'

'It was urgent.'

'Sorry, Father Yardley. We need more than that.' The peanut face creased. 'If you're not prepared to enlarge now, we may have to ask again. And again. Mrs Talbot may well have been the murderer's target. You don't need me to spell out—'

'That my words to Dr Baxter put me under suspicion?' Yardley smiled. 'Personally, Superintendent, I'm indifferent to my reputation with the local constabulary. However, it's my priestly duty to avoid scandal. I'd a phone call from a friend this evening, if you must know. Church organist. He's just been threatened with dismissal if he doesn't conform to the whims of his new vicar, whom I know to be a musical ignoramus. My friend's determined to argue his case all the way up to the Diocesan Synod if necessary, and I wanted to catch the Bishop's ear before the vicar did.'

'I see. You went to the Talbots' bedroom. Go on.'

'The room was in darkness, but the door was fractionally ajar. I knocked. No reply. Thought I'd leave Jon—the Bishop—a note. So I switched on the light—and saw what your wife saw, Chief Inspector.'

'Tell us,' Baxter said coldly.

'The body I took for Mrs Talbot's—lying spreadeagled, face down. The blood on the head and neck and on the floor. An artificial flower on the floor near the body, and further away a bloodied candlestick. I rang the Lakes' quarters straight away. Saw no one until Dr Baxter came.'

'To whom you said, "She was an occasion for sin." What did you mean?' Baxter asked.

'Another question you'll put again and again if necessary? Very well. I've known Jonathan Talbot since he was a boy. Almost from our first meeting I realized he'd a vocation for the priesthood and a vocation for celibacy. Lucy—that spoilt, sanctimonious child—came between Jonathan and the divinc purpose. I can think of no greater sin than shutting one's ears to God.'

'Not even murder?' Baxter asked.

'Of course not.' Yardley spoke tetchily, as if to a dull pupil. 'The part is less than the whole.'

'Thank you for your help, Father Yardley,' the Superintendent put in.

'I'm free to go?' A flash of resentment, perhaps of thwarted martyrdom, distorted the peanut face.

'For the time being.'

Highcroft had transferred his attention to his graph paper before the priest left the room. Baxter saw that it now contained an assortment of geometrical shapes filled with shorthand squiggles and interconnected with dotted and solid lines.

The Superintendent intercepted his inquiring gaze.

'Germ of my Major Inquiry Graphic System, mark one. Tell you more when it's online. Any input you'd care to suggest?'

'Milky coffee and toast. Like me to arrange it?'

'If you feel the need, Baxter, I'll keep you company.'

Baxter appealed to Frances Lake, at whose suggestion hospitality was extended all round. Several volunteers, under PC Browning's supervision, withdrew to the kitchen to prepare snacks. Annie Urquhart, who had predictably failed to offer her services for this domestic chore, followed Baxter out of the parlour.

'Who's next?' she asked.

'Don't think the Superintendent's decided.'

'Then could you decide for him, Richard?'

Painfully aware that Highcroft must be receiving every well-projected syllable, Baxter looked her in the eye. 'State your case, Dr Urquhart.'

'I've remembered something potentially important. Didn't register when I talked to you earlier, but—'

'Stay there. See what I can do.'

Highcroft was persuaded with a little difficulty to postpone the interview with Coulter Dryden.

Annie stuck in essentials to the story she had already told Baxter, with one significant addition.

'I'd just settled down in my bath when I heard this car starting. Bloody irritating. I was finalizing the structure of a paper I'm presenting in Stockholm next week when this fool started abusing an ignition system. Went on for two or three minutes maybe.'

'What time would this be?' Highcroft asked.

'Five to eleven—something like that.'

'Can you be more specific about the engine type?'

'Quite specific. Like the bathroom we share, our bedroom's on the north side of the house, overlooking the car park. Ordinary engine noise I'm used to. Don't ask me about all the comings and goings this weekend. I didn't register them. Ignition trouble's different. It's the on-off-on feature that gets to you, I suppose. First time this godawful row started up was after supper yesterday. I looked out of the window. It was a dirty white little van with a sign on the side. Too dark to read it.'

'Registration?'

'Didn't get that either. And I didn't see much of the driver, because of the way the van was facing. What I did see was Patricia Gorridge—the housekeeper here—in the front passenger seat.'

'Sure of this, Dr Urquhart?'

'Quite sure. There's something else . . .' She hesitated.

'Go on, please.'

'I think I heard the same vehicle start much later yesterday evening, about eleven. But faintly, farther away. On the road maybe. I was on my way to the loo at the time. That was just before I discovered our room had been gone over.'

Frances Lake was waiting outside with a tray when Annie took her departure.

'If you want to question me, could we possibly get it over with?' she asked as she poured coffee. 'Dr Baxter has been most kind, but I'd like to get back to my granddaughter. As you may know, something upset her at supper.' She twisted her rings.

Highcroft invited her to sit down. Her evidence added nothing to Sarah's, until she was asked about Patricia Gorridge's travel arrangements.

'Her son gave her a lift home yesterday. He was helping out here.'

'Name? Occupation? Address?'

'Nigel. Self-employed computer maintenance engineer, when he's anything. Better at spending money than earning it, according to local gossip. Don't know his address, but you'll find it in the Yellow Pages under Fennycom, I expect. That's the name on his van.'

'Can you describe the van?'

'White Ford transit. In appalling condition, considering Gorridge's mechanical skills.'

'He's helped out here before?'

'Occasionally, when his own business was slack. But he doesn't like getting his hands dirty, and he expects better pay than we can offer. He's good about giving his mother lifts, though. Seems genuinely attached. Whatever Nigel Gorridge's faults, I don't see him as a murderer.'

'There's a chance—a slim chance, I agree—that the crime was manslaughter.'

'But *whose* manslaughter?' Frances's voice rose. 'This business has put an awful strain on everyone, not least my husband and myself. The uncertainty doesn't help. Who was this Karen East person? Surely we've a right to know.'

The detectives exchanged glances. 'You will as soon as the next-of-kin has been located and informed,' Highcroft said. 'I'm sure you'd appreciate that courtesy if the victim were a relative of your own.'

Without warning, Frances Lake began to weep. When, after a brief interval, she made an apologetic departure, Highcroft conferred with Baxter. Armstrong was radioed with a request to add Nigel Gorridge's name to the list of those wanted for questioning.

Coulter Drysdale was preceded into the buttery by an officer carrying a plastic-wrapped Smith and Wesson revolver which had been found in his breeches pocket. The man himself, who was shown in a few minutes later, looked to have regained his normal body temperature. Although not yet sober, he had the manner of a self-aware inebriate. When Highcroft's first question forced him to look up, the flabby face below the velvet cap was expressionless.

'Is this your weapon?'

'Yes, Superintendent.'

'Are you aware that it is illegal for a private citizen to carry such a weapon?'

'Yes, Superintendent.'

'Why were you carrying it tonight?'

'Because I'm a man of substance and I don't have a bodyguard. Success entails vulnerability.'

'Had you any special reason to feel vulnerable tonight?'

'None.'

'Why did you go to the deceased's room?'

'I had questions to ask him.'

'*Him*, Mr Dryden?'

'David Sharrock. Hadn't meant this to come out—for Deb's sake. But I'm not quite sober enough to tell a convincing lie.'

'What sort of questions?'

'First and foremost, why he was got up as a woman.'

'Why should that concern you?'

'He was an acquaintance—a business associate. I'm not an old fogey. Don't like old or young fogeys round me. But you have to draw the line somewhere. And cross-dressing in public places is out of line.'

'So Sharrock was an acquaintance. A friend?'

'I did Dave a few good turns on his way up. Saw his potential when others didn't. Latterly, we collaborated in a number of joint ventures that brought us together socially. We came to know and like each other. He was almost like a son to me.' Dryden brushed his eyes.

'When did you last see him before this weekend?'

'Three or four weeks ago—I can't be sure.'

'Where?'

'For dinner at my house. He was passing through on his way to Fenfantasy—his new theme park near Fenport.'

'Did you entertain him often?'

'Once a month at least.'

'Did he give you any indication he'd be coming here this weekend?'

'None.'

'Did he know you planned to come?'

'Not as far . . . Wait, though. I believe Deborah mentioned it over dinner one evening. The idea of us dressing up in Tudor costume seemed to amuse him.'

'When did your paths first cross this weekend?'

'Last night at supper.'

'Recognize him straight away?'

'More or less.'

'And your wife?'

'Didn't suspect a thing. She'd have told me if she had, I'm sure of it.'

'And you didn't enlighten her? Why not?' It was Baxter's question, and he watched the reaction with interest.

'It would have spoilt her weekend, especially with Dave making up to the Bishop's wife the way he was. Deb's seen a lot of the world since we married. But she's an old-fashioned girl at heart. Goes by the standards they taught her in Sunday School.'

Highcroft reclaimed the interrogation. 'Did Sharrock know you were coming to his room tonight?'

The briefest of hesitations. 'No. I wanted to take him off guard.'

'Tell us about your trip home this morning.'

Dryden shifted on the hard bench. 'I've already made a statement to your colleagues on that subject.'

'Which we haven't yet had time to check. We understand you called in for some papers?'

'That's correct.'

'Which you found?'

'I did.'

'Leaving your car at the Fourways Garage?'

'Correct again.'

'Are you sure you picked up nothing but papers from your house?' Baxter interposed.

'Quite sure. I don't get the drift of the question—'

'Did you pick up your revolver, for instance?'

'No—absolutely not. I already had it on me.' Dryden looked and sounded relieved as he gave his final answer. What question, Baxter asked himself, had he been expecting?

CHAPTER 8

Baxter picked up Highcroft's chirruping radiophone.

''Lo, Bill.'

'Where's the Super?'

'Gone for a pee, minus his handset. Reckon he's a hang-up about doing official business in a state of undress. What've you got?'

'It's good. Gorridge has a juvenile record, for starters. Shoplifting at first. Then a credit card job in 'eighty-two.'

'Like Sharrock.'

'His offences were in Cambridge, Gorridge's in Holtchester. No evidence of a criminal association, but they'd been mates. Not being a first offender, Gorridge got three months' youth custody. Sharrock, as you may recall, was put on probation.'

'Enough to end a beautiful relationship.'

'Seemingly not. Pair of them signed up for Tekbridge about the same time.'

'That's neat—very neat. Any later links?'

'Only thing on record is that Sharrock paid a fine of Gorridge's four years back—motoring offence.'

'Where's Gorridge now?'

'No trace. Certainly not in the flat over his business premises in Fen Holton. Want us to try his house in Cambridge? Or his mother's?'

'Just put both houses under surveillance. The search for his van and for Mrs Talbot still takes priority. Any sightings?'

'No. Someone's spotted the Bishop's car, though. Heading your way. I've had a word with Mrs Claverhouse, but I couldn't get an estimate of his departure time out of her. She was asleep when he left, she says, and she doesn't want her husband disturbed.'

'Hold off, then.' Hearing purposeful footsteps, Baxter ended the conversation.

'Mrs Dryden next,' Highcroft decreed, when he had been brought up to date.

Whereas Coulter Dryden had regained something of his self-possession before being interviewed, Deborah seemed less assured than on their last encounter. She looked physically uncomfortable in the too-tight overall—borrowed perhaps?

'Do you know the identity of the deceased?' Highcroft asked after the preliminary formalities.

She nodded. 'David Sharrock. My husband has just told me.'

'But before that? Had you any suspicion that Karen East might not be what she seemed?'

Deborah laced her fingers. 'It crossed my mind that she and Lucy Talbot might have met before.'

'Why was that?'

'They laughed a lot when they were together—as though they shared some sort of private joke.'

'How well do you know Mrs Talbot?'

'We've hardly ever met outside the Historical Dance Society. Lucy's been coming for the last six months.'

'How did you find her?'

'A very nice girl—lively, kind, outgoing.'

'Would you say her behaviour in David Sharrock's company was typical of her?'

'No. Lucy's a strong sense of humour but it isn't like her to be cliqueish—to shut people out.'

'What about Sharrock? Was it in character for him to—er—cross-dress?'

Deborah fiddled with her rings. 'I've no idea what makes people do that sort of thing, Superintendent. Exhibitionism, perhaps. David certainly liked attention.'

'How long have you known him, Mrs Dryden?'

'Seven or eight years.'

'Can you remember how you first met?'

'Through Jonathan Talbot, oddly enough. You've heard of Tekbridge—the rehab scheme he started for young offenders? Quite a few industrialists—East Anglian people especially—became involved, my husband among them. Coulter helped out for several years with finance and employment opportunities. David Sharrock was one of the youngsters he gave a start to.'

'And took a personal interest in.'

Deborah fingered her pendant. 'My husband takes a personal interest in any charity he supports financially.'

'But Sharrock, we understand, became your husband's friend. And yours?'

Deborah sighed. 'David was a frequent visitor—quite often, a house guest. I did my best for him as a hostess for my husband's sake. He'd missed out on affection as a child—I made allowances. Superficially, he could be charming. But underneath I felt he was sneering at us—using us. Friends? No, Superintendent. It would be dishonest to say David Sharrock and I were friends.'

'Enemies, then?' Baxter put in quickly. 'Did you regard him as an enemy?'

Deborah shook her head. 'I don't think of anyone in those terms. I honestly don't.'

Darting a disapproving glance in his subordinate's direction, Highcroft reverted to the events of the evening. Deborah's earlier responses had persuaded Baxter that she liked, where possible, to be truthful. Yet her account of her recent activities was stilted and unconvincing. Her evidence supported what they had already heard, but added little.

'Well?' Highcroft smothered a yawn as the door closed behind her.

'Alibi's not quite right. These last five minutes she wasn't speaking her own lines.'

'Whose, then?'

'Her husband's or Lake's or both, I'd say.'

'Maybe it's something she's got going with Lake? Maybe she's just trying to spare Frances—'

'Maybe.'

'Won't go down well at Shire Hall if we muckrake unnecessarily, Richard. The Chief Constable tipped me the wink. The Lakes and Drydens between them have put a lot of money into Cambridgeshire. Lake's in line for a deputy lieutenantship.'

'And Sharrock in his idiosyncratic way has done the state some service.'

'The anti-drink ads? The Think European campaign? Self-advertisement, if you ask me. Count me in with Mrs D, Baxter. Fogey I may be, but I'll never understand—'

Voices were raised in the passage. A knock. PC Browning opened the door a scant foot, his coffee mug uplifted in a gesture of deterrence.

'Excuse me, sir. The Bishop of Fenport—'

'What's going on, Superintendent?' The voice was brusque but not unpleasant. 'I can't get any straight answers. What's all this about a murder? Whose murder? And where's my wife?'

'Very well, Officer.' Highcroft looked and sounded at the end of his tether. 'Show the Bishop in.'

The man in the damp black raincoat was taller than Baxter had remembered him. A strand of greying hair straggled across a conventionally handsome face. He clutched a document folder.

'Care to tell us where you've been, sir?' Highcroft began.

Talbot's eyebrows shot up. 'An alibi? You're asking me—?'

'We're asking everybody, sir,' Highcroft soothed. 'Normal routine.'

'Yes, yes, I'm sorry. Don't think I'm trying to pull rank —that would be farcical in present circs. It's just this all seems so unreal, and my prime concern is for Lucy.'

'We've an alert out, sir, but at present we've next to nothing to go on. We need your cooperation.'

'Very well. I left here for Cambridge immediately after supper. Spent the evening at Starlings. That's a house on the Madingley Road—don't remember the number if I ever knew it.'

'With a Mr and Mrs Claverhouse?'

Talbot nodded. 'If someone's going to question them, could they do it gently, please? Henry's terminally ill.'

'So his wife tells us.'

A quick frown.

'And you drove straight to Cambridge and back?'

'Absolutely.'

'Times of arrival and departure?'

'Eight and eleven-thirty at a guess, but it would only be a guess. The Claverhouses and I hadn't met for three or four years. We talked a good deal, played bridge.'

'All three of you?'

'Sometimes, and sometimes Henry and I chatted on our own while Madge caught up with her chores or rested. She was asleep when I left. Now please—can we get back to Lucy?'

'We'd like you to check your wife's belongings later, but as far as we can see she left Hare Holt between ten and eleven-fifteen without anything except the clothes she stood up in.'

'Her period costume?'

'No, sir. She was wearing her own Tudor shoes, apparently, with the period costume belonging to the deceased, the person who went by the name of Karen East. For some reason they did a swap.'

'Karen East? That gawky young woman Lucy befriended?' Talbot's surprise seemed genuine.

'Never met her before this weekend, did you?'

The Bishop shook his head.

'Remind you of anyone you'd met?'

'No. I didn't see much of Ms East, of course. Didn't give much thought to her either, to be frank. But if she was in Lucy's clothes, is it possible that she was killed by mistake? That someone—oh my God!—was trying to kill Lucy?' He covered his face in his hands.

'It's a possibility we can't exclude, sir.'

'But why? I love my wife, so I'm partial. But ask anyone who knows her. Lucy's good. The sort of person to whom goodness comes naturally. And fun to be with. Funny and attractive and very much ali—Please God she's alive.'

'No need to give up hope, sir. Did you notice anything to suggest—with hindsight—that your wife knew Karen East before this weekend?'

'No. The girl seemed to be a loner. Lucy's always nice to loners.'

'Did Mrs Talbot say anything to you about Karen?'

'No. Perhaps because I didn't give her a chance. Ironic, really. I'm always trying to sell my clergy the concept of a listening Church, but I'm all too conscious that I haven't been much of a listening husband since my preferment. The job's rather taken over—the new demands and the new opportunities. Maybe I've been trying to do too much too soon. Henry Claverhouse told me I was always a competitive bastard.'

'Housing is among your interests, I gather?'

'Yes, but how—'

'Your working-party report.'

'Which I intended to show Toby French before I discovered I'd left it at home. At least, I assumed . . .'

'Here you are, sir.' Highcroft passed the envelope and its

contents across the table. 'Mr French says it was given to him here this evening after you left for Cambridge.'

'Given? Then it must have been stolen.'

'Any suspicions about the culprit?'

'None. But what does it matter? Nothing matters now except Lucy.'

'Try to think where she might have gone, Bishop.'

Talbot rubbed his forehead. 'Everything's a crazy jumble.'

'Cup of coffee?' Baxter suggested.

'Wouldn't help. The dress-swapping doesn't make sense for one thing, unless it was some kind of joke. Lucy's a strong sense of humour. What was this Karen East's other name? You've implied she had one.'

'Would it surprise you to know it was David Sharrock?'

'A man in drag? No, surely not! *The* David Sharrock? Of Sunnyscene?'

'The same.'

'I'm astounded. Horrified. Are you quite sure?'

'For all practical purposes, yes. An acquaintance of yours, we believe?'

'A client of Tekbridge seven years ago. You know about the rehab outfit I helped to get going? We cooperated with the prison, police and probation services. David's referral's on his police file, I presume?'

Highcroft nodded. 'Any subsequent contacts?'

'With me? No. Didn't expect any. David seized what rehab had to offer, and used it to good advantage. But he felt humiliated by it, I think. He didn't make a secret of his criminal record later on, but he liked to give the impression he'd pulled himself up by his own shoelaces.'

'What contact did your wife have with Sharrock—in his Tekbridge days or later?'

Talbot flushed. 'Lucy came down to our clubroom from time to time—helped out with the coffee bar, played squash, that sort of thing. And yes, she met David. They got on well—we both got on well with him. He'd plenty of charm on tap.'

'And more recently? Has your wife—?'

'Met him? Yes. I'd forgotten, until you asked just now. Lucy told me she'd run into him a couple of months ago when she took the children to Fenfantasy—that's the new theme park David's opened near Fenport. It seems he was down on a tour of inspection.'

'Any subsequent meetings?'

'He called in at the Cathedral one day when Lucy was working there. Made a very generous donation to the Restoration fund. Took her out for lunch.'

'Did they meet again?'

'No. No, I'm sure Lucy would have told me if they had.' Talbot's hands twisted. 'Or at least would have tried to tell me. The truth is—I suppose—that I've been running away from Lucy these last months. Everything she does for the Church seems to come so easily, so naturally. I didn't want her to see how tough things were for me. Didn't want to burden her with my worries and self-doubt, I told myself at first. Later I realized that was sheer conceit. That I needed to be frank with her, needed her understanding. That's why I let her persuade me to come here. It would be a chance for us to relax—to open up without worrying about the kids.

'Who are where—?'

'With Lucy's mother.'

Baxter noted the address and phone number.

'Does the name Nigel Gorridge ring a bell, Bishop?' Highcroft continued.

'Another client of Tekbridge. But you'll know that. Why do you ask?' For the first time, Talbot sounded evasive.

'Because he was here this weekend.'

'Yes, Lucy said something about him helping his mother out on Friday. I know Mrs Gorridge slightly.'

'Nigel gave her a lift home on Friday evening. But there's evidence to suggest he came back later. A candidate for the theft of your article. *Scandals of the Suburbs* is a catchy title. Maybe our friend thought he'd stumbled on something a provincial hack would pay for. Maybe you were just unlucky —other rooms appear to have been gone over. Any reason Gorridge should owe you a grudge, sir?'

'No—I can't think . . .' Talbot wasn't much of a liar, Baxter decided.

'Have you or your wife had any recent contact with him?'

'None.'

'Gorridge's van was heard leaving the car park here again tonight, about the time of Sharrock's killing or shortly after.'

'And you think he may have taken Lucy? Forced her to go with him? Oh no. Please God, not that. There's something I must tell you, though I promised Lucy I never would. She was convinced the incident was a one-off. Blamed herself.'

'What incident?'

'It was seven years ago. In Cambridge. In the Tekbridge clubroom coffee bar. Lucy'd been on her own checking stock. Nigel came in—offered to help. Then, quite out of the blue, he made a pass. Lost control, started to tear her clothes. There's no doubt in my mind that he'd have raped her if David Sharrock hadn't come on the scene and forcibly intervened.'

'And you let Gorridge get away with it?' Highcroft couldn't disguise his disapproval.

Talbot flushed. 'The episode didn't reach the ears of his probation officer, if that's what you mean. But he took some tough talking. He was a decent lad at bottom, Nigel, like many of the kids we worked with. David was different, sicker but tougher. He'd learned to split off his inadequacies, deny them if you like. He'd already got a hold on Nigel. As a result of this incident, the hold was probably strengthened. But that wasn't my main concern, as you can imagine.'

'How did your wife cope with the trauma?'

'Bravely, but I'm sure it left scars. She avoided the subject. I couldn't bear to expose her to the risk of a repeat performance, so I persuaded her to stay away from the clubroom. I was deeply committed to the project, unwilling to give it up. But the situation became absurd. My family and I were seeing almost nothing of each other. So I resigned—more abruptly than I should, I've been told.'

'By Dr Urquhart?' Baxter put in.

'Among others. And my new parochial responsibilities

didn't leave me much time for supporting a successor. Ironic, isn't it, that Nigel was indirectly responsible for the demise of Tekbridge. I used to hold that against him. Now the only thing that matters is that he hasn't hurt Lucy. There's nothing else? You're not holding out on me?'

'No, sir.' Highcroft stifled a yawn. 'You'll want to go home, I expect?'

Talbot shook his head. 'Not yet. Not without knowing.'

'As you wish. We'll do all we can, believe me. A photograph of your wife would be useful.'

Talbot produced a snapshot from his wallet.

'Thanks. And would you see the Senior Scenes of Crime Officer upstairs, please? We'd like you to check our inventory of your wife's clothing. Is that the document case your report was taken from?'

'Yes, as a matter of fact. Been handling it myself a good deal today, though.'

'Don't suppose the thief would be daft enough to open it without gloves, but they'll give it the once-over upstairs.'

'You think the theft and the killing are in some way connected? That Gorridge was implicated in both?'

'Speculation's not my style, sir.' Highcroft clasped his hands as if to conceal his graphics from unauthorized eyes. 'Rest assured that we'll be in touch as soon as we've news of your wife.'

Talbot stood up, brushing back the stray lock of greying hair for the first time in the interview. 'Thanks, Superintendent. Not your fault the assurance doesn't help much. *And this is hell, nor am I out of it.*'

As soon as the door had closed behind Talbot, Highcroft stretched. 'Looks bad for friend Gorridge, doesn't it?' The words came out in an extravagant, three-note yawn.

'Thinking of calling it a day, sir?'

'Never was a night bird. Don't late hours get to you, Richard?'

'On my second wind, by the feel of it.'

'Then I'd like you to hang in for another couple of hours. I propose to knock off until six. Alert me if they find

Gorridge. Otherwise, report to the incident room here at nine. 'Night, Richard.'

''Night, sir.'

Left to his own devices, the Chief Inspector sought the Senior Scenes of Crime Officer on the first floor.

'How goes it, Trevor?'

'Most of the real work's behind us. Packing and labelling should be finished inside the hour.'

'Good. Spare time for a quick walkabout?'

They began in the Talbots' bedroom. Baxter contemplated the chalked outline of the corpse and trail of dried blood which had led to the candlestick.

'Fingerprints?'

'Prints that look to have been Lucy Talbot's all over the show. Including that bathroom—' Bly jerked his head. 'And the bedroom beyond—Dr Baxter's.'

'My wife's friendly with Mrs Talbot.' Baxter tried to keep his voice steady. 'Seems reasonable that they should have popped in and out of each other's rooms.'

'Sure. Mrs T's prints look odd, though. Come through here.'

Bly led the way through the bathroom to Sarah's room where he paused by the window. 'Two very clear palm-marks three feet up from the sill. Big smudge lower down. Scrap of fancy-looking fabric caught in a splinter on the window-sill. There you are.' Bly indicated a plastic packet on the dressing-table.

It was white stuff, with a black and brown pattern.

'Sharrock's Tudor dress, presumably?'

'Looks like it. Nothing like it in any of the wardrobes.'

Nor, to Baxter's recollection, in the winter parlour. So Lucy had stood, tarted up as Karen, pressing herself against Sarah's window, but not banging it. Desperate to be seen but not heard. He shivered, imagining Sarah in a like predicament.

'What other prints?'

'Three clear sets in the Talbots' room. The Bishop's—his were in the bathroom too, as you'd expect. The dead man's. And A. N. Others's.'

'Nigel Gorridge's, if we're lucky. They've got his dabs on record at HQ. Could we have them checked soonest?'

'Sure. We've an identical set—partly overlaid—from one of the downstairs doors. A. N. Other seems to have exited to the car park.'

'And Mrs T?'

'Nothing on the door or frame. Several sets of footprints in the downstairs corridor. Just inside the presumed exit there's a real jumble of prints—far too messy for identification, I'd guess. Could indicate a struggle, do you think? Want a shufti?'

'I'll wait for the photos. Sharrock's room next, please.'

Baxter turned his attention to the dead man's effects. The former contents of the chest of drawers and dressing-table were those of a young woman of limited means and conventional tastes. Marks and Spencer shirts, sweaters, panties, slip and tights. A headscarf with a washed-out pattern of wildfowl. Boots tissues and make-up. A sponge-bag containing soap, toothbrush and Femina razor. A mending kit.

A young woman with conventional fantasies too. One or two of the commercial and copied tapes beside the personal radio recorder carried the names of Tudor dances, but most were country 'n' western tear-jerkers. There were also a couple of magazines—*Bella, Woman's Story*. And a Jessica Stirling historical romance.

A lovat tweed coat and skirt and a lemon jumpsuit had hung in the wardrobe. A high-necked, Victorian-style nightdress had been tucked under the pillow. A full-length padded housecoat had hung behind the door. The zipped travel bag was unlocked and empty. The handbag had contained only twenty pounds in cash, a powder compact and car keys.

'What about the car?'

'Hired Mini. No sign of the hiring papers, though. More mushy tapes in the front pocket. Five hundred cash, cheque-book and credit cards in Sharrock's clothes in the boot. Odd mixture, really.'

'How d'you mean, odd?'

'Pricey silk undies, but chainstore shirt, shoes and pinstripes. Tinted specs in the jacket pocket where we found the driving licence. Jacket isn't in great condition. Snagged —nearly torn through here and there.'

Sharrock had, however, taken every step to frustrate curious visitors to his bedroom. How many, Baxter wondered, had there been? Coulter Dryden's drunken fumblings would have effectively obliterated evidence of earlier searches. The policemen were on the point of entering the Drydens' room when Baxter's radiophone reclaimed his attention.

A taxi had just deposited Gorridge's wife at her home in Gwydir Street, Cambridge.

'I'm staying on here,' Sarah said, when he went to say good night to her in the winter parlour. 'You don't mind, do you?'

'Yes, but I'm not surprised.'

'We've been talking among ourselves. Most people want to carry on with the course. Lucy would want us to, I think. You will find her, won't you?'

'We'll do our damnedest.'

'There's another thing. Early this evening I promised Frances I'd take a trip to London with her and her granddaughter on Monday morning.'

Sarah paused and glanced sideways. Several course members, including Annie Urquhart, were within hearing distance.

'Something's been upsetting the little girl. Frances feels, as I do, that professional help may be indicated. She wants me to have a word with her son on the subject. I've cleared it with the Super—don't know if he mentioned it?'

'He's a lot on his mind.'

Annie Urquhart, overhearing, snorted derisively. Ignoring the implied insult to his superior, Baxter kissed his wife and left. He wondered briefly as he walked across the damp car park what else Sarah might have told him in confidence. But as he drove off, with the car window at his elbow fully open to admit refreshing lungfuls of moist, mild air, he concentrated on the tangled evidence already at his disposal. As always, at this stage of an inquiry, the data and their implications seemed to have a life of their own. A confusing, wriggly mass, like the seaweed he had prodded in the rock pools of his childhood, and the nameless creatures hidden beneath it.

He made good time to Cambridge.

CHAPTER 9

'Nigel? Not at home, I'm afraid.' The girl in the flowery dressing-gown and fluffy white mules looked at first glance as immaculate as the hall and staircase behind her. Wholesome was the word for Beverley Gorridge. She reminded Baxter a little of the girl on the old-style Ovaltine advertisements. It came as a surprise to realize that her plump, fair-skinned face was still made up, and the hand that returned the ID cards was less than steady.

'Know where we can contact your husband?'

'Not if he's not in Fen Holton. At his workshop or his mother's place.'

'We've tried. Expecting him home soon?'

'Not until tomorrow—today, that is. Why? Something wrong?' Beverley coloured, running a ringed hand through her tawny hair. 'Sorry to be in a mess. Don't know when I've gone to bed without cleaning myself up. Hardly ever go out on my tod either. Engagement do—one of the girls in the office. Nige backed out—rush job, he said—and Sue's a special friend. So my sister said, "Go on, why not?" She took the kids—they really like it at her place. I didn't drink anything hardly, but I've no head for booze. Nige is always taking the mickey . . . But you don't want to know all this, do you? What's wrong? Why do you need to see Nige?' She teetered and subsided on to the stairs.

'Close the front door, shall we?' Baxter suggested gently. 'Wouldn't you rather we talked in your sitting-room with a cup of black coffee inside you? Detective-Constable Browning makes a good cup of coffee.'

Baxter and Browning, a recent and enthusiastic recruit

from the uniformed branch, had rendez-voused between the Victorian terraces in Gwydir Street. Dolls' houses, most of them, cosy pads for childless couples, but a tight fit for families. A stack of red plastic toyboxes occupied one corner of the Gorridges' sitting-room, a tricycle the other. Most of the remaining floor-space was occupied by a squidgy tan three-piece suite.

'Dave Sharrock's been killed. Honest? Not having me on, are you?' Beverley said a few minutes later. 'No, of course not, you wouldn't.' She leant forward from her seat on the settee and deposited her empty mug on a glass-topped coffee table.

Baxter shook his head.

'Thank God. Terrible thing to say, isn't it?' She began to cry.

'Then why d'you say it, Mrs Gorridge?' Baxter asked. Browning blushed and glanced away from her disregarded thighs.

'Because I love my husband. And our marriage didn't stand an earthly as long as Dave Sharrock was alive.'

'Can you spell that out?' Baxter asked quietly.

Beverley blew her nose. 'Dave had star quality, I remember reading somewhere. Too right. Below the smarm, he was cold and glittery and out of reach even if he was right beside you. And Nige, poor sucker, was his number one fan.'

'So you'll have seen quite a lot of Sharrock over the years?'

'Since we were all at the Tech. Six years ago, that'd be. Nige had known him far longer. Nige and Dave and a bloke called Stuart Kerr hung out together.'

'All clients of Tekbridge?'

'Not Kerr.'

'So what'd they have in common?'

'Not a lot. Dave was doing business studies, the others were into electronics and computer engineering. Dave was ambitious, even then. I reckoned he cultivated them so he could have cheap expertise on tap any time he needed it. Julie Kerr thought the same.'

'Kerr's wife?'

'Sister. Stuart's gay.'

'Sounds like we ought to contact him. Did you and your husband keep up the friendship?'

'Not since Stu moved to London four years ago. We only hear from him at Christmas. He's a sight more stickability than my Nige. Topped up his HND with an MSc. And he's done well on the job front. He's something fancy in the City, Julie told me the last time I saw her.'

'Tell us about your husband's recent dealings with Sharrock.'

She shook her head. 'Not something Nige would tell me about.'

'Sorry, Mrs Gorridge, but this is a murder inquiry.'

'And you think that Nige . . .? No way.'

'If you want to help your husband, help us.'

Beverley sighed. 'OK. We'd this showdown three years ago, Nige and I, when I saw how much harm Dave was doing him. Dave was in the money, even then. Every time he'd been down here or we'd been up to his London place, Nigel'd talk of nothing else but Dave's new car or his new furniture or his new sound system. Audio is Nige's big passion. Whatever Dave had, Nigel wanted. And he wanted it straight away.'

'Women included?'

'Women didn't mean much to Dave, far as I could make out. Not that he was gay. Don't suppose he was ever short of a woman to wine and dine and sleep with. But no strings. Never had a living-in girlfriend that I heard of. Nige couldn't make sense of that.'

'Tell me about the showdown.'

'Not much to it. I told Nige Dave wasn't doing him any good. He'd have to choose between him and me. Should have stood my ground. All that happened was Nige didn't insist on us all going out together, didn't bring Dave here.'

'But he talked about him?'

'Not much. I didn't encourage it. So I don't know the details, only that Dave was still seeing Nige, still using him. About six months after Nige started up on his own, he got a subcontract for control systems maintenance at Fenfantasy.'

'Sharrock's theme park near Fenport?' Baxter put in for Browning's benefit.

'Uh-huh. Nige stopped working from home when that came up. Wanted a base that was convenient for Fenport as well as Cambridge, he said. His mother heard about a place going cheap in Fen Holton. Flat over an office. Building plot attached.'

'But you stayed put?'

'For the time being. I wanted to be sure things were working out before I uprooted the kids. We're cramped in this house. Neighbours are eggheads—not my sort. But I've family and friends to fall back on in Cambridge. Part-time work too, when I need it. Nigel's had financial problems before. Besides, I wasn't happy about the Fenfantasy contract. Nige has been putting too much time and effort into it when he should be expanding his clientele. And I loathed the idea of running our home on Dave Sharrock's money.'

'That lady's a motive, if she's to be believed,' Browning observed as they headed back for the car.

'And an alibi.' By the end of the interview Beverley had been clear-headed enough to name a baker's dozen of the pub party.

'I'm not saying she did the deed,' Browning persisted. 'But suppose she put someone up to it? Sort of girl a man might kill for, if he was that way inclined. I mean, I couldn't help noticing . . .'

'And I noticed you noticing, Gary.' Baxter opened the front passenger door of the police car and handed Browning the keys. 'But I'd expect a bloke who was gone on Beverley to target Gorridge, not Sharrock. Let's forget the fairy stories, shall we, and get us some facts.'

He rang HQ on the car radio.

'Is it good, sir?' Browning asked at the end of a long series of grunts.

The Chief Inspector unwrapped a soda mint. 'They've found Gorridge and his van in the back of beyond—Fen road near Manea. Seems he took a corner badly. Van ended up on its side in a ditch. Gorridge's concussed. Out cold. On his way to Addenbrooke's Hospital.'

'And Mrs Talbot?'

'Gone. Vamoosed. Little doubt but she was in the van, though. There was a piece of brocade—white with a black and brown pattern—between the seats. Torn out of a sleeve, maybe. Lipstick on Gorridge's shirt.'

'Not nice.'

'Not nice at all.'

'Next stop Addenbrooke's, sir?'

'Next stop HQ.' Baxter rubbed his stomach to assist the progress of the alkaline. Then the basic minimum of paperwork. Then bed. He remembered with a pang that it would be empty.

Next morning had a surrealistic feel. At eight Baxter and Armstrong sat facing Highcroft in his cubbyhole in the mobile incident room which had been set up at one corner of the Hare Holt car park. A red wooden griffin was framed in the window behind the Superintendent's head. This and the more distant garden conceits distracted Baxter's attention from his senior's homily on Investigation as Learning Experience.

'May I take your silence as agreement, Chief Inspector?'

Baxter grunted, suddenly aware that Highcroft had shifted from generalities to specifics, and feigned interest in his briefing sheet.

'I'd have preferred to do more interviewing myself, but the CC feels strongly I should be free when the media descend.'

Uniformed officers were already in place outside the house's six entrances. Others waited in readiness to defend the grounds.

'Mass invasion's inevitable, I suppose, now Sharrock's name's been released.'

''Fraid so.'

A knock. The office manager handed Highcroft a note.

'Ah, good. Word that Gorridge has regained consciousness. You agree, I take it, both of you, that he's our prime suspect.'

'Our prime information source, at least,' Baxter hedged.

'Don't suppose you'll get anything from his mother, but as she's at the hospital, you and Armstrong may as well see her there.'

'The thought had occurred, sir.'

Highcroft coloured. 'Do you also agree, Chief Inspector, that early visits to Sharrock's London flat and business HQ are indicated?'

'Certainly.'

When the detectives entered the private ward, the remains of a liquid breakfast were being wheeled away. Below its thatch of light red hair, Gorridge's broad face was pale. A colourful bruise on his forehead was the only visible injury, but they could see the upper edge of a bandage round his midriff.

The policemen took chairs on either side of the bed.

'How d'you feel?' Baxter asked, after the introductions.

'Lousy.'

'You don't look so bad. Bruises—cracked ribs, isn't that right? You got off lightly.'

'That's what they tell me.' Gorridge attempted a shrug and winced.

'Did Mrs Talbot get off as lightly?'

'What do you mean?'

'There was a piece of material in your van. White with a black and brown pattern. There'll be a photo of it for you later. Sound like what she was wearing?'

Gorridge nodded stiffly.

'Yes or no, Mr Gorridge?'

'Yes.'

'Like to tell us how it came to be there?'

'No idea.'

'No?'

'Tore it when she got out, I suppose.'

'Got out where?'

'Just before the crash. It was her made me go off the road, silly bitch.'

'Why'd she do a thing like that?' Baxter asked very quietly. 'They've been over your clothes, Gorridge. To put it politely, it looks like you got excited.'

'OK, so what's that prove? I'm twenty-four years old, for God's sake. She's an attractive woman.'

'And an old acquaintance?'

Gorridge laughed harshly. 'I was waiting for that. Re-bloody-habilitation. When I hear the word I want to puke. Who gave you the story—Luce or the Reverend Jon?'

'Mrs Talbot's gone missing, Mr Gorridge. That's one of our purposes in interviewing you. We very much hope you can give us a clue as to her whereabouts.'

'Let's get one thing straight, shall we? I didn't pressure Luce into leaving Hare Holt with me. She begged me to get her away from that house, would you believe? Got into that van of her own free will.'

'Why?'

'She wanted me to take her home. And I said no, not until she'd answered some questions. My mate was dead, wasn't he? We've had our ups and downs, but Dave was my mate all right and he was dead. She knew who'd killed him, I reckoned. And she wouldn't bloody tell me.' He began to weep.

'Your turn, Bill,' Baxter said after a brief interval.

'Why'd you go to Hare Holt last night, Mr Gorridge?' the Inspector asked in the Belfast accent that had survived twenty years' exile from his native land.

Silence.

'Why'd you go back on Friday night after leaving your mother home?'

A second silence.

'We've got the Bishop's report,' Armstrong went on. '*Scandals of the Suburbs*.'

'Report? You're talking riddles, Inspector. First I heard of any report.'

'In that case, what brought you back to Hare Holt on Friday night?'

'Who said—'

'Your van was heard leaving.'

Gorridge sighed. 'I went back to see Dave. Gave my mother a hand earlier Friday evening—you'll know that. Helped her serve and clear the supper things. Came as a shock, seeing Dave rigged out as a woman in that dining-room, and with *her*. Last place in the world I'd have expected to run into him.'

'Recognize him right away?'

'No. Wasn't paying much attention to the people in the dining-room, you see. Middle-aged bunch, mostly. Not my type at all. It was Dave's laugh made me look twice. Then he swivelled his head—a way he had—and I knew him right away.'

'So?'

Gorridge cleared his throat. 'Knocked me sideways, seeing him in that gear. With her. He'd always had a thing for her, ever since Tekbridge. That's why he was so mad when I—look, I don't know what the Rev's told you.'

'Does it matter?'

'To me it matters. To Bev if it comes out. I'm a family man, Inspector. Want to stay married. Seven years ago, I was a kid. Seventeen. Hadn't met a woman like Lucy Talbot before. Misread the signals. And she was sending signals, all right, whatever her old man told you. *I'm not getting enough*—that was the first part of the message. Ask her—ask her when you find her. Can you blame a kid of seventeen for not waiting for the ifs and buts?'

'Friday night,' Armstrong said sharply.

'Took my mother home after supper. Eight-thirty or thereabouts.'

'Tell her about Sharrock?'

'No. I was too churned up. Went back to my own place in the village. I'd unsettled business with Dave. He was my mate, but it wasn't all sweetness and light between us. I won't pretend different. Didn't see so much of him once he got into the big money. Nature of things. Bev said he was only interested in me for what he could get out of me. Something in that, but it wasn't the whole truth.'

'What *could* he get out of you?'

'Computer systems knowhow. May not have many fancy certificates to my name, but I've a fair knowledge of software as well as hardware. I've had my hands on most of the business systems in current use in the UK, sussed out their strengths and weaknesses. Picked up enough to help Dave keep tabs on his purchasing departments and systems staff when he was on his way up. Saved him a few expensive mistakes before he could afford high-powered consultations.'

'And later?'

'Later, when he could afford to splash out on tailor-made networks, I was out of my depth. Be the first to admit it. Sound systems excepted. Always been a hobby of mine—music synthesis, voice synthesis, you name it. Kept up with developments there. Dave got interested in fancy sound effects when he went into theme parks. I saved him a bob or two when he was choosing systems for Fenfantasy and the rest.'

'This what you wanted to discuss with Sharrock on Friday night?'

'In passing. My Fenfantasy maintenance contract expires next month, and I haven't been able to get a straight answer on renewal from the local management. So when I saw Dave, I decided I'd ask him to get things moving. My boy's birthday's next week, mortgage payment on the Cambridge house is due week after that. Thought I'd touch Dave up for an advance when I was at it. Considering the help I'd given him for free over the years, I reckoned I'd earned it.'

'What time did you arrive back at the house?'

'Couldn't be sure. Elevenish. Left the car on the road.'

'How'd you get in? Those your mother's keys you had on you?'

'Lord no.' Gorridge sounded genuinely shocked. 'Last thing I'd want to do would be to implicate Mum. Took a set from the back of a cutlery drawer Friday supper-time when her back was turned. Shouldn't think anyone's missed them. Let myself in by the kitchen door.'

'How'd you know where to look for Sharrock?'

'I'd heard someone call him Karen at supper, so I checked the room-list in the screens passage. No one else of that name.'

'OK. You went up to his room. Unobserved?'

'Far as I know.'

'Go on.'

'I knocked. No reply. Door wasn't locked, so I went inside to wait for him.'

'How long before he came back?'

'Ten—fifteen minutes maybe.'

'Boring for you. How'd you pass the time?'

'Sampled a couple of country 'n' western tapes he'd left lying on the dressing-table. Smoochy numbers—not the sort of stuff I'd have expected Dave to go for. Part of the act, I suppose.'

'Look around the room?'

Gorridge flushed. 'Didn't nick anything.'

'Looked, that's what I said. Curiosity would be natural in the circs, wouldn't it?'

'Wardrobe door was ajar. Could see a bit of his fancy dress, so I peeked inside. Other things were women's clothes. Nothing special.'

'The dressing-table?'

'Drawers were shut. I left them that way. Dave wouldn't have appreciated it if he'd caught me rummaging. When he came back, he made a scene about me playing his tapes, would you believe? Always been touchy about people going through his things—ever since he was a kid.' Gorridge's voice cracked on the word.

'OK. Sharrock came back. Say where he'd been?'

'Showering, which was true, I guess. He'd a spongebag and towel—smelt of toiletries.'

'How'd he react to your being there?'

'Not too well. Like I said, he made a scene about the tapes. Riled me, that did. I'd meant to keep things jokey, low-key. But I found myself asking straight out what he was doing in drag, what he had going with Luce. That's what we all called her in Tekbridge. If she didn't like it, she never said. Dave blew his top good and proper when I asked. Told me it was none of my business. If I'd my best interests at heart—my family's interests—I'd better forget I'd seen him and forget it quick.'

'You're quite sure that's what he said?' Baxter took over the questioning.

'Oh yes. It stunned me. He'd never threatened me in that way in his life. Didn't mean it, I'm sure. But at the same time I saw red. So I told him he'd have to pay me to forget. New contract within the week. Five hundred up front. Dave said he'd no cheque-book with him—only a few quid. He was going abroad on Tuesday for a week or two, but he'd see me right when he got back to London. Then he asked me to leave.'

'And did you?'

'Wish to God I had. But it bugged me—him hustling me out. Blokes in Dave's position don't have problems raising the wind. I told him I was skint. The contract could wait, but the cash couldn't. So he said he'd see what he could do, providing I didn't split. He'd ring Saturday evening to tell me when and where to collect. Best deal I could do, I reckoned. David checked that the landing and stairs were clear. I left.'

'For home?'

'For my pad in Fen Holton.'

'Where did you spend Saturday?'

'Job with Anglia Nuprint in Holtchester. It'd been on my books for some time, but my mother doesn't know that—or Bev. Stayed there till five. Then I rang Bev. Told her I'd be working that evening. Sunday morning too, maybe. No sense in my going home that night, and I'd have to cop out of her office friend's booze-up. Worst thing I ever did, far as Bev was concerned. Too right, it was.' Gorridge rummaged in the tissue box on the bedside locker.

'Straight back to your Fenport place after work?'

'Via a video library and a Chinese takeaway. I was watching this grotty video about the sex life of Robinson Crusoe when Dave rang. Last time I heard his voice. Oh Christ.' He dabbed at his eyes and stared at the tissue as if its dampness were not of his making.

'Go on when you're ready,' Baxter said gently. 'What did Sharrock say on the phone?'

'Don't remember exactly. Gist was that I could have the cash if I came straight away. And there was something jokey about a bonus. I was to come to the Talbots' bedroom, not his. He told me where to find it. The Bishop would be in Cambridge until late, he said. Didn't mention Luce, and I didn't ask. I couldn't believe he'd be in her bedroom with her consent, but Dave had surprised me so many times anything was possible.'

'What time did he ring?'

'Ten-thirty-five.'

'Sure?'

'Yes—I'd been checking my watch all evening. Told him I'd be over in five minutes—as it turned out, it was more like fifteen. Ignition trouble. Then when I did make it to the kitchen door of the manor, I saw shadows on the blind.'

'Whose shadows?'

'People in Tudor costume, that's all I could say. Two at least, a man and a woman. Could have been others—I didn't stop to find out. Beetled round to the north-east door. No lights showing on the ground floor of the East Wing—that's where the Lakes hang out.'

'Go straight up to the Talbots' room?'

'More or less. Had to hang back a couple of times to avoid being seen.' Gorridge reached for the glass of water on the locker. 'This doesn't get any easier.'

'Take it bit by bit. Bedroom door locked again?'

'Shut, not locked.'

'Tell us what you saw.'

'This figure on the floor in fancy dress, face down with its arms spread out. I was sure it was Luce at first. The dress was red and white—nothing like the dress in Dave's wardrobe.'

'What else did you see?'

'Candlestick rolled into the corner of the room. Far right-hand corner from where I was standing. Blood on the floor.' He retched. 'Nothing else.'

'No knife? Think hard. Nothing like a knife?'

Gorridge shook his head. 'Unless it was under the body, of course.'

'And no Mrs Talbot?'

'Not at first. I said something—"My God", I think, when I saw the body. She must have heard me, for she unlocked the bathroom door the moment I said it. Came into the room just as I was kneeling down beside him. I knew him soon as I got up close. I knew him from the back of his neck.

'It was a shock all the same, to see her standing there in his fancy gear.

'"Don't touch him," she said. "It's too late to do anything for him. He'd have killed us both, if someone hadn't killed him first. Please take me home."

'It was the word home that made me give in to her—that and the childish way she spoke that made me think of our Paula. She was in shock, I suppose. So was I, maybe. All I wanted to do was to get away from that body—tried not to think of it as Dave's body. But I hadn't a hope in hell of leaving the house on my tod. Luce was clinging to me now, tearing at my clothes. Chances were, she'd scream the place down if I didn't take her with me.'

'Anyone see you leave?'

'Not that I know of. We'd one narrow miss when this old bloke came out of a ground-floor loo. That was all. Most people were in the winter parlour, Lucy said.'

'What else did she say?'

'Nothing—well, next to nothing. Just that she hadn't killed Dave and didn't know who had. It wasn't good enough. When we got into the van, I told her it wasn't good enough. Told her I'd been as close to Dave as anyone had been. I'd a right to know everything she knew. But no go.'

Another sip of water.

'In the end, when Luce twigged I wasn't heading for Fenport, she made a grab for the wheel, forced me to brake. Then she scarpered. I made the next bend—attempted a U-turn. Car came out of nowhere doing a ton. Must have swerved to avoid it. Ended up in the ditch, they say, but the next thing I know I'm here. Been thinking since I came round. Asking myself if there was any truth in what she said. If Dave had had it in for me. Got himself up as a decoy. If that's true I should be grateful to the bugger who removed him from the scene, who saved my life. But I'm not. I'm bloody not.' Gorridge broke into loud, angry sobs, succeeded by shamefaced apologies.

'OK,' Baxter said quietly. 'You've a right to your feelings, Mr Gorridge.'

But not to put the screws on Lucy Talbot. Who might at that moment be somewhere even less comfortable than a National Health Service bed.

CHAPTER 10

Beverley Gorridge, red-eyed and obviously unslept, was pretending to read *Woman* as the detectives passed through the waiting area. Her mother-in-law, who had introduced herself before their ward visit, was making a more convincing show of reading the *Guardian.*

'He's all yours, now.' Baxter bent to retrieve the magazine Beverley had let slip through her fingers.

'Going to be all right, is he? I mean, the doctors would tell you . . .'

'No more than they told you, I'm sure. Shock, bruises, concussion. They want to keep him in until tomorrow for observation, but that's not unusual.'

'And he's in the clear far as you're concerned?'

'We don't want to ask your husband any more questions for the foreseeable future. Beyond that, no promises. Best I can do—sorry, Mrs Gorridge.'

Her mother-in-law took over. 'Enough to be going on with, isn't it, Bev? Run along, dear. Tell Nigel I'll look in later. You'll want to talk to me, I expect, Chief Inspector?' As Patricia Gorridge folded her *Guardian*, Baxter saw that she had solved more than half the crossword.

The administrator's office that had been put at their disposal was sparsely furnished but very, very hot. Patricia slipped out of the jacket of her grey chalk-striped suit and hung it carefully on the back of one of the three typist's chairs. She clipped her gloves into an attachment on her handbag.

'You know the purpose of this conversation, Mrs Gorridge?'

'I can guess. My daughter-in-law rang me after you'd been to see her. I phoned Mr Lake.' Patricia's voice thickened, and she cleared her throat. Sharrock evidently meant something to her. But what, exactly?

'As Mr Lake may have mentioned, we're in process of interviewing everyone who was at Hare Holt yesterday. So you won't be surprised if I ask you about your activities.'

'Where do you want me to begin?'

Baxter requested and received what sounded like an accurate summary. At Frances Lake's insistence, Patricia had been relieved of clearing and setting tables, and of serving food. She had therefore been based almost entirely on the kitchen and had met only those course members who had visited it. 'Karen East' was not among their number. She couldn't even remember the name being mentioned. The first she knew of David Sharrock's presence was from her daughter-in-law. She had left Hare Holt at about 8.30 on Friday and Saturday evenings, and returned home where she had read, done household chores and listened to Radio Three. Alone. No alibi, she smilingly confirmed. It was then Baxter noticed the black rings under her eyes that were not almost but not quite camouflaged by masking cream.

'One black mark against me, you see. And I may as well tell you before you dredge it up that it's faintly possible there might be another.'

'Oh?'

'Eight years ago, when he was eighteen, David Sharrock made, or said he made, a will in my favour.'

'Not many eighteen-year-olds make wills.'

'An extravagant gesture. David was given to extravagant gestures. I didn't take it seriously. Felt sure there'd be other gestures, other wills.'

'He must have been fond of you, all the same.'

Patricia bit her lip. 'In his way. I was a resource he

needed at the time—that he didn't want to lose. But mainly, the will was to spite the uncle who'd paid for his schooling. David had convinced himself he could persuade him to finance his university education too. The day he told me about the will was the day he learned from his uncle's London solicitors there was nothing doing.'

'Still alive, this uncle?'

'Died two or three years ago in Australia. No doubt the solicitors could confirm. Horsfall and Sturridge—Knightsbridge area, I believe.'

'When did Sharrock first meet your son?'

'Nearly fourteen years ago. Nigel was ten-and-a-half, David thirteen. It was his first Christmas holiday from Winton.'

'The public school? Four-figure fees even then, I'd guess. The uncle can't have been short of a bob or two.'

'He'd a managerial job in a Perth canning factory. My guess is that the fees for Allenguard—the prep school—and Winton must have left him skint.'

'So extravagant gestures ran in the family?'

'You might say that. I left Fen Holton with my parents as a young child. My mother didn't move back until she was widowed, and what I know of the Sharrocks' past history comes from my aunt. Graham never hit it off with his father, apparently, and made a complete break with his parents when he emigrated. But he'd had a soft spot for Sandra, his kid sister, and David's mother. Took the news of her death badly—felt guilty about walking out on her, perhaps.'

'Who was the boy's father?'

'Nobody knew—Sandra included, by all accounts. There was a rumour he was someone she met at the Square and Tassel, here in Cambridge. She was just sixteen when she got pregnant, twenty-one when she died. A motorbike accident. When Graham heard the news, he contacted his parents through the solicitors and offered the financial package. An all-or-nothing arrangement. He specified the schools—he'd taken professional advice, it seems. University wasn't mentioned. School fees would be paid direct, but

Graham would top them up with a maintenance allowance to be paid to the grandmother. The grandfather didn't like the idea, but he liked the prospect of the boy being taken into local authority care rather less, so he gave way.'

'Lucky Sharrock.'

'Not as I saw it.'

'Why so?'

'The gulf between those schools and that home was too great. Fen Holton was a poor village then. People worked on the land or on the railway. David's prep school manners didn't fit. By the time he moved up to Winton, he'd lost what local friends he had. That's why my aunt felt sorry for him—asked my husband and me to have him in Holtchester for a week that Christmas holiday. Every holiday he stayed a little longer. By his last year at Winton he was spending more time in Holtchester than in Fen Holton.'

'So he and your son were close?'

'To begin with, yes. Neither of the boys was athletic, but they liked swimming and ice-skating. And they joined in the historical pageants George Summers and I used to get up for the local kids. David loved dressing up, even then. Later, they diverged. Nigel lost interest in school—Browne was under-equipped for the technical subjects he did best at. David's termly reports were excellent. He planned to read History at university with an eye to a political career. At seventeen he was offered a place at Trinity College, Cambridge.'

'So what went wrong?'

'What David needed from his uncle was a positive, permanent relationship. What he got was a fruit machine. There were chatty letters to begin with, photographs, promises of future meetings. David kept the letters in a folder, boasted about the farm his uncle would buy one day, fantasized about emigrating. But the letters petered out. By the time he was fourteen, they were reduced to stilted notes at Christmas and birthdays. When he was fifteen there was a wedding photograph.

'What went on coming sporadically were gifts of cash. The maintenance allowance increased with the years, but

stick was a possible, but by no means the only possible, murder weapon.

'Last paragraph,' Highcroft said tetchily.

Baxter read it. The evidence suggested that the blows to the forehead had been delivered first, those to the base of the skull after the victim had fallen.

Baxter grimaced. 'Self-defence can't account for that lot.'

'There's more.' Highcroft passed over a clutch of blown-up photographs.

'The candlestick?' Odd how unfamiliar the components of common objects could be when enlarged.

'*A* candlestick—not *the*, according to our friends in Forensic. Pattern of bloodstains is wrong for this to have been the weapon, they say. Too regular. Looks as though this one has been dipped in the wound—rolled in it.'

'Yuk. And the stains on the floorboards?' Baxter contemplated the three shots of them.

'Mostly caused by the real weapon, they reckon. Which the killer evidently let drop or threw down, so that it rolled across the floorboards. But look here and here and here.' Isolated splotches had been marked on one of the photographs.

'They won't commit themselves until they've done the re-creation job and the computer analyses. But they're pretty confident there's been a substitution.'

'Other pewter candlesticks been gone over?'

'They look to have been thoroughly cleaned.'

'By Mrs Dryden and Mr Lake?'

'Quite. Mr Lake, of Lake's. Deputy Lieutenant in waiting. A sensitive situation, you'll agree. I've consulted with the Chief Constable.'

Baxter's eyebrows rose. 'At breakfast-time? On a Sunday?'

'He advised me to raise the matter first with Mrs Dryden.'

Who was not and was never likely to be a deputy lieutenant.

On entering Highcroft's tiny office, Deborah Dryden extended a plump hand and almost immediately withdrew it.

'Greasy paws, I'm afraid.' She giggled. 'Been making puddings.' She removed a tissue from the pocket of her white nylon overall and wiped her fingers.

'You keep yourself busy, Mrs Dryden.' Highcroft made a business of settling her in a chair.

'With Frances and her other stalwarts away, it seemed natural to give a hand. Any news of Lucy?'

'I'm afraid not.'

'Poor girl. I do hope she's all right. One feels so helpless.' Deborah's brown eyes darted from one face to the other.

'Perhaps you can help Mrs Talbot by helping us,' Highcroft began.

'I don't think I quite—' Deborah's stubby fingers tightened on the tissue.

'Can we talk about candlesticks?' Baxter said brusquely. 'The candlesticks you were cleaning last night. Why were you so anxious to clean them?'

They could see how clumsily she had applied her rouge, now her face was drained of natural colour.

'It was a nasty job for anyone to come down to next morning.'

'No other reason?'

She shook her head.

'Then we'll talk about this candlestick, shall we?' Highcroft held up one of the photographs.

'Is that what killed him?' She choked on the words.

'It's the candlestick we found in the bedroom. The one we were meant to find. Any comment, Mrs Dryden?'

'All right, I'll tell you. But take the photograph away, please. *Please.*'

Highcroft replaced it carefully on the pile on his desk blotter. With equal care he issued the formal warning against self-incrimination.

'This will destroy Coulter, you know. Losing David was bad enough . . . That's why I lied to you before. Don't think I was trying to save my skin. To avoid paying the penalty.'

'The penalty for what?' Highcroft prompted.

'For killing him, of course. I hated David Sharrock. I killed him.'

'With your husband's knowledge?'

'Good God, no. Coulter doesn't even know I recognized David on Friday night. I'd have recognized him in any disguise, I think. Hatred's like love, I suppose. Another sort of obsession.'

'What did you have against him?'

'I couldn't take the father-and-son game Coulter played with him. The way David exploited it. I'd wanted children when I married. So had Coulter. But there were reasons—' she hesitated—'nothing to do with me. It wasn't something we could talk about, but I felt cheated. I used to envy friends their young children. Now I envy them their grandchildren.

'The bogus relationship rubbed salt in the wound. Coulter couldn't understand—wouldn't. I tried to shake it off. Took up new interests. Historical cookery was the one that stuck. But it wasn't enough. When David was around the strain was still intolerable. Then over the last couple of months we saw less of him than before. I began to hope he was getting bored with us—that he'd stay away.

'That's why it was the most awful shock to see him here in drag, chatting up Lucy Talbot. Trying to ruin someone else's life. Confident that neither Coulter nor I would recognize him. I decided right away at supper-time on Friday that I'd kill him the first chance I had.'

'Without taking anyone into your confidence?' Baxter took over the interrogation.

The question seemed to surprise her. 'That's right.'

'Why wait until Saturday night?'

A brief pause. Then the words came in a rush. 'I couldn't think how to do it, you see. What to use as a weapon. Didn't know where Coulter hid his gun. Even if I had, I wouldn't have known how to use it. Didn't think of a candlestick until I was in the kitchen on Saturday morning. I'd hoped to smuggle one out—kill him while Coulter was in London. Then the call came about the suspected burglary, and I had to make the trip home. That gave me time to think. I realized it would be safer after dark.

'When I saw David leave the candle dance soon after Lucy, I knew it was now or never. Two or three minutes after they'd left I told Coulter I'd a headache—was going upstairs for a lie-down. He'd had a few drinks. Probably didn't take in what I was saying. My Tudor dress is very loose, so it wasn't hard to hide the candlestick.

'After I'd changed my clothes, I went to David's room. Listened. Nothing. Then I tried the Talbots'. I could hear the two voices—Sharrock's and Lucy's. His more than hers. I waited. Five, ten minutes. Then I heard the noise of water running in the bathroom. I took a chance that Lucy was using it. I tried the handle of the bedroom door. It gave in my hand.

'The curtains were drawn and the electric light was off, but there was a lit candle in a candlestick on the dressing-table. At first I thought it was Lucy standing there in her coral and white dress, looking out of the window. Then I heard her voice in the bathroom. David Sharrock called to her to shut up.'

'Anything in his hands?'

She hesitated. 'No—could have been, I suppose. Didn't take time to look. I had to do it quickly or not at all. I just hit him on the back of the head with the unlit candlestick —two or three times, I'm not sure. He cried out the first time, very softly. Then he staggered and fell forwards. I half-expected Lucy to hear, to come through. But she didn't.

'When I'd finished, I threw the candlestick down. Then I thought about fingerprints, and what it would do to Coulter if I was convicted. That's when it occurred to me to swap the candlesticks. I blew out the candle on the dressing-table. Luckily, I'd a couple of handkerchiefs in my pocket. Proper linen ones. I used one to pick up the clean candlestick. It was horrible, bloodying it. I used the second handkerchief to wrap round the base of the candlestick I'd used as a weapon, so it wouldn't stain my clothes.'

'Mrs Talbot remained in the bathroom throughout?'

'Must have—I suppose.'

'Making no noise?'

'I—I couldn't be sure. Isn't it awful? I was so concerned about Coulter that I didn't think how poor Lucy would feel if she was the first to find it—him.'

'Go on,' Highcroft said coldly.

'It was quite hard to hide the candlestick under my cardigan. Luckily, I didn't meet anyone on the stairs on the way down. There were people in the kitchen when I went in.'

'Mr Lake included?'

'Yes, but he—none of them was anywhere near the sink, you see. And there were other dirty candlesticks on the draining-board, so it was easy to do what I had to.'

'What did you do with the handkerchiefs?'

'Cut them up and flushed them down the nearest downstairs loo. Disgusting. It's all disgusting, isn't it? I don't expect you to understand. I don't really understand myself. And now, I suppose, you'll want to take me into custody.'

Highcroft hesitated. His pale eyes met Baxter's. He hesitated again.

'No, Mrs Dryden,' he said at last. 'For the time being, you're free to leave.'

The Chief Inspector breathed a sigh of relief. Deborah Dryden looked uncomprehending.

'I can't face him,' she said at last in a small, childish voice. 'I can't face my husband. Please don't ask it of me.'

CHAPTER 11

'I take it you think she's innocent, sir,' Baxter said when Wendy Powers had persuaded Deborah to leave.

Highcroft was activating his computer graphics system. 'Of the killing, yes. Pretty obvious she was covering up. Agreed?'

'Provisionally. But covering for whom?'

'Her husband looks like the prime candidate from where I'm sitting. Hang on a sec. 'Highcroft typed something on his terminal. The screen display, which was beyond Baxter's reading distance, convulsed colourfully. 'Who else might she be shielding?' Highcroft asked, fingers poised over the keys.

'Lucy Talbot? Robin Lake?'

Highcroft sighed, tapped again with evident reluctance. 'The Bishop's wife? The prospective deputy lieutenant? The CC'll take it badly if we make a wrong move in either of those directions.'

'There's always the chance, though, that Mrs Dryden was mistaken in her attribution of guilt.'

'Of course, of course, Richard.' Highcroft coloured, frowning at the VDU as if uncertain of his system's capacity to handle such complications.

'Care for a summary of our hospital interviews?'

'And your impressions?' the Superintendent asked afterwards.

'I've a hunch Nigel Gorridge is innocent. His mother could well be guilty.'

'But unwilling to confess? Did she strike you as a woman without scruples?'

'No. But she might have kept silent for the same sort of reason as Deborah Dryden put forward. To save her son the distress of knowing his mother had killed his hero.'

'Women,' Highcroft said bitterly. 'Criminal investigation would be one hell of a sight easier if it wasn't for women, Richard. Off the record, don't you agree?'

'Can't say I do, sir. Been well advised by women before now. By DS Powers, for instance. By my wife. Which reminds me. There's a fair lot to squeeze into the London trip. It would help if we could take Wendy along. Unless you've other plans for her?'

Highcroft, it seemed, had none.

With a fountain at its centre, the atrium of Sunnyscene House, London WC1, would have been a typical sample of post-modernist corporate architecture. It was, however, dominated by twelve-foot-high replicas of Hereward the Wake, St Etheldreda and Fen Tiger cartoon characters, familiar to Baxter from advertisements for the Fenfantasy theme park.

The detectives were ten minutes early for their rendezvous with Helen Worth, David Sharrock's personal assistant.

Baxter, whose first impression had been of a small, wan girl, discovered as he followed her into the lift that she was a healthy-looking young woman of almost his own height. His eye, he concluded, had habituated to the scale and brightness of the plastic giants.

In Sharrock's penthouse, which was divided into official and private quarters, the eccentricities were more discreet. Armstrong's fingers recoiled from a chair-arm. Baxter grimaced sympathetically. There were hide armchairs in his house, as in the Inspector's. Like his junior, he wore leather shoes. But encounters with intact horns, hooves and shells embedded in domestic artefacts repelled him none the less.

'Spooky, aren't they?' Helen smiled a quick smile. 'David said they were his talismans against things that went bump in the night.'

'Did they work?'

Her eyebrows arched. 'Did he sleep well, do you mean? Wouldn't have told me if he hadn't.'

Baxter doubted if that was the whole truth, but it would do for now.

'Been his PA for long?'

'Four years. Since the launch of Sunnyscene.'

She wasn't quite the woman Baxter would have expected Sharrock to employ. The turquoise gaberdine suit looked right, so did the shapely legs and narrow feet in their filbert-shaped pumps. But Helen's long-chinned Edwardian face was handsome rather than beautiful. Her twist of reddish hair was insecurely clasped. Her speech was flat, South London. She had poise, though. No flap, no useless emoting. He guessed she had been good at her job.

'You want to see his papers, I understand. Mr Collard's due back at Gatwick just after midnight. He asked me to ask if it could wait.'

'Sorry, but it can't.'

Helen smiled as if at a point scored off the deputy chairman. 'Where'd you want to begin?'

'Where'd Mr Sharrock keep a will?'

'In his wallsafe, if he'd made one, which I very much doubt. If David ever thought of his death, he didn't let on.

He took enormous risks, physical as well as financial. Acted as if he were invulnerable.'

'Who else knew the combination?' Baxter watched as Helen opened the safe.

'No one.'

'So he trusted you?'

'As much as he trusted anyone. God, it sounds weird, past-tensing him like that. Whatever else David may have been, he was a today-and-tomorrow person. Look, I've given up smoking, but I really feel the need . . . Do you mind?'

'Please go ahead.'

She helped herself from a carved box on the table.

The detectives gave their attention to the interior of the safe. It contained several dozen large, sealed and well-stuffed envelopes, which bore the typed names of commercial enterprises. Baxter broke several of the seals and looked inside.

'Did you know what was in here, Ms Worth?' he asked over his shoulder.

'Stock and share certificates. His private private portfolio, he called it. The one his Sunnyscene accountants didn't meddle with—or his personal financial advisers. He prided himself on beating the professional analysts at their own game.'

'And did he?

'Sometimes, I believe. But I wasn't interested. He'd ring up every now and then when he was out of the country if he wanted to buy or sell. My job was to post certificates wherever I was told—he used lots of different brokers—or lodge the incoming documents he'd post to my home address.'

'So he *did* trust you!'

She shrugged. 'Wealth frightens me. David knew I'd no interest in money beyond what I needed to live where I wanted with the man I wanted. My husband restores old clocks. He can't just work anywhere—he needs the right temperature, the right humidity. There's no way we could have scraped up the deposit for our Kent place without

David's help. My keyboard skills aren't brilliant, or my languages. I'm thirty-two. I doubt if many other bosses would have done as much.'

Baxter worked his way through the envelopes. Not all of them, he discovered, contained securities.

'Never tempted to break a seal, Ms Worth?'

'No. Dave warned me against it, and I took him seriously. I wasn't indispensable. And if he felt his interests threatened, he could be cruel, very cruel.'

'Can you give instances?'

'No. It was the way he talked about people now and then—the things he laughed at—that gave me the creeps. The little-boy image he presented to the media had a darker side. I could imagine him tearing wings off flies.' She shivered.

From one of the sealed envelopes Baxter had extracted a his-and-hers passport. The names on the cover were those of Joseph Anthony and Marian Villiers. The man's face was a close-cropped David Sharrock's, the woman's Lucy Talbot's. She wore a candy-striped sports jerkin. Her chin was lifted, her black hair windblown. The dark angel. An occasion for the sin of murder, after all? But whose sin? 'Seen her before?' he asked Helen.

'No. Not a face you'd forget in a hurry.'

Lucy's description hadn't been released to the media. Not yet.

'Did Mr Sharrock ever talk of marriage?'

'Never without a wisecrack. An absurd institution, he said. He slept around, discreetly. With women who knew how to look after themselves.'

Helen Worth included, Baxter decided.

'I don't know, though,' she volunteered a few moments later. 'He did make a joke three or four months ago about the love of a good woman. I didn't take it seriously—maybe I should have. He changed in other ways this past year, so why not that?'

'What sort of changes?'

'He became more secretive and more purposeful. His twenty-fifth birthday—his quarter-century, as he called it—was a big landmark. It wasn't until then, I think, that he really believed his success would last. "Next year I'm going to make things happen," he said at his birthday party. We all assumed then he was talking about business. Later, I wasn't so sure. So yes, there might have been a woman who mattered.'

Baxter completed his inspection of the envelopes. Securities and more securities. And a scarf—a woman's headsquare in a clear plastic bag, its one visible corner decorated with a partridge's head. On a label inside the bag a date had been written in a bold, faded hand. March 3, 1968.

'Seen this before?' Baxter showed it to Helen.

'Sorry. Sort of thing my grandmother wore when we were kids. But it doesn't ring specific bells.'

'And the date? The handwriting?'

'They mean nothing.'

'Sleeping area next, I think.'

The fitted wardrobes held the polychromatic range of designer label sportswear that had helped to create the Mr Sunnyscene image and a dozen hand-tailored business suits. In addition there were several fancy-dress outfits, of which the most preposterous was a Hereward the Wake ensemble with the green iridescent finish of the caricature figure in the foyer.

'Dressing-up looks to have been a hobby,' Baxter prompted.

'An obsession.'

'Cross-dressing included. Does it surprise you that he died in drag?'

'Not especially. It wasn't a compulsion, but he'd a freewheeling imagination. Look at those sci-fi costumes—animal, vegetable, mineral—he liked to cross all the boundaries.'

'Did you help him with shopping for clothes?'

'Occasionally.'

'Including the Tudor dress he brought to Fen Holton? White dress with black and brown embroidery?'

'No. I'd have remembered. Actually, I'd no idea he was going to Cambridgeshire this weekend, but that's not unusual. He'd often go abroad without telling me beforehand and phone in from all sorts of unexpected places.'

'Remember the last outfit you bought for him?'

'Easily. It was only last Wednesday. One of his slumsuits, as he called them. The sort of chainstore outfit he wore in the street when he wanted to be incognito.'

'Can you describe this one?'

'Blue, pinstriped number. Still got the receipt, if it helps.'

'It might. Was the suit in good nick when you bought it —no snags or tears, for instance?'

'No. I'd have noticed, or David would. He opened it out when I handed it over.'

'Wednesday, you said.'

'Wednesday lunch-time. Last time we really talked. Thursday and Friday he looked into his office a couple of times to sign letters, deal with messages. Told me he was taking a long weekend off. Going to Switzerland on Tuesday.' She bit her lip.

'What was his mood?'

'I got the impression there was a small cloud on his horizon last Wednesday and Thursday. He hummed a lot —a habit when he was uptight. Friday morning, he seemed more relaxed. He'd fixed some deal, I guessed.'

Or some dealer? Baxter brooded on the worn and torn condition of the suit in the Mini boot. Leaving Wendy Powers to complete the search of the penthouse, he and Armstrong made tracks for Star Street police station.

'Nineteen-sixty-eight,' the Inspector said as he drove out of the car park. 'Year Sharrock's mother died, wasn't it?'

'From all we've heard, he wasn't the type to treasure relics.'

'Why date it, then? Why wear something very like it at Hare Holt?'

'Your guess, my dear Bill, is as good as mine.'

'No two opinions about the fake passport. Mrs Bishop is in this up to the neck.'

'Always assuming she knew about it.'

'Oh, come on. Don't tell me her old man didn't see this

coming. That it wasn't the real reason—' Armstrong braked to avoid a Sunday skateboarder.

'Cool it, Bill, for the sake of our health. At least until we've heard Lucy's side of the story.'

If they ever did. Baxter's first action on arrival at Star Street was to ring the Fen Holton incident room. No Mrs Talbot yet. No sightings.

'Your visitor's waiting,' said Theo Andrews, the duty sergeant and an old acquaintance from the Chief Inspector's Met days. 'He didn't register as you came through. Take it you're not personally acquainted?'

'Not yet.' The detectives peered through the frosted glass at the shapeless figure of Gideon Poynter, whose ex-directory phone number had been wrested with some difficulty from his masters at the *Clarion*. The photographer's criminal form, they had ascertained, was limited to occasional punch-ups.

'Canteen first,' Baxter decreed. 'Poynter doesn't look the type I care to confront on an empty stomach.'

Fifteen minutes and two cheese rolls apiece later, they joined the photographer in an interview room that, like most in the station, was overdue for redecoration.

'Good of you to come,' Baxter murmured.

'To which intro every good boy says "delighted to be of help"? Well, I'm bloody not, to be frank. A scoop that wasn't and half an hour's heel-kicking haven't done anything for the happiness rating. You can have my pics of Sharrock, such as they are, when they're processed. Don't see what else I can do for you.'

'You might just do something for yourself, Mr Poynter,' Baxter said quietly. 'Like telling us why you left Hare Holt last night.'

'On your list of suspects, am I?' Poynter laughed. 'Accused of murdering a whizzkid I didn't recognize? All right, all right. I left because I was bored stiff with the mock-Tudor inanities. And because Sunday's the only day the girlfriend's still in bed when I surface. Enjoy lousing up other people's weekends, don't you, gentlemen?'

'No comment. What time did you leave Hare Holt?'

'Ten past ten at a guess. Countrywide Car Hire will confirm.'

'Drive all the way up to Town?'

'Yep. My car's in dock, so I'd trained down to Cambridge on Friday and been picked up by Annie Urquhart and Toby. Fancied a quicker trip back.'

'Make straight back to London?'

'More or less. Stopped for a jar at the Fowler's Nest. Ten miles or so from Fen Holton, isn't it?'

'Witnesses?'

'Dozens, but some weren't seeing too straight, I'd surmise. Place was overrun by a wedding party.'

'How long were you there?'

'Five minutes at most. Din was appalling.' Poynter rubbed his chin.

There's something else, Baxter thought. What sort of something?

'Any other stops?'

'Cross Lanes service station for a leak. Bog was empty. I doubt if anyone noticed me go in.'

'Then straight home?'

''Sright. Arrived just before the late film. Russian thing. Like the storyline in words of one syll?'

'It'll keep,' Baxter growled.

'In which case you've squeezed me dry.' Poynter stood up.

'One last thing,' Armstrong put in. 'Anyone you knew in the crowd at the Fowler's Nest?'

Poynter paused, brushed the Star Street dust off his cords, smiled a slow smile. 'Now you ask,' he said, 'I do remember spotting Derwent Lake.'

'Know the Great Wen's not your favourite place, Bill,' Baxter said when their witness had taken a sullen departure. 'All the same, seeing as we're here—'

'We might as well chase up Derwent Lake?'

'Not today, I think Not just on Poynter's say-so, though I'm bloody glad you asked the question. Stuart Kerr seems a safer bet.'

'The boyhood chum of Sharrock's?'

'And employee of Lake's Bank. Precisely. Colindale address, as I recall.' Baxter consulted a scrap of paper in his wallet. 'Come on.' He led the way back to the foyer where he announced his intention to Andrews and requested the use of a London *A to Z*.

'Kerr—Stuart Kerr, you said? Got a feeling you're too late, Dick. Wait a tick.' The duty sergeant's fingers activated a computer display that was mercifully more comprehensible than Highcroft's brainchild. 'Look. Ordinary sort of name. Ordinary sort of killing, too, poor bastard.'

Stuart Kerr's body, they read, had been discovered battered and stabbed in a public lavatory on the Star Street patch shortly after 9.0 on Friday morning. Post-mortem investigation indicated that death had occurred about an hour earlier. There was evidence of a struggle. The deceased had been identified on Saturday by a Mr Neil Allingham who shared his home. A wallet and ring were reported missing.

A phone call to the investigating officer established that the Mid-Anglian detectives were welcome to interview Allingham. A second phone call secured Highcroft's rather more grudging consent.

When they arrived at the stucco and brick semi-detached villa, someone was hoovering overhead. Through the draped curtains of the lounge they saw the set of a 'thirties film, but in colours. Fondant colours. The house, like the public rooms of Hare Holt, had been furnished in period. But this was a light, bright, Art Deco period.

The young man who answered the door wore an unexceptional black polo and white drill pants. But his dark, slicked-down hair had a 'thirties look. 'Yes?' he said. A dog barked overhead.

Before the detectives had time to answer, a small white Yorkshire terrier had hurtled itself downstairs and upon them. The young man bent to retrieve it. 'Hush, Bet. It's not Daddy,' he said, holding the little creature high, and kissing the top of its head.

'Mr Neil Allingham?'

The young man nodded, and cast a dull eye over the ID cards.

'I don't understand. What's the Mid-Anglian Constabulary to do with Stu?'

Mention of David Sharrock's death roused little interest in the questioner.

'Heard of the guy, yes. All over the ads, isn't he? Never set eyes on him. Stu knew him once, I believe. Yonks ago, in Cambridge. But Sharrock was a go-getter, wasn't he? Nothing like Stu. I doubt if they were ever friends—real friends.' His face twisted.

'Odd coincidence, though, isn't it?' Baxter persisted. 'Two teenage mates killed within two days of each other.'

A low moan. A yelp. 'Sorry, Bet. Come inside, will you? You'd better come inside.'

Allingham led the way into the living-room, where they sank into various components of the pink, sculpted suite. Released, the Yorkshire terrier leapt on to a piano stool, from which she looked down at them.

'She was Stu's before she was mine,' Allingham said. 'Looking after her's all I can do for him now. That and keeping the house nice. He loved this house.'

'Was there something else you wanted to say?' Baxter began gently. 'About Mr Kerr's mur—'

'Don't use the word. I can't bear it. Couldn't, yesterday, when the Met officers used it in the morgue. That's why I didn't tell them about the knife.'

'Knife?'

'Stu's flick-knife. It wasn't with the belongings they asked me to identify. That's what the bastard must have used. I can see it—hear it. I thought maybe if I kept quiet about the knife, I'd blank it out. But I couldn't. Glad I told you. Thought a dozen times this morning about ringing the investigating officer.'

'So why didn't you?'

'Thought they'd take the line that if he carried a knife he deserved what was coming. That I couldn't get across over the phone the kind of guy he was. Stu wouldn't have hurt anyone except in self-defence. Never carried a weapon until a couple of weeks ago.'

'Something happen to change his mind?'

'Someone.'

'Someone you didn't mention to the Met?'

Allingham sighed—the Sisyphus sigh of the deeply depressed. 'Stu'd warned me the bloke was dangerous. He was afraid for Bet and me—for the house.'

How ludicrous they were, Baxter thought, these attachments to particular configurations of brick and mortar, from which he was certainly not immune. 'Would you like to begin at the beginning?' he said.

Another sigh. 'Last August it started. I blame myself. I'd gone mad in the July sales—new curtains and carpets. Then I lost one of my best clients.'

'Clients?' Allingham looked too conventional for a hairdresser. A chiropodist perhaps?

'One of my authors. I do research—for biographers, mostly—Newspaper Library's just across the road. Stu used to say I was the ghost of a ghost. Not that my income went far at the best of times. Stu made good money—enough to cover all our expenses in the normal way, but he hated us being in debt. Said he'd have to think of moonlighting when he heard about my spending spree. Then, a week or two later, he told me he'd run into an old friend who'd fixed him up with something.'

'Old friend? No details?'

'No. Thought he might have been a former colleague. Stu never talked much about his work or his colleagues.'

'Was he happy at the bank?'

'Fair to middling. He'd been passed over for promotion. Anti-gay thing, he reckoned.'

'How'd it go—this spare-time job?'

'OK, for the first couple of weeks. Bloke who was employing him was a bit crazy, he said. Assignment was some kind of practical joke, for which Stu was supplying the computer programming, I suppose. Anyhow, his cash advance was more than enough to clear my £1500 credit card bill. Then things seemed to go sour. How, I don't know. But Stu gave me the impression he was locked into something he wanted out of. There was trouble at the bank around the same time.'

'How long did this go on?'

'Three or four months, I suppose. Stu seemed his old self again when we went on a ski-ing holiday to the Tyrol. First time ever—oh God.' Allingham's nails dug into a pink grosgrain cushion.

'Drink of water?' Armstrong offered.

'No, thanks. Rather get it over with. That was that until about a month ago. Then Stu came home late one evening looking washed up. Couple of days later—a Saturday—he said he was going to Cambridge to see his sister. He'd looked so rough before he left here that I tried to persuade him not to go. Rang his sister's number twice—he wasn't there. He'd lied to me. First time. It wasn't like that between us —was it, Bet? We were . . . committed.'

Another short silence.

'Stu never said where he'd been that day, but he'd been drinking before he came home. The flick-knife fell out of his pocket when he was undressing.'

'Can you describe it?'

'Silver or silver-plate handle five or six inches long, engraved with convolvulus.'

'Ask him about it?'

'Yes, but all he would say was he might need it if he was pushed further than he was prepared to go. "There are things I'd never do," he said. "You know that, don't you, Neil?" I told him, yes. "I'd never hurt a kid," he said. "You know that." "I know," I said. That was all. He was very drunk, you see.'

'And next morning?'

'Next morning I told him straight out to break with whoever was putting the boot in. "This bastard owes us," he said. "Why should he get away with what he owes us?" That was that, until last Friday. I woke up to find a note on his pillow. Gone swimming on the way to work, it said. Friday night, he didn't come home. But you hope—you go on hoping, don't you? Saturday morning, I rang the police.'

CHAPTER 12

Around 4.0 Baxter, Armstrong and Wendy Powers recrossed the Cambridgeshire border under lowering clouds. To judge by the state of the gutters, heavy rain had preceded them through the village of Fen Holton. Never a hub of activity on winter Sundays, the High Street showed minimal signs of habitation. One bedraggled pedestrian trudged along the ill-lit pavement. Several seconds elapsed before Baxter recognized his wife.

Armstrong braked and reversed.

'Well timed.' Sarah clambered into the back of the car. 'What's this?' she asked, pointing to the plastic-wrapped object that separated her from DS Powers.

'Sharrock's state-of-the-art speech synthesizer. Wendy can't wait to put it through its paces,' her husband said. 'What's up with you, love? Renault packed in?'

''Course not. I'd a letter to post and thought I mightn't have time tomorrow. Besides, I felt in need of fresh air.'

'What's been happening up at the house?'

'Not a lot you'd be interested in. People are still reacting to the shock. Everyone's worried sick about Lucy.'

'But the show goes on?'

'Yes. It feels the right thing—I don't know why. Thank God it's a *branle* day. They're rather jolly dances. More country than court, with simple steps and lots of mime. You pretend to be washerwomen and popping peas, etcetera, etcetera. Haviland's been working his damnedest and everyone's rallied round.'

'Everyone?'

'Well, almost. The Drydens have gone home. Poor Jonathan Talbot's been haunting the incident room. Still no sightings of Lucy?'

''Fraid not. We've just come off the car radio.'

'And how was London? Oh, Bill, I don't usually cross-examine him—really. But I feel involved in this case—

because of liking Lucy and having to certify that sad, mixed-up young man. Don't tell me anything you shouldn't, Dick.'

'I'll ask you a question, then. Remember Sharrock wearing a headscarf?'

'With wildfowl motifs? Oh my God, does it matter?'

'Might do.'

'Should have told the Super last night, but it slipped my mind. Besides, such a nice woman . . .'

'Who's such a nice woman?'

'Oh, sorry. I'm gabbling like one of my less coherent patients. Lack of sleep, I suppose. Deborah Dryden. When she saw Sharrock's headscarf hanging on a coathook on Friday evening she nearly passed out.'

'Without knowing whose it was?'

'Yes. But she asked me and naturally I told her. What's it mean, Dick? OK, forget I asked.'

'I can honestly say I haven't the faintest idea. Another thing. Did Lucy Talbot ever mention travel plans?'

Sarah frowned. 'She said she'd had wanderlust when she was living in London, that's all. But why—?'

'Tell you later. Much later. OK?' The gate-lodge of Hare Holt was in sight.

'OK and good luck, love.'

Richard curtailed the parting hug out of consideration for Bill Armstrong. Public display of private emotion elsewhere than on the football field offended the Ulsterman's sense of decency.

On re-entering the incident room, the Chief Inspector found three differently timed phone messages instructing him to ring Highcroft, who had been summoned to the Holtchester Headquarters for a conference with the Chief Constable and his deputy. Fortified by a cupful of milky Bovril and a cream cracker, Baxter picked up the phone.

'On your own, Richard?' Highcroft whispered.

'Yes, sir.'

'Good. CC wants this kept from the media boys and anyone who might blab to them. For your ears and the Bishop's, then. Mrs T's been located.'

'Alive? Unhurt?'

'To all intents and purposes, yes. Spent the night in a windmill, would you believe? Post mill half a mile south of Long Fenton.'

Baxter consulted a wall map. 'And within a few miles of Gorridge's accident.'

'Three, to be precise. Outfit's an industrial museum. One of the voluntary custodians found her a couple of hours ago when he arrived to open up.'

'And nobody thought to search the place earlier?'

'No signs of life, I'm told. No evidence of forced entry. Mrs T had been shown over the place not so long ago. Knew where the keys were hidden.'

'So where is she now? Hospital?'

'Bishop's House, Fenport. Bishops' wives are a protected species, it seems. Mrs T knew the bloke who found her. Talked him into driving her straight home, talked him out of putting us or her husband in the picture. Wanted time to wash and change, she said. Chap had the wit to contact a neighbour—wife of a sub-dean or some such—who called in Dr Ganji.'

'Who is a police surgeon?'

'Right. He informed us and insisted on a hospital check, but she discharged herself afterwards.'

'Want me to do the interview?'

'You and DS Powers. But proceed with caution. The CC's anxious about reactions at Lambeth Palace.'

'There's a complication.' Baxter reported the discovery of the fake passport.

'Bloody hell! Crunch-time for the Talbots, would you say?'

'Or the Lakes or the Drydens. Want a rundown on our London interviews?'

'Get Armstrong to fax me an interim report.'

Baxter transmitted the order to his less than enthusiastic colleague. Curious about Talbot's response, he himself walked over to Hare Holt to convey the news. The Bishop, with whom he spoke in the empty screens passage against competition from crumhorns, giggles, and foot-stampings, seemed genuinely delighted. But the mood passed quickly. As Talbot turned away, shoulders hunched, to collect his and his wife's bags, Baxter had the impression of a man whose heaviest baggage had still to be offloaded.

Before leaving for Fenport, Baxter returned to the incident room and rang Lou Mercier's home number. When he'd tried it from London, Jo had told him her husband was on duty. His office number had, however, been engaged.

This time Lou answered, thickly. Supper-time, Baxter surmised. He gave the gist of his interview with Neil Allingham. 'Tell you what bugs me,' he added. 'Can't shake off the notion that Kerr's out-of-hours assignment and therefore his death might have been connected with his work for the bank.'

'Why me, Dick?' Lou moaned, slurping liquid comfort. 'Only a cog in the City wheel, aren't I? Temporary cog. You know this'll have to go upstairs.'

'So it shall, old son. In triplicate or whatever. But not yet, if I can help it. You've read the papers, Lou. You know we've a little problem down here—'

'Yes, but—'

'I've a hunch our interests overlap.'

'You do?' Somewhere behind Lou's cynicism, Baxter detected the curiosity of the born bargain-hunter.

'When I told you on Friday morning Sarah was weekending with the Lakes, you pricked up your ears.'

'Did I now?'

'You also dropped hints about a simmering financial scandal.'

'Don't know what your Cambridge eggheads tell you. Far as I'm concerned, two and two still make four.'

'OK, but I've been informed that Derwent Lake was in the vicinity of Hare Holt at the time of last night's murder.'

A pause. 'Off the record, I'd rather you didn't interview him before tomorrow afternoon.'

'All right, if it's all right with Highcroft. But why so?'

'Not over the phone, mate. Pop round to my office tomorrow lunch-time, and I might have something.'

'OK. There's one snag. Frances Lake has asked Sarah to

go up to London with her and her granddaughter tomorrow morning to thrash something out with friend Derwent. I gather she's concerned about the kid's emotional health. Sarah's been roped in in a semi-professional capacity.'

'So?'

'In the light of subsequent events, I'm not happy about her going, but she thinks she's duty-bound, so I haven't a cat in hell's chance of stopping her—'

'And you'd like us to put in a spanner from this end? Sorry, chum. Mrs Lake's probably set the visit up with Derwent. He might get nervous if they backed out. If it's any consolation he's been under obbo since nine this morning.'

It wasn't. 'Curiouser and curiouser.'

'Stop fishing. Tomorrow afternoon, then?'

'Right, mate, and thanks. Grateful for small mercies.'

Baxter's last act before leaving for Fenport was to request from Holtchester HQ a search of case files and newspapers for any incident involving Deborah or Coulter Dryden on March 3, 1968.

A visibly more cheerful Jonathan Talbot put his head round the door of his study before Baxter and Wendy Powers had completed their inspection of his bookshelves. 'She'd like to talk to you now.'

He led the way to the open door of a big, underfurnished Georgian sitting-room. The sub-dean's wife, a rounded Tiggy-Winklish figure in a bilberry velour tracksuit, had beaten them to it.

'You've been marvellous, Andrea,' Lucy was saying. 'But Evensong must be over, and Harry—'

'Will be snoozing over the Sunday papers. Shan't budge till I've seen you both fed and watered, dear.'

'I'm perfectly capable—' Talbot began.

'Can you do soufflés, Bishop? Thought not. Light texture—delicate flavour—that's what the system needs when it's stuffed full of sedatives. You could manage a spoonful of leek soufflé, couldn't you, Lucy?'

'Several.'

Andrea scuttled kitchenwards.

'What should we do without our unreconstructed Marthas? Be in the study if I'm needed, love.' Jonathan took a seemingly reluctant departure.

Lucy, in sweater and flannels, sat on a rocking-chair, with one bandaged foot on a low stool. She looked paler than Baxter remembered her from their sole encounter at a fund-raising dinner for a local nursery. 'Feeling OK, Mrs Talbot?'

'Physically? Fine, thanks. Came off the hockey field in worse condition many a time in my schooldays. But I feel bad—I really do—about giving so many people so much trouble. Please forgive me.'

'Let's take it from here, shall we? You know why DS Powers and I are here, I presume?' Wendy's neat black head was already bent over her notepad.

'Yes—yes, of course. I heard a local radio news bulletin. Confession's cleansing, isn't it? I couldn't talk to you until I'd cleaned up physically. And I can't talk to Jon—not really talk—till I've cleaned up inside. Does that make sense?'

'Confession, you said?'

'And you thought . . .? Yes, of course. That's how a policeman would think. Funny, Sarah's husband being a policeman. Your wife's a fine person, Mr Baxter.'

'Agreed.'

'I didn't kill David. I've been cowardly and stupid, and my cowardice and stupidity may have contributed to his death. But I didn't kill him.'

'Do you know who did?'

Lucy shook her head.

'Did you know he'd be attending the course?'

'Not really.'

'Yes or no, please.' Baxter spoke gently.

'He'd said last December he might come. But I assumed he was joking, fantasizing. It was hard to tease out fact from fantasy in anything David told me.'

'When did you first meet?'

'Seven years ago.'

'In Cambridge? At the Tekbridge Centre?'

Lucy flinched. 'Jon told you that? Then why go over the same ground?'

'We need your version, Mrs Talbot. We need any information you may possess about Sharrock. Sure you hadn't met him before Tekbridge?'

'Quite sure.'

'And you first met Nigel Gorridge at the same time?'

'Yes.' She cleared her throat. 'As Jon may have told you, I helped out in the coffee bar.'

'How would you characterize the relationship between Sharrock and Gorridge at that time?'

'David was the leader, Nigel the incompetent follower. But they got on quite well.'

'With occasional friction?'

'Yes.' Lucy flushed, visibly distressed.

'And one rather spectacular row in which you were involved?'

'If Jon told you that, he shouldn't. All right, Nigel made a pass at me. I expect he'd have raped me if David hadn't intervened. It was my own doing. I should have read the warning signs, but I hadn't had much experience of adolescents in those days. It was totally unconnected with . . . what happened last night.' She fumbled in her trousers pocket.

'Are you sure of that?'

'Nigel didn't kill David last night. Didn't try to rape me.'

'What made you jump out of his van, then?'

'Fear. Terror. He was very angry. I thought he thought I was the killer—that I'd tried to frame him, maybe.'

'I see. Let's go back. How did your relationship with Sharrock develop after the coffee-bar incident?'

'There hadn't been what I think you mean by a relationship. David had been one boy among a couple of dozen. I caught him staring at me now and then, but he didn't have an obvious crush like Nigel and one or two others. After the attempted rape, Jon begged me to stay away from the centre. For his sake I agreed.'

'I see. When did you next meet Sharrock?'

'Not until one Saturday last October. My children had heard about the Fenfantasy Theme Park from some of the locals. Jon said he'd take us, but something cropped up to prevent his coming.'

'Know Fenfantasy was part of the Sharrock empire?'

'Not beforehand. It was pure chance that David was on a tour of inspection the day we visited. He seemed delighted to see us. Sent kind messages to Jon. Treated the kids to any free rides they fancied. Took snapshots of all of us—there's one over there.'

'May I?' Baxter got up to inspect the silver-framed photograph on the bookshelf. The boy's and girl's faces were obscured by towering glasses of ice-cream. But Lucy, sitting between them at a café table, was unmistakable. She was laughing at the photographer, her black hair windblown, her Florentine angel's face uplifted, her candy-striped shirt open at the neck.

'That shirt you were wearing. Is it a favourite?'

Her eyebrows rose. 'For summer. It was an unusually hot day for October.'

'Worn it since?'

'Don't think so . . . No, I'm sure I didn't. Why?'

'Never mind. When did you next see Sharrock?'

'Early December. He turned up at the cathedral gift shop where I help out sometimes. I may have mentioned it, the day we went to Fenfantasy. It was twelvish and he asked me out for lunch. Said he was looking for a property in the area and wanted advice.'

'From a newcomer?'

'I was brought up in Fenport. That had come out too the day we visited the theme park. He was so easy to talk to—to laugh with. All right. I was attracted. For which reason I was doubtful about lunching with him. But trade was slack that day, and I allowed myself to be persuaded.

'We ate prawn patties in a pub near Godmanchester, and drank *vin rosé*. Giggled over the purple prose in the estate agents' handouts David had provided himself with. Surveyed the exteriors of a couple of stately homes and found them wanting.

'It was a quarter to three when he left me off at the cathedral. I'd promised to be back at two, but David's cheque for £500 made an impressive peace-offering.'

'Meet Sharrock again?'

Lucy sighed. 'Only once, before this weekend. It was late December. I'd a follow-up appointment with my former London dentist. The reminder had come on the morning of my lunch with David. I remember him saying he'd keep his fingers crossed for me on the day.

'But when I got out of the train at Liverpool Street, there he was on the platform with a bunch of freesias. Said this was the sixth Cambridge train he'd met that morning. He was very tanned. Said he was just back from Switzerland.

'I was embarrassed, angry, excited—all sorts of things that don't matter to you. He insisted on driving me to the dentist's. Afterwards, he helped me hunt for sale bargains. He begged me to have lunch with him again.

'I agreed because I thought things were getting too heavy, because I wanted to sit down across a table and tell him so. We had a heavenly salad in the lounge of Brown's Hotel. You know it? Panelled walls, old-fashioned armchairs. Not at all David's natural habitat, I'd say. Clever of him to guess it would be mine.'

Wendy Powers turned a page of her notebook.

'I'm talking too much—sorry. It's the dope.'

'Never mind. Go on.'

'Things didn't work out at lunch the way I'd intended. Most of the time David talked nonsense—seduced me into talking nonsense. In the middle of it he said: "You do know I adore you, don't you?" When I reminded him I was happily married, and intended to stay married, he asked me if I was holding out for an actor. Bishops fell for actresses, didn't they, so obviously bishops' wives . . .?

'I hoped he'd got my message, that the joke was his way of backing off without losing face. I asked him about Switzerland—he'd plans for a theme park near Geneva, he said, a joint venture.'

'Any developments in his househunting?'

'I did ask him if he was still planning to settle in Cambridgeshire, but he became evasive. Said something was in the offing but it might bring bad luck to count chickens. He asked me how I spent my spare time in Fenport. Didn't seem interested until I mentioned the Hare Holt dance course. Then he really lit up. It was extraordinary. He seemed intrigued with the idea of historical dance, talked about taking classes in London, asked me for details of textbooks and records.'

'And announced his intention of attending the course, you said.'

'Yes, but that was almost an aside, when we were saying goodbye at Liverpool Street. The train was drawing out. I said, "Take care," and he grinned and blew a kiss and said, "See you at Hare Holt," as though we'd already agreed it. And before I could get out the word "No!" he'd turned on his heel and was walking back to the ticket-barrier. As though my "no" didn't matter. As though nothing I'd said that day had mattered.'

CHAPTER 13

'I thought of writing—asking him not to come,' Lucy went on. 'But Jon would be there, plus several dozen other people. Just the occasion to get things on to a friendly basis, especially if David was coming to live in Cambridgeshire.'

'Had he mentioned knowing anyone in the county?'

'Yes, the Drydens. Deborah's involvement in the Dance Society was news to him, though.'

'No one else? The Lakes? The Gorridges?'

'No.'

'OK. Let's get on to the dance course.'

'Oh God.' Lucy covered her face.

'Fancy a glass of water?' Wendy Powers offered. 'A coffee?'

She took her hands away. 'No, thanks. I felt very tired suddenly. The medication, I expect.'

'Or lack of sleep?'

'No. There were sacks in the mill. It took some time, but

I slept in the end. The dance course, you said. Friday. I'd so looked forward to having time with Jon, helping him unwind. But he didn't even stay for supper that first evening. I was at the table, feeling rather sorry for myself, when David appeared—in drag.'

'Recognize him immediately?'

'When I heard his voice, yes. There was an empty seat on the bench beside me, so he came straight over. He'd made a good job of the make-up. And he moved the way he looked. Like a gawky, self-conscious young woman. A type but not a caricature.'

'But his voice was unconvincing?'

'When he laughed, it was his own laugh. Anyone who knew him well would have recognized it. But it didn't worry our neighbours at the supper-table. They didn't seem to notice either when he whispered to me, begging me not to give him away, not to spoil the joke.'

'And you went along with that?'

'That first evening, yes. I was curious to know how long it would be before the Drydens rumbled him. Or Nigel Gorridge. He was helping at table on Friday. A surprise to David as well as to me, I gathered.'

'And after supper?'

'I decided to get things straight with David. That meant having a word on our own. So I offered to show him up to his room.'

'A move that might have been misinterpreted?'

Lucy's short upper lip stiffened. 'I made myself very clear. Told him that if he wanted to involve me in his practical joke, he mustn't embarrass me—mustn't dog my footsteps. If my husband or anyone else asked me who Karen East was, I wouldn't lie for him.'

'How'd he take that?'

'Quite well. He did mutter something about bishops and ham actors being brothers under the skin. But then he assured me he'd mind his P's and Q's. What he wanted to talk about most of all was Hare Holt. The house enchanted him. He asked me how I'd feel about living there. Guilty, I told him. "That'll soon wear off," he said.'

'"Will", not "would"?' Wendy checked.

'Yes. Should have seen that red light, shouldn't I? But I went back downstairs. Whatever David did that evening, I didn't see him again. And he paid no attention to me at breakfast on Saturday.'

'By which time several bedrooms had been given a going-over?'

'So I gathered from Sarah after breakfast. I wondered if it was part of David's practical joke. Challenged him on the subject before the morning dance session.'

'With what result?'

'The news seemed to irritate him. He insisted he'd no part in the incident, but he gave me the impression he'd guessed the culprit.'

'Then you danced together?'

'Yes, we were learning the pavan, *Belle qui tiens ma vie*. David told me he'd been mugging it up from one of the dance manuals I'd recommended. There's this dreamy song to go with it. Very sad, very Platonic. The tenor was singing as we danced.

'I'm ashamed to say it, but I shut my eyes and imagined how wonderful it would be to be worshipped. Then I opened them and saw David's made-up face under the frowsty wig. It was tense, hungry. And it frightened me. I'd this feeling something dreadful had started to happen, and I was letting it happen.'

'But you didn't take any action?'

'No. When the music stopped, and we all straggled out for coffee, everything seemed so blessedly normal. I avoided David without difficulty until supper-time. Most of us were in costume then. David's Spanish-style costume was magnificent. He was at the foot of the main staircase as Jon and I went into the dining-hall, but he kept his distance during the meal.'

'See anything of Marina Lake's anxiety attack?'

'Not much. David was embarrassing me at the time—strumming on the table and humming *Belle qui tiens*. I felt sure people were listening, staring at me.'

'Then more dancing?'

'Yes.' She shivered. 'The experts did some demonstration dances, then the candle dance began. I watched at first. It was beautiful, but eerie, like watching half-length portraits bobbing up and down. I'd drunk too much at supper, and alcohol depresses me. I felt Jon should have seen how much I needed him. Should have put off his visit to the Claverhouses. Sarah tried to buck me up, but still I felt alienated from all those other costumed people, even my friends among them. You're like Sarah, Sergeant. Professional, competent. How you must despise women who get into my sort of mess.'

'There but for the grace of God . . .' Wendy murmured.

'Just a phrase to you, I expect. The awful thing is, I believe God's grace is there for the asking. And I didn't ask. Just went on feeling sorry for myself and thinking how little I knew about the people in those fancy costumes, David least of all. When we danced he tried to make me laugh, but it didn't help.'

'Did you stay until the end of the dance?'

'Almost, I'd guess. I wanted to get away before the lights went up—didn't want to mingle. Before I left, I told David I'd played his game long enough. That I'd put my husband in the picture as soon as he got home.'

'He asked me when that would be, and when I said possibly midnight, he urged me to put off telling Jon until morning. "Something I want to sort out before I come clean," he said. "Can't hurt to leave the Rev in the dark a few hours longer, can it?"

'And I thought it couldn't. I honestly thought it couldn't.' Lucy's tissue was a small, soggy ball. She hobbled over to a bureau to find a replacement.

'So like a fool I agreed. Told David I wanted an early night. Couldn't believe it when I answered a knock on my bedroom door two or three minutes later—before I'd begun to undress—and found him standing there. Couldn't believe it when he pushed in past me. He'd never touched me, you see, never so much as kissed me.'

'Did one of you bring up a candlestick?'

'David. I asked him why for the sake of something to say.

Keep him talking, I told myself. Humour him. He laughed and said it was to protect him against things that went bump in the night. It wasn't funny, the way he said it. He'd locked the bedroom door by then—pocketed the key.'

'What time was this?'

'Ten, five past ten—something like that.'

'Go on.'

She leant back, gripping the arms of the rocker.

'I begged him to leave. But he just stood there, smiling. Then he took off his black wig and headdress and said he'd something to tell me first. He arranged the two chairs to face each other. We sat down.'

'Any sign of a weapon?' Baxter asked.

'Not then. But he scared me all the same.'

'So why didn't you call for help?' Wendy put in.

'Later, I thought. When I heard footsteps. Nobody seemed to be coming upstairs yet . . . I just sat there, watching David's eyes. He didn't say anything at first, just hummed the music of the Torch Branle.

' "Nice tune," he said.

'I nodded.

'Then he hummed a few bars of *Belle qui tiens*.'

' "Our song, isn't it?" he said like an actor in an old B-movie. "Our dance?"

'I just stared. Then he reached forward suddenly and grabbed my wrists.

' "Say it, duckie. Say it."

'Dear God, he's mad, I thought. So I said what he wanted. He kissed the undersides of my wrists.

' "Nice house this, if it was done up," he said.

'I suppose I agreed.

' "You'll like living here, won't you, love?"

' "Me?" That stunned me completely.

' "You and me, sweetie. And the kids, if you like. Plenty of room for the kids."

'I realized he was trying to drag me into some crazy dream. So I shouted "No!" and pulled away, expecting a struggle. And he dropped my wrists, just like that, and stood up. Very white, but smiling.

'"My little joke, Bishopess," he said. But I knew it wasn't. It was some kind of test and I'd flunked it.

'I stood up too, and asked him to give me the room key. That was when he produced the knife.'

'What sort?' Baxter asked.

'Flick-knife, with a silver engraved handle five or six inches long. Flowery design. Odd that something so horrible should be so pretty. There was blood, dried blood in the crevices.'

'What next?'

'He said: "You're going to be sensible, aren't you, Bishopess?"

'"You're the one that's being silly," I said. The way I might have said it to a child. That's what he was, I think. A crazy child. He jabbed at my stomach. Lightly. But it pricked me through the layers.

'He pulled some coins out of his pocket, and said he'd a phone call to make. "One or two things I've got to sort out with my old mate, Nigel Gorridge," he said. "In his best interests. Funny bloke, Nige. You know that, don't you, Bishopess?"

'I blushed, and hated myself for blushing.

'He came closer, not touching, but staring.

'"I'm going to ring old Nigel and you're coming with me, Bishopess. A little heavy breathing down the blower wouldn't come amiss. Anything else and you'll get the length of this useful little gadget between your shoulder-blades. Understood?'

'"Understood." And he warned me that if I didn't co-operate, Jon would pay for it too. Then our children. And I believed him, you see. I'd told him earlier the children were at my mother's. So—so I . . .' She covered her mouth.

Wendy got up to touch her shoulder.

'Easier if I plough on. He checked if the corridor was quiet, and when it was he made the call from the payphone. Stood behind me. Made me dial the number he told me—hand him the receiver in his gloved hand. Can't remember what he said exactly. Something about giving Nigel what he'd promised plus a bonus he'd appreciate. He nudged me with his elbow and I knew he was planning to humiliate me—to watch while Nigel . . . Sorry, I can't say it.'

'Never mind. You saw no one on the corridor or on the stairs?' Baxter prompted.

'Not a soul.'

'Go on, please.'

'I don't know what I'd expected when we went back into the room. Certainly not that he'd ask me to swap clothes.'

'Did he give a reason?'

'To take the mickey out of his old mate, he said. I pointed out that Nigel hadn't seen our Tudor costumes, but David said he must have when he gave the bedrooms a going-over.

'I thought the real reason was that David wanted to see me undress. But no. He let me use the bathroom, but he propped the door open with a chair, and told me to push my clothes through. He stripped his own top layers double-quick, shoved his things through to me, and told me to hurry or he'd do the job himself. When I came through, he was splashing on my perfume, inspecting himself in the dressing-table mirror.

'"Neat job, eh?" he said. "Better stay in the bathroom while Nigel does his double-take. I'll give you a shout when we're ready.'

'It was only when I saw his right hand go to his pocket, that I knew he'd the knife in there. That he was going to use it. If Nigel assaulted me it would be the last thing he'd do. And his blood would be on my gloves and my Tate Girl dress.

'But all I could do was back away into the bathroom. This time I turned the key in the door and he didn't seem to notice. I listened. Heard him cross the bedroom and unlock the door leading to the corridor. And for the first time that evening I was able to pray. I just sat on the loo seat in the Spanish dress, praying. That I would hear Nigel coming in time. Would scream in time.

'Then I remembered the bathroom had two doors. David hadn't guessed. No reason why he should. Very slowly, praying the lock wouldn't squeak, I tried the door leading to Sarah's room. It opened. No sounds from David. No sounds at all. I kicked off my shoes, tiptoed across Sarah's room. The corridor door was locked.

'I went over to the window, pressed against the glass, looking. It was raining. There was a little moonlight, very little. It seemed an age before I saw anyone, but it might only have been five or ten minutes.'

'Description?'

'A man—that I'm sure of. He was wearing something that could have been a cycling cape and a peaked cap. Must have had fancy dress underneath. I could just catch the gleam of his buckles.'

'Heading in which direction?'

'Not heading anywhere as far as I could make out. Walking to and fro along the terrace with his head down. Almost as though—'

'Well?'

'It sounds crazy to say it, but as though he was a prisoner in an exercise yard. Every time he came past the window I did the SOS signals in semaphore, willing him to look up. The fifth or sixth time he did, but only for a second. I don't know if he saw me, but he stopped in his tracks and headed back for the house.'

'But you'd seen his face?'

'Not properly. Because of the cap, you see, and because of something over the lower part. A scarf, or possibly a beard. Very soon after that David tried the bathroom door. I made it back from Sarah's room before he asked me what I was doing. Praying he'd come to his senses, I said. He laughed and said that in his experience nonsense paid off better than sense.

'It all happened so quickly then. The squeak as our bedroom door opened. The sound of a blow, a gasping sound, a thump. Of his body falling, I suppose. Then other soft, muffled sounds. And more blows.' Her voice broke.

'Please try,' Baxter said. 'Go on trying.'

She sighed. 'I let murder happen. David's murder, but it might as well have been Nigel's. I couldn't scream, couldn't move. Not even after it was over. Not even when the corridor door opened again. I crouched on that loo with my head down and my hands over my ears. So I didn't hear what they said, you see.'

'They?'

'The woman who asked the questions and the man who answered them. They weren't there long—three or four minutes, perhaps. Then the woman left. Came back almost immediately. Another minute or two and they'd both left. Then I forced myself to go out of the bathroom. To face what had to be faced. To wait for Nigel.' Her head slumped sideways.

Wendy Powers ran forward. Baxter went to the kitchen for water. He returned to find his witness stirring, his sergeant kneeling on the floor. The two black heads almost touching, one neat, one tousled. Conspiratorial.

'You've cleared Becher's, Mrs Talbot,' he said briskly, when she had drunk her fill. 'Home straight in sight. Try please to describe what you saw when you left the bathroom.'

Sketchy as her description was, nothing in it contradicted Sarah's.

'Notice the flick-knife?'

She shook her head. 'It wasn't there. Not unless it was in his pocket or underneath the body. Nigel arrived a few minutes later. He went to touch David, but I knew it was too late. I told him to leave him in peace.'

'What else did you and Gorridge talk about?'

'Sorry. I was so desperate to get away, I didn't pay attention. I just kept begging Nigel to take me home. I couldn't face Jon in that room, in that house. It was horribly selfish of me, I know—'

'People in shock are apt to be selfish. What next?'

'We made it downstairs somehow without being seen. There was a lot of noise going on—I remembered there'd been talk of a party. When we got into the van, Nigel humoured me. Pretended he was taking a short cut to Fenport. But he kept pressing me to talk about what had led up to the killing. I couldn't, I just couldn't. I felt his anger, I saw it.

'When I realized we were on the wrong road, I panicked.

Waited till the van had slowed down before a sharp bend. Nigel made a grab for me as I opened the passenger door, but he missed. I jumped. He nearly lost control of the wheel but he made it round the next corner. I felt so bad when I heard about his accident. I hope I'd have gone to help if I'd known. But there are so many things about myself I don't know any more. Anyhow, I'd no idea he'd gone off the road. There was no screech of brakes—nothing. Just the headlights of a car coming in the opposite direction at top speed. Too fast for the driver to spot Nigel's accident, I suppose. I threw myself face down in the ditch and the car went past without slowing. Then I picked myself up and started walking along the verge, until I came in sight of Long Fenton.

'And the prospect of help?' Wendy's exasperation was obvious.

'I couldn't face people in the Tudor dress—David's. It oppressed me. I turned into a fen track with no idea where it led. Five minutes later I saw the smock mill. I'd been there before, but we'd come by a different route. Everything went so smoothly I couldn't believe it. The key under the stone I'd remembered. And inside, overalls to change into, sacks for extra heat.

'Eventually I slept. God kept me alive for a purpose—I don't know what. No doubt He'll tell me in his own good time. Any other questions, Mr Baxter?'

'Not for the present. You'll want to talk to your husband, I expect.'

She nodded. 'I do now. I really do.'

'Believe her?' Baxter asked in the car afterwards.

Wendy frowned at her tired face in the driving-mirror. 'Think so, sir, but I wish to hell I didn't.'

'Why's that?'

'If that flick-knife should turn out to be Stuart Kerr's, it looks like Sharrock used and then killed one old mate, and plotted the death of another. Threatened and humiliated and tried to frame a woman he'd claimed to love. Far as I'm concerned, whoever topped a monster like that was doing a good turn—to Sharrock as well as to society. Who knows how much more damage he'd have done if he'd stayed alive? And from all I've read, shrinks can't make over that sort of psycho.'

'Not today, maybe. But there's always tomorrow. Sharrock was a young man. Besides—'

'Know what you're going to say, sir. "Murder is murder is murder."'

'Deny that and you're on the slippery slope to genocide. Agreed?'

Wendy sighed, shifting her grasp of the steering-wheel. 'Been a hard day, sir. Maybe I'm not thinking straight. First thing tomorrow, I'll probably agree with you. OK?'

'OK, Sergeant.' Baxter relapsed into silence. The rest of his journey back to base was spent among the weedy pools of his private imaginings.

CHAPTER 14

At eight next morning a watery sun streamed through the windows of the incident room and across the two readers of the *Clarion*.

'Makes a difference, doesn't it?' Toby French tapped page four for the second time in two minutes.

Baxter reread the illustrated text:

On the day of David 'Sunnyscene' Sharrock's mystery death (see page one), his host Robin Lake was snapped tripping the light fantastic (far right). Taking steps to improve his vital statistics, perhaps? City analysts predict hard times ahead for the 90-year-old Merchant Bank. Rumours of computer system cock-ups recur in the wake of the Healthicrunch and Zilkinglas share issue flops. The loss of several large corporate accounts is widely reported.

Chairman Edward Lake is here pictured (right) communing with his laptop after a working lunch with senior advisers. Tough Ted, as he is known to Square Milers, is said to be planning a purge all the way up to board level in a desperate bid to restore client confidence.

Will the axe fall on Derwent, Cousin Robin's son and the third Lake among the current board of directors? Father-to-be-Derwent, shown below slurping his Saturday minestrone in a hostelry not ten miles from the family seat and scene of the recent tragedy, could well be in the soup in more senses than one.

'Makes a difference about what, Toby?' Baxter asked, po-faced.

'About my sense of loyalty to Poynter. *Clarion*'s bought all rights on this lot. Colour supp project's out of the window, he told me when I rang just now. Never was anything more than a cover, I'd guess.'

'So you'll be out of pocket?'

'That's the least. Local journalists need local goodwill. Lakes are never going to believe I wasn't in on this. It was hard enough to persuade Annie.'

'My commiserations,' Baxter said absently. His attention was held by the shot of Derwent Lake which might or might not provide him with an alibi, depending on the length of time the diner had lingered. Lucy's evidence had suggested an unlikely though not impossible motive. Suppose Derwent Lake had got wind of Sharrock's interest in Hare Holt?

Toby cleared his throat. 'In view of developments—in view of Annie's reaction—I've decided to add to my previous statement.'

'Good for Annie. Half a sec.' Baxter summoned Wendy Powers from the outer office. 'Let's have it.'

'For starters, Annie thinks her evidence may have led you to suspect Nigel Gorridge of nicking the Bishop's report.'

'And he didn't?'

'Not unless he passed it on to Poynter. That's who slipped it to me after supper on Saturday.'

'A joke?'

'Suppose so. Muttered something like "For what I am about to owe you," which begins to make sense. You'll appreciate I'm not eager to finger a fellow-tradesman, but Gideon's put himself way out of line.'

Baxter grunted. 'For starters, you said.'

'The other thing may not matter, but it's been puzzling me.'

'Go on.'

'Saturday afternoon I nipped down to the village to buy wine at the off-licence for Annie and me and a couple of others. I'd been feeling parky—bedroom radiator had conked out—and the walk to the village got the circulation going. Heading into the wind on the way back wasn't such fun, so I took the short cut through the car park behind the Bull. Not many cars, but one was a red Mini I thought I'd seen at Hare Holt. There's a phone-box at one corner of the car park, and I could see a woman in it with her back to me. I was almost past before I recognized "Karen East".'

'Time?'

'Church clock was striking a quarter past three when I left the off-licence.'

'Remember what Sharrock was wearing?'

'Greenish-blue tweed coat. Boots, I think.'

'Nothing on his head?'

'Not at first. That's the odd thing, you see. When she—he came out of the phone-box he was putting on a headset.'

'Odd? Personal stereos are thick on the ground.' Baxter unwrapped a soda mint.

'The oddity is what she—he'd—been doing. I'll swear Sharrock had been holding the headset to the telephone mouthpiece—playing a tape down the line.'

'Interesting episode if true. Why the delay in sharing it?' Baxter asked crossly.

'Sounds stupid, but it's been hard to unthink "Karen". I asked for a lift back to the house. "Karen" said she'd another errand to do in Holtchester, but she'd drop me at the gate-lodge. I'd rationalized the phone-box incident before we got there.'

'On the basis of what was said?'

'No. Practically nothing was. She—he—put a cassette on the car player. Johnny Cash. And the other tapes on the shelf carried the big country 'n' western names—Earle, Rogers, Griffiths, Wynette. What came over was a soft-centred, inarticulate girl. Playing schmusic down the wire to a boyfriend would be in character, I reckoned. And a call-box offered more privacy than Hare Holt.'

'Reactions, Sergeant?' Baxter asked on French's departure.

Wendy considered. 'Looks like Nigel Gorridge told the truth when he denied searching the bedrooms. If so, other aspects of his evidence should be taken seriously.'

'Such as?'

'Such as the fuss he said Sharrock made when he thought Nigel'd been playing his tapes. Seems to me we ought to check whether the labels match the contents.'

'Any specific hunches?' Baxter helped on his soda mint with a covert abdominal massage.

'Wild, I agree. But from what Helen Worth told me, that speech synthesizer could do all kinds of everything. Sharrock used to bug office parties.'

'Popular corporate joke.'

'Yes, but he'd feed the tapes into the machine. It can break down input into syllables, recombine them into new words or phrases. Helen told me a lot of technical stuff I didn't take in about compensation for contextual effects. But the gist is it can generate new but convincing intonation and pause patterns.'

'Which could fool the voice print analysts?'

'That's what I thought.'

'I'm sold, cleverclogs. Play over those tapes. Find out what else you can about the synthesizer. Nigel should be able to fill us in. I'll try to find out who tipped off the *Clarion*.'

The editor had, however, taken evasive action. Not for the first time, to judge by the guardians of his public and private peace in the Isle of Dogs and Godalming. Baxter left peremptory messages with both, and replied to a summons from his newly-arrived senior officer. Bill Armstrong was already in attendance.

'A pity you didn't leave that one for me,' Highcroft

complained. 'The CC takes a dim view of this splurge. I've undertaken to complain in person when we're up in London this afternoon.'

'We, sir?'

'Yes. The CC's had a request from the City Force. The *Clarion*'s disclosures have embarrassed them as well as us, it seems. They intend to arrest Derwent Lake rather earlier than they had intended.'

'Arrest? On what charges?'

'No details yet, I'm afraid. But the CC got the impression they'll include fraud.'

Lou Mercier had hinted as much.

'This meeting I've set up . . .'

'A commendable initiative. The present consensus is that if such a meeting proves necessary, there should be representation at superintendent level.

'If?'

'You must surely agree that in view of what happened on March 3, 1968, our next interview with Mrs Dryden could clinch the case.'

Baxter nodded. Highcroft, to do him credit, seemed to take little joy in the prospect. Before leaving, he assigned the lately arrived Armstrong the task of updating his experimental database.

'You think that system's a load of codswallop, don't you, Richard? Be honest,' Highcroft said as they drove off.

'Let's just say I'm not a visualizer.' It was easier than describing the flora and fauna of the weedy pools of his own ruminations, or attacking techniques that organized tangled evidence too simply and too soon. With another colleague he might have spoken honestly, but social lies were essential if he and Highcroft were to maintain a tolerable working relationship. And Baxter cared enough about his work to want that.

The sun streamed through the windows of *Bali Hai* and across the road maps on the coffee table in the drawing-room. As the police car crunched on the gravel, Coulter

Dryden raised his head. He was at the front door before they rang.

'Planning a journey, Mr Dryden?' Highcroft smiled uneasily. Absurd, Baxter reflected, to feel threatened by this out-of-condition Gulliver. The model villages that surrounded him in the square entrance hall were proof enough of their owner's insecurity.

'Deb needs a break,' Dryden said as he ushered them in. 'Didn't sleep a wink last night, poor girl. Don't know what you put her through yesterday, but—'

'You've come for me, haven't you?' Deborah emerged from what Baxter took to be the kitchen, holding a tea-towel and a saucer. 'It's all right, darling. I have to go. Want to go, you see.'

'All we propose to do just now is talk, Mrs Dryden,' Highcroft said with surprising gentleness. 'Where would be convenient—the kitchen?'

She nodded.

'No!' Dryden's tomato face creased. 'You're not getting her in there on her tod.'

'Mrs Dryden?'

Her plump hands gestured vaguely. 'All right. Coulter's got to know sooner or later, hasn't he?'

Dryden stared at her. 'Doesn't realize what she's saying, you see. Cracking up. Come on, then.' He led the way into the sunny drawing-room. More model villages interspersed the chintz and mahogany and blocked access to the calf-bound contents of the bookcases. As the others sank into the feathery depths of the three-piece, Baxter brought forward a piano stool.

'We'd like to ask you about a headscarf, Mrs Dryden,' Highcroft began. 'A headscarf with a design of game birds belonging to Karen East.'

'Balderdash!' Dryden put in. 'Out of consideration to Deb I shan't put it more strongly. Why are you subjecting her to this nonsense?'

'Remember, Mrs Dryden? We've been told you nearly fainted at the sight of that scarf last Friday.'

'I'd been on my feet too long . . . in the kitchen.' She was paling, patchily: her cheeks already wan, but the loose flesh of her neck almost as pink as her raspberry sweater.

'Done in—still is.' Coulter touched her knee.

'Let's go back, shall we?' Highcroft went on. 'To the 3rd of March, 1968. Ring any bells, Mrs Dryden?'

A little moaning sound. 'Then you know—?'

'These dickheads don't know a thing,' Coulter interrupted. 'Sniffer-dogs, that's what they are. Never mind that they're on the wrong scent. Thing is to keep noses down and tails up—to be visibly busy. Name of your game, Superintendent?'

'If you could read aloud the *Cambridge Evening News* headline for the relevant date, Chief Inspector?'

'"Fenport Finance burgled. Ordeal of proprietor and clerk."'

'I remember,' Deborah Dryden said flatly. 'Never a day but I remember.'

'I've read that report too,' Dryden put in. 'It doesn't begin to describe what Deb went through. All right, old Rowley Sutton was a loan-shark. A bloodsucker. There were plenty who would have said he deserved his come-uppance. But Deb took it badly—knowing it had happened with her sitting there.'

'Bound and gagged. You were gagged with a duster, according to your evidence, Mrs Dryden,' Highcroft continued.

She nodded.

'And Sutton with his own woollen scarf? By persons unknown to you?'

Deborah stared at the gros-paint flowers on her firescreen. Coulter gripped her wrist.

'You've no right to put her through this. Don't answer him, pet, don't answer.'

'I must warn you, Mrs Dryden . . .' Baxter doubted whether either of them was registering Highcroft's words.

Then, at a signal from the Superintendent, he showed her the headsquare taken from Sharrock's penthouse, and still wrapped in polythene.

'Recognize this, Mrs Dryden?' Highcroft leant forward, his pale leyes on her face.

'Yes, but I don't understand . . .' Her voice tailed off.

'No matter. Tell us what happened—all of it.'

'All right. Sutton was gagged with that scarf—my scarf—to begin with. He didn't remember because he was unconscious. A push, that was all. It happened the way I told the police afterwards—I swear. A push and he'd stumbled, caught his head on the corner of a filing-cabinet. But afterwards, when he was gagged and bound, his face went grey. I thought for a minute he might be dead. So I said we'd better look.'

'*Said?*' Highcroft echoed. 'So you weren't gagged?'

'Not until later.'

'One last question. This package was found in Sharrock's London flat, but I doubt if the label's in his writing. Take a look. Take a good look.'

One glance was enough. Deborah shrank back in her seat, both hands clenching the tea-towel.

'All right, Highcroft,' Coulter said. 'I wrote the bloody date. She's had enough. Can't you see she's had enough?'

Another caution. Coulter listened impatiently. 'Let's get it over with,' he said.

'Changed your tune, Mr Dryden?'

'Love my wife, you see. More than this house, this county, more even than the business.'

'What happened on March 3, 1968?'

'I raided Sutton's place.'

'Unaided?'

'So help me. OK, I'd pumped Deb the six months we were courting. About the times of collections, bank deposits. About the cash that stayed out of the local bank—that lay under the floorboards for months at a time. About the times she was alone with the old man. But she hadn't a clue what I had in mind. Not until I showed up that Friday evening. All right, she didn't make trouble, but only because she was too scared—'

'That's not true.' Deborah spoke with surprising firmness. 'It was because I loved him. Because I knew he'd make better use of the money than that horrible old man. I never wanted to work there. But jobs were hard to come by in Fenport in the 'sixties. When I found out about Sutton's methods—about his collectors' threats, the ways they conned clients into taking on new loans—I tried to resign. But he told me my married sister was on his books and behind with her payments.'

'You weren't to blame, love.' Coulter patted her knee. 'You weren't to blame for any part of it.' He turned to Highcroft. 'I'd no thought of using Deb's headscarf as a gag until I saw it on the office coatstand. Better shape for the job than his own muffler, I reckoned. No intention of hurting the bastard. Afterwards, when we thought he'd conked out, poor Deb was terribly upset. So I replaced the headscarf with Sutton's muffler, shoved the scarf in my pocket, told Deb I'd destroyed it.'

'And why didn't you?' Highcroft persisted.

'Yes, Coulter, why?'

'Love—insecurity. I've no right to ask you to understand, Deb. You don't, do you, gentlemen? You've never breathed in brickdust on a building site, have you? Eaten bacon and eggs fried on your dad's shovel and pretended to like it? The Lump's where I started. Squaring up to the big boys with the best of them, but bloody lonely, bloody afraid.'

In a world he never made, Baxter reflected. Remaking it had cost Coulter dear.

'I'd come a long way by 'sixty-seven, the year I met Deb. Served my time. Collected a good few City and Guilds. Got some junior management experience under my belt. Knew what there was to know about the British construction business. With Deb beside me I knew I could make my mark. I'd saved a fair bit, but not enough to launch myself. Sounds incredible now, but the five grand I took from Sutton made all the difference. Made me creditworthy, for Christ's sake. Creditworthy!' He threw back his head and laughed. 'But I needed Deb too, you see. I couldn't risk ever losing her. It wasn't blackmail—I swear I never thought of the scarf as blackmail. I just thought, if ever she wanted to split,

I'd show her . . . remind her what we'd been through. Prove to her that we had belonged.'

'I gave you no reason,' Deborah said in a small, cold voice. 'I never wanted to leave you.'

'I know, love. I've known for a long time.'

'Then why keep the headsquare, Mr Dryden? Perhaps you'd prefer to continue in your wife's absence?'

'No!' Deborah answered for him, reaching for his hand.

'I kept it at the back of a filing-cabinet at home. Deb never meddled with my things. I never looked at it. Out of sight, out of mind, or nearly. Once in a blue moon I'd think—supposing I died? Suppose someone had to make an inventory? I'd remember it then. Tell myself I must get rid of the thing. But I'd this superstitious fear that someone would catch me at it. That I'd be punished for letting Deb face the music all those years ago.'

'Did David Sharrock have access to your filing-cabinet?' Highcroft asked.

Coulter nodded sadly. 'When we moved here, I kept it in my basement office. That's where we'd go to talk business after dinner when Dave visited us. I don't hold my drink like I used to. Sometimes, I'd go to sleep. He could have taken the cabinet key from the desk, I suppose. I trusted him, you see.'

'Did you call home on Saturday morning to check your filing-cabinet?'

He nodded. 'I'd recognized Dave at supper on Friday, like I told you. It wasn't until we were in bed that night that Deb told me about the other scarf. She'd said it wasn't quite the same as hers, but I wondered if she'd got it wrong after all these years. If Dave was playing some kind of trick. I made an excuse that I wanted a drink of water and I went downstairs to look in the screens. The coatpegs were empty. I thought of going to Dave's bedroom—asking him straight out. But I had to be sure.

'Even when I'd ransacked that filing-cabinet, when I'd convinced myself the scarf had been stolen and only Dave could have stolen it, I didn't want to believe the worst. It was a crazy stunt, I told myself. Just as the cross-dressing was a crazy stunt. A joke aimed at me. What's the first thing he'd think, coming on that scarf in a packet with the date on? Souvenir of some long-lost dollybird, he'd think. No reason why he should link it with Deb. No reason why he should do any detective work on it.'

'Anything happen to change your mind?'

'I came straight out with it at the dancing session after supper on Saturday. Asked him what the hell he was doing dressed up like that, what he'd done with the scarf. He ignored the first question—told me I'd taken a long time to pick up his signal about the scarf. Asked why it mattered. When I mumbled something about sentimental value, he laughed and said poor old Sutton mightn't have shared my sentiments. "Do your homework and the other chap's if you want to get ahead," I used to tell Dave. And he had. He bloody had.

'Then he said the scarf—the real one—was in London. I could have it back at a price.'

'What price?'

'I don't know how much of this you've believed, but you're certainly not going to believe this. Dave asked me to buy Hare Holt for him when it came on the market. "No chance of that happening," I said. "Frances is determined to gift it to a trust." "Frances doesn't hold the purse strings," he said. "And the money's running out." It could just have been true. There'd been rumours that Lakes Bank was on the slide. I asked Dave why he couldn't buy the place for himself. He said he wasn't the type the Lakes would do a deal with. They'd suspect him of wanting to set up a theme park in the grounds, he said. "And would you?" I asked. He laughed. Said: "I'll keep them guessing."

'Then he started to lean. He wanted to answer straight away. I agreed, for Deb's sake. It seemed to me I'd no option. "Good old Coulter," he said. I knew you'd give me what I wanted. No hard feelings?" That's what clinched it. Dave all rouged up in drag and saying that. Twisting Deb and me and the Lakes and God knows who else round his little finger and expecting us to ask for more. And I'd let him. All those years I'd let him. Treated him like a son, when he'd no interest in being anybody's son. I did have another option. Later that night I went to his room with every intention of taking it. Of shooting him. So what happened? I went to sleep, didn't I? I bloody went to sleep.'

CHAPTER 15

Frances Lake wiped off her granddaughter's orange juice moustache. 'Dr Baxter and Daddy and I have things to discuss. Why don't you run upstairs and talk to your mice?'

'I don't *talk* to them,' Marina objected. 'It's more like a very high singing. Grown-ups can't do it.'

'Then they've been missing you,' Derwent Lake put in. 'Run along, darling. We'll all come up to the playroom later. OK?'

'Knock the door before you come in, won't you? They don't like grown-ups overhearing.'

'Promise.'

'More coffee, Mother—Dr Baxter? Why the deputation, may I ask? Sorry to sound inhospitable, but, as you know, I came out of a meeting to be here.'

An unscheduled meeting, apparently, which had forced Derwent to leave a message at Queen Charlotte's Hospital, apologizing for failing to meet his visitors there and asking them to make their own way to the house in Highgate. The part-time domestic help had delayed her departure to let them in and serve coffee.

The kitchen was a large, cheerful room in a lightened and brightened Victorian semi. Here as elsewhere the chief sources of brightness were flowering plants and flower paintings. 'Uncle Vanni's,' Marina had explained, enlarging on the cicadas, lizards and bullfrogs which were for her the chief attractions of her uncle's Ligurian garden.

Her father, who sat across the kitchen table from his visitors, looked in need of Italian sunshine. He was a fair-skinned young man with receding brown hair and a new beard. His still-visible jawline reminded Sarah of someone else's. His father's, most likely. The bruise on his right cheekbone—product of a collision with a hospital swing-door, he told his mother—was all his own.

Frances, more obviously anxious than her son, gabbled her preliminaries. She apologized for coming on a day when he had other worries. Her misplaced trust in Poynter had probably added to them. A friend had rung to warn Robin of the *Clarion* article, Frances explained. She'd bought a copy at the hospital bookstall.

'So that's it!' Derwent sounded amused. Relieved, even. 'You've come to warn me that DCI Baxter's put me on his blacklist. To show Dr Baxter what a nice guy I am—'

'Nonsense, dear. No doubt you'll be questioned like the rest of us. I know perfectly well you've good reasons for whatever you did on Saturday night.'

'And you aren't a teeny-weeny bit curious?' Sarah picked up a note of panic under the flippancy.

'Derwent, please! We've come about Marina. Go on, Sarah, I can't.'

'Briefly, Mr Lake, your daughter has shown signs of acute anxiety during this visit to Hare Holt. On Saturday evening she was terrified by some reminder of a traumatic experience you'd forbidden her to talk about. In my opinion and her grandmother's, you should withdraw that veto. By imposing it, you put at risk your daughter's mental health. Anything you want to add, Frances?'

'No—that's it in a nutshell, Derwent. Whatever frightened Marina, it was too much for her to cope with alone. Tell her she can share it with us. Now. Before she's the new baby to adjust to.'

Derwent got up and crossed the room as if to distance himself from the women. '"Mother knows best,"' he said. 'You always thought you did. Give me credit, for God's sake. Don't you suppose I didn't realize what I was putting Marina through? Didn't care? Didn't cuddle her when she woke at night in a cold sweat?'

'Then why?' Frances asked.

'If she talked—if it got out, I could lose her.'

Frances got up, a little stiffly. 'Look me in the eye,

Derwent.' The words, like the movement, were effortful. He obeyed. 'Are you saying, she'd be taken away from you for her own safety? That you'd lose a—a special relationship?'

Derwent jerked his head. 'You're asking me if I *abused* her? How could such a thing even occur to you?'

'Ten years—five years—ago it wouldn't. But I watch television, read the papers. Sorry, darling, but the question had to be asked. Sarah?'

'If your mother hadn't asked it, Mr Lake, I should.'

'And reported me to the police if I'd refused to answer?'

'More probably, to the social services.'

'Think how much harm an official investigation would do, darling,' Frances urged. 'To Marina, Gaby, your father. To the bank.'

'The bank!' Derwent laughed. 'That's funny—you don't know how funny that is, Mother. All right. You've boxed me in, the pair of you. For the record, I didn't molest my daughter. No one did. I've had it checked out by Dr Herring-Smith, a pædiatrician and a family friend. Ring her if you like, Dr Baxter.'

'For the present, I'll take it on trust. But we need to know what prompted the referral.'

Lake resumed his seat at the table. 'How can I be sure I know this won't go straight to your husband?'

Sarah's colour rose. 'I'm here as your mother's friend, and as a doctor.'

'Apologies. OK, I'll take the risk. I know I put too much on the kid. And I mayn't be around when she needs to talk. About a month ago she was abducted.'

'The poor lamb.' For the first time that morning, Marina's grandmother wept.

'Could have been a lot worse. They only kept her for six hours. Bloke who was left in charge was a humane type. Played games—told her stories.'

'Where did they take her?' Frances asked.

'Empty flat somewhere in London. Two hours' car journey, she thinks, but they could have been driving in circles.'

'Starting from where?'

'Angel Walk, Hammersmith.'

'Hammersmith!' Frances made it sound like Outer Mongolia.

'It's on the route between the hospital and Marina's violin teacher. It had become a Saturday afternoon routine on Kirsten's weekends off for us to park there. I'd nip into King's Mall for whatever bits and bobs Gaby wanted and popcorn for Marina.'

'Leaving her alone in the car? A six-year-old?'

'I know, Mother, I know. But Angel Walk's such a little road, with Regency dolls' houses and a pub. Reckoned there'd always be someone to keep an eye out.'

'So what happened?'

'She'd been told not to let anyone into the car—to stay put if strange men approached her. But he didn't approach her, this bastard got up as an octogenerian. He tottered down the street clutching a Safeways bag full of dog food, and dropped it so the cans rolled over the street. Marina, good little Brownie that she is, leapt out of the car to oblige. Whereupon the fat bloke who looked to be sleeping in the Volkswagen in front sprang into active life. The two of them bundled her into the VW, hid her under a rug, reversed and drove off. As far as I know, nobody noticed anything.'

'And you didn't call the police? Why on earth not?' Frances asked.

'Because I'd been warned not to.'

'Warned by whom?'

'By a mystery man who'd rung me about four that morning. Told me I was in for a shock that weekend. If I wanted a happy ending, I'd await further instructions. No mention of Marina, you see. That was clever. If I'd thought for one minute that Marina or anyone other than myself was involved I'd have sought advice straight away from Dad or my solicitor or somebody.'

'Why not the police?' Frances persisted.

Derwent looked uncomfortable. 'This berk had done his homework. Knew too much about bank affairs for my comfort. If there was to be an investigation, I felt it should be private. I'd report the call to the Board Monday morning, I told myself.'

'So what did you do when you discovered Marina had been taken?' Sarah asked.

'Drove home. Waited. If I hear nothing inside the next hour, I told myself, I'll contact the police. The call came in twenty minutes. From a phone-box, probably. Marina told me later they stopped the car once on the way to the flat. Different caller this time.'

'Who specified the ransom?'

'Yes. It wasn't money—it was something I had to do. I did it. "It's dead easy," this guy said. "It'll not cost you more than a little embarrassment." It's cost me a bloody sight more, but it was worth it. He said Marina would be waiting for me in Trafalgar Square that evening when I'd finished. And she was, Mother, she was.'

'It must have struck you that something like this might happen again,' Sarah said quietly.

He nodded. 'I've had half a dozen more calls to warn me that it will if I squeal. Last was only last Thursday. Different voices each time—but the funny thing is, I don't think any of them belong to the bod who's pulling the strings.'

'Why's that, darling?' Frances asked in tones that suggested she was beginning to doubt Derwent's sanity.

'It's the way they talk. Fluently, when they're giving me my sermon for the day. But when I ask questions, they become hesitant. As though Mr Big was listening in—dictating the right answer. Not good for morale, feeling you're up against some sort of private army.'

'I can imagine.' Sarah touched his sleeve. 'Let's all go upstairs, shall we? Ask Marina what frightened her on Saturday evening?'

He shrugged. 'If you think it'll help.'

'That tune.' Marina hugged herself as she said it. 'That tune the lady was humming.'

'Which lady?' Frances prompted.

'The one in the white dress with black and brown things. Who was meant to be Elenora de something.'

'Remember the tune, darling?' Frances followed up. 'Did it go with one of the dances I'd taught you?'

'No, but he'd sung it in the car. And his voice was like the lady's. And he tapped out the tune on the dashboard like the lady did.'

'*He?* The driver?'

'The other one. The old man who'd spilt the dog food. But when he talked I knew he wasn't old really. He talked when I pretended to be asleep, but in French and very fast, so I suppose they weren't sure if I was asleep or shamming. The song was French, too.'

'Can you sing it, darling?'

'Only bits. He only sang little bits of it at a time, under his breath, as though he didn't know what he was doing. It went like this, sort of.'

She hummed the first quatrain of *Belle qui tiens*. Sarah's eye caught Frances's.

'Get any of the words?' Frances asked.

'Not many, but *belle* came into it—that means beautiful. And *yeux*—that's eyes. Anne-Marie—this friend of mine at school—is half French, and she's taught me parts of the body.'

'That's good—that's very good.' Sarah shared Frances's obvious relief. Yet the truth, if Derwent was to be believed, was almost as horrible. 'What did the man who sang in the car do to frighten you, Marina?' she asked.

'Nothing, really. But it was scarey the way he went on at Sid—the fat one, the nice one. Sid helped to bundle me into the car, but I'm sure the other one made him.'

'And you didn't hear the other man's name?'

'No. Sid's wasn't the nice one's real name, either, I don't think. He just told me to use it when we were playing games in the flat. I don't suppose Bet was her real name either.'

'Bet? You didn't mention a woman,' Derwent put in.

'Bet was Sid's dog. I don't think he meant to let that out. So I shouldn't have told you, should I?'

'Don't worry, pet. Don't worry about a thing.' He hugged her. 'Now why don't you give Dr Baxter a rundown on your mousery. Gran'll want to hit the road soon, and I've my boring old meeting to get back to.'

Sarah followed him out on to the landing. 'May I steal another minute from your fellow directors?'

'From the City of London police, you mean.'

'I'd no idea—I'm so sorry.'

'Didn't intend to let it out. Don't say anything to Mother, will you? She's been through more than enough this weekend. I'd like to keep my troubles from her until the new grandchild's safely delivered.'

'Of course. What I wanted to say may or may not be of any practical help. But I feel you should know it was David Sharrock who hummed *Belle qui tiens* at supper on Saturday. Marina's in no danger from that quarter now. Another thing, from what I've heard of him, I don't believe Sharrock was anyone's puppet. Maybe you're out of the wood.'

'Thank God—oh, thank God.' Lake backed against the wall. 'I can't think why he'd want to do it, but I'm past caring. We turned down a loan application from him years ago—remember seeing it on file. But that was out of all proportion. Oh, what the hell. I'll talk to the police. It'll be an incredible relief. Tell my mother, will you? And thanks.'

As he turned away to go downstairs, Sarah realized who he reminded her of. A chilling coincidence, if it was a coincidence. She hurried back to Frances and Marina and the white mice.

'Like to keep this informal, if I may.' Detective-Superintendent Shrubsole of the City of London Police beamed at his three Mid-Anglian visitors in the seminar room at Wood Street. 'DI Mercier knows more about the Lakes case than any of us, so I'll ask him to make our presentation. You won't mind interruptions, will you, Lou?'

Mercier, uncharacteristically brusque, took over. 'Let's cut the cackle, OK? Two hours ago, Derwent Lake gave us evidence which, if supported—and that's a big *if*—could destroy our case against him. It'll save time and effort if you read transcripts of his statement.'

Baxter and Wendy Powers made short work of the two

sheets of A4. Highcroft, pausing occasionally to embellish a new diagram, took a little longer. He then recapitulated:

'Lake's kid is abducted. By David Sharrock or a joker who shared Sharrock's taste in early dance music, if the kid's to be believed.'

'By a man now dead,' Mercier added.

'Or by two men now dead,' Baxter amended. 'Stuart Kerr had a dog called Bet.'

'That's rich. Could be Lake found out Sharrock was going to Hare Holt. Could be he concocted the abduction story when we started breathing down his neck. Coached the kid to throw her panic.'

Baxter shook his head. 'Don't buy it. Other factors apart, she'd crumble under interrogation.'

'Reckon Lake did what he's now representing as the ransom price?' Highcroft asked. 'Went into the bank that Saturday evening. Signed a blank credit transfer instruction?'

'Possibly. We know that a fraudulent computer-printed document was created—almost certainly by Stuart Kerr—' and signed by Lake. As a result £5,500,000 was misdirected. Until this morning, I'd have said firmly that Kerr took his instructions from Lake. That if the form was blank at the time of signature, Lake checked it afterwards to make sure it was completed according to his specification.'

'Perhaps you'd better backtrack,' Shrubsole suggested.

'OK. Here's a photocopy of a note I received last Wednesday.' Mercier waved it. 'London postmark. Forensic are getting nowhere fast with the original.'

They read: *You may be interested to learn that £5,500,000, earmarked as a loan from Lakes Bank to Verdegon Pharmaceuticals, is on its way to the pocket of a Lakes director.*

'No idea who could have sent it?' Highcroft asked.

'Someone working for another finance house, I guessed. Things have been tough since Big Bang.'

'Tough enough for a bank director to risk his future for £5,500,000?' Highcroft hesitated between purple and tan felt-tips.

'Lakes have had more than their share of bad luck this

last year. Rumour has it, board members have been pouring in private capital and taken whopping salary cuts. Harder on some than others, no doubt. Chairman wasn't to be drawn, of course, when we chatted.'

'Took the bull by the horns, did you?' Baxter tried unsuccessfully to visualize the scene.

'With a minder from the Serious Fraud Office in case things got tricky. We'd checked with Verdegon beforehand —without retailing the criminal allegation. They're an Anglo-Swiss company, currently developing ecologically friendly cleansing products, and an old customer of Lakes. A hiccough had occurred, they admitted. Payment into their numbered account at the Crédit Rougemont, Geneva, hadn't been made on the due date. But Lakes had now rectified the omission, and as far as Verdegon were concerned, the matter was closed. We rather gathered they didn't want to put their golden goose off her lay.

'Liaison with Swiss banks is improving, but we needed something better than an anonymous letter to get what we needed out of the Crédit Rougemont. When we visited Lakes, we found that an internal investigation was in progress. And that's how the chairman would have liked to keep it, of course.'

'To maintain public confidence?' Highcroft made a bold, yellow swirl.

'Of course. Our anonymous friend had put a spanner in the works, so they had to settle for damage limitation. They'd a problem, but they reckoned they'd an expendable scapegoat. The late Stuart Kerr.'

'Why so?' Highcroft reverted to purple.

'When Verdegon complained, three days after the due date of payment, Edward Lake had personally examined the credit authorization in his hard-copy company file, and discovered a discrepancy between the account number quoted there and in the document from which it had been copied.

'Payment had been made to account number 311789 at the Crédit Rougemont instead of account number 311367. This was an online funds transfer, you understand, and the number was what determined destination. No cheques—no cheque clearance delays either. When Lakes contacted the Rougemont the money had been dispersed to a variety of first stage locations—mostly exotic, but including the Isle of Man.'

Wendy Powers suppressed a giggle.

'Yes, I'd hopes of the Isle of Man. But that was stage one, remember. God knows where stage two was. Anyhow, Ted Lake's first assumption was that the account number had been input wrongly by the data preparation clerk, and that the mistake had been overlooked by the colleague responsible for verification.'

'Some coincidence,' Highcroft complained.

'True. But it's happened before. DP clerks get fair pay, but they don't get much status. Treat a sparky kid like a computer peripheral, and what do you expect? Ted summoned his head of information processing from Tenerife for a crisis conference. Twenty-four hours elapsed. The IP bloke reminded his boss of extra security devices that had been built into the computer system after its teething troubles last autumn. These included an online diagnostic package, to which none of his junior staff had access.'

'Do you mean they couldn't use it or didn't know about it?' Highcroft asked.

'Neither. In fact, no one else in the bank knew about the facility except the chairman and head of internal auditing. Using it, the IP man was able to show that the Verdegon account number had been input correctly and duly verified, and that a correct credit transfer authorization had been printed on the Friday afternoon before the Monday when payment was due. This must have been the document which Derwent Lake, as the only Board member in the building, had signed before witnesses late on Friday evening.

'Shortly after eight p.m. the following day, Saturday, the Verdegon computer file was opened, the account number altered online, and a new authorization printed. If Lake is to be believed, on the blank form he had already signed. Steps were taken by the criminal to obliterate the online record of the alteration from the computer's memory—steps which would have been effective if it hadn't been for the new security facility.

'The original document was stored in a safe over the weekend, pending the funds transfer on Monday morning. It seems likely that the switch was made first thing Monday, after it reached the cashier's in-tray.'

'Could Derwent Lake have altered the file online?'

'No. Especially not in view of the attempted camouflage. The only people with sufficient skill and unsupervised access to the system were three senior members of the data processing department. Internal inquiries had indicated that the late Stuart Kerr was the only one of that number with a less-than-watertight alibi. He was also the only one in the bank's employment at the time of the computer cock-ups last autumn. Edward Lake is now prepared to admit that the experts he called in diagnosed sabotage.'

'So he wanted you to put the boot in?'

'Emotionally, yes. But he appreciated that if Kerr already had a grievance, he'd react badly to unjustifiable harassment. So he agreed to let us use his evidence in an approach to the Crédit Rougemont, who hadn't yet named the second account-holder.'

'And you got your info inside a fortnight?' Highcroft was visibly impressed.

'Inside ten days. Swiss laundries ain't what they used to be, thanks to the war on the drugs trade. The account had been opened six weeks before in the name of Ombrelles Anglo-Romaines. A fictitious company, it would now appear. Sole director was one Marcus Aylott.'

'Also fictitious?' Baxter asked.

'A character in his own fiction, if you like. Con-man with the talent to reach the top, but a reckless spender. The Rougemont security videos didn't mean anything to the Swiss police, but we knew him straight away. He's wanted in Ireland and France as well as the UK. By now he's probably chucking his tranche at a roulette wheel in the Bahamas.'

'Any positive link with Derwent Lake?'

'Early days, and we need more facts about the money

movements. But how's this to be going on with? Derwent Lake belongs to a European financiers' committee that meets fortnightly. Last meeting took place the day the Ombrelles Anglo-Romaines account was opened. Afterwards, Aylott and he overnighted at the same hotel. Neat?'

'So's a classy frame-up,' Baxter growled.

'OK, but when we started talking to Derwent he got nervous. Really nervous.'

'No wonder, if he told the truth about the phone threats. Can we hear the tapes he brought?' Wendy asked.

'If you like. But faking phone messages is a doddle, compared with the computer stuff.'

'*Some* phone messages.'

'You've lost me, Sergeant.'

Highcroft nodded. 'Tell them.'

'David Sharrock possessed a sophisticated speech synthesizer. He was seen to transmit a pre-taped message by phone from Fen Holton on Saturday afternoon. At precisely the same time, we learned on our way here, the Features Editor of the *Clarion* received an anonymous tip-off that Derwent Lake was under suspicion of fraud.'

'Got the *Clarion* recording?'

'Scrubbed. Editorial policy, they say.'

'So you can't prove it was from Sharrock. Or that he used his box of tricks to create it?'

'No. But we know that between four-forty-five and five-fifteen Sharrock re-used a tape he'd labelled as a Tammy Wynette to record a half-hour chunk from the BBC programme, *Saturday Sequence*. Odd mix of chat and pop, but a blank tape might have seemed odder to a snoopy friend. Maybe he'd something to hide in a hurry.'

'*Maybe?* Need more than that, won't we?'

Wendy smiled demurely. 'Of course. Which is why we'd love to hear your tapes, Mr Mercier.'

There were three—the three last in the sequence, Lake had attested. Two men's voice and a woman's. Baxter, who had heard many such threats, noted the well-judged mixture of intimate specifics and ominous generalities. Hospitals, he reminded himself, are penetrable institutions. Even an observer without Sharrock's talent for disguise could easily have found out what Gabriella Lake ate for supper on a given evening, what colour of nightdress she was wearing. But retailed by unseen and malign strangers, such personal trivia must have deepened their hearer's sense of helplessness.

Wendy Powers was sitting forward on her chair. 'Could we have the middle one again? The woman?'

Mercier obliged.

Wendy turned to Baxter. 'Sound familiar?'

'Yes and no. Helen Worth—reconstituted?'

'That's what I thought. Could we have them all again? So we can concentrate on the pause patterns?'

'I go along with Lake,' Shrubsole said afterwards. 'Sounds to me like there's a silent third party, prompting.'

Mercier shook his head. 'Not quite. The responses to his questions are delayed, but when they come, they come smoothly. Too smoothly for twitchy underlings transmitting truths from on high.'

'Agreed,' Wendy said. 'The phrases sound machine-made. Like phrases generated by a speech synthesizer in interactive mode.'

'You go along with this, Victor?' Shrubsole gazed in awe at his visitor's graphics.

'Worth taking expert opinion. Richard?'

'I'd second that. I'm inclined to take Lake at face value, but it's possible he rumbled Sharrock at some point before he died. If so, he's a prime suspect for the murder. Pity your obbo didn't start twelve hours sooner, Lou.'

'Could be he spent some time here on Saturday night. Look at our video still.' Mercier tapped a blurred black-and-white shot, one of several, which showed Lake getting out of his car. 'Maida Vale address. Lake went straight round after he left the hospital Sunday evening. See the girl at that window?' They saw.' Kirsten Sondstrom, the kid's ex au pair.'

Baxter fished out his reading glasses. 'Who marked Lake's face, and when? No sign in the *Clarion* pic.'

'You're right. And there's the bruise in our first Sunday

morning shot. Hospital swingdoor, he told us, which can't be true, unless he went there late Saturday evening.'

Highcroft pocketed his paper and pens. 'Valuable exchange, Shrubsole. Much appreciated. You'll excuse us if we get about our business? Coming, Richard?'

A WPC intercepted them at the doorway of the seminar room. 'Phone message for DCI Baxter,' she said.

CHAPTER 16

As Baxter read the message, Highcroft asked the City DS to check on Derwent Lake's whereabouts. He was, it appeared, at Queen Charlotte's where his wife was now in labour.

'Hardly the time or place for a showdown. Best if we tackle Ms Sondstrom first. Coming?' If the Superintendent was disappointed, it didn't show.

Baxter made his apologies with some reluctance. But his message was from Len Wardle, an informer who had given value for money in Baxter's Met days. It concerned dealings between Sharrock and the late Olly Brentwood, ex-CID sergeant turned private eye. If Baxter was interested, he should contact Wardle at the Square and Tassel pub in Cambridge.

'Why does that name ring a bell?' Highcroft asked.

'Haunt of Sharrock's mother's, according to Mrs Gorridge. Could be coincidence. Len Wardle was doing bar work, last I heard. All the same . . .'

'Very well, Richard.' Highcroft's fishy mouth tightened in distaste. 'Hardly a case for an ex-nark, I'd say, but you know your man. Wendy stays with me.'

'Money doesn't enter into this, Chief Inspector,' Len Wardle began. 'Let's get that clear from the start.'

Baxter nodded. 'If you say so.' Len had always had a moralistic streak. The pew-like snugs of the pub seemed an oddly appropriate setting.

'I've said goodbye to the old game. Gave my word to the daughter. But when I read in the paper about poor old Olly last September, I went to see Moira here. Moira Brentwood, she was then. Mrs Gray—DCI Baxter.'

Baxter shook hands with the small, bright-eyed fortyish woman.

'A terrible tragedy—my condolences.'

'Did you know Olly?'

'Slightly—before he left the Force. He was well liked.' And pitied. He hoped that didn't show. Moira didn't look the sort who would welcome patronage.

'Olly had his faults,' she began, clasping both ringed hands round her lager glass. 'But he didn't deserve to die like that. I saw him afterwards. They said the fumes got to him first, but all the same . . .'

'These things can take years to fade.' Baxter recalled his own first sight of scorched human flesh. He turned to Wardle. 'Where do I come in?'

'David Sharrock was Olly's last customer. I saw the payoff. Reckon Olly didn't give him everything he wanted, but he gave him something. I saw the look Sharrock gave him afterwards, and it wasn't pretty.' He recounted the August scene at London Airport. 'If I'd had any inkling the bastard would kill . . . But I hadn't. Not until I came back from holiday and read about the inquest in the paper. Even then, I wasn't sure until I'd gone round to Moira's.'

'There's no evidence,' she said sadly. 'Nothing that would stick. It was just they said Olly could've dropped a lit cigarette. But he'd given up smoking. Out in that garden he told me, day before it happened.'

'Mention this in court? To your solicitor?'

She shook her head. 'Didn't think it'd do any good. And Olly'd dinned it into me that I mustn't get involved in his cases. Too risky. For the kid too, he said.'

'You were living apart, weren't you?'

She nodded. 'For three years before he died. Sweet man when he was sober. But when he hit the bottle . . . We stayed friends, though. Went out every so often as a family.

He knew about Gary—my second. Knew I might want a divorce one day.

'It was a birthday treat for Julia, the Cambridge trip. I hadn't been for yonks, but my grandmother was a bedmaker at Gaunt College and I spent a week here with her every June when I was a kid. Stuck in my memory—Midsummer Fair, picking strawberries at Chivers. So when Olly said he'd been going down on a job—'

'For Sharrock?'

'He didn't talk about the case—except to say he hoped to wind it up that day. And he kept Julia and me away from the people he talked to. When he was doing his rounds in Cambridge, we picnicked. When he made his Linton call, he left us at the Zoo.'

'So you've no idea who he interviewed?'

'The last one was a Linton woman called Fleet. A Catherine Fleet. I only know that because I overheard the name. We stopped here first. Julia and I had to stay in the pub garden. When I came in to find out why Olly was so long getting the drinks I spotted him with his back to me, talking to an old man in that booth over there. At least, Olly was talking and the old chap was shouting. I realized straight off it was business, and popped into the Ladies before they saw me. But I heard the words Fleet and Linton—couldn't miss. And that Linton call was the last one he made.

'Olly was on Cloud Nine when he picked us up afterwards at Linton Zoo. "Payday tomorrow," he said. "This one'll be a biggie." And he told Julia to help me make out a shopping list. The money went up in smoke, I suppose. They found nothing—nothing except a bloody electricity bill.' Moira blew her nose.

'We've checked the phone book,' Len put in. 'Only Linton Fleet is Fleet Salad Growers.'

'Sounds a good bet—thank you both very much.'

Moira buttoned her coat. 'It was Len's doing. I wanted to speak out, but I'd never have had the nerve, if he hadn't egged me on. It hasn't been easy . . .'

'I appreciate that,' Baxter said.

'Drink up, girl.' Len patted her sleeve. 'You've done the

right thing. Fancy showing me the sights before we hit the road? My first time in Cambridge, remember.'

'My last. Let's go home, Len. Let's both go home.'

'Mind if we stay in the kitchen—I'm rather mucky.' Soil clung to Catherine Fleet's boots and dungarees.

'This is fine.' Baxter meant it. The mix of old and new —oak, Mason Ironstone, checked red gingham, white appliances and white modern china—struck him as pleasant and sensible. So too did his hostess.

'How can I help?' She unpeeled her rubber gloves.

'A man called Brentwood came here one Thursday last August.'

She sighed. 'Yes.'

'Asking you what you knew about David Sharrock?'

'One thing.'

'Did he tell you how he'd got hold of your name?'

'From a customer at the Square and Tassel. Told them he was writing a history of the place. I worked there when I first came to Cambridge.'

'Did you tell Brentwood what he wanted?'

'Yes. I'd no right. But he seemed honest. And I didn't want David Sharrock coming here in person.'

'You knew him?'

She shook her cropped head. 'Met him once as a child. But I knew of him from the media. Go-getting type. I didn't want him here—pestering. Besides, what good does it do, raking up the past?'

'Was his mother a friend of yours?'

'What makes you think that?'

'Someone told us she patronized the Square and Tassel.'

Catherine twisted her wedding ring. 'Sandra died over twenty years ago. Brain damage from a road accident. A hard death. Why can't you leave her in peace? How'd you got hold of my name anyhow? Brentwood promised—'

'And seems to have kept his word. The day he passed a message to Sharrock he was burnt to death.'

'Because of that? Because of me? Oh God.' She covered her face with strong, scarred hands.

'Open verdict. But we do know that Sharrock himself was murdered at Hare Holt last Saturday night.'

'I saw it in the paper. Dreadful. But if he did that to Brentwood perhaps he deserved to die.'

'Come, come, Mrs Fleet. You're a market gardener. You surely don't endorse the laws of the jungle?'

She sighed, pulling off her muddy boots. 'OK, but I need a G and T. Join me?'

He shook his head. 'Go ahead.'

She padded off and rejoined him a few minutes later. 'I want to put this in context. What I told Brentwood was what Sandra Sharrock told me in hospital six weeks before she died. She might have been lying.'

'Why should she?'

Catherine shrugged. 'To tease me, make me guilty. Or because Ray looked richer than her other lovers.'

'Ray was his first name?'

'Not the real one, she was pretty certain. He was a bad liar, she said. And a boring man, which was why she'd refused to identify him to her parents. She'd wanted nothing further to do with him.'

'Surname?'

'She hadn't any idea, except that it began with L. She remembered the letters RSL on his briefcase. So did I.'

'Where had you met him?'

'In the Square and Tassel. *Met*'s putting it strongly, though. It was very much "Hello—goodbye." I was moonlighting there, because my husband and I were scraping up the deposit for this place. Graham Sharrock, Sandra's brother, was a friend. I'd lived in Fen Holton until I was ten, and Graham and I had been schoolmates.

'Sandra was fifteen when Graham emigrated to Australia, and he asked us to keep an eye on her. There'd been friction at home between Graham and his father, which was what drove him into the Army and then to Australia. Apparently Mrs Sharrock was so busy trying to keep the peace, that Sandra had free rein.

'When she started work as a shop assistant in Cambridge, we tried to befriend her. Went on trying for several months for Graham's sake. Maybe if we'd had more spare time and patience . . . been closer to her in age . . . As it was, we found her promiscuous, provocative, manipulative. In short, impossible. So finally we gave up on her.

'I'd warned her twice about drinking in the Square and Tassel. She looked eighteen, so there was no danger from a police visit. But one of the other customers might have recognized her. And there were the moral issues. But I'd learnt the uselessness of raising moral issues with Sandra.

'After our second set-to on the subject, she avoided the pub for at least three months. Then she turned up about nine one wet, blustery evening in November. You know what those booths are like?'

Baxter nodded.

'Sandra wasn't very tall. I didn't spot her until the man she was with was carrying the drinks back to their booth. Not her usual type. Square, as we said then. Businessman rather than don. Thirtyish, receding hairline. Cashmere topcoat, sharp grey suit. Pricey briefcase with RSL on it. And a ring-mark on his wedding finger.

'"Ray," Sandra said, before I could get a word in. "Ray—Cath. Cath's my guardian angel, aren't you, love? Sees I don't hit the hard stuff more than I oughter." And on she rattled about the yummy meal Ray had just stood her, and about missing her last bus home. Could she sleep on our sofabed, she wanted to know? She might be starting 'flu, so an early night would be a good idea. To my eyes, Ray looked a lot more flu-ey than she did. Embarrassment, I guess.

'What I should have said would have embarrassed him further. "Ray," I should have said," Sandra's sixteen. Over the age of consent, but only just. A year ago her brother asked me to keep an eye on her, and I don't think he'd be happy about her having sex with a married man."

'What's the point? I thought. It might put off this bloke. But what about the next one, and the next?

'So all I said was: "Sorry, Sandra. Ian doesn't like me handing over the spare key. Besides, if you're starting 'flu you'll be better off in your own bed. I'm sure Ray'll drive you home if you ask him nicely.' He looked more embarrassed than ever, but they left.

'Ian and I bought this place soon after that. I wasn't often in the City Centre, so it didn't surprise me that I didn't run into Sandra. Didn't hear about her baby until I ran into a schoolfriend when he was three or four months old. Surprised me that Sandra should get herself pregnant, still less go through with it.

'Things weren't working out too badly, my friend said. Sandra still got out and about, although there wasn't any sign of a steady boyfriend. At her father's insistence, she was working only part-time now, and in Holtchester. So she'd time to play with her son, although her mother coped with most of the child-rearing. Her father worked long hours, so he didn't have much to do with his grandson. Good thing, my friend thought. The old man was sourer than ever.

'Ian and I kept in touch with Graham Sharrock off and on. He got a job as works manager in a canning factory, but hoped to set up in fruit farming. In one letter he said Sandra had sent him a photo of her little boy, David. That made me feel guilty about our lack of contact. Ian said Sandra could have got in touch if she'd wanted to, and I suppose he was right.

'All the same, when I read about the motorbike accident, I felt I had to visit her in hospital. I'll never forget the first time, when her face was just eyes and mouth and bandages. It was on the third or fourth visit that Mr and Mrs Sharrock and David came into the waiting area when I was there. Sandra already had another visitor. Her mother went to buy fruit, leaving David with his grandfather.

'The child—he was about four—seemed to switch off the minute his grandmother left them. So did the man. I tried to make conversation. Mr Sharrock told me he'd been made redundant from his job on the railway. His bitterness was obvious. It was horrid to think of a child exposed to that coldness and bitterness day after day. That's why I asked Sandra if she'd made contact with David's father.

'"Told the parents I'd forgotten all about him," she said, with the little grunt that was the nearest she could get to a laugh through the bandages. "Damn nearly true. He was a wimp, a bore. Why saddle David with a God-Almighty bore for a father—his grandad's enough to be going on with, poor little devil.'

'I said I was thinking of practical help—money for a holiday with David perhaps when she was better.

'"If and when," she said. But she agreed to think it over—to tell me next time I came. And wanted to know when that would be. It surprised me that she should care, but I suppose making schedules—any schedules—dims the prospect of death. She'd already had major brain surgery at that point and knew more might be needed.

'Next week, the day before her second visit to the theatre, she agreed to name a name. She made me promise I wouldn't attempt any contact unless she died, and wouldn't pass on the name to her parents. Not, she pointed out, that the name would do any of us any good. He'd said it was Ray, but he'd obviously been lying. Such a boring lie and such a boring lover. I asked what she knew about him. Very little, apparently. They'd first met in a bar at the University Arms earlier that evening. He'd said he lived in London. She rather thought that might be true.

'*Ray*. I remembered the voice and the face and the clothes and the briefcase. RSL. I asked her if she was sure. And she swore she was. The 'flu she'd complained of had materialized. And she'd been housebound for three weeks as a result.

'At first it looked as though the second operation would succeed, then an infection set in. I never spoke to Sandra again alone.

'I felt it would be a terrible waste not to use the information she'd given me. RSL had looked as though he could provide more for his son than an occasional holiday. But finding him wasn't going to be easy. I knew that an approach to the Social Services or voluntary agency might lead to a paternity suit which could do the child more harm than good. I couldn't afford a private detective. I spent a few hours flicking through old newspapers in the reference library, but without success.

'Then, five or six weeks after Sandra's death, I struck lucky. In an *Illustrated London News* in our doctor's surgery, where I'd taken one of the children for a measles immunization. A photograph of a wine-and-cheese party in a new extension to an art museum in Manchester. The extension was to be called the Lake Gallery, and had been funded by Lakes Bank. And there, representing the directors, was RSL—Robin S. Lake. Robin Stanford Lake, as I later discovered.

'It didn't seem wise to ring Robin Lake at his home, and I'd quite a job getting through to him at the bank. But when I did and mentioned Sandra's name he agreed to a meeting straight away. Stood me lunch at St Ermine's Hotel. He seemed quite genuinely distressed—made no attempt to contradict her story or disclaim responsibility.

'I explained about my promise to Sandra. After asking a few questions about the boy's family circumstances, Lake said he wouldn't be doing David any kindness by getting personally involved.'

Baxter raised his eyebrows. 'Sounds like self-interest, I know. But I don't think it was just that. Lake had one child—a legitimate son—a year or two older. His wife wasn't likely to have another. Try as she might, he felt she'd find it impossible to treat the two boys equally.

'Boarding-school wasn't an ideal solution, but it was the best we could think of. My idea was that the fees should be paid anonymously. But Lake pointed out that the Sharrocks—and later David—would identify the donor as the father. The boy would fantasize about his origins to no good purpose.

'It would be better, we agreed, if the payments were believed to come from a friend or relative. Someone who could develop a personal relationship with the boy.

'Lake asked if my husband and I would be prepared to take on the role, but we wouldn't have deceived anyone. We couldn't afford fee-paying schools for our own children, let alone anyone else's. And the Sharrocks, as far as I knew, had no well-heeled friends. Graham was the only possible candidate.

'I rang him up—from the hotel—straight away. He didn't take much persuading. The idea of playing the successful Australian uncle appealed, I think. He was a bachelor then. He wanted to take over full financial responsibility in a year or two. And he agreed it would be easier when David started asking questions if he could truthfully say he didn't know the father's name. You think we were wrong, don't you? You think a child should know his father.'

'I'm not here to pass judgement.'

Catherine poured herself another drink. 'Maybe I *was* wrong—Ian said so at the time. But I did what I believed to be right. Robin Lake too. Whatever his faults, he didn't deserve this horrible thing that's happened to him.'

CHAPTER 17

Re-established at his desk in the Hare Holt incident room after a quick supper, Baxter rang Sarah.

'Time to pop over for a natter?' she asked.

'Better not. How goes it?'

'At a sinking pace!'

'Come again?'

'English corruption of the *cinq pas* of the galliard, so Haviland says. Bloody apt. Galliards, voltas—they hit where it hurts. And I've only had half a day of them. My admiration for Elizabeth I knows no bounds.'

'How's morale among the dancers?'

'Good on the whole. There've been a few squabbles—about arm-swinging, for instance.'

'Arm-swinging?'

'Mm. Mabel Dolmetsch fans approve—some of the others say it's un-English. We've had hassles about tempo, too. Haviland's been trying to speed up Father Yardley—with little success. Annie and Toby continue their private scraps.'

'Talbots back in action?'

'No—Lucy felt she'd better stay in Fenport and hold Jonathan's hand. The media have descended on them in full force.'

'And the Drydens?'

'Coulter's caught some sort of 'flu bug, Deb told Frances. But she sent over spiced beef for supper. Glad that's over—too much like a replay. Poor Marina. You'll have heard about the abduction?'

'Uh-huh.'

'How goes the case? End in sight?'

'Who knows? I've one hunch—Highcroft's another. If either's right, people you like could get hurt.'

'I see,' she said quietly. 'Not your fault, Richard. Get yourself some sleep, sometime. Promise?'

He promised. Five minutes later, Highcroft returned his call. Kirsten Sondstrom, he explained, had come home thirty minutes before.

'With Derwent's alibi?'

'Sort of. But she wasn't awfully convincing. Says she didn't notice the black eye.'

'Maybe she'd her own reasons for protecting him?'

'Maybe, but I doubt if her boyfriend shares them. Teacher in the language school she's been attending.'

'You've talked to him?'

'Not yet. Visiting his mother, she says. No contact number. Wendy reckons she's on the phone to him now. We'll watch a bit longer. Two City men are minding Derwent at Queen Charlotte's.'

Highcroft listened in silence to Baxter's report of the Linton interview. 'CC's going to hate this,' he said afterwards. 'Puts Robin on the spot and no mistake. Adultery's one thing, one-night stands with teenagers are another. If that sort of skeleton tumbled out of his cupboard, he might well slam the door.'

'Frances likewise. Or Derwent. Sandra Sharrock might have confided in a Cambridge friend—or a hospital nurse. If so, an interested party could have dug up the truth without involving Catherine Fleet.'

'We know perfectly well that Frances—'

'Didn't commit the murder. But she's a fixer. Might have used someone. Yardley, for instance. Maybe that's who Deborah was protecting?'

'You know bloody well it wasn't,' Highcroft barked back, with a rare flash of empathy. 'You know it's going to come down to Derwent or Robin. Got yourself paperwork to be getting on with?'

'Plenty.'

'Then stay on duty until I ring back. Put officers on the gates if you consider it necessary.'

Baxter looked across the shadowy gardens. Lights shone from many windows. Every now and then he caught a glimpse of plumes, ruffs, and brocade. 'Don't think we need bother, sir. They'd not either of them run.' He hoped he was right.

Two hours later, Highcroft had not rung back. Baxter's eyes were scratchy, his back aching, his duodenum pricking. He split a carton of raspberry-flavoured milk with Bill Armstrong, who looked very healthy, very wide-awake. Switching on his personal radio, he went out for a breather.

His conversation with Wendy Powers the previous evening came back to him. 'Murder is murder is murder,' he told himself. Knowing what he knew now, he found the mantra glib, meaningless almost. Subhuman was not a word he used often, but when he thought of Sharrock's twisted talents, of the precision with which he targeted his victim's weaknesses, he saw a creature as grotesque as the plastic caricatures in Sunnyscene House. And yet, and yet. The child Catherine Fleet remembered from the hospital waiting-room was surely no monster. Something sometime had gone terribly wrong for him. A piece was still missing from the puzzle.

The moon was up now, three-quarters full, in a cloudy sky. Cheated of colour and dimensionality, the garden topiary and ornaments looked like stage scenery. Absurd, but no more absurd than the E-shaped house, with its mini-turrets, its barley-sugar chimneys, its initialled parapet. The very name was absurd. A holt was a wood, and hares were meadowland creatures.

Perhaps Denys Leveson, the house's first owner, and a Londoner by birth, had drawn his knowledge of wildlife from an unreliable bestiary. Ignorant and egotistical the old merchant may have been, but he had built to last. Baxter walked round the house, and out on to the main avenue for a better view. The front elevation, darkened now, was an awesome sight. From this viewpoint, he had no view of the room where Sharrock had died. He shivered, none the less.

Clouds drifted across the moon. Something else moved against the skyline. A stick figure, passing quickly behind the parapet of the East Wing. Then it halted. Baxter advanced quickly and quietly, straining for detail, seeking the cover of the box hedge that bordered the Tudor gardens. When he was still twenty yards away the figure bent double, scuttled towards the stone initials. For a second—through a loss of balance, perhaps—an arm stuck out from behind the L, giving it the bizarre semblance of a pound sign. Then disappeared. Baxter saw nothing more. Heard nothing. He waited for fifteen minutes. Twenty. His pocket radio chirruped. He wouldn't mention this to Highcroft, not yet.

But Highcroft hadn't rung back. Robin Lake was in the incident room, Armstrong told him. Asking for him by name.

Lake sat, very upright, on a plastic stacking chair in the Superintendent's cubbyhole, clutching a small brown parcel. His navy Guernsey and cords showed few signs of wear or tear, but the hand that shook Baxter's was grazed.

'See me on the roof just now?' he began.

'I saw someone up there, yes.'

'Went up for one last look. No intention of jumping, you know, leaving a mess for poor Frances . . . No intention of coming here this evening. Tomorrow, I thought, after breakfast, after the dancers have cleared off, I'd tell Fran quickly and go. But I knew it couldn't wait when Catherine Fleet rang.'

'When was that?'

'An hour ago. You'd just left, she said. Quite a shock, hearing her voice after all this time. I blurted everything out to Fran afterwards, but I felt—we both felt—I should keep quiet until after Gaby's baby was born. Then Derwent rang from the hospital. Another girl. Fran's disappointed, but Derwent sounded over the moon. But he said the Superintendent had been checking his alibi with Miss Sondstrom. That being so, I'd no option but to come to you.'

'For what purpose, Mr Lake?'

'You must be perfectly well awa—'

'In your own words.'

They came slowly. 'To confess to the murder of David Sharrock. Of my son.'

That said, his whole posture loosened. Baxter summoned Armstrong and administered the caution against self-incrimination.

'You must think I've much to answer for, Chief Inspector,' Lake began.

'Not our business to judge.'

'So many mistakes. I'd no idea Sandra Sharrock was so young. Not until I left her off at her home and saw her face under the street-lamp. Until then she'd seemed like other girls I'd slept with. Girls who enjoyed good food and good sex, who could look after themselves. There weren't many. I tried to be faithful to Frances, but the early years of our marriage weren't easy. She was stuck at home doing the dual-parent act and I was charging round the country assessing the prospects of potential clients, justifying my presence on the Board to my late, lamented father.

'Been visiting a Newmarket stud the day I met Sandra. Owner was half-Irish, with the gift of the gab. I'd a suspicion he'd talked me into offering him twice as big a loan as I should, and I didn't look forward to defending my decision to the Board next day. An evening with an old friend in Cambridge was a more appealing prospect than the latest instalment of Fran's toilet-training saga. When I saw Sandra in the University Arms I revised my priorities.

'Dynamism . . . charisma, the standard words sound silly.

It was little things—her laugh, the way she used her hands when she told jokes. I sat there for half an hour. Making the drinks last, wishing I could hear the jokes. Maybe some of them were about me.

'Later, after we'd made love in the car, and I'd made my usual speeches, she didn't even try to reciprocate. Said she'd a splitting headache, which was possibly true—her forehead was burning. Asked me to drive her straight home. Next day, when I rang the Cambridge number she'd given me, I got through to the Cattle Market.'

Armstrong suppressed a grunt of approval.

'I winced and laughed and tried to forget her. But every so often I'd be reminded of the way she told jokes, the things she did with her hands. When Catherine told me she'd died, I was overwhelmed with guilt—neurotic guilt. If it hadn't been for me and men like me she might have thought more of herself, taken fewer risks. Do you understand, Chief Inspector?'

'Does it matter?'

'No—no, of course not. The habit of self-justification dies hard. I tell myself I'd have shared Catherine's news with Frances, told her of my involvement, if I'd felt less guilty. But I don't know. Derwent was six—at pre-prep. school. Fran had just started a course in interior decoration. I was in line for the chairmanship.

'When Catherine showed me a photograph, I'd no doubt David was mine. The mouth and the chin were so like Derwent's—his eyes were my mother's. I'd no doubt of my responsibility to make provision—the phrase my father and grandfather would have used. But the boy obviously needed more than money. Catherine has told you of our arrangement?'

'In outline,' Baxter said.

'It should have worked—would have worked if Graham Sharrock had pulled his weight.'

'When did you know he hadn't?'

'Not until David's last term at Winton. I'd kept my distance, didn't even receive a copy of the school reports that my solicitor sent to Australia.'

'Weren't you curious?'

'Of course, but I fought it. Once, I gave in. Read a Winton magazine I'd found at a friend's house the year he was fifteen. There was a photograph of the Junior school play—*Henry V*. David in chain mail with his hair cropped was in the lead. Very handsome, very angry.

'Later, when I read his aunt's letter—he'd shown it to my solicitors and they'd sent me a copy—I remembered that angry image. It was a bitter letter. Graham had upped sticks a year before, his wife wrote, leaving a stack of unpaid bills but no forwarding address. Never had any money sense, never had an English bank account. He'd told her early on about the arrangement with Catherine, which she spelt out for David's benefit. Enough was enough. David had had more than her kids ever had. If he wanted icing on his cake he'd better track down the supplier.'

'But he didn't? Not right away?'

'No. My solicitor, on my instructions, must have done an effective stone-walling job. Convinced David that he'd never disclose his client's name. His client's relationship to David wasn't mentioned, but the boy must have guessed it.

'Cowardly of me, I know, but I couldn't bear to face my son in the Mr Moneybags role I'd cast myself in. How could I tell him I was withdrawing funding for his good, when his good had never been my prime consideration? And if I changed tack, continued support, I felt in my bones he'd want more and more.

'If he ever tracks me down, I thought—asks me about the relationship—I'll come clean. But it didn't happen like that.'

'How did it happen?'

'Five years ago, he applied to us for a bank loan in connection with a windsurfing project. The application was turned down before I heard of it. Rightly so, by our normal business criteria. It was badly drafted, inadequately documented. Had I reversed my colleagues' decision, I'd have given them grounds to doubt my sanity. I wondered if David had chosen Lakes deliberately. Wondered and waited for him to make a personal approach. Half wished it, half dreaded it. But nothing happened.

'It was a year later, at a party at the Drydens', that I first saw David in the flesh. Coulter's an old client and it was on his recommendation that we'd bought Hare Holt. Frances fell in love with the house from the start. I'd been reluctant, but I made inquiries and established that David's grandparents were dead. He himself didn't visit Fen Holton.

'It was a shock, then, when Coulter pointed out this blond young man at his party. To hear about David's criminal record, which hadn't made the national press. He was, no question, the centre of attraction. A raconteur, a mimic. Talking with his face and his hands and his body the way his mother had.

'It came as no surprise when Coulter told me David had made a good start in the leisure business. When he enthused about their mutual rapport, my gut reaction was anger. How could a redneck like Dryden claim a special relationship with my son? Unreasonable, don't you think, Chief Inspector?'

'Understandable.'

'I told myself I'd no right to interfere. I avoided visiting the Drydens, although Deborah came here quite often to see Frances. But I couldn't escape from David. The media took him up. Hardly a week but I didn't see him on TV or in the papers.'

'"Mr Sunnyscene."'

'Yes. All those sporty poses. His exhibitionism began to worry me. Reminded me of Derwent on the climbing frame when he was six. I'd tell myself David wanted me to look, to make contact. I'd tell myself I was being a fool. Then the card came.'

'What sort of card? When?'

'Birthday card—last September. No secret now that the bank computer system was playing up. The system Derwent had advocated.'

'Sabotage?'

Lake hesitated. 'That possibility was considered. As a

non-executive director I wasn't privy to the details. There was a black-and-white drawing on the front of the birthday card, showing a VDU and a procession of bugs crawling out of it. And the printed message inside read *Happy Birthday, Daddy*.'

'Show it to anyone?'

'Derwent. He thought it had come from a colleague with a grudge. I tried to believe he was right.'

'When did you know he wasn't?'

'Last Saturday evening. It began when I looked into my granddaughter's bedroom. When she told me about her abduction.'

'Breaking her word to her father?'

'She was half asleep when she began, muttering. The phrases reminded me of what she'd said in a nightmare a few nights ago. Combined, they gave me the gist. The rest I coaxed out by explaining that her father hadn't wanted her grandmother or mother to be upset by the news. That telling me didn't count.'

'What then?'

'I guessed the ransom might have been in some way connected with the Verdegon business. I tried to ring Derwent without success. I rushed down to the great hall—I'd already changed into Tudor costume, and I didn't take time to change back. My one aim was to confront "Karen East" when the dancing was over. To challenge her with Marina's story. I still thought of Karen as a woman, an accessory to an unknown principal. Extraordinary that it should have been Deborah Dryden—dear, dull Deb—who put me right.'

'When?'

'When we danced—after Sarah left the hall. Not that I felt like dancing, but Deborah's undemanding. Motherly, too. So I wasn't altogether surprised when she said: "Poor Lucy—I *am* worried about her." Lucy was dancing with "Karen" a few yards away from us.

'I tried to keep it light—asked Deb if she didn't approve of women dancing together.

'"*Women!*" she said. "Don't you know who that is? Use your eyes, Robin!'

'When I looked hard, I recognized him straight away. But I had to hear her say it. "Who?"

'"David Sharrock," she said. "He frightens me, Robin. He's dangerous."

'My bright, shining son. And I, more than anyone, was responsible for whatever he'd become. I stayed in the hall until the dancing was over—helped clear away for a bit. But as soon as I decently could, I escaped into the garden to get control of my emotions—to rehearse our interview. I've no idea how long I'd been there, pacing the length of the terrace, when I looked up and saw her.'

'Her?'

'Lucy Talbot. At a darkened bedroom window—the bedroom your wife was using, but I didn't know that. Her costume didn't look right, but the light wasn't good, and I couldn't be sure. But I could see her face pressed to the glass and I could see her arms waving. SOS. SOS. I ran into the house and upstairs.

'I tried the bedroom door handle, found it locked. Thought I'd got the wrong room. Tried the next handle, opened the door and there he was. At the window, with his back to me. In Lucy's dress and gloves and wig. I'd have been deceived, if I hadn't heard this little, muffled sigh from the bathroom. A woman's sigh.

'All my preparations went by the board. "David." I got it out for the first and last time.

'He spun round, said: "Daddy! What a nice surprise."

'I asked: "First Marina, then Lucy? Is that it?"

'He laughed and said: "Christ, no, Daddy. Nothing so boring. That's the one thing my mum told me about you. That you were a goddamn bore. But you're a coward, too, aren't you? And I don't much appreciate having a Dad who's a coward. Spoils the image."

'Then I saw he'd a flick-knife.

'I asked him what he'd been trying to do to Derwent.

'And he said: "To see how my big brother takes a joke. Badly, I can tell you."'

'I asked what he wanted of me, and he said nothing I could give him. After that everything seemed unreal. I heard myself offering him Hare Holt and him telling me that was already taken care of. Then Lucy whimpered again.

'David said: "Sorry, Daddy. Come at a bad time, haven't you?" and made a lunge at me.

'Somehow I sidestepped. Grabbed the candlestick. Caught him off balance. He staggered, stunned, fell forward. When I knelt beside him, I remembered him in the school photograph. Sword in hand, ready for the slaughter. My bright, shining son—my bright, shining monster. I imagined all that anger stored up inside him. Remembered Marina crying in her sleep and Lucy whimpering next door. And I knew only one way of stopping what I'd started. So I hit him again and again.

'I wanted to stab myself, but I thought of Frances having to cope—of Marina being here. Then Deborah came in. I shouldn't have agreed to her swapping the candlesticks, but I didn't want the truth to get out until the course was over—until Gaby's baby was born.'

'So you left Mrs Talbot to find Sharrock?' Armstrong's Belfast voice was razor-edged.

'Unforgivable, I know. When she disappeared, my instinct was to come clean. But I'd no idea where she'd gone or why. You'll want this, I suppose.'

He handed over the manilla envelope. Baxter opened it carefully to expose a flick-knife with an engraved handle.

'There's blood on it,' Lake remarked with a little shudder.

'Blood and fibres.'

'Ugh. I don't suppose you can tell—?'

'Not yet.' Baxter caught Armstrong's eye and saw that he too remembered the manner of Stuart Kerr's death and the snagged suit in the boot of the Mini.

'No right to ask. You've been very patient, Chief Inspector. Anything else you want of me tonight?' Lake sounded at the end of his tether.

'Nothing that won't keep.' The arrest was made. Arrangements were made for the prisoner's transfer to Headquarters.

Half an hour later Highcroft came online. 'Took some doing, but we made it, Richard. Miss Sondstrom's boyfriend's due for promotion. Which is why he doesn't want an assault charge on his record.'

'But Derwent Lake has presumably no intention—'

'Our chum wasn't to know. He'd set up the Saturday night meeting because he suspected a connection between Kirsten's sacking and a payment of £25,000 into her bank account. Derwent's denials failed to convince. The boyfriend lashed out and subsequently regretted it. Kirsten organized the Sunday night get-together so he could apologize.'

'Money part of the frame up, do you reckon?'

'Looks like it. Isle of Man source, we've established. We'll know more tomorrow. Time to home in on Lake Senior, don't you think?'

'He's saved us the trouble. Confessed.'

'Really? Good God.' Papers rustled as Highcroft's visual aid received its latest embellishment.

CHAPTER 18

'It's a compromise, of course. If we hadn't needed the money now we've no other income, I'd have insisted on gifting the whole property to an English organization. But things might have turned out worse, don't you think?'

Sarah examined the sketch-map of Hare Holt that Frances had just drawn on the paper napkin supplied by the Old Bakehouse, Holtchester. A wasp was circling the coffee cups and the butter was melting in the August sunshine.

'I'm glad you set aside the nature reserve.'

'Deer park would have been the proper thing, of course. But Patricia's outfit weren't prepared to stock and maintain it.'

'The Fen Holton Trust? Mrs Gorridge wouldn't like you to give it her name, would she?'

Frances snorted. 'Like it or not, money talks. Coulter

Dryden chipped in with an advance on the reserve, but the lion's share of the Trust's funds will come from one quarter.'

'And ultimately from David Sharrock's estate?'

Frances winced. 'Yes. Quite how much the solicitors don't know yet. But eight figures at least, one hears. And most of it's to go on low-cost village housing. Frightfully worthy, but a mite uninspired, don't you think?'

'How does Robin feel about it?' Sarah asked gently. Although the trial was fresh in her mind, she found it hard to envisage the banker in Wormwood Scrubs.

Frances shook her head. 'You'll think I'm an awful coward, Sarah, but I can't bring myself to talk to Robin about . . . David. About what happened. Not yet.'

'It might help him if you could.'

'That's what his probation officer says—perhaps later. I've told him all about SERS, though.'

Sarah looked blank.

'French acronym for the European Society for Renaissance Studies—you know. Group that's bought the house and gardens. We're both so pleased they agreed to retain the Tudor layout of the gardens. Derwent's contracted to pop over from Italy twice a year, expenses paid, to advise on any problems.'

'How's his hotel going?'

'Well. Early days, of course, but he says it suits him far better than the bank. That he'd felt like a square peg for years.'

'Aren't you pleased he's found his niche?'

Frances sighed. 'I try. I try very hard to be pleased about Derwent and Gaby and the children. I try to be pleased about SERS and Robin's nice probation officer and the new flat in Putney and the voluntary work I've started at the Victoria and Albert. Next year, perhaps, I needn't try quite so hard, and the year after that . . . Method acting, you know. Which reminds me, Sarah, you haven't brought me up to date on Emma's career.'

*

At ten to eight that evening Richard Baxter poked his head round the door of his living-room in Kings Covert. Sarah, already showered and perfumed and wearing her filmy, blue-and-white Anokhi dress, was tidying the pile of magazines which lay beside the overflowing canterbury.

'You're late, darling.'

'Rang the surgery an hour ago. You were out on a call, they said. Didn't you get the message? Clay's sick. No dinner.'

'No dinner at the Warrens,' she corrected. 'So what do you say to a twosome? My treat. A celebration, sort of.'

'Celebration of what?'

Sarah hesitated. 'Tell you afterwards. You won't laugh, will you? It isn't funny.'

Richard and she dined pleasurably off cucumber soup, salmon en croûte and raspberry mousee in a restaurant overlooking the Great Ouse. Back in Kings Covert, they drank decaffeinated coffee on the terrace that had been two summers in the making.

'Any twinges?' Sarah checked. 'Propitiatory soda mint?'

'Definitely not. I feel great. The tum feels great. Vote of thanks from us both. I'm just a little bit confused, though. Seem to recall a strongly worded resolution about belt-tightening between our Salzburg trip and Christmas.'

'I'd a phone call from Deborah Dryden this morning. She was supposed to be meeting Fran Lake and me for coffee, but Coulter had to go to the States on business at short notice, and she's going with him.'

'They get around.'

'Not recently, they haven't. Deb was pretty euphoric, actually. Burbled something about the Crown Prosecution Service dropping a case. Seemed to assume I'd know what she was on about.'

'Want to be told?'

She considered. 'No thanks. Not really.'

'How'd you find Frances?'

'Marvellous, everything considered. All the same, darling, I'm awfully glad I'm not married to a murderer.'
'Me too, darling. Me too.'
She was glad he hadn't laughed. She kissed him.

Fringe Ending

CHAPTER 1

Six inches of corduroyed leg—a left leg. To its right and in parallel, one green wellington boot.

Hardly the stuff of an identification that would stand up in court. But more than enough for Detective Chief Inspector Richard Baxter, who surveyed the scene through the kitchen window of his home in Kings Covert, Cambridgeshire. The coffee tray had already narrowed the possibilities: few of his wife's visitors rated Bernard Leach pottery. Fewer still would be allowed to rummage among the foliage of the Baxters' dear but decrepit mulberry tree, while Sarah held the ladder. Besides, on his way home, the Chief Inspector had spotted Rupert Parsingham's battered brown station-wagon in the parking space by the village green.

Richard turned away from the window and sought solace for the morning's frustrations in a mug of tepid coffee and the latest edition of *Collectors Guide*. Sarah's horticultural guru was much in demand on spring Saturday mornings, so with luck he wouldn't have long to wait.

Nor had he. In faded green dungarees and sweatshirt, with a triangular headscarf slipping off her reddish-brown hair, Sarah looked absurdly young. Typecast, he didn't dare tell her, for the rancher's helpmeet in a 'forties Western.

'Pear midge, cladosporium, clear-winged moth,' she muttered, evading his hug. 'Let me get that down, will you?' In large scale and felt-tip on the memo board her medico's scribble was just about readable.

'Sounds ominous. Have we got all of them?'

'Not yet, but I doubt if I'd recognize the early stages,

and prompt treatment is essential. Wanted Rupert to run over the symptoms today, but it would have taken too long on top of the more urgent stuff. So I daren't forget next time round.'

'Why so? He'd fit in an extra visit, if you asked him nicely.'

'That's the snag.' Sarah scrubbed her hands at the kitchen sink. 'He's retiring in July. Quite cut up about it, poor man.'

'Lucky man, I'd say. So why's he going? *Ann. dom.?*'

'Partly.' Sarah flopped down in a basket chair. 'He's turned seventy, so he'd need medical backing to renew his driving licence. And his GP's warned him he won't play ball. Glaucoma's not responding to treatment, apparently. Already, he's lost some peripheral vision. Add that to arthritic hands—'

'And he's better off the roads? Take the point, darling. But surely mobility isn't essential for his job? I'd have thought he could've expanded his clientèle in Cambridge City, maybe even offered a 'phone advice service to his farther-flung customers.'

'Wouldn't be fair to his successor, he said, when I suggested something of the kind. Got quite shirty, as a matter of fact. Came across True Blue Camford for a minute or two—just like his sister.'

'Oh Lor'.' May was high season in Cambridge for protest demonstrations, and Eve Parsingham Wells featured colourfully and noisily in most of them. 'Maybe that's what getting him down—not being able to put a dozen miles between himself and Sis when the fancy takes him. Poor bugger. But there are worse fates, so don't let him spoil the rest of your weekend, love. More coffee?'

'*Our* weekend,' she amended as he poured it.

Their first shared free day-and-a-half in three months. He grinned. 'I hadn't forgotten.'

'Feel like a trip to Newmarket? 2,000 Guineas day, Rupert tells me.'

'Let's pick something we both like.' Sarah had no doctrinaire objections to horseracing, but it wasn't one of her favourite things. 'What say to a breath of sea air? Overnight stop in Aldeburgh or Sheringham?'

'Or Southwold? I really fancy Southwold. I'd say great, lovely. We could lunch on the road. But meantime let's slow down. Let me enjoy my cuppa. Besides, you know what rushing does to your duodenum. Your turn to off-load the mental baggage. How was the crime-busting pow-wow?'

Richard pulled a face. 'Funny, if you'd been a fly on the wall. Vic Highcroft's fancy new pattern-detection program has come up with the answer the rest of us arrived at weeks ago. On present evidence, there's no pattern to the jewel thefts, except that the merchandise is all top quality and the scenes of crime are in the Eastern counties.'

'So you reckon they're not the work of one gang?'

'I reckon we need more evidence. Doorstepping's getting us nowhere fast, so why not start at the other end, say I. Put tabs on the fences that could handle that class of goods.'

'Good thinking.'

'Ta. Highcroft's slapped me down every time I tried to implement it. This regional get-together was my first chance to side-step him, to fly the kite outside a Mid-Anglian forum.'

'So?'

'So the Norfolk lads cut me off in mid-sentence. Seems they'd got there first. The six fences they named coincided with my own first guesses. Three turned out to be in the slammer over the relevant period, one's gone straight, one's in a psychiatric hospital. But number six, who looked in many ways to be the best proposition, left the country in a hurry less than a fortnight ago. Day after the Norwich Ecclesiastical Museum job. Cross-Channel contacts suggest he's lying low in Holland or Belgium. On past form he'll dispose of the hot stuff long before he resurfaces. So we're back to square minus one—back to the doorstepping.'

'And what's wrong with that?' Sarah teased. 'Honest, labour-intensive employment. Keeps people off the dole. Speaking of which, here's a letter from Emma that should cheer you up.' She tossed it across the table and went upstairs.

The airmail envelope had, he noticed, a Leningrad postmark. The three scribbled pages began and ended with apologies for brevity. The rest was mostly taken up with a tongue-in-cheek précis of the Russian tour by the Merseyside theatrical company in which his daughter served as assistant director and dogsbody.

Then, almost as an afterthought, came the news that the company would be splitting up when their current tour ended in late May. Emma had a London-based job in prospect, but not before the autumn. Which was why she'd said yes to an SOS from a college friend—Paul somebody—the squiggly surname defeated her father. He'd persuaded her to take over the direction of a musical show in which he was involved, a fringe event at the Cambridge summer Festival. Since nothing more than pocket money was on offer, and if her parents didn't mind, she proposed to base herself at Kings Covert for June, July and August. *Mind!* Letter in hand, Richard went out into the hall.

'She'll be at home for her birthday,' he yelled above the hiss of Sarah's shower. For the first time in six years—no, seven. God help them, she'd be twenty-three.

Sarah made enthusiastic noises.

'Who's this Paul she's on about?' he shouted back, still unable to make out Emma's squiggle.

He didn't make out Sarah's reply either. But it could

wait. He picked up the East Anglian tourist guide from the hall table and began looking up hotels in Southwold.

Bang-clinkety-bang.

'Come on, Trickstep, COME ON! Give it to him, you dozy bastard—let him know who's boss. COME ON!' Bang-clinkety-bang.

Rupert Parsingham listened and loathed. *Look thy last on all things lovely*, De La Mare had urged, and Rupert Parsingham had come to Newmarket this May afternoon to do just that. Next to horse chestnuts in flower, he could think of few things more beautiful than thoroughbreds at full stretch. And thanks to the complimentary ticket passed on by his employers, he had a rare front-of-grandstand view of the races.

Bliss unalloyed, until the unspeakable woman on his left had started to shout and bang the railings. Thank God she hadn't edged forward until after the classic, the 2,000 Guineas. Bang-clinkety-bang above the roar of the crowd. OK, there was greed in that roar—open, childish greed. Greed, suspense, disappointment. But there was joy as well—collective joy in the spectacle of speed and grace and horsemanship.

Bang-clinkety-bang. 'Faster, you bastard. Get off your bum, can't you? Get stuck into him!' No joy there.

Half-turning, Rupert took in a pair of royal blue gaberdine sleeves, ageing scarlet-tipped hands, and the sapphire-and-diamond bracelet that was doing the clinking.

Bank-clinkety. Bang-bang. As he turned away something flashed in the left-hand blur of Rupert's visual field. He checked. Two blue sleeves, two scarlet-tipped fists. No bracelet.

Bang-bang! 'TRICKSTEP!' Silly bitch hadn't noticed a thing. Rupert wanted to laugh out loud.

He turned away from her again, swivelling clockwise for a glimpse of the row behind. His eyes were caught and held by a commonplace checked shirt collar and a commonplace Adam's apple. Above, a thin, tanned face set apart by black circumflex eyebrows and an expression of total concentration. The blue eyes focused on the front runners just as forty years ago they had focused on Rupert's diagrams of stag beetles. And twenty years ago on a sentencing judge at the Old Bailey.

'Simon! Simon Drinkwater!'

A frown. Then the quick, remembered smile.

'Bear! My apologies—Mr Parsingham.'

On the race-track below Trickstep had increased his lead from three yards to ten.

'All over bar the shouting, isn't it?' Drinkwater said. 'Any winnings to collect, Mr Parsingham?'

Rupert shook his head. 'And Bear—please. It's what all your lot called me, isn't it?'

The other laughed. 'Never knew you knew that. Changed monickers myself—for business reasons, you understand. I'm Dunnett now, Sam Dunnett. What say we get out of here, Bear, while the going is good? Fancy a jar?'

'Delighted.'

Dunnett, accelerating unobtrusively, reached the back of the stand before applause marked the end of the race. Above it, Rupert caught a screech of anger from the front row to which those in his immediate vicinity gave no reaction. Head down, he hurried after his ex-pupil.

'Out-of-town boozer might be more peaceful,' Dunnett said on the way to the car park. 'Any suggestions?'

Fifteen minutes later they were settled at a quiet corner table in the White Cygnet, Exning.

'Still schoolmastering, Bear?'

'At seventy? Have a heart. No, actually, I gave up that lark years ago, not long after your first—er—um—'

'My first conviction?' Dunnett's lips curved behind his brandy glass.

'Sorry—'

'Don't be. Boot's on the other foot, matter of fact. Your letter to me in prison, the offer of a reference . . . Bloody-minded of me not to reply.'

'Water under the bridge. You were eager to stand on your own two feet, I expect?'

Dunnett smiled again. 'Something like that. So you gave up teaching—for what, Bear?'

'Horticulture. Bought myself a nursery out Trumpington way on the strength of a small legacy.'

'Ah yes. Flowers were always your passion, weren't they? Though you did your duty by the horrid fauna we kids used to propagate in matchboxes. Was your degree in Botany?'

'Mmm, but a Third. A blot on the family 'scutcheon.'

'It comes back to me. Wasn't there a *Sir* Rupert Parsingham? Eminent Cambridge Victorian?'

'Yes, Great-Grandpa did pioneering work on the flora of the tropics. I love plants as much as he, I dare say, but I've no talent for theorizing about them—or selling them, for that matter.' Rupert contemplated the foam on his beer and was reminded of meadowsweet.

'So your horticultural venture ran into trouble?'

'Deep trouble. Luckily, I found a buyer with commercial flair but little specialist knowledge, who took me on as an employee. Phil tarted the place up, turned it into a garden centre, and the crowds began to roll in. He's learnt a lot about plants over the years. Might have given me the push long ago, I dare say, if his wife hadn't talked him into putting me on to after-sales service.'

'As for consumer durables?'

'More or less. Customers call me out if they're having problems with plants they've bought from us. Well, that's the theory. In practice, I try to answer any gardening question they care to put.'

'And you like that—nosing around your clients' gardens, pointing out the errors of their ways?'

'Love it. Can't face the prospect of packing it in in July—that's when I retire.' Rupert's face twisted. 'D'you know, Si—Sam, I've got the details of our regular clients' gardens mapped out in my brain. I could summon up any one at will and see it as clearly as I see you across the table—or that sapphire and diamond bracelet you nicked twenty minutes ago.'

'Now look here!' Dunnett reddened.

Rupert smiled wryly. 'I'm looking. At the man who was the boy I taught party-tricks in 'fifty-seven. Sleight-of-hand seemed a harmless therapy when you smashed your knee early in the cricket season. But I'm also looking at the boy who stole a wallet from the Chairman of the school governors the following Speech Day.'

'You can't prove that,' Dunnett whispered, paling.

Rupert shrugged. 'Who else had the chutzpah and the skills? You'd have broken down under police interrogation, I suspect, if I'd chosen to publicize your accomplishments.'

'Sir Archie Spooner wouldn't miss what he lost, the old bastard. And he *was* a bastard. His fault poor Stinks got the push for thumping the Fitzwinton kid.'

'So rumour had it.'

'One of the other Fourth Formers overheard the row at the Governors' meeting. Stinks was no great shakes as a teacher, but he was our form master and we felt protective. Besides, the way the Fitzwinton brat messed around in Chemistry, he could have got us all blown up. That kid was a born attention-seeker, real pain in the arse.'

'And a sadist. I remember the smirk on his face the time he told me the groundsman's Alsatian had got at the First Form hamsters. Cage door must have been left open accidentally, Fitz said. I knew he was lying and I knew he knew I knew. His smirk said it all.'

'Which is why you didn't finger me over the wallet business, I presume?'

Rupert nodded. 'Never could abide cruelty to animals.'

'Unattractive, I agree, even by proxy. So we'd both do better, wouldn't we, to forget the exhibition that bloodthirsty bitch made of herself this afternoon? If she did lose a few sparklers—*if*, please note—then by your book and mine, Bear, she had it coming.'

'Come clean, Sam. Evasiveness without good cause is scarcely more appealing than cruelty. I'm ready to forget what I saw in the stand—*everything* I saw—if you're prepared to be honest.'

'Now look here—' Another attempt at bluster.

Rupert sighed. 'You're cornered, dear boy. That barman over there's ex-Army, an old friend and a fitness fanatic. I know the number of your car. You've no option but to trust me.'

The younger man hesitated, then made a laughing gesture of surrender. 'OK, sir, Dunnett dunnit. That what you wanted?'

'I'd like to see the bracelet.'

'Why the hell?'

'A whim. *Look thy last on all things lovely*, the poet said. Apt philosophy for a man who'll be dead in three months, don't you think?'

'Dead? Good Lord! Awful sorry, Bear. You look good. What's the trouble? Something inoperable?'

'Nothing I want to talk about. But you'll indulge a dying man? One quick dekko.'

A handkerchief changed hands under the table. Rupert opened it on his lap and made a brief inspection of its contents. The sight depressed him. Two blue-eyed and diamond-spotted reptiles were intertwined in death or ecstasy. Sapphires and diamonds were lovely things: crowded into fanciful settings their beauty was dishonoured. As an ornament for day wear, the bracelet was absurd. Even by candlelight it would have been disagreeable. '*Un embarras de richesse*,' he punned, returning the handkerchief and bracelet to his companion.

Dunnett laughed—a little nervously, Rupert thought. 'Riches embarrassing? Wouldn't know about that, Bear. Never had much disposable cash. Anything I can spare goes back into the business.'

'The old business?'

'God, no. Horse-breeding. Strictly legit. Been running a stable near Buenos Aires for the past ten years. Steered clear of the UK up till now, but a fungus infection last year lost me my best stock, so I'm over here to raise replacement capital. Just enough to keep the show on the road, you understand.'

Rupert raised an eyebrow.

'Couldn't resist a trip to the Guineas. Don't know what came over me when I saw that bauble on Cruella's wrist. Challenge to prove I hadn't lost the knack, I suppose. A one-off. Put it down to the male menopause, if you like. And she deserved it. She bloody well deserved it.'

'Did your other victims?'

Dunnett grimaced. 'Below the belt, old man. I've paid my dues in the slammer.'

'For this season's activities?'

'I'm not with you, Bear.' Dunnett's blue eyes signalled injured innocence but his fingers tightened on the brandy-glass.

'Come on, Si—Sam. What the hell. You can put up with "Simon" from a man under death sentence. According to reports in the local media, which my dear sister is forever forcing on my attention, there've been a dozen or more jewel thefts in East Anglia this spring. Always top quality stuff, but assorted methods—con jobs, burglaries, simple dipping. The hacks' current theory is that more than one gang is responsible. But I've read the reports of your trials over the years, Si. Felt a mite responsible, to be honest. And you're nothing if not versatile.'

'Likewise non-violent. Never hurt or threatened anyone, have I? Never nicked anything the owner couldn't afford to lose?'

'Not to my knowledge.'

Simon rotated his brandy-glass. 'Speaking hypothetically, mind, if I *had* been playing my old game by my old rules, would you say I deserved to go back inside?'

Rupert considered, surprised that the other man had so nearly compromised himself. 'I'd need to know your motive.'

'Only way I can raise the wind to restock. Don't expect you to believe this, Bear, but horses are the be-all and end-all with me. Never had much luck with human relationships. Nags aren't as demanding as women, and to my eyes they're far more beautiful than overpriced baubles that spend ninety-five per cent of their lives in a safe.'

Rupert smiled. 'There's a flaw in your argument somewhere, but I shan't try to winkle it out. Life, as they say, is too short.'

'Look—about that—' the other man cleared his throat. 'Sorry if I'm speaking out of turn, but something you said earlier set me thinking. Retirement is on your horizon, you say. A time when most people could use a little extra cash.'

As if money mattered. Rupert was repelled by the other's insensitivity.

'Don't suppose you're one to spend much on yourself. But a little extra—five grand, say—could come in handy, couldn't it? For unexpected expenses or your favourite charity?'

Or a gift. A surprise gift to the woman Rupert loved. A farewell gift. That prospect pleased him. 'Am I to understand, Simon, that you're offering to pay me for my discretion?'

'Funds don't rise to that, old chum. Wish to God they did. No, what I have in mind is a little business proposition.'

Rupert began to feel like a character in the schoolboy comics he used to confiscate. The sensation was novel, but not unpleasant.

'Spell it out,' he heard himself saying. With three months to live, what had he left to lose?

CHAPTER 2

'Great—lovely—toodle-oo, my sweet.' Eric Finchley watched in silent self-consciousness as his fellow-diner put away his pocket phone and cleared his elbows from the path of the approaching waiter.

'Yesterday's footage came out a treat, Corrie tells me. And she's a hard girl to satisfy.'

Aubrey King's smirk suggested a joke. Not the sort of joke Eric indulged in. Nor, even for the waiter's benefit, did he propose to massage Aubrey's ego by inquiring further into the relationship between the TV documentary maker-cum-presenter and his senior camerawoman. Instead, he witnessed in straight-backed silence the delivery of his duck pâté and Aubrey's seafood mélange.

'Let's hope their bugs don't bite.' Aubrey jabbed a fork platewards. 'And before I forget, Corrie loved the fishy shots better than anything. Fishy—Her very word! Out of the mouths of babes and sucklings . . . Hasn't a clue, of course. Six years' collaboration and she hasn't seen through me once.'

The waiter disappeared behind the service hatch, leaving

them, his first customers of this mid-May evening, alone in the stuffy dining-room. Eric grunted. Over the four years of their own professional relationship he had come to recognize Aubrey's expansive manner as a mask, an artifice.

Two hours earlier, Eric, as Director of the Parsingham Institute for the Scientific Study of Tropics, had taken a public farewell of the public Aubrey King and his team at the close of their third videomaking visit to Eric's workplace in Downing Street, Cambridge. On this, as on the earlier occasions, Aubrey had insisted that their private business should be transacted outside the Institute and the university city. The Ruffled Feathers, near Royston, which even in May was little patronized by tourists, was their usual rendezvous.

'You've a message?' Eric took the initiative and despised himself for it.

Aubrey's sharp-featured face softened into his screen smile. 'Several. First, as they say, the good news. Our friends liked your last batches of data, especially the gen on marine pollution.'

'A gift for Detoxicon, properly exploited.'

'There was, alas, one slight snag—'

'Not at my end, I can assure you. Went over that stuff with a toothcomb. Rechecked every crucial computation. Otley's work's outstanding—in a class of its own—'

'That, old man, is the snag. Term cognitive style ring a bell? Read any psychology?'

'Never had the occasion.' Not quite true. Once, a long time ago, Eric had tried. It hadn't helped. He had learnt to deal with his pain in his own way, but the memory distressed him. He reached for the wineglass.

'Pity. Good management course would give you most of what you need—'

'I am paid to administer, not to manage.' Eric faked anger to mask his unease.

'Really? Dear Camford! No business of mine, of course, but, given the mutterings I overheard from some of your younger staff over lunch in the Grad Pad, you and your Board might do well to drag yourselves into the twentieth century.'

The Grad Pad—the University Centre. So that's where Aubrey and half Eric's junior colleagues had sloped off to at lunch-time. *Carte blanche* was *carte blanche*, but all the same . . . Better not brood, though. 'Cognitive style?' he prompted.

'Ah yes.' Aubrey parted herring-bone from flesh. 'Cognitive thumbprint might be more accurate in this instance. I'm talking about a way of thought specific to one or a very small number of high-flying specialists in a given field of study, which would be instantly identifiable to other specialists in the same field.'

'Fuzzy sort of concept, by the sound of it,' Eric complained.

'As clear as most of the hunches we run our everyday lives by. And it can be quantified, if you know which features to select for a given discipline and how to weight them. In a science such as marine microbiology—'

A pause to let the penny drop. Eric focused on his bread-roll.

'Elements of experimental design would count, I'd guess. Plus features of conference and journal reports. Idiosyncrasies of syntax, imagery—'

'Imagery? Metaphors, similes, all that Eng. Lit. rubbish? For crying out loud, Aubrey. Sort of thing your TV fans expect, maybe, but unlikely to loom large in serious scientific communications.'

'No? Take a closer look next time you're in the library, old boy. You'd be surprised.'

The library? A veiled insult? Just what had the Young Turks been saying? 'Where's all this leading?' Eric asked.

Aubrey munched slowly and washed down his last mouthful before replying.

'To Julian Otley, I'm afraid.'

'The Pacific pollution project? You're saying he's let something out? Never. OK, he's an awkward customer, as you may have seen for yourself. Restless, too. But ideologically he's an infant. Believes in the potential of the UN, Third World regional collaboration, the lot. He's totally committed to that research programme.'

'Nobody's saying he isn't. But he's ambitious, isn't he? Goes to conferences—reads papers.'

'Nothing that matters on the Pacific project—nothing sensitive.'

'That's not the point. Among those attending the same conferences there's an Anglo-German bird called Dagmar Andersen—a marine toxicologist. Know her?'

Eric shook his head. 'Toxicology's off my personal wicket.'

'Since last April Andersen's been on the payroll of Detoxicon, Munich.'

'Oh my God.' Eric's butter knife slipped from his fingers.

'Seems she's been aware, for some time, that Otley was researching Pacific pollution. She also read two or three of his publications and heard him read a conference paper on some theoretical issue or other. Don't ask me what, but she was impressed. Emotionally as well as intellectually, perhaps. Impressed enough to request a transcript and his phone number.'

'No more?'

'She said not. I prefer to believe not. But taken in combination that was enough for her to guess he'd written the last experimental report you sent me—the stuff that hit her desk in Detoxicon six weeks ago.'

'Unmarked.' Eric's throat tightened. 'I'll swear that

report left my office unmarked.' But could he be a hundred per cent sure—of his secretary, for instance?

'My Munich contact assures me it remained unmarked, except for a *Commercial Confidence* stamp which was added by him. Nobody in Detoxicon knew its origin. All their local linkman has is a hot line to yours truly. Which he used pronto when dear Dagmar tried to check its provenance by ringing Otley at the Parsingham.'

'Christ.' Eric poured himself Malvern water. It tasted warmish, sweetish.

'Fear not, old chum. Her call was blocked, and it's highly unlikely to be repeated. Her impulsive tendencies have yielded—permanently, I feel certain—to arguments suggested by yours truly. Gentle art of persuasion and all that. You won't press me for details?'

Eric shook his head, sickening. *Oh, Mumsie. I never wanted anything like this, never. But I did it all for you. You know that, don't you? Tell me you know that, Mumsie.* No reply. Not to be expected in the Ruffled Feathers. There was only one place where she talked to him. And he'd never relinquish that. Never.

Aubrey repeated his small-screen smile. 'Accentuate the positive, dear boy. Consider the might-have-beens from which you have been delivered. All the same . . .' He leant forward, heavy brows knitting, as if inviting a close-up.

Eric dispatched urgent memos to his digestive system.

'All the same, my dear chap, you'll appreciate that this episode makes things difficult for Barney.'

'Meaning what, exactly?' Eric heard himself ask. The sort of inelegant construction he'd schooled himself for years to avoid. The Malvern water flowed uselessly over the greasy pâté in his stomach. Bile rose to his throat.

King reached forward to pat his hand. '*Nil desperandum.* Barney wanted you to know he isn't proposing a permanent rift—just a back-off. Keep the show on the road for another two years and he might well come up with something even better.'

'*Might?*' The word conjured forgotten yearnings for a spaniel, a waterproof watch, a bicycle. Eric's boyhood had been studded with aborted *mights*.

'Only one thing's certain in this life, old son.'

Eric shuddered. Mumsie had never liked to think about death, not even in the last long weeks in hospital. Neither did he. But sometimes you had to.

'In the meantime, how does this look by way of a consolation prize?' King passed over a long envelope. £300,000 was typed on the sheet inside. Nothing else. 'I'm authorized by you-know-who to make this sum payable to any offshore account you may care to nominate.'

'Money! Does Bryce really believe that's what I went out on a limb for? Do you, Aubrey? Bloody money!'

Eric's urge to vomit had been overtaken by a more pressing urge to weep. Rising, he pushed past the returning waiter and hurried across the still-empty restaurant to the men's room.

Three or four minutes later, he emerged from a cubicle and sluiced his blotched face in a basin. He reached blindly for a paper towel, patted the features that he'd never quite come to terms with. The strong nose and soft, off-centre mouth. Footsteps disturbed him. A second face was reflected in the cloakroom mirror. Thin, freckled, vaguely familiar.

Had they met before? Eric returned slowly to the dining-room, his self-control shaken anew by this uncertainty.

'Finchley didn't say anything about Friday night—didn't hint, even?'

'Not a squeak, love—I told you,' Valerie Gates murmured into the receiver and beamed reassurance at the photograph of Norman in his new blazer that she'd taken from her handbag. 'There's no way he could've recognized you, is there?' No need for Norm to know her boss might have caught one or two glimpses of that snapshot. He'd worries enough, and he was a born worrier.

'Can't help remembering the funny look he gave in the Gents,' Norman persisted.

'Fancied you, maybe?' She forced a giggle, fingering the cleft in his photographed chin.

'This'd be no laughing matter if it got to Trish, Val. Not after me giving her the overtime story to get out of supper.'

Trish, always Trish. Norm's only daughter and her late mother's champion, with Views on the indecency of early remarriage. 'No reason it should ever get to her, love.' Valerie's eyes slid from the snapshot to her wristwatch. She was already ten minutes into her lunch-break. Five minutes, it would have been, if that silly old fool in the outer office hadn't delayed her phone call. 'Listen,' she went on. 'If Doc Finchley didn't see us together, there's no way he could have made the connection. And I'll swear he never looked into that brasserie Friday night when we were there. Why should he? Stands to reason he ate in the dining-room, if his car was in the dining-room car park.'

When Norman had returned, grey-faced, from the men's room, she had slipped out—unobserved, she felt sure—to check the numbers of the parked cars.

'I keep telling you, love,' she went on. 'If the Doc looked odd when he saw you, I'll bet you what you like it was nothing personal. He was tense, wound-up all the time the TV crew were here. And he was like a bear with a sore head when I tackled him about my pay rise this morning. Money troubles, if you ask me.'

'D'you mean he refused?'

'Yes and no. Tell you when I see you tonight.' A Christmas wedding, they'd agreed. Thirteen months, that would be, since Enid's death. Val thanked God she'd her mortgage nearly paid, Norm being in a council flat. But there were things needed doing to the house before he moved in.

And she wanted a classy wedding dress this time round, informal but classy. Fine cream wool, she'd decided, like the one in last month's *Good Housekeeping* Look for a Life-style. 'You look good in cream, Val,' Norm had told her once. 'You've the skin for it. Most women your age haven't.' She loved the way he noticed things like that. If he wasn't up to much in the other department, well—she had her memories, hadn't she?

'Don't brood, poppet,' she urged. 'If the Doc gets sticky, I'll think of something. Val always thinks of something. 'Bye, now.'

This morning, when Finchley had hinted that the future of her job was uncertain, Valerie's thoughts had flitted back to the confidential tasks that had earned her those nice little Christmas and birthday presents and the promise of promotion. Then forward to the Friday evening meeting in the Ruffled Feathers between two men who had said a long goodbye in her presence earlier the same day. She hadn't told her lover that she'd recognized Aubrey King's car as well as Finchley's in the restaurant car park. She might never tell him.

Time to get moving. Valerie slipped Norman's photograph into her handbag and replaced the Institute Director's desk phone beside the jade statuette of his wife. Then she sprayed herself with White Satin toilet water and went into the outer office.

'No sign of your sister, Mr Parsingham?'

'Not yet, Mrs Gates. Punctuality never was Eve's strong suit, I'm afraid.' Rupert smiled apologetically above the copy of *Nature* he had taken from the magazine rack. Strange to realize that this dumpy, weatherbeaten little man in faded denims had anything to do with the oil paintings of the Institute's founder and his son whose portraits, in full academic fig, hung on either side of the entrance. Something about the faces, though. Teddy-Bear faces.

'Afraid I'll have to pop out now if you'll excuse me,' Valerie said. 'My lunch-break, and I've shopping to fit in.'

'Of course, Mrs Gates.' Rupert Parsingham beamed. 'Don't worry about me. Perhaps Dr Finchley . . . ?'

'Won't be back before three-thirty, I imagine. Going straight from lunch at Landers College to a Faculty meeting.'

'Another time.' Rupert began to grope in a pocket of his jacket. Valerie knew what he'd be up to the minute she'd left. That bloody pipe. But you couldn't ask a Parsingham not to smoke in the Parsingham Institute, any more than you could ask him to wait with *hoi polloi* in the entrance hall.

'Your sister will be on her tricycle, I suppose?'

'Most probably.' Another apologetic smile, almost as though he guessed about the trouble they had with the cleaners over the tyre-marks. Poor old bugger. You could almost feel sorry for him, living with a sister like that.

Whatever am I thinking of, getting sentimental about a Parsingham, Valerie asked herself, as she went out into the corridor. It's people like them that run this town, not people like Norm and you. Look out for yourself, girl. When Hardy comes to Hardy, their sort won't.

CHAPTER 3

The Vice-Chancellor and University Senators, still robed and manacled, clanked offstage. The sparse audience in the school hall applauded. The final dress rehearsal of *Spin City*, which had been protracted by a traditional sequence of fused lights, torn tapes, jammed zips, missed entrances and other last-minute crises, was finally over.

'So?' Stacey Caldwell, scriptwriter, prompted her left-hand neighbour in the front row.

'So jolly good show, my dear! Isn't that what they say in these parts?'

Shit.

Clive Sinton must have seen her face tighten. 'You've the makings of a good playwright in you, Stacey. But smart little scribblers scare the hell out of has-beens like me, if I'm honest. So you won't mind if I slope off to the boozer?' He was already on his feet, smiling apologetically. If it wasn't for the jaundiced complexion and the scar on his forehead, Stacey thought, he'd have made a good stand-in for Clint Eastwood.

Niggled by an incipient headache, she minded about his defection quite a lot. Two months ago, when Paul Sinton had first suggested inviting his playwright father to the preview, she'd been the sole member of the production team to oppose the idea. Now she'd a clearer idea of where she wanted to go as a dramatist, and a firmer belief in her own talents, she felt ready to use the criticism of a fellow-writer. Especially one with a reputation for straight talking. And Sinton was copping out.

Emma Baxter, who'd been sitting on their guest's other side, intercepted his escape. 'Are we good enough for Edinburgh, do you think?'

'So Cambridge Festival is second league!' Sinton flashed eyebrows in mock reproach. 'Bet you don't give that one to the local press.'

If Emma was irritated, Stacey didn't hear it in her voice. 'Edinburgh gets better media coverage,' she said sweetly. 'And their best fringe performance award would be worth having.'

'You're in for that with a chance, I'd say, but you'd do

well to rub down a few rough edges in the script and the production.'

'Such as?' Emma's clipboard was at the ready.

'Not now, my love. Get your local run over first.'

'And afterwards you'll lead a workshop session for us? Care to fix a date?'

'No diary on me. Bring it tomorrow night—OK, I promise.'

With that, Sinton squeezed past Emma and the others in the production team still seated in the front row.

'Eight a.m. swim, young Paul?' he called to the stage manager, now emerging from the wings, before hurrying out of the hall.

The Victorian paterfamilias role. As far as Stacey could gather, roleplay was the junior and senior Sintons' only means of intercommunication. How wearing. How sad.

'On stage, everyone!' Emma bellowed.

The Victorian dons, students, bedmakers, porters, shoeblacks, city councillors, tradesmen, prostitutes and street urchins who made up the cast of *Spin City* obeyed with varying degrees of reluctance. The backstage team mingled self-consciously with the actors. Emma, successor to an apathetic director, who had been smitten with late-diagnosed glandular fever, had in past weeks taken a tough line with the amateur company.

Tonight, Stacey noted with relief, she was mostly dispensing reassurance. No last-minute changes were proposed to the spoken book, and only a two-word substitution in the tongue-twisting lyrics of the shoeblacks' chorus.

Stacey didn't much care for the change, and she'd fight for its reversal before the Edinburgh run. But fatigue and her twingeing temple persuaded her to submit in the short term. As Emma turned her attention to the actors, she slipped thankfully into the wings and headed for the tiny backstage kitchen.

She was sitting there reading the fire emergency procedures and waiting for the paracetamol tablets to dissolve in a mugful of water when Paul Stinton joined her. He filled and switched on the electric kettle.

'Coffee, Stace?'

She shook her head. 'I'm checking out when I've downed this lot. Post-mortems aren't my scene at the best of times. Anyways, Julian's due to pick me up.' She glanced at her wristwatch. 'Overdue.'

'And he doesn't like to be kept waiting. You know, Stacey—'

'Lay off, Paul. Don't give me the Agony Uncle stuff tonight. Please.' *A one-track lab rat like Julian Otley's bad medicine for a creative type like you.* It had been some months since she'd heard the spiel but she'd sat through it a dozen times when she, like Paul, had been a research student in the University History Department. There had been some truth in the diagnosis, but her relationship with Julian had been more complicated and more rewarding than Paul could have guessed. Now that its end was in sight, she was in no mood for 'Told you so.'

It came as a relief, then, that Paul took her no for an answer. How little of his father there was in his appearance, she thought, watching his fair-skinned face and shock of straw-coloured hair as he cleared away the detritus of earlier rounds of coffee.

'Your dad didn't give much away at the end of the show,' she said. 'D'you think it got across to him—emotionally, I mean?'

'Your guess is as good as mine, Stace. I was backstage, remember.' Paul concentrated on the disposable beakers he was stacking.

'But you talked at the interval—I saw you.'

Paul laughed. 'About map shops. Dad's planning to see the sights while he's here. Revisiting the scenes of his misspent youth, I suppose.'

'Oh, great. Why don't you tag along with a tape-recorder and camera? Newspaper feature could get the show some good publicity.

'No go.' She watched Paul tip the beakers into the trash can and wash his hands at the sink. He turned back slowly to face her, paper towel in hand. 'We're not what you'd call buddies, Dad and I. Good thing, maybe. Blokes with big talents can overwhelm their offspring, if they come too close. We go swimming together, play chess now and then. But conversationally, there are quite a few no-go areas. And Dad's early life in Cambridge is one of them.'

'He's never written about it?' Stacey cast her mind back through those of Clive Sinton's black comedies she'd seen or read.

'Not yet.' Paul poured himself a coffee and sat opposite her at the formica-covered table. 'To the best of my knowledge he hasn't visited the place since he left in 'sixty-six. You don't know how I sweated to get him down for this show.'

'For which I for one am duly grateful.' Stacey, her curiosity aroused, recalled the glimpses she had sneaked of Sinton Senior in the course of tonight's rehearsal. The snorts of impatience at the assorted cock-ups, the barks of laughter when satirical lines came over the way she'd intended, the lacing of fingers in the few moments of unalloyed pathos. 'I think we got through to him. Thanks again.'

Stacey squeezed Paul's hand briefly before gulping down the dregs of paracetamol.

'So there you are!' Julian Otley was at the door, padded helmet in hand, his thin face pink and windblown from his motorbike ride across town.

Not a bad advert for her TLC, Stacey told herself, as she returned his hug. Six months ago it would have been a sarcastic 'Am I interrupting?' But maybe, if she were honest, he'd have said that six seconds ago, when she and Paul were tête-à-tête. The stage manager muttered that he had to see Props and departed. Julian pulled a chair close beside hers and sat down.

'Coffee?'

He shook his head, threw his arm round her shoulders. 'How was it?'

'Endless. Balls-up after bloody balls-up, so we overran. You'd have seen the last couple of scenes if you'd come when you said.'

Julian consulted his watch. 'Eleven-forty! Sorry, love. I was checking some calculations. I'd simply no idea!'

'Heard that line before some place, haven't I?' She kissed the tip of his elegant nose. 'Time was, you couldn't wait to quit the Parsingham. Now it seems like you'll never bring yourself to make the break.'

'Fair's fair, Stacey. You know my gripe was always against Finchley, not my research assignment.' He tweaked a strand of her short, curly hair.

'Go easy—my head hurts. Best if I crash soonish. Like to give me a ride back to Plumtrees?'

'Now?' The spaniel eyes registered dismay. 'Without stopping by at the flat, you mean? Oh, sweetie!' He buried his face in her T-shirt.

'Yes, now, Julian.' She pushed him away gently and stood up. 'Eve's expecting me before midnight. No reason why you shouldn't come too, though. She's told me often enough you'd be welcome.'

He jumped up to face her. 'At Castle Bloody Parsingham? No, Stace. No, thanks.'

He'd refused the invitation to sleep at Plumtrees several times before. The refusals and their bitterness had puzzled Stacey, hurt her. But she had put no questions.

Tonight, tired and needy, she asked 'Why not?', gripping

him by the elbows, forcing him to look her in the eye.

Julian flushed. He spoke softly, hesitantly. 'It's been so good between us these last few weeks, hasn't it?'

It! Sex, you mean, you dumb British bastard. S-E-X. So why can't you say it? Aching for him, she relaxed her grasp, let him pull her closer, talk over her shoulder.

'But I couldn't . . . manage . . . at Plumtrees, you see. And it'd be hell, wanting you the way I want you tonight and knowing we'd so little time left together, and not being able . . . Stay at the flat tonight.'

'Oh, knock it off, Jule.' She pulled away sharply. 'Snap out of the self-pity routine. Think of someone else for a change. Eve Parsingham Wells is an old lady who's been kind to me, who's got a hole in her roof, who's alone.'

'Not quite alone, surely? Why doesn't she root little brother out of his cottage to keep her company?'

'Fat lot of good Rupert would be in an emergency. He's eye trouble, plus arthritis, plus he's really depressed about retiring this month. But you know all that, Jule. Tell you straight, I don't like the way you talk about Rupert. After all—'

'After all what?'

'Nothing. It's just that I don't comprehend your attitude to that poor old man.'

'Dirty old man, don't you mean?'

Her anger flared. 'No I damn well don't. And if you know different, tell me.'

He shook his head. 'Forget I said it.'

'No way, Jule.' She looked up into his drawn face and wondered if hers was as pale. 'Mudslinging makes me sick to the stomach. Forget about giving me that ride. What difference does a couple of months make, anyway? Best if we made a clean break now, sorted out our priorities. I'll pick up my junk from your place tomorrow.'

'No, darling. No, please.' His fingers dug into her shoulders. She held herself rigid. 'It's him, isn't it? That old bastard Parsingham talked you out of coming to Karachi with me, didn't he? Now he's put you up to this.'

'You're crazy!' The word came out before she'd time to think, the word she'd told herself she'd never use against him. Without daring to check his reaction, she wrenched herself free from his grasp and ran out of the kitchen.

'Don't!'

Startled, Di Beresford let go of her nightdress and stubbed her toe on the bedside table.

'Phil, you bastard!' She advanced on the bed threatening her husband with her pillow. They tussled briefly, giggling.

'Oh sorry, sweetie.' Phil kissed the bruised toe. 'When last did I get the chance to watch you undress?'

The question was serious and she answered it seriously as she curled round him. 'February? In Madeira?'

Their holiday, their last holiday for how long? The Beresfords' home routine, imposed by the demands of the Middlefields Garden Centre, was almost invariable. Phil rose at six, Di at six-fifteen. At bedtime, she went up first at eleven. More often than not she was out for the count when he followed. They made love hurriedly, exhaustedly, in the wee small hours, reminding each other of their need for sleep.

Tonight was above par. Far above.

'Sure that film your mum took you to was a 'forties tear-jerker?' he asked her afterwards.

'*Random Harvest?* Couldn't be weepier. And incredibly relaxing. Just what you could do with, a weepie.'

Phil rolled on to his back. 'What I—what we could do with right now, my love, is a Landscaping Services Manager.'

'What about White, then?'

'Backed out, would you believe?'

'Oh no, not again. Not after the bloody interview.' On the Beresfords' first two attempts to make the appointment, candidates had withdrawn before they had selected their short list.

''Fraid so. He rang around eight. Usual story for a Northerner. He'd just got round to checking out Cambridgeshire house prices.'

Di groaned. 'Cheer up, love. Our fallback candidate shouldn't present that problem. From Huntingdon, as I recall. What was her name again—Stamford-Halley?'

'Stammer-Halitosis would be nearer the mark if her interview performance was typical. Rang her immediately White hung up. Can't say I was sorry to hear she was now unavailable. Witchford Gardenplan signed her up the day before yesterday.'

'She tell you how much they were paying?'

'Thousand more than we offered.'

Di wrinkled her sunburnt nose. 'Where do we go from here, then?'

'Way I see it, we buzz the half-dozen local folk we fancied who backed out last time round or the time before. Tack a thou on to our salary offer and check their reactions. Interview those who show willing soonest—tomorrow for preference—and on their own patches. OK?'

'OK, if we can afford it.' Even before the latest hike in interest rates, they had agonized over the costs of launching the landscaping venture.

'We'd have to cut the frills, certainly. Trips abroad. Sunday shop staff, now Chrissie's got the hang of the till.'

Di groaned. 'With her GCSE exams coming up?'

'I know, love, I'm sorry. But it's up or under. We'll be in Queer Street if we don't recoup the building costs of the new office pretty soon.' Di didn't know the half, thank God. Left the books to him and their accountants—and Camcross Financial Services.

'OK, Phil. You win.' Yawning, she snuggled back under the duvet. 'Oh hell!'

'Whassat?' Her drowsiness had infected him.

'Rupert's last day tomorrow.' Parsingham had been on sick leave for the last fortnight of his employment. 'I promised to see him. I was going to take him his leaving present, remember? But I can't go off base, can I, with you talent-scouting?'

'About that present—'

'We can't afford it? That what you're going to say, Phil?'

'You know we can't. Not with this latest development.'

'We've got to—we owe him. Think how much he's taught us.'

'Taught me, you mean.' Di, the daughter and granddaughter of college gardeners, had had little to learn from the old man whose instruction Phil had so bitterly resented and despised himself for resenting.

'What have you against Rupert? Can't you tell me, now he's retiring?'

He felt her eyes on him. 'Nothing, don't be silly.' How could he make her understand that learning from her kindly, self-mocking Rupert had felt like learning from Granddad. Granddad, fifty years a cabbie, who had night after night drummed into him the names and locations of the several thousand streets of London. The Knowledge, he and his mates had called it. Granddad who knew every way under the sun of humiliating a kid whose skin was several shades darker than anything in his pattern book.

'Nothing personal,' he said in the careful voice in which he'd always spoken of and to Rupert Parsingham. 'Thing is, the old boy said himself he owed us for baling him out when he went on the rocks, for keeping him on all these years. He's not on his beam ends. He's got his State pension, if nothing else. And I don't suppose he pays rent to his sister.'

'Not the point.' She was sitting bolt upright now, brown arms folded beneath her little white breasts.

''Course it's the point, Di. OK, we give him a prezzy. Prezzies. A cheque plus that picture your dad wants him to have. Deliver them myself between interviews tomorrow. No problem. But a cheque for £50, not £500.'

'Oh, come on, Phil. £500's less than his month's salary.'

'And more than we can spare. Bet he wouldn't take if he knew how we were placed—'

'And you're not telling him. If you do, I'll find out, Phil, and I'll never forgive you.' Her face puckered.

'OK, OK you win. 'Night, sweetie.' He couldn't bear to see her crying. But he couldn't bear to part with half a grand either. There had to be another way. Pretty soon he'd hit on it.

CHAPTER 4

'Should see her right for you, love.' The photocopier engineer hauled his bulk to a standing position. 'Lend me a brush and pan and I'll leave everything shipshape before I push her back.'

Valerie Gates stopped typing. 'I'll sort that out, thanks.' New man, or he wouldn't have made the suggestion. You'd never believe how careless some people were about the stuff they let fall behind that photocopier. Checking up on that sort of thing was one of the little extras Dr Finchley appreciated. Her next boss too, Valerie hoped. She glanced at her wristwatch. Three-thirty. The Board meeting would be well under way. Maybe Finchley's appreciation wouldn't count much longer, if things went the way the Chairman's secretary had whispered they might. Still, she wasn't one for crossing bridges . . . 'Cup of tea?' she offered.

'I'll not say no.'

The way the engineer's eyes homed in on her V-neck as she cleared her desk, Valerie guessed there were other things he wouldn't say no to either. Get a grip on yourself, girl, she warned her reflection in the cloakroom mirror as she filled the kettle.

Heat did this to her. Couldn't settle her mind on her work in this dull, sticky July heat. Every window in the Director's suite shut. And she didn't dare open one in his absence, not at this time of year. Tough luck on his wife to live in a hermetically sealed house, but the air-conditioning at Appletrees was probably a sight more efficient than the three miserable office fans.

Valerie rinsed her face. Only Tuesday. Three-and-a-half days before the weekend. Feel better when she'd got home, maybe, had a shower and a change. Madrigals on the Backs tonight if the rain held off. Best part of the Festival, as far as Valerie was concerned. Norm wasn't so keen but he'd come to please her.

No more worries about being seen together, now Trish had been told. Last Saturday they'd gone shopping for the engagement ring. Valerie gave it a peck to cheer herself up on the way back to the office with the kettle. But what she saw in her mind's eye was that tapestry three-piece suite in Eaden Lilley's sale. Outside their price range, she and Norm had agreed. A good four hundred outside. Dare they, daren't they?

Afterwards, when the mechanic had left and she'd washed up the cups and saucers, Valerie hauled out the Hoover from the cupboard under the stairs and advanced on the photocopier.

*

Eric Finchley couldn't wait to get away after the Board meeting. A swim had been his first thought, but he felt too frazzled, too weary to brave the crowds in the pool just yet. Better go home to Appletrees first for a shower and change of clothes. Then to Parkside by bicycle. He risked cycling on summer evenings. Then the swim, a small snack and straight back to the Parsingham.

I tried, Mumsie, I tried, he assured his invisible companion, as he steered his Volvo into the rush-hour traffic. He had indeed tried his damnedest to win the Board over. And almost won. The senior members, holders of established Chairs and Professorial fellowships in the colleges that counted, had a sentimental affection for the name of Parsingham. Few would wish to go down in the annals of the University as traitors to the memory of the late, great Sir Rupert and destroyers of the Institute created in his memory.

Eric's rhetoric had delicately, oh so delicately, mined that sentimental vein. Then half way through his speech he'd heard the sound he'd feared for longer than he could remember. A buzz, now rising, now fading, as its maker circled first near the window and then homed in on the sugar bowl.

His language generators had stalled. A mere bluebottle, as it turned out. No cause for alarm from that quarter. But the spell had been broken. He had stumbled through the remainder of his prepared text, exposing the thinness of his argument, his disbelief in it. His hearers' eyes had avoided his. The brief ensuing discussion was dominated by the younger, tougher-minded Board members. They argued that nostalgia was a luxury beyond the University's present means, and not one of their seniors spoke or voted against them. None was prepared to fight for a higher grant from central sources. An axe hung above the Institute polished and ready to fall—in one year, or two, at most, unless a seven-figure benefaction materialized.

Don't worry, Mums, I haven't finished yet. Tell you later, Eric reassured, as he waited for the lights to change at Northampton Street.

As he turned into his drive, he remembered the invitation he'd refused to his next-door neighbour's garden-party. A couple of months ago he'd have fought his physical dread of such functions and accepted, for fear of offending a Parsingham. Not now. Not since he'd gone cap-in-hand to Eve and been turned away empty-handed.

He hoped to surprise Dolores, to catch that lovely, idiosyncratic startle response he'd married her for. But because she was at the kitchen sink, she'd seen him park the car and greeted him calmly, with her ready Filipino smile. It irked him to find her, floury-armed, in the butcher's apron that reached almost to her ankles.

'You made all this?' he asked after the ritual kiss, his eyes ranging over assorted sweets and savouries.

'Not all today. I raided the freezer. Eve rang me in a panic at lunch-time—caterer's let her down. One of her lame sheep, I think. And with her electricity off—'

'Surely Stacey could have made herself useful?'

'Eve felt it wasn't fair to bother her, not before the first night.'

'So it all falls on you.'

'Don't fuss, Eric. I've nearly done. Like me to pour you a drink?' There was already a half-full tumbler on the working surface beside her.

'No, thanks, Dolly. I'm perfectly capable . . .' He helped himself to a gin, ice and lime from the dresser. 'It's just that—you know I hate to see you overdo.'

'In case someone should take me for a mail-order bride?'

The words stunned him. He'd given her so much in the eight years of their marriage, asked only tact and good humour and a comfortable home in return. Until a few months ago, he'd had all in good measure. Now, every so often, she'd come out with something like that. Something disturbing. 'You're tiddly, Dolly,' he said.

She shrugged. 'If you choose to think so, Eric. When do you want to eat?'

What had got into her this year? Six months ago she'd have asked what kind of day he'd had. He'd have known she didn't care, would have told her nothing that mattered. Even so, the anodyne exchanges had been comforting. An assurance that they were a couple, as nearly normal a couple as made no difference.

'Thought we might have a late supper after the noise has died down next door,' he said. 'Haven't had my swim yet, and I'll have plenty to keep me busy at the Institute after that. Don't put yourself out. Just wrap me up a bite of something to eat at the pool. Leftovers will do nicely for supper.'

'Oh, I think we can do better than that, Eric.' She raised her brows as if mocking his frustrated martyrdom. 'Let's have a leisurely supper, shall we? There are things I need to say to you.'

Things . . . About her life or his? His professional secrets were safe from her, surely. So too, please God, the personal. Eric checked that everything was in order in his darkroom before going upstairs to shower.

Fifteen minutes later he descended, refreshed and strengthened with a new resolve. He fiddled about in his study until he heard Dolores's bath water running overhead. Then he left the house by the back door. He strolled uphill across the lawn that Dolores had replanted with flowerless evergreens, under Rupert Parsingham's guidance.

A somewhat futile gesture, given the jumble of flora in the old man's own fenced-off plot. As he walked, Eric surveyed the west-facing front of Rupert's cottage. Its curtains were drawn as they often were in summer against the setting sun. The notice on the door was a rarer, but not unprecedented, phenomenon.

Eric left the grounds of Appletrees by the back gate that opened on a service road. A few yards took him to the garden gate of Plumtrees Cottage, a few more to its front door.

The message on the door was what he had expected. PLEASE DO NOT DISTURB. He knocked, all the same.

'And another.' Clive Sinton waited for the second black coffee and scowled at the mirror in the public bar of the Signal Box. His reflected face scowled back. Scarred, yellowish from things he'd done to his liver, puffy-lidded from things he'd done to his kidneys, in need of a shave. Who'd want a monicker like that in a first-night audience? But Paul did or said he did. Hence the sobering-up routines.

They wouldn't quite work—never had. 'Why the binge?' Paul's eyes would ask. He'd long ago given up asking that question out loud, thank God. For Clive, a wordsmith by trade, couldn't begin to frame an answer.

To say he couldn't face the Second Court of Princes' College or the Northside caravan site stone cold sober would have prompted other questions. Questions he could never have answered, not even at one of those rare Scrabble or chestnut-roasting sessions when he and Anne and Paul had functioned like your five-star, impregnable nuclear family.

His lunch-time alcoholic anæsthetic had worked this afternoon—or maybe it hadn't even been necessary. Maybe what had counted was the recollection of Anne's words from '66, repeated like a mantra under his breath this afternoon as he walked through the housing estate that had been built over the caravan site, trying to work out the spot where their van had stood. 'He didn't touch me. That's all that matters, isn't it, love? He didn't touch me.'

No one had built over the Second Court of Princes', which he'd skirted in one of the few bright intervals of this dull, sticky day. A-24 had caught his eye as it had when he'd worked on the scaffolding outside it in '66, but for very different reasons. Today each of its windows glinted silver with a grotesque metallic artefact, and other objects of the sort lurked in the interior. Sculptures, people still called them. Daft name for things that hadn't been carved, but rather sliced and twisted. From what? Steel? Aluminium?

Then he'd spotted the raw materials on the shelves that had once held Eric Finchley's books—or rather, Eric Finchley's uncle's books. Row upon row of beer cans.

'Look, Mother,' an old Suffolk voice had croaked behind him. '*A-24. Ms B. Selwick. Fellow-commoner in Creative Arts.* That's what it says on the little old notice board. Creative bloody arts!' Clive had turned, and was included in. 'Have to laugh, don't you, mate?'

And he had—oh, he had. Finchley's image had been well and truly exorcized from his old lodgings. If it lingered anywhere thereabouts it was surely overhead, among the petrified and powerless gargoyles.

The Dining Hall of Princes' was something else again, the focus for Clive's worst guilt and his worst shame. But it drew him nevertheless. He would go there tomorrow.

He sipped at the second coffee, muddy and probably carcinogenous. His head was clearing, but slowly. When he leafed through the *Cambridge Evening News* that someone had left on the counter beside him, the small print looked blurry.

The headers were clear enough, though. Typical provincial menu: COMMUNITY CARE PROTESTS, FESTIVAL BUDGET ROW, CHANGES AT MIDDLEFIELDS GARDEN CENTRE.

And the photographs. Straightforward shots of local faces, mostly. Nothing arty-farty. He made a child's game of it, spotting animal resemblances, checking names. Councillor Vera Potterswade, vixen. The Vicar of St Peter Paul, crocodile. Then a Teddy-bear face—called Rupert, for God's sake. Rupert Parsingham. Clive laughed out loud.

Then he looked again. It wasn't possible, he told himself. It didn't fit. *The retirement of Mr Rupert Parsingham, horticultural consultant (left) coincides with major organizational changes at the Middlefields Garden Centre, Trumpington. Mr Parsingham, who is the great-grandson of Sir Rupert Parsingham . . .*

It fitted. The old man was one of Them, with God knew how many rights to a place at the High Table of Princes' that night in '66. But no right at all to get out of his seat and stare at Clive the way he'd stared that night. The way he stared still in his nightmares.

Tomorrow, you bastard. Why couldn't you leave me in peace until tomorrow? Clive gulped down the dregs of his coffee, and checked his watch. Plenty of time before the curtain-up of *Spin City*. The dress rehearsal had moved him almost to tears more than once. And tonight the image of Parsingham's stupid, bearish face would be among those of the clownish dons on stage, staring down at him as though he was subhuman. He couldn't face it, not without something to kill the pain. But he'd promised Paul, and he couldn't let Anne's son down either. Not here in Cambridge.

With no thought but to distance himself from alcohol, he left the pub and turned right into Mill Road. A stale, warm breeze blew dust and litter in his face. He walked faster, hoping to wear himself out, for exhaustion was also an anæsthetic. Already he could smell his own grime and sweat. He'd have to stop soon, freshen up.

Then he remembered that the pool where he and Paul had swum that morning was only yards away. His togs were still in his shoulder-bag. He crossed over.

CHAPTER 5

Eleven-thirty. The first-night garden-party at Plumtrees was warming up. Not so the Stage Manager of *Spin City*.

'It wobbled, I tell you. The minute Larry put his weight on it, that bloody pinnacle wobbled.'

'OK, Paul, if you say so,' Emma soothed. 'Point is, though, the audience didn't give a monkey's.'

'Absolutely not!' Their hostess—a short, sturdy figure in a striped caftan—bore down on them. 'Everyone, but everyone, who saw that show has been praising it to the skies. Hear me, Stacey?' Eve beckoned the scriptwriter, who obeyed the summons a little wearily. 'A smash hit. Just what I prophesied at dress rehearsal.'

Stacey's face lost some of its strain. 'Thanks for the ego-boost, Eve. Audience was great, but my hunch is they were mostly buddies of the cast. Maybe I'll take you more seriously when I read the reviews.'

'Better stoke up with a few hundred calories before then, my dear. Aren't I right, Dolly?'

Dolores Finchley, who had changed into a traditional Filipino tunic-dress in embroidered coral silk, was carrying a trayful of savouries wrapped in lettuce leaves. As she joined the group, Paul muttered an excuse and withdrew, with Emma in tow.

'Let's sit down for a bit.' A low table was found for Dolores's tray. Eve subsided thankfully on to a rusty metal chair, and the younger women sat on the parched grass at her feet. Relax, Eve urged herself. The party, like the show, had been a success. She'd been right, absolutely right, to go ahead.

'Haven't had a chance to thank you two angels properly

for all you've done. I'm not one to panic, Lord knows, but when I got that call from the caterers—'

'It's Dolly we should both be thanking. This yummy finger food!' Stacey helped herself to a second leafy package.

'Absolutely delish!' Eve followed suit. 'But the decorations were your doing, Stacey.' She looked round with real pleasure. The patchy light from the several dozen coloured paper lanterns was suitably festive, whilst concealing the scars inflicted on the Victorian house and gardens by her recently departed lodgers.

'No big deal.' Stacey retrieved a blob of spiced spinach from her flowery pants. 'Actually I found it therapeutic, having something to fiddle with during rehearsals. Great show, great party, Eve. And you're the one who's making it fizz. Only thing that bugged me was not seeing Rupert around tonight.'

'He just can't cope with parties. Never could,' Eve said firmly. Or with the sight of Plumtrees in its current run-down condition.

'So he told me. But I'd counted on seeing him at the show. He more or less promised he'd make the first performance, when he turned down the invite to the dress rehearsal. Thought I'd let him know how things had gone.'

'But you didn't?' Eve was struck by the sharpness in Dolores's tone.

'No—not when I saw the notice on his door. Thought maybe he'd taken something to help him sleep. He's had some low spells recently, hasn't he, Eve?'

She nodded. 'He told me the only good thing about being away from work this last fortnight would be dodging goodbyes from his clients. But they've been calling in shoals, so he tells me.'

'Yes,' Dolores confirmed. 'When I'm at my kitchen sink

I can't help noticing the comings and goings. Phil Beresford called around lunch-time today.'

Eve nodded. 'Official presentation, I expect. Di told me some weeks ago her father wanted Rupert to have an old engraving of Princes' gardens.'

'He'd like that,' Dolores said.

The tone was authoritative, proprietary even. Eve stifled a rare pang of jealousy.

'The presentation may have felt like the point of no return, all the same,' Dolores went on. 'Anyhow, Rupert must have stuck up the DO NOT DISTURB notice soon after Phil had gone. It was there half an hour later—stopped me in my tracks on my way to see him.'

'Leavetakings can be hell,' Stacey volunteered between nibbles.

'Don't brood, dear,' Eve said more sharply than she'd intended. 'Rupert wouldn't want to blight your big night. Up you get, now, and meet someone who's absolutely dying to meet you!'

Eve semaphored energetically to a slim, blonde woman in pale blue. The type who had been wearing chambray for twenty summers and making anything else look overstated. 'Zoë Grayling, drama critic for the *Sentinel*. Stacey Caldwell, our clever scriptwriter.'

Zoë nodded graciously. Stacey pulled a face.

'Excuse the possessive,' Eve went on. 'But as a founder Friend of the Fringe and Stacey's landlady—'

'I'd say you're entitled.' The journalist flashed shapely eyebrows above her wineglass.

'Zoë tells me the show's really enlightened her about our Town-Gown scandals,' Eve went on. 'Never even heard of the Vice-Chancellor's Court, had you, my dear? Not to mention our Victorian poverty statistics.'

'Nor had I until six months ago,' Stacey protested.

'Rabbiting, aren't I?' Talking had always come easier to

Eve than listening. 'You'll want to slip off somewhere quiet for your natter. Conservatory, I suggest. And, Zoë, you absolutely must persuade Stacey to write a sequel!'

Stacey made small protesting noises, but departed in the journalist's company. Something accomplished, something done, Eve told herself. She would sleep well tonight. It came as a shock to see that Dolores was sober-faced, sad even.

'I was really sorry to see Rupert's DO NOT DISTURB notice this afternoon.'

Not that again. 'Why? He's put it up before—when the children's noise got on his nerves, for instance.'

'I know, and I've always respected his privacy—this time too, of course. It's just . . .' Dolores hesitated, biting her lip. 'Just that something cropped up since I saw him this morning. I'll be taking an early train to King's Cross tomorrow—too early to disturb Rupert—and I hate not being able to say goodbye to him.'

'Goodbye?' Eve was stunned. 'I don't understand.'

'I've had bad news from London. A young woman I've come to know quite well has tried to commit suicide. She's going to need a lot of help these next few weeks.'

'A Filipina? A domestic worker?'

Dolores nodded.

Eve knew better than to press for details. Dolores was well aware of her scorn for the immigration laws that had for so long bound immigrant servants to their employers on pain of deportation. Even so, she had been resolutely tight-lipped about the Kensington-based support groups she had been visiting weekly throughout her stay in Cambridge.

'I'm sure you've done all you could, Dolly.'

Dolores shook her dark head. 'No. Once I might have kidded myself you were right, but not any longer. Not now I've more time on my hands.'

More time? Eve didn't understand. But there was so much about Dolores she didn't understand.

'Chita will need to see someone on a daily basis for several weeks—someone to be within reach round the clock in a crisis. My grandparents live in the village she grew up in—I can speak her dialect. I'm the obvious person to help, but I can't do it from Cambridge.'

The truth but not the whole truth, Eve guessed, and mocked herself for playing detective.

'You'll be away for several weeks, then? Keep in touch, won't you? I'll miss you. Especially if Stacey takes wing. She's talking of heading back to the States after the Edinburgh Festival.'

'Really? I'd no idea.' Dolores laid a hand on the older woman's arm. 'I'd be sad to think of you here all alone.'

'Not for long, I'm sure.' Eve already regretted her brief display of vulnerability. 'Rose and Jean-Pierre sent a card from Burgundy promising to come back after the grape-harvest, and Steve and Ruth are booked in for the Cherry Hinton Folk Festival next weekend. Haven't heard from the others recently, but they're not all good communicators. Anyhow, the place isn't fit for children until we get the roof repairs finished and the rewiring done.'

'About those roof repairs—' Dolores began.

'Not tonight, please. Slating's a marginally more cheerful subject than damp-rot, I grant you, but it doesn't make good party-talk all the same.'

'Forgive me, Eve. But autumn's just round the corner. I'd hate to think of you shivering under a sheet of plastic with frost on the ground. And considering your young houseguests left you in the lurch with the job half done—'

'They'd their reasons. The tourist season's when most of them earn their living.'

'Are you sure laziness didn't come into it, Eve? What happens if they cop out again?'

Eve's anger flared. 'I shall have a word with my bank

manager. Listen, Dolly, I don't want to squabble. But my domestic arrangements are really none of your business.'

'That's true.' Dolores's black eyes filled. 'I don't like interference myself, Eve, and I hate to sound interfering. But you've been a kind neighbour and I just couldn't leave without speaking out. I really feel you should get the job done professionally. Eric feels the same. I'm not sure if he's approached you himself, but if there are insurance problems—financial problems of any kind—I know he'd be delighted to help. He's not a man to show emotion, Eve, but I know he's genuinely concerned about you and Rupert—'

'Concerned? About us?' Eve laughed shortly. 'Sorry, my dear. I don't doubt your own motives. Tell me honestly, now. This London trip of yours—there's more involved than helping Chita, isn't there?'

Dolores nodded, fiddling with her silver bracelets. 'There are so many other Chitas. And changes in the immigration law won't solve all their problems.'

'Could the weeks stretch into months, years even? Are you thinking of leaving your husband?'

Dolores got to her feet, visibly distressed. 'No comment. Sorry, Eve. But you do understand that if it came to that, Eric would be the first to be told.'

'Not Rupert? And you've always been so close!' Eve heard herself saying.

Dolores stared down, angrier than her neighbour had ever seen her. But she spoke very quietly. 'Go on, Eve. You're not usually one for innuendoes. Ask me what you want about my relationship with your brother.'

But Eve didn't. She daren't. The younger woman walked away.

'Stacey about?' a man's voice asked.

Eve swivelled to confront the gaunt figure of Julian Otley, stooping even more than usual under the weight of a rucksack and bedroll. A welcome distraction. 'Come to shack up with us? Good-oh!'

Julian turned pink. 'If it's all right—if you don't mind, that is.'

'Open invitation. Glad you've taken it up at last.'

'Thanks—but I should have warned . . . forgot about the party. Came straight from the lab, you see. Meant to ch-check things out with Stacey.' Julian's pink deepened to crimson.

Eve flashed him a quick diagnostic stare. 'Last seen with a critic in the conservatory. Do investigate. And come back later for a nightcap, both of you.'

Emma and Paul had helped themselves to ices labelled *makupuno*, which turned out to be a delectable species of coconut, and had taken possession of two deckchairs in a small summerhouse.

'Cast an eye over this lot!' Paul exclaimed after a long period of companionable silence. He toed a pile of battered toys, tricycles and dismantled swings. 'Where you have kids you have clobber.'

'*Some* kids,' Emma corrected. 'I was obsessional about tidying up my messes when I was little. D'you know, I actually begged my dad to buy me a miniature chest-of-drawers when I was seven.'

'And did he?'

'Not the one I'd fallen in love with. Hadn't occurred to me before that police sergeants' pay didn't stretch to antique mahogany. But it registered that he was really upset about palming me off with plywood. Would you believe, I've never been able to tell him what I'd like for a birthday from that day to this.' Emma's throat tightened. It mattered. Silly that it should matter.

'I'd believe you. Dads . . .' Paul's voice trailed off.

'You haven't forgiven yours for opting out of this shindig,

have you? That's bugging you more than a wobbly bit of scenery that a nail will put right in the morning.'

Paul shrugged. 'Maybe. He should've made the effort. It's nothing personal, mind. One thing this exercise has told me is that I'm not cut out for stage-management. And I know *Spin City* won't make or break your reputation, Em. But it might be important for Stacey. Dad could've done her good here by mingling with the critics—persuading those who haven't seen the show yet that it's worth their attention.'

'Mm. Give him credit for turning up at the performance, which is more than my Ma or Pa managed. Quite honestly, from the way he looked when I spotted him in the Signal Box, I was amazed to see him in the audience. I'm not surprised he didn't feel up to theatrical chit-chat afterwards.'

'My guess is, the name of Parsingham may have put him off as much as anything.'

'Really? Some personal grudge?'

'Shouldn't think so. But he worked here as a mason and scaffolder, don't forget. He's always been scathing about Camford élitism—including the cult of the famous academic families.'

Emma laughed. 'Quite right too. But it's hard to think of Eve or Rupert as members of a University mafia.'

'She doesn't look the part, I admit. Do you know her well?'

'Only by reputation. Which, according to my mother, was curate's-eggy. I gather a great sigh of relief went up throughout the peace movement when Eve's enthusiasms switched channels. She was super in headline-catching stunts, it seems—wire-cutting and paintspraying *doubles-entendres* on F-111s. But apt to tread on her sister's ideological corns in the long night watches at Greenham.'

'Speaking of which—' Paul yawned, a mite unconvincingly, and leant across to kiss her. 'This chair's doing terrible things to my vertebrae. What say we shove off, now we've done our social duty?'

'Nice.' And it would be. Emma allowed herself to be pulled to her feet. She'd been wary of reviving the short, sweet affair, interrupted two years before when both had graduated from Lancaster. Throughout rehearsals for *Spin City*, she'd commuted from her parents' home in Kings Covert.

But this morning her ten-year-old van had broken down two miles outside Cambridge, and was still under repair. With both her parents on duty and unable to fetch her, she could think of no good reason to refuse Paul's offer of overnight hospitality. And as he hugged her tight in the summerhouse and asked her to sleep with him, she could think of no good reason to refuse that offer either.

The party-goers had thinned out considerably as Emma and Paul headed downhill towards the front gates. Someone hailed them from the shadows. It was Stacey, her round face uncharacteristically grim. She was wheeling a tricycle. *The* tricycle—so Emma deduced from the slogans plastered on its every available surface. Eve's battle chariot in many a nominally non-violent action.

'Seen Eve?' Stacey asked.

They pleaded ignorance. 'Something wrong?' Paul inquired—redundantly, to judge by Stacey's glare.

'Found the trike outside the kitchen door—that's what's wrong. And Eve promised me faithfully she'd put it under lock and key every evening before sunset.'

'Spate of cycle thefts?'

But Paul's last question remained unanswered. For Stacey's gaze, horrified now, was fixed on someone else. Someone coming up the drive behind them.

Emma turned to see a boy of perhaps eighteen in black leathers, carrying a tote bag. His blue-green hair was stiffly lacquered and his face and hands were tattooed. But the face beneath the tattoos had an amiable expression.

''Lo, Stace,' the newcomer said. 'Whose thrash? Any nosh going?'

Stacey let go of the tricycle and ran forward to grab his arm. 'Not for you, kid. Not any more. Think all you have to do is to walk back here and give Eve the old babyface crap, do you? No way, you filthy little murderer. No way.'

The boy swore, spat and tugged himself free. Then he turned on his heels and ran down the drive.

CHAPTER 6

'My professional instincts tell me . . .' The Chief Constable of the Mid-Anglian Constabulary tapped his newly cultivated moustache as if acknowledging the message. 'My instincts tell me this will turn out to be suicide—a common-or-garden coroner's case.'

Another time the all-too-apt metaphor might have reduced DCI Richard Baxter, the most junior recipient of this early morning briefing, to silent giggles. But he and more especially his wife Sarah had heard the news of Rupert Parsingham's death with real sadness. Besides, his daughter had said something about a first-night party at Plumtrees. With her first musical production on her hands Emma needed involvement in a murder case like she needed a hole in the head.

Not that poor Rupert had died from a hole in the head. Reports from Bill Armstrong, the duty DI at the scene of crime and from the police surgeon, pointed clearly to carbon monoxide suffocation. Hose plus exhaust pipe—common enough suicide method. Ironic that the old station-wagon whose loss Parsingham had so dreaded should have done him this final service.

'The break-in at the cottage complicates matters, of

course, but we've no present reason to believe it was any more than a coincidence.' Francis Montgomery's hairy hands bore down on the afrormosia conference table which dominated his room at Holtchester Police Headquarters. 'The ACC concurs. Right, Littleton?'

The Assistant Chief Constable (Criminal Investigation) made the strangled noise that Baxter had learnt to interpret as agreement.

'But DI Armstrong has doubts.' Montgomery's Norman nose wrinkled, as if he had named a disease transmitted by policemen of the lower sort. 'And Victor Highcroft has convinced me that it would be prudent to be seen to take his doubts seriously.'

Detective-Superintendent Highcroft's fishy face quivered pinkly.

Baxter found the Chief Constable's polysyllabic prose heavy going at 7.30 a.m. on top of a hurried breakfast. As far as he could make out, the essentials were (a) the dead man was a Parsingham and therefore only a little lower in the Cambridge University Pantheon than a Newton or a Darwin, and (b) his sister was an unpredictable trouble-maker. Montgomery laboured both themes emotionally and at length. Had he cancelled his scheduled attendance at the week-long pow-wow of European Chief Police Officers where Victor Highcroft was to accompany him as a technical adviser? Was he planning—God forbid—to take personal charge of the case?

No on both counts, it transpired.

'ACC Crime and I are agreed that territorial considerations must be waived in a case of unusual sensitivity. Our first requirements for the Acting Senior Investigating Officer are relevant CID experience and knowledge of the academic scene. An Oxbridge graduate of suitable seniority would be ideal—but lacking any such candidate, you're the obvious choice, Richard.'

Baxter, toughened by an eight-year sojourn in Cambridgeshire to insults to his redbrick Alma Mater, grunted acquiescence.

'You'll report direct to the ACC during Superintendent Highcroft's absence. Been cleared with Cambridge City, of course. Any objections?'

As if they'd count. 'What about the jewel thefts investigation, sir?'

'Back burner until our return, pending unforeseen developments. Victor has a new strategic proposal in the pipeline, which I'll cast an eye over between other commitments in Geneva.'

Highcroft smirked, obviously revelling in his honorary elevation to the ranks of the CPOs.

'Look forward to hearing more, sir,' Baxter murmured. Now that he no longer expected the Superintendent's computerized brain-children to yield useful results, he rather welcomed them as diversions from the daily grind.

'That's that, then.' The CC collected his papers. 'We'd better hit the road for Heathrow, Victor. No rest for the wicked, eh?' A standard Montgomery joke, a standard ripple of sycophantic laughter.

Baxter was surprised, then, when the old man paused for a private word on his way out. 'Extraordinary bloke, Parsingham. Finicky, too. Used to get down on his hands and knees, the wife told me, to pick up every scrap of foliage after he'd shown her one of his fancy pruning techniques. Damned embarrassing for Georgie. With him being who he was, don't you know?'

'Maundy Thursday-ish, sir?'

'What? Oh, hardly . . .' If Montgomery suspected irony he wasn't letting on. 'We've been clients of his for years, you know. Georgie's taken his death badly. She'd like to think the Force was doing its best for him.'

'So'd Sarah, sir.'

'Miss him myself, come to that. One of the few men in the county who really understood alpines.'

As Baxter drove the ten miles from Holtchester to Cambridge he reflected that his Chief might metamorphose into someone altogether more honest and likeable if he were to take early retirement and devote himself exclusively to his rockery. As to the task in hand, the Chief Inspector felt none of Montgomery's qualms about disturbing the peace of Academe. Especially not since his dealings with the sometime Warden of Gaunt College.

He'd always had qualms about working off patch, however. Official clearance with Cambridge City Division was one thing, the hurt feelings of locals were quite another. At least he'd have no problems of that sort with DI Bill Armstrong, his second string at Holtchester for the last eight years, and already on temporary assignment to Cambridge City. Or with DS Wendy Powers, whose services he had secured before leaving Headquarters.

Besides, Montgomery might just be right. Maybe this would turn out to be a coroner's case.

The garage adjoining Rupert's cottage was Daimler-size, most probably a former stable. Which was just as well. When Baxter arrived it already housed Dr Stallburn, the pathologist, Bill Armstrong and three Scenes of Crime specialists as well as the vehicle which contained the mortal remains of Rupert Parsingham.

'Like to move him as soon as poss, Baxter.' Stallburn, a tall, heavy man, backed away from the open door of the station-wagon.

Baxter peered briefly at the figure slumped in the driving seat, a garden hose still lying across his lap. 'No doubts as to cause of death?'

'Immediate cause, no.' Stallburn peeled off his plastic

gloves. 'For the rest, we'll have to wait until we get him on the slab, won't we?'

Baxter, whose absence from autopsies on several previous occasions had made him the butt of the pathologist's unsubtle sarcasm, knew there'd be no escaping this one.

'Time of death?' he asked, peering at the corpse.

'Twelve to sixteen hours ago, at a guess. He's quite stiff. Stomach contents might narrow the range.'

Baxter's own insides were protesting against the effects of his hurried breakfast. He helped himself to a sodamint as he moved away from the van.

'Your lot done their stuff on the corpse?' he asked Trevor Bly, Senior Scenes of Crime Officer.

Bly nodded.

'Best get him away, then. Any sign of a suicide note?'

It was Bill Armstrong who answered. 'In an inside pocket. Here, guv.' He handed over a pencil-written page, already sheathed in plastic, which had obviously been torn from a pocket diary. No address—only the previous day's date near the top of the page in the same small, neat script as the message that followed.

Baxter squinted and read:

My dear Pudding,

Rotten of me, I admit, to cop out, but the time was ripe. You know how I felt about packing the job in. That was why. No cut flowers at the funeral, please, but if you want to make my ghost happy ask one of your motley crew to water my geraniums.

Bear

'Shown this to Mrs Parsingham Wells, Bill?'

Armstrong nodded. 'She's sure it's authentic. Handwriting's definitely his, and Pudding was his name for her when they were kids. Eve's Pudding, you know.'

'Yes—yes.' Baxter suppressed sick-making memories.

'Besides, she says it wasn't altogether a surprise. Her brother'd been very low since he knew he'd have to give up his job. Yesterday was the official retirement date, but he'd been on sick leave for a fortnight.'

'So what's your problem?'

'This place, for starters. When'd you last hear of a suicide mopping up the ruddy garage before doing the deed?'

Baxter shrugged. 'He was a finicky type—you've that on the authority of your Chief Constable, no less. Besides, look around you.'

The garage had evidently doubled as a storage shed. A fairly standard range of household maintenance and gardening equipment was stowed in an orderly fashion on its walls and shallow shelves. The paint tins were firmly lidded, the half-used sacks of fertilizer and compost tightly tied.

'Take your point.' The DI flushed, as if recalling the cheerful chaos of his own outbuildings. 'Not just that, though.' Baxter's Ulster-born junior could be as mulish as any of his compatriots when he got going. 'What about the method? This bloke had arthritic wrists—gave him a fair bit of pain, his sister said. So why'd he mess around fitting a garden hose to his exhaust pipe—even supposing he had the wrist power to make the connection.'

'Prints around the join?'

'Oh, his. Both hands—nice and clear. Ditto on the inner door handle. But who knows what was wiped off before he made them? Who knows that he didn't make them under duress or to oblige an accomplice?'

Baxter laughed. 'Going all round Will's mother's, aren't you, as they say in these parts?'

'Parsingham was—my next point. All he had to do was start up the engine. With the garage door shut, the fumes would've done for him sure enough anyway.'

'But not soon enough, perhaps. In twenty minutes, say, as opposed to five. Maybe he wanted to get it over fast in case he'd second thoughts or in case he was interrupted. If Stallburn's anywhere near the mark in his estimate, this was a daylight job.'

'Which raises another question.' Armstrong's square face had the eager-beaver expression that cut twenty years off his forty. 'Why not wait until after dark if his time was his own? Then there's the break-in.'

'Nothing taken here in the garage?'

'Doesn't look that way. We might get Mrs PW to check later on, mightn't we, once she's got over the shock of finding him. But I don't suppose she'd much occasion to use the place.'

'Anything else in his pockets?'

'Nothing out of the way. Wallet with nearly £40 in crisp notes and coins, cheque-book, Natwest Switch card, Access card, driving licence, keys to his house and garage.'

'Both locked where his sister found him?'

'So she says. Want to give the cottage the once-over? Mrs PW made such a song and dance that I asked the SOC team to confine their activities to the window and living-room. OK?'

'OK for the present. And Trev'll request some tests on the muscle power needed to fit that hose exhaust connection, won't you, Trev?'

Bly made a note.

Smiling his 'just-you-wait' smile, Armstrong led the way towards the adjacent cottage. Its style was that of Plumtrees—late Victorian in red brick patterned with blue, with a fancy wood trim under the eaves. All the curtains were drawn. The PLEASE DO NOT DISTURB notice was still stuck on the open, blue-painted front door. To its left a prints man was at work on the frame of the ground-floor sash window through which the intruder had evidently entered.

'Any joy?' Baxter asked him.

'Not a lot, sir. Marks have been wiped inside and out. Given all the living-room surfaces the once-over, so feel free to reccy, but please steer clear of the soiled rug under the window. Garden compost or something. Inspector Bly's sending a bloke across later to take scrapings.'

'No sign of a forced entry?'

'Uh-uh. Window must have been unlocked, if not open. Might be something itsy-bitsy stuck to the curtain, I dare say. You can see the fibre caught on the catch for yourself.'

Sludge-green, Baxter would have called that colour. No doubt it was known as something prettier in the current rag trade. A lot of it about.

'Could be something for you down there, as well.' The prints man jerked his head towards some trampled foliage in the herbaceous border to the left of his ladder.

Inside, a photographer was packing his gear. The original kitchen and parlour had been merged, Baxter guessed, into the living-room whose shabby charm showed through its present disorder. The plain repp curtains had faded to the older blue of the Oriental rugs. Time had assimilated the yellowish-browns of the pine and yew and fruitwood furniture. There was a bowl of sweet peas among the old willow-ware on the table laid for one, and pots of geraniums on the window-sills. A few pieces of jade and coral among English fairings in a corner cupboard were the sole tokens of the family's tropical connections.

It wouldn't take much time or effort to put the room to rights, Baxter thought. The traces of the intrusion—if such they were—were curiously random. One of several bookshelves had been emptied of its neatly labelled contents, a table lamp had been overturned, a box of slides spilt, a desk drawer pulled out. But the Staffordshire dogs on the mantelpiece stared unscathed at the framed engravings of garden plans on the wall opposite. Eighteenth-century draughtsmanship, possibly French, probably pricey. A more recent engraving of a garden with college buildings in the distance lay in half-opened wrappings beside the ancient typewriter on the big oak desk.

'Amateur job, would you reckon, Bill?' Baxter asked, as the photographer took his departure.

'An amateur in a hurry or a flap.'

'You'd be in both if you'd left a dying man in the garage.'

'Looks to me like our friend was after something specific,' Armstrong suggested.

'Which usually means cash. Let's follow his trail.' Baxter removed the top desk drawer which had been left open and placed it gently on the floor. Using his fingertips, he removed and inspected its contents.

Here he found a mixed collection of stationery and writing materials, neatly arranged. As well as paper, pencil sharpeners, ball points, whitener and other items evidently in current use, there were a few oddities. A faded box of sealing-wax, half used, a folder full of blotting-paper, an ancient tobacco tin containing an assortment of rusting pen-knibs, holders and fountain-pens. Parsinghams had been hoarders, it seemed, long before conservation became fashionable.

Baxter held one nib to the light and squinted. 'Waverley . . . that takes me back. *They come as a boon and a blessing to men—the Pickwick, the Owl and the Waverley pen.* There was this rummy old enamel sign in a corner shop I used to visit when I was a kid in Birmingham. Edwardian, shouldn't wonder. Ads were made to last in the old days.'

Armstrong cleared his throat. A sudden thought struck his senior. 'Had breakfast yet?'

'No, but I'm not bothered, sir.'

Knowing Bill for a good trencherman, Baxter was disbelieving. With the help of a ruler, he worked his way quickly through the remaining contents of the drawer. Right at the bottom there was a cardboard box that had once contained Mars bars. And now double foolscap, he guessed, having already found samples of most other writing papers, ancient and modern.

Instead, he found banknotes.

Shifting the box from the floor to the desktop, he checked the amount. Nine packs of £50 notes, neatly banded, ten notes to a pack, were stacked two on two. And there was a tenth pack on its own, containing four £50 notes. 'Four thousand six hundred quid.'

Armstrong peered over his shoulder and whistled. 'Parsingham wasn't the sort, was he?'

'Sort for what?'

'For stashing money in the house. OK, he was a hoarder. But nearly five grand that could have been earning interest?'

'Tax-dodging's a possibility.'

'I suppose,' Armstrong conceded. 'But it doesn't fit with the old boy's background and reputation, does it? See the piece about him in yesterday's *News*?'

'No, but I knew him slightly.' Very slightly, Baxter was beginning to suspect. 'Agreed, it wasn't in character. So why'd he stow it? And why £4,600? Looks like £400 was nicked. If so, why so little?'

Armstrong, who was parting the notes with a pencil tip and noting their serial numbers, didn't answer directly. 'Mixed lot—impossible to trace their life-history, I'd guess.'

'Most obvious conclusion would be that he acquired the loot gradually. And if not through saving . . .' Baxter hesitated.

'Blackmail, do you reckon?'

The DCI sighed. 'I don't want to believe that of him, but what else . . . ?'

'Maybe we should take a squint inside the drawers our trespasser didn't bother to unlock?' Armstrong suggested.

'Didn't or couldn't.'

'Look.' His junior pointed to something glinting under the old Underwood manual typewriter on the desktop, and retrieved a set of desk keys. 'One of the commonest hidey-holes. So our friend didn't make the effort to look. Shall I do the needful?'

'Later.' Baxter wrapped the keys in polythene and stowed them in an inside pocket. 'Time I paid my respects to Rupert's Pudding.'

CHAPTER 7

'Sarah Baxter's husband!' Eve Parsingham Wells erupted from the back door of Plumtrees and intercepted the detectives on their way to the main entrance. 'Front doorbell's out of commission—this way, if you please.'

She turned on the threshold to inspect Baxter's identity card and subject his face to close scrutiny. Her own was blunt-featured like her brother's, and just as weather-beaten. The pepper-and-salt mop might well have been cut by her own hand. There were no obvious traces of weeping. Her denim jeans and cheesecloth shirt had seen better days.

'Well, well.' Eve pursed her small mouth. 'Frank Montgomery could have sent worse, I suppose, though I'll never understand why a nice woman like your wife should get spliced to a copper.'

'Don't see Sarah as much as I used to,' she went on and she led the way through a dim back passage to a large kitchen. 'Still on the anti-nuke warpath, I suppose? Tell her from me, will you, that the Bomb isn't the number one enemy any more. Tell her that as a medic her place is in the front ranks of the war against poison!'

'Perhaps you'll give her the message in person some time?' Baxter murmured, as he took stock of his surroundings.

The walls and cupboards were covered with bogus tourist posters bearing slogans such as 'Come to sunny Stinkport' and depicting the sewage and other nasties that awaited the incautious bather. Eve's propaganda might have carried weight with Baxter in a more salubrious setting. But the sink gave off a whiff of rancid dishcloth, burnt-in spillages disfigured the Aga cooker and mouldering crumbs were scattered underfoot.

'Coffee?' Their hostess gestured towards a chipped enamel pot. Both detectives declined.

'I will if you won't, then.' Eve poured herself a murky mugful and laced it with brandy. 'Do me a sight more good than the sedatives that twit of a doctor tried to ram down my throat. Sit down, both of you. Can't do with hoverers.'

Eve climbed on to the highest available seat, a stool that doubled as a stepladder. She watched and waited until the detectives had disposed themselves on Windsor chairs facing her.

'Well then, Chief Inspector. I trust you've been able to open your colleague's eyes to the truth that's staring us all in the face.'

'Truth, Mrs Parsingham Wells?'

Her face reddened and contracted. For a brief moment she pressed a tissue to her mouth. When she spoke, it was more softly. 'No word games, please. My brother killed himself. I knew the minute I saw him this morning. I'd seen it coming, ever since he knew he couldn't drive any longer. That's what I told the Inspector. How many times do I have to say it? How long are your people going to be trampling over the garage and the cottage? He'd have hated that, Rupert. *Please do not disturb*. Not much to ask, is it? But you did disturb him—you bloody well did.' Eve's voice almost failed her.

'I'm sorry,' Baxter said after a brief pause. 'And that's not just a form of words. I only met your brother once or twice, but I know how much my wife learned from him, how much pleasure his visits gave her. Perhaps he did take his own life unassisted. If we were sure of that beyond reasonable doubt his death would be a matter for the coroner. But Inspector Armstrong has raised questions which in my judgement deserved to be aired. For instance, had your brother the strength to fit the hose to the exhaust pipe?'

'Strength can come from despair.'

'Perhaps. If we're lucky, the forensic scientists may give reassuring answers to this and related problems within days if not hours. In that event, we shall trouble you no further.'

'And if not? Weeks and months and years of irrelevant questions? Sorry to be blunt, but I for one have better things to do than sit here answering them. Once Rupert's death becomes public knowledge, I'll be deluged with letters and phone calls.'

'Are you alone in the house? Shouldn't you have someone—'

'Not that again, please! First the WPC, then Eric Finchley, then my doctor whom Eric rang without my knowledge or consent. No, no, no. I'm alone, and for the present I prefer it that way. If and when I feel the need of company, I'll make my own selection. Understood, Chief Inspector?'

'Certainly.' What he also understood from the heightened pitch of her voice and her laced fingers was that she was fighting off a fit of weeping. 'Who, by the way, is Eric Finchley?'

'Director of the Parsingham Institute and my next-door

neighbour. He spotted the police at the cottage. Called on me on his way to work. Eric's always very *attentive*.' A half-smile, a tightening of the lips. Why? Baxter wondered.

'I trust DI Armstrong will agree that I answered his questions fully and frankly earlier,' she went on. 'No doubt my answers are on record, but in any event I've absolutely no intention of being put through all that rigmarole twice in one morning for your benefit, Chief Inspector.'

'Of course not,' Baxter soothed, conscious of his junior's mutterings. 'A very few questions, then. It could save us all time and trouble if you'd be good enough to answer.'

She sighed. 'Cut the cackle.'

'Was your brother right- or left-handed?'

'Left, like me.'

'For all purposes?'

'Yes. Why should that matter?' There was a hint of anxiety in her tone which Baxter couldn't account for.

'It may help in interpreting his fingerprints. I noticed the fork was to the right of the knife on the table he'd laid for supper.'

'Breakfast.'

'Really? You didn't say—'

'The Inspector didn't ask. Rupert was a creature of habit. Breakfasted at six-thirty, the only meal he ate at the table by the east-facing window. Same time every day, even on Sundays, when he wasn't leaving for work at a quarter to eight. Snack lunch at twelve if he was home. High tea—his big meal of the day—at five. Nursery tea, I used to call it. But he ate that from a trolley-table by the west window in summer or near the fireplace in winter.'

Which he or someone else must have cleared before he died. A check of Rupert's kitchen waste-bin was an urgent priority.

'I see. It would seem from our preliminary inspection that theft may have been a motive for the cottage trespass.

That cash may have been taken. Please regard this as confidential—there are puzzling features. I emphasize the *mays*. Any comments?'

Eve had relaxed visibly, as though eager to accept the suggestion. Too eager? 'Theft seems the obvious motive for the break-in,' she said. 'An alcoholic in search of drink, poor devil, though he wouldn't have found much of that in Rupert's place. There've been other incidents in this neighbourhood. We're close to Alexandra Gardens and Jesus Green, where some of the winos congregate. The DO NOT DISTURB notice would have attracted attention, and with the window open . . .'

'Perhaps.' Most winos of Baxter's acquaintance would have left messier visiting cards. 'Did your brother normally keep substantial sums of cash at home?'

'No, no. I'm sure he didn't.' She frowned. 'Sort of thing he was always lecturing me about. What little capital he had was in his building society account. A few hundreds, I imagine.' But the question had clearly unsettled her.

Armstrong raised an eyebrow, but Baxter frowned discouragement.

'I can only suppose,' Eve went on, 'that he made a withdrawal when he decided to kill . . . end his life. As an intended gift for a charity or a friend, perhaps.'

'Any friend in particular?'

'No idea.' Eve shook her head firmly. 'Our circles hardly overlapped, Rupert's and mine. He was a popular man in his quiet way—made many friends through the Garden Centre. There've been plenty of callers this last fortnight that he's been on sick leave, or so he told me. But I can't give you details. I'm out a great deal in the daytime. Besides, Rupert's front door is out of sight from Plumtrees. Our great-grandfather was quite advanced for his time. Thought his coachman deserved a little privacy. Appletrees wasn't thought of when the cottage was built, of course.'

Eve seemed more relaxed now. All the same, Baxter felt he'd better not push his luck. Besides, poor Armstrong looked in need of nourishment.

'One last question, then. Who, to your knowledge, visited your brother on the day of his death?'

'I did. Just after breakfast.'

'Who else?'

'I saw no one enter or leave the cottage.'

'That's not a straight answer.'

'I'm sorry, Chief Inspector, but it's the only answer you're getting from me this morning. It's absurd to suppose that the cottage was broken into in broad daylight, and I refuse to believe that any of his daytime visitors was responsible for a later break-in.'

More bluster, but the distress behind it was obvious. Eve's voice was strained now and high.

'There's more than the trespass to be considered,' Baxter reminded her.

Eve sighed. 'I firmly believe that my brother did away with himself, and that any properly conducted forensic tests will back me up. But I'm not God. We were at one on some issues, Rupert and I. We both felt free to kill ourselves if life became unbearable. And agreed that each of us must judge our own time. We'd no dependants, you see. Rupert is a childless widower. My daughter Ginnie and I have never been close. The young people who share my house and my resources come and go. I'm fond of them, of course, but I avoid over-involvement. Also, Rupert and I agreed to help each other commit suicide if so requested.'

'A serious offence in the eyes of English law.'

'Even if the suicide is terminally ill and the helper a qualified medic. Don't I know it! And in that respect, as in many others, the law's an ass. It hurts me to think that Rupert might have turned elsewhere than to me for help, and I've no reason to suspect it. But if I should be mistaken, the last thing in the world I'd want is for his helper to stand trial. For which reason, I refuse to amplify my answer to your question about visitors.' Her hands were fisted now, bearing down on her plump thighs.

'I don't have to tell you, Mrs Parsingham Wells, that it's an offence to hinder the police in the course of their duties.'

'That's right, you don't.' She jumped down from her perch, smiling defiance. 'Do you really suppose, Chief Inspector, that I can be browbeaten with threats of prison? I've been to Holloway three times, remember, for deliberate violations of laws I didn't respect. If the need arises, I shan't shrink from a fourth visit. In fact, it would be a comfort to use Rupert's death to advance the cause of voluntary assisted euthanasia. I like to think he would have approved.'

Baxter, disinclined to bang his head against this particular brick wall, brought the interview to a close. He was surprised, but considerably relieved, that Eve made no difficulties about a visit to the path. lab. later in the morning to identify the body.

'Euthanasia!' Armstrong repeated as soon as they were out of earshot. 'Strange that she didn't for one minute entertain the nastier possibilities.'

'Oh, but I think she did.' Once or twice, very briefly, before pushing them back under the surface. The first time—for reasons Baxter couldn't begin to fathom—had been right at the beginning of the interview when she had told him her brother was left-handed.

CHAPTER 8

'Tea and toast, please.'

'Make that two.'

Baxter couldn't remember seeing Bill Armstrong walk

past sausages, bacon and tomatoes without so much as a sniff. 'Stomach trouble?'

'Fadge trouble.'

'Come again?'

As they took their seats in the half-empty canteen of Cambridge City District HQ, the Inspector obliged. 'Last night's fadge—Ulster potato bread. We've Maureen's grandmother staying while Ma-in-law spends a few days with her sister in Slough. Old doll takes the line that no woman's fit to be a wife and mother unless she produces a batch of home-baked bread every other day. Maureen, like a fool, plays up to her. Everything was fine until Gran discovered Maureen couldn't do fadge. So she set about teaching her. And Maureen, to Gran's mind, is a slow learner. So it's try, bloody try again. Also waste not, want not. Irishwomen of Gran's generation have a folk memory of the famine, I reckon. Anyhow, there's been fadge on the supper-table four nights in a row, and I'm stuffed to the gills with it.'

'Talking of food . . .'

'If you must.'

'The PM should give us a lead on the time of Parsingham's death, if nothing else. Assuming he had high tea at five, as per usual.'

'About the only lead we're likely to get from what we've collected to date.' Armstrong did battle with a miniature milk carton.

'Something I want to check on downstairs when they've sorted things out a bit.' A large office on the floor below was to serve as an incident room, and Baxter, as Acting Investigating Officer, would have the use of a smaller office next door.

When they poked their heads round the door ten minutes later, the incident room looked if anything more chaotic than on their first visit.

'High tech, they call it!' The fiftyish Office Manager gestured helplessly at a man in British Telecom overalls on hands and knees before a floor socket and a uniformed PC who was disembowelling a computer terminal.

Baxter's eyes roved over the telephones, modems, fax machine and other assorted hardware. 'Look good when it's finished, Terry. Superintendent Highcroft's going to love it. That media release . . .'

'Got it out OK, sir. Used the 'phone next door. Here's your copy of the transcript.'

'Good man.' Baxter had kept it as low-key as possible. *Mr Rupert Parsingham was found dead early this morning at his home at Chesterton Lane, Cambridge. A police investigation of the circumstances of his death is in progress. A fuller statement will be made today or tomorrow.* 'Great. Word for word. And no comment, mind, when the newshounds come baying. Everyone clear on that?'

'Of course, sir.' The Office Manager's lower lip protruded in a wastn't-born-yesterday pout.

'Fine. Be out of your hair in a minute, Terry. At the path. lab., if anyone's asking. Let's have a shufti at this lot first, though. Over here, Bill.'

He led the way to a corner desk where a young WPC was numbering packaged exhibits. 'Mind if we have a quick riffle, Officer?'

He could sense her resentment as his clumsy fingers muddled her neatly sorted piles, but he persevered until he found the packaged suicide note.

'Look there, Bill.' He pointed at a dirty mark to the left of the page, two-thirds of the way from the bottom. 'Half-registered it when Bly showed me this in the garage, but I couldn't be sure. Not sure enough to mention it to his sister.'

'So what's so special? Fingermarks—where he'd steadied the paper. Oily and dusty, which'd fit if he'd written the note after fitting the hose connection.'

'Or trying to fit it and failing? Go on, Bill . . .'

'Afraid I'm not with you.'

Baxter smiled at the unwillingly immobilized WPC. 'Be glad of a peek at the prints that were lifted from this note, Officer, plus all the others from the garage. Assuming you can locate them quickly, that is, things being as they are in the office.'

'No problem. Filed them myself. Shall I bring them next door, sir? You'd be more comfortable.'

An eviction order. Baxter, mindful of the territorial struggles of his own years at a corner desk, went quietly. Within a couple of minutes he had the prints in front of him.

'OK, Bill. The suicide note, first.' Armstrong peered obediently over his shoulder. 'See what was bugging me?' The oily print had been joined by a host of others undetectable to the naked eye.

'Wrote the note with his right hand, that's for sure. And his sister swore he was left-handed.'

'So?' Baxter prompted.

'So—I dunno.' Armstrong's eyes roved to the other prints. 'Could've hurt his left wrist twisting the hose, d'you reckon?'

'In which case, why'd he use it on the mop and the driver's door of the van?'

'Mm . . . Hey, something wrong here as well!' Armstrong was squinting at the prints from the hose and exhaust pipe.

'Wrong how?'

'If you twist something tight, you go like this, don't you?' Armstrong clenched air, fingers bent and bunched, thumbs extended. 'Look at those prints—they're nowhere near right. Fingers splayed, thumb balls hardly making contact. Whether or no Parsingham could've fixed that hose, he wasn't doing it when he left this lot. That's holding, for Pete's sake, not squeezing.'

'After someone else's prints had been wiped off, d'you reckon?'

'Why else?'

'But if that someone had been there at Parsingham's request, helping him on his way and risking imprisonment, you'd think the old boy would have done a decent cover-up. He wasn't stupid—must have guessed prints might be taken. So maybe he wasn't trying.'

'And the suicide note? Reckon he could've used his right hand there to arouse suspicion?'

'Let's take it up with his sister, shall we? After the post-mortem, and after we've given that cottage a proper going-over with Wendy's assistance.'

'Wendy—DS Powers?' Armstrong brightened visibly.

'Pizza dough, wouldn't you say, Baxter?' Dr Stallburn, the forensic pathologist, held up something half-digested between a long pair of tweezers.

'Take your word for it, if you don't mind.' The Chief Inspector was concentrating on his deep-breathing, anti-nausea routines.

'Olives, Parma ham, tomatoes, mozzarella—and, yes, a sprig of dried basil. Nice, light pastry. Green salad—lettuce, fresh chives and basil, if I'm not mistaken. Raspberries with yoghurt dressing. Coffee? Harder to be sure of the liquids till we've tested. But yes, I'd say coffee.' Armstrong, po-faced, made detailed notes, keeping his eyes on his notebook.

'Makes me feel lunchish myself, actually.' The pathologist's bleak face softened. 'Nice to think the old boy had such a tasty meal before the end.'

'How long before the end?' Baxter managed.

'From his meal-time, do you mean? An hour—an hour-and-a-half. The Parma, you see—'

'OK. We understand he normally ate at five. Would a six to six-thirty death fit your other data?'

'Very well.' Stallburn nodded approvingly at the corpse as if at a cooperative patient. 'Tissue analysis suggested a time between five and seven.'

'And he died where he was found?'

'No marks to suggest otherwise. No sign that anyone else laid hands on him. Carbon monoxide suffocation pure and simple, so to speak.'

'Arthritis in both wrists, you said earlier. Bad enough to affect his grip?'

'Bad enough to prevent him fixing that hose, you mean. I'd say so, but without taking specialist advice I couldn't be sure. Major systems were in fair shape for his age and if the adrenalin was flowing . . .'

'Not to worry—it probably doesn't matter.'

Over sherry in the more congenial atmosphere of the pathologist's office, Baxter elaborated on the prints evidence.

'Suspected murder, then? You'd wonder why. Poor old bugger—a maverick, but well liked. We don't have much time for gardens, Polly and I, but to judge by the buzz when the word got round half my fellow-consultants seem to have taken his advice on matters horticultural and personal. Guide, philosopher and friend type, they'd have me believe. But the *Nil nisi bonum* syndrome may have been at work. Ready for a fill-up?'

They refused. Baxter stood up and Armstrong followed suit.

Stallburn extended a well-scrubbed hand to each in turn. 'Got your colour back, both of you. Couldn't send you out the way you were—bad advertisement. Poor old Parsingham. As I say, you'd wonder why. Your job to winkle that one out, I suppose!'

As if truth were a gallstone. Probably was, in some modern poem or other, Baxter reflected as he passed the Festival posters in the hospital foyer. The Parsingham case had put paid to his chances of seeing *Don Giovanni* and *Spin City*. The Mozart opera would be an undiluted loss, but he'd have gone to the fringe show purely for love of Emma. Musicals, in his opinion, had gone steadily downhill since *My Fair Lady*, Sondheim always excepted.

'Keep wondering about that blackmail theory,' Armstrong said as he, Baxter and DS Wendy Powers foregathered outside Parsingham's cottage. 'Doesn't fit with anything we've dug up on the old guy to date.'

'So let's keep digging.' Baxter used the keys under the typewriter to unlock the two remaining drawers and the dead man's desk. 'These and the waste-bin for starters—take your pick.'

Wendy inspected the confettied contents of the bin. 'Bags this, if nobody minds—I'm not bad at jigsaws.'

The drawers were considerably less challenging. Baxter's drawer yielded a Cambridge Building Society savings book, which recorded transactions for the previous five years. Rupert had put away monthly sums increasing over this period from five to twenty pounds, making small annual withdrawals at Christmastime. The account stood at £387.

There were also manilla folders with date labels containing correspondence. Baxter flicked through three of the most recent. They held letters on gardening topics, mostly, some apparently arising from talks Parsingham had given on local radio. Reply dates had been noted on all, but there were no copies of the replies. The horticultural correspondence was interspersed with a few letters and Christmas cards from friends and relatives, but none suggested emotional intimacy. Two of the folders in Armstrong's drawer contained the typed texts of talks delivered on radio or to local horticultural societies. A third held cuttings of gardening articles by Parsingham and others.

Here and there, both detectives found items which had apparently been filed at random, and perhaps in haste. These were mainly discount vouchers for petrol and other consumables, but there were also a few betting-slips and race cards.

'Guilty conscience, do you reckon?' Armstrong asked. 'Don't suppose his sister's a lover of the Turf.'

'Hardly. How are you doing, Wendy?'

She looked up, flushed, from the side table on which she had spread the scraps of paper. 'Give me a few more minutes, will you, sir? This could be important—it really could.'

The others made a superficial study of the contents of the bookshelves. Popular biographies, thrillers, travel books—secondhand or paperback for the most part. More gardening manuals for the common reader than heavyweight texts on horticulture. The collection of a man of modest means and modest scholarship. But a houseproud man. The books and shelves had been dusted within the last few days.

The two men went into the kitchen which had evidently been made out of a Victorian larder and pantry. In one corner they found the folded tea-trolley, a few tiny crumbs still adhering to its surface. There was a milk carton and an empty pizza packet in the waste-bin. The uneaten half of Parsingham's last meal had been stowed in the table-top fridge and a scent of coffee hung around the sink.

They went upstairs. The smaller of the two bedrooms had evidently doubled as an office. Its contents included a typist's chair and desk, on which stood a projector and word-processor. Boxes of slides were ranged on one shelf, ring-bound folders on another.

A camel dressing-gown hung behind the door of the larger bedroom, and the bed was made up. There were several dozen family photographs dating from the dead man's childhood and much earlier. That recurring whiskery figure, often in tropical kit, must be Sir Rupert. The silver-backed brushes on the dressing-table bore Edwardian hallmarks.

The most recent wedding photograph had been taken in the nineteen-fifties, to judge by the tight-bodiced dress with its long, swirling skirt. The bride, who looked far younger than her groom, was holding out her left, ringed hand to the photographer. Her right tugged at Parsingham's sleeve, as though urging him into the future. For reasons that he couldn't analyse, that image moved Baxter more than anything he had seen in the garage. He wondered when and why she had let go.

'Look here!' Armstrong's nasal rasp recalled him to the present. The Inspector was kneeling on the haircord carpet in the landing, sniffing at a minute brown mark. 'Peat, like they found downstairs. There's another spot just inside Parsingham's bedroom, and in the bathroom.'

Where the hand towel hung askew on the rail and a sheet of tissue floated in the loo bowl. Hardly Parsingham's style.

'Time for Bly's boys and girls to extend their activities.' Baxter rang HQ Control on his handset and left a message for the Senior Scenes of Crime Officer. 'And for us to have another go at poor old Eve.' The prospect gave him little pleasure, as he led the way back to the living-room.

'SOCOs should be back within half an hour, Wendy. Will you please make a thorough search of the bookshelves down here, when you've finished with the waste-paper basket? Could be some private papers tucked away. Then the upstairs shelves and cupboards, once they've been fingerprinted. Any luck with that litter?'

She straightened, shaking her black hair out of her eyes. 'Nearly done, sir. Bit hard to read, because the scraps of paper won't lie flat, and I've one or two gaps to fill. But all the same . . . Look.'

It was a photocopied letter. Baxter took in at a glance the preprinted heading of the Parsingham Institute for the Scientific Study of the Tropics, a March date and a STRICTEST CONFIDENCE directive. The addressee was a Professor G. T. Warleybridge, Head of the Department of Microbiology in the University of the North Pennines, to whom a Dr Julian Otley had evidently made a job application. The writer was Dr Eric Finchley, Director of the Parsingham Institute, where Otley was employed—or had been at the time of writing. The tone of the reference was more-in-sorrow-than-in-anger, its content damning. Baxter re-read the salient phrases: *long history of psychiatric illness . . . at least two serious recurrences since graduation . . . undoubted brilliance . . . unpredictability . . . aggressive outbursts . . . lapses of concentration . . . failure to verify data.*

'A hatchet job, wouldn't you say, sir?'

Baxter nodded. And there was something else. In the lower left portion of the reconstituted page, there was the photocopied print of a man's left hand. He looked again at the spatulate fingers, the swollen thumb-joint, and matched the image against others they had seen that morning.

'Well, Bill?'

'Parsingham's—bet you what you like.'

Wendy looked into each of the men's faces in turn. 'He copied this, do you mean? He kept it? But why?'

Armstrong reminded her of the assorted £50 notes.

'Blackmail? You mean the old man blackmailed Otley? But that's horrible. Enough to push the poor chap over the edge, if there's any truth in Finchley's assessment of his mental state.'

'Horrible and possibly untrue. So we'll keep it under tabs for the present, shall we? Get the photographer to snap this when he comes, Wendy. God knows how long they'll take with the professional reconstruction. Now for Eve.'

Mrs Parsingham Wells was in the kitchen as before, but no longer alone. Another elderly woman, like enough to have been her sister, but more conventionally dressed and coiffed, was helping her wash up lunch dishes at the sink. As the detectives entered the house, a wall phone rang.

'Don't worry about a thing, dear! I'll cope!' The visitor sprang into action. Eve made a face as she led the way from the kitchen to a larger room at the front of the house. 'Thank God for a diversion! Cousin Esther loves coping. Misses her lost status on the Bench, I suspect. Sit!'

They were all at eye-level this time, in 'forties-style tub-chairs of patched imitation leather. Baxter spotted chewing-gun on the arm of Armstrong's and hoped the seat of his own pants was unscathed.

'Your cousin is a magistrate?' Baxter flicked in vain through his mental register of the local judiciary.

'Was—not is. Retired. And she sat in Surrey, alas. I rather relished the thought of being brought up before her for a breach of the peace, but no such luck. Ever since she's moved back to Cambridge, she's been abominably interfering. I rang through Rupert's obit notices to the papers just now with heavy emphasis on *House Private*. Did Esther take the hint? Did she heck! Kindly meant, but one longs to be alone. You are here, I take it, with a purpose?'

'You may remember I asked you which hand your brother used,' Baxter began very quietly. 'The left, you said.'

She nodded, stiffening as she had at the formal identification.

'The evidence we've collected so far supports your statement—with one exception. The note that was found in his pocket was written with his right hand.'

'You're sure?' It was almost a whisper.

'Quite sure. Why should he have done that, do you suppose?'

Eve fisted her stubby hands and pressed them together. Tears filled her faded brown eyes. 'To tell me he wasn't ready to go. To tell me he was being murdered.'

CHAPTER 9

'I half expected it,' Eve said after a long silence. 'The geraniums, you see.'

'The geraniums your brother wanted you to water?' Baxter prompted.

'Yes. What Rupert grew were pelargoniums. Same family, but he was a stickler for the general name. Old schoolmastering habit, I suppose. Told myself at first he'd been teasing, but he wouldn't have . . . not at a time like that.'

'But why use his right hand?'

'We'd this game when we were children. We were both left-dominant, but somewhat ambidextrous—Rupert especially. We taught ourselves to write with our right hands as a means of sending coded messages. Statements written with the right hand were untrue—so you had to guess which hand had been used in each sentence before you could decode a letter. We became fairly adept. There were giveaway signs if you looked closely, but the grown-ups were unaware.' A quick smile, as quickly clouded.

'Do you want us to find your brother's killer, Mrs Parsingham Wells?' Baxter asked.

The question seemed to take Eve by surprise. Then: 'Yes—yes, of course! He wanted to go soon, I'm sure. But if he wasn't quite ready . . .' There could be no doubt that this hypothesis caused her deep distress.

Baxter nodded. 'Then we'll need your cooperation. Did your brother make a will?'

'Shouldn't think so. As I told you before, he'd nothing worth . . .' Again, her voice trailed away.

'Could you give us the name of his solicitor?'

'Garbutt, Garbutt and Castle. Mind you, Harrison Garbutt's the only one of the bunch I'd trust, and he's on holiday. Anyhow, I don't suppose Rupert had dealings with them since his business folded.'

'I must ask you again the question I asked earlier. Who, besides yourself, saw your brother on the day of his death?'

'No one who could conceivably have killed him.'

Baxter counted five under his breath. 'At this stage we're looking for pointers, not criminals. If Mr Parsingham let something drop to a visitor . . .'

She sighed. 'You won't let this go, will you? All right. One was Dolores Finchley—Eric Finchley's wife and a very good neighbour to Rupert and myself.' Eve paused as if to let the encomium sink in. 'Dolly told me she'd looked in yesterday morning to see if Rupert wanted any shopping done. He didn't. You won't find her at home, by the way. She'll be in London for some weeks. Voluntary social work in Kensington.'

'I see. Who else?'

'According to Dolly, Phil Beresford called at the cottage around lunch-time. He's Rupert's ex-employer. Owner of the Middlefields Garden Centre, Trumpington.'

'Any others?'

'Only Stacey Caldwell, to my knowledge. She popped over about twelve—before Beresford, I imagine—to collect some cutlery Rupert had promised to lend me for my party. First-night party for *Spin City*. Emma will have told you?'

Baxter nodded curtly.

'Caldwell with a "d"?' Armstrong checked. 'And her address?'

'Stacey sleeps here and she spent most of yesterday here too, making decorations for the garden-party. Normally she spends her days at Julian Otley's flat. Quiet for her work, she says. Green Street—not sure of the number, but it's over a shoe-shop.'

The detectives exchanged glances.

'Julian slept here too last night, as a matter of fact. Both of them left early this morning before . . . before I found Rupert. Julian works at the Parsingham. Stacey's American—historian turned playwright. But you must know this, Chief Inspector. She's a friend of Emma's. Wrote the book and lyrics for *Spin City*.'

'*That* Stacey? Sorry. Didn't make the connection.' Irrational anger swamped Baxter's pity. What right had this garrulous old woman to drag his daughter's name into a murder investigation?

'No more questions?' Eve's bluster had failed her. She looked shrunken, exhausted.

Baxter tried to speak gently. 'Not now. The Scenes of Crime team will be back, I'm afraid, to complete the search of your brother's home. You'll appreciate why?'

She nodded dumbly.

'Good. We shan't trouble you further today.'

Eve reached for his sleeve. 'There's something else.'

Obedient to her gesture, Baxter resumed his seat beneath a poster of Nelson Mandela.

'Last thing I wanted to come out, but I must put in my oar before Stacey does. Wonderful young woman, clever too, but not the world's best judge of character. English character, anyhow.'

'No?' Baxter belched discreetly.

'Fact is, someone cut the brakes of my trike a couple of months ago.'

'Good God!'

'Camouflaged the damage with insulating tape—not a

brilliant job, but good enough to deceive me without the benefit of my reading specs. First thing I knew I'd lost control half way down the drive. Zoomed straight out on to Chesterton Lane and into the path of a lorry. That would have been that in the morning rush hour, my usual time for leaving the house. But it was only seven-thirty—I'd decided late the night before to attend a Deep Green meeting in London. The road was quiet and the lorry-driver managed to take evasive action. Welsh chap—frightfully shaken up. Found myself recommending hot, sweet tea. Real WRVS stuff.'

Baxter caught Armstrong's eye and raised interrogative eyebrows. The Inspector shook his head. 'You failed to report the incident?' Baxter checked.

'*Decided* not to. Lorry-driver didn't argue the point for long—he was already behind schedule.'

'Didn't the chap who repaired the tricycle ask awkward questions?' Armstrong put in.

'Chap, Inspector! I was stripping down car engines long before you were thought of. Bertie, my late husband, was a qualified mechanic. No, I bought replacement brakes—did the job myself. My bad luck that Stacey caught me at it and insisted that the police must be told.'

'But you silenced her?' Baxter asked, amused in spite of himself. 'How and why?'

'Emotional blackmail, I'm afraid. Not a weapon for a feminist to be proud of. Why? Who'd want police and reporters swarming all over their place?' Especially not if there were druggies among their houseguests, Baxter reflected.

'But we're talking about criminal damage with intent to endanger life,' Armstrong put in. 'Surely, as a responsible citizen—'

'I'd been irresponsible to leave the trike out at night. A temptation to some unfortunate psychopath.'

'Who might do more damage to the next victim?' Armstrong's Belfast brand of moral indignation had a cutting edge.

'That occurred to me afterwards. At the time, I was concerned to protect Damien Ronson. Former member of our collective with a petty juvenile record. Stacey suspected him, and I guessed she wouldn't be alone, but I *know* he wasn't responsible.' Eve's left hand decapitated an invisible objector.

'No? So why did Stacey disagree?' Baxter asked.

'There'd been a row among four members of our community who were working on the roof repair. According to the other three, Damien wasn't pulling his weight. He was hauled over the coals at House Meeting—not for the first time. I'd pleaded for special consideration in the past—he's just eighteen and he's spent half his childhood in care. This time I felt the censure was justified, so I let the "Conform or get out" ultimatum go through without comment. Next morning poor Damien and his van had departed.'

'Was that when you found your brakes cut?'

'No. Twenty-four hours later. I'd left the trike under cover in one of the outhouses on the evening of the House Meeting. Rain had been forecast. Stacey's line is that Damien couldn't find it straight away when he left, and was in a hurry to get off the premises. Came back the next night, according to Stacey, to administer my personal punishment.'

'Which makes some sense if he'd anticipated your support at the House Meeting,' Baxter suggested.

'He'd want to hit back—of course he would. I can see him slashing the brakes, but not applying the sticky tape. Lacked the guile, for one thing. Besides, you'll never persuade me he was a murderer. Never!'

'But you expect Stacey to finger him? Break her word to you after two months' silence?'

'Because of Rupert's murder . . .' Her mouth twisted. 'You'll soon be issuing a new media release?'

'Yes.'

She sighed. 'When Stacey hears the news, she'll be on to you straight away. It's absurd, of course, to make that connection. Damien had nothing against Rupert. And, besides, if he'd . . . done either of us any harm, he'd have been daft to show up last night.'

'He was here? At your party?'

'Would have been, but for Stacey. She met him on the drive, she told me. Sent him packing.'

Once back in the police car, Baxter radioed a request for an all-stations alert, and massaged his stomach. Life, his insides were telling him, was becoming altogether too complicated.

The plump receptionist at the Parsingham Institute marked her place in *Seventy Summer Suppers*. 'I'll try Dr Otley for you.' But not too hard, Baxter suspected. 'What name shall I say?' Her fingers hovered over an intercom keypad.

If the Chief Inspector's rank and occupation sparked a flicker of curiosity, she wasn't letting on. 'Down in a tick, he *says*,' she reported in a tone that might have been cynical or plain bored. As she resumed her study of Macaroni Magic, Baxter pottered about the spacious entrance hall with Detective-Constable Gary Browning in his wake. In his present weary state, he was guiltily glad of a companion too junior to draw attention to weaknesses in his conduct of an interview.

The interior of the Institute was superficially more attractive than the Downing Street frontage in its present state of grime. But there was nothing inside to match the mélange of palms and serpents and elephants' heads on the area railings, or the exuberantly carved foundation date, 1887, which was also the year of royal jubilee.

Perhaps, Baxter mused, the stuffed crocodiles and allegorical marble maidens for which he had hoped were tucked away behind the door labelled DIRECTOR/DIRECTOR'S SECRETARY. This waiting area, with its models in well-lit showcases, blown-up colour photographs and TV monitors offering on-demand video presentations of the Institute's recent achievements, might have been part of any modern museum.

With a sense of having seen all that too often before, Baxter turned his attention to the leafy banisters of the staircase. He was kneeling on a low step lecturing Browning on the finer points of the wrought-iron foliage when he was interrupted by throat-clearings. He got up hastily, brushing dust off his knees. Damn sneakers. The thin young man was wearing them—who wasn't, nowadays?

'Dr Otley?'

The newcomer grunted, frowned. 'What can I do for you, Chief Inspector . . . Black, is it?'

'Baxter. Be grateful for a few minutes of your time, in connection with the death of Mr Rupert Parsingham.'

'Parsingham?' The tone was chilly. 'Don't want to sound disobliging, but I'm hellishly busy, and I hardly knew the old chap.'

Nor liked him, Baxter surmised. 'But you knew he was dead?'

'Well, yes. Stace—a friend—mentioned it on the phone at lunch-time. Did himself in, she reckons.'

'I fear not.'

'You mean someone . . . God! That's incredible.' Julian clapped a hand to his mouth, as if to adjust its expression, 'Poor bastard. All the same . . . don't see where I fit in.'

'You spent last night at Plumtrees, I understand?'

'Yes, but I didn't see the old boy. That's when it was done, was it?'

Baxter avoided the question. An elderly couple in shorts

and sunhats had come in by the front door and were bearing down on the receptionist. 'We'll be interviewing everyone who was in the vicinity of his cottage yesterday, Dr Otley. Routine. Now is there anywhere we can have some privacy? Your office?'

'Shared.'

'Come out for a cuppa, then? Thirsty weather. Where'd you suggest?' Baxter, who had lunched late off cheese sandwiches in the police canteen, spoke from the heart.

Julian, still clearly reluctant, conceded that Tattie's, if approached through the grounds of Downing College, could be reached within five minutes and might, at this off-peak hour, provide a quiet table. This they found on the balcony screened by a sycamore. Baxter gazed through its branches at the pinky-gold collegiate buildings in the classical style which he found most congenial.

'Fire away, then!' Julian blew on his black coffee. Not his first that day, to judge from the smudges under his reddened eyes.

Browning took a clean page in his notebook.

'Care to give us a run-down of your activities yesterday afternoon and evening, Dr Otley.'

'Worked in the Institute lab and my office till around seven-thirty. Biked home for a snack. Back to the Parsingham until eleven or so. Home again to pick up some gear before biking to Plumtrees.'

'Any witnesses?'

Julian frowned. A handsome face, half way between Michael Ignatieff and an emaciated Keats. The look that appealed to maternal women of Baxter's acquaintance. 'Bloke who shares my office left for the day around five. Guess the other staff on my corridor had gone before I did, too. Didn't see anyone as I let myself out and in again. I've a key to one of the back doors. Next time I saw anyone I know was at the Plumtrees party. Remember speaking to

Mrs Parsingham Wells and Paul Sinton and Emma Baxter. No relation, I suppose?'

'My daughter,' Baxter replied tersely. 'There's something else, I'm afraid. We found the torn-up copy of a letter which concerned you in Mr Parsingham's cottage. Any comment?'

'I'm bloody astonished, that's all!' But also embarrassed, to judge by the sudden flush.

'Can you suggest how it came to be there?'

'Not a clue. What kind of letter?'

'A reference written by your Director.'

'Good God!' Surprise, but relief as well. 'Can I have an eyeful? Brought it with you?'

'No, and if I had I wouldn't be prepared to let you read it at this juncture. It was written in strictest confidence.'

'But surely you can give some indication of the contents?' Julian's angry colour had faded. He took his first sip of coffee.

'Only to say I could understand your concern about the letter falling into the wrong hands.'

'A bad reference, then.' Julian chuckled. 'But you drew the wrong conclusion. Six more weeks and I shake the dust of the Parsingham off my feet. Couldn't give a toss what lies my present employer cooked up about me. Said I was mad, shouldn't wonder?'

'Are you?'

Julian sipped more coffee and smiled. 'Why should I answer that?'

Baxter drank tea and smiled back. 'You don't have to. On the other hand, I'm conducting a murder inquiry and I need to evaluate the trustworthiness of the evidence I collect. You might save me some time and yourself some embarrassment if you came clean.'

'OK, just testing. Only too ready to come out of the psychiatric closet, so to speak. Condition goes by the name of post-traumatic incident syndrome. May sound a mouthful, but I can tell you I was bloody glad when they came up with a correct diagnosis and effective treatment programme. Just six months ago, that was. Problem goes back to when I was nine. Car accident. Schoolfriend's father was driving, his mum was in the passenger seat. She went through the windscreen—died instantaneously, so they said. The father took longer. Hell of a lot longer.'

'Before your eyes?'

'Yep. My friend and I were trapped in the back. Tim banged his head—no compulsory seat-belts then—and passed out.'

'You remained conscious?'

'Uh-huh. Broke a few ribs—medics patched those up OK. They didn't do such a good job on the nightmares and daymares. All sorts of stimuli would set them off—a wooded hill like the crash site, a flowery design like the pattern on Tim's mother's dress. My parents didn't always notice. When they did I couldn't find words to explain. Sounds daft.'

'No.' Baxter recalled his own childhood horror of a tiger skin rug and his fear of naming the fear.

'Symptoms eased off gradually during my grammar school years. Next instalment came my second October in Cambridge—one of those blue-and-gold Michaelmas days.'

'Another car crash?'

'I was sitting in the front seat of a bus in a traffic jam on Castle Hill when a cyclist twenty yards ahead tried to overtake the jam and swerved into the path of a lorry. Girl with buck teeth and red hair and a Newnham scarf. Nobody I knew. Red hair and redder blood. They held up the bus to make way for the ambulance. They'd have let me out, I suppose, but I couldn't budge. It felt as if I was trapped in the back of Tim's father's car again. Waiting and watching. They carried me out in the end.'

'To hospital?'

'Uh-huh. More shrinks. More hospitalizations. More drugs. Nobody seemed to get to the nub of the problem. Having gone off the rails rather flamboyantly at one of my Tutor's sherry parties and again in Chapel, I guessed some mention would be made of my medical history when I sought a post-doctoral post at the Parsingham. Dr Finchley's weapon was sent gift-wrapped, as it were.' Julian laughed.

'What gave him cause to use it?'

'Fear of the brain-drain, I guess. When an academic outfit loses too many research staff in a short space of time it begins to lose credibility.'

'There've been other recent defections?'

'No more than from other British university institutions, perhaps. But Dr Finchley takes these things very personally. I guess anyone who's been fundraising and publicizing day in day out for twelve years is bound to be ego-involved.' A guarded note had crept into Julian Otley's replies.

'Why are people leaving?'

'The usual reasons, mostly. Pay, conditions, promotion.'

'You hope to better yourself in these areas?'

Julian smiled. 'In Karachi? Not financially, anyhow. Other factors have influenced some of us. Ethics, if you like.'

'Oh?'

'Nothing dramatic. Just the feeling that PISST—bloody apt acronym—is an anachronistic relic of Empire. That a tropical research institute should be sited in the tropics. I've met undergrads who wouldn't dream of taking a post there. For some of us, conversion to their point of view came later. On a fieldwork assignment two years ago, in my case.'

'That's when you started trying to make a move?'

'Oh no. I'd the psychiatric problem, remember. Also, although I'd ceased to believe in the legitimacy of the organization, I'd no doubts—still haven't—about the legitimacy of the project I was heading.'

'Can you fill me in on that?'

'Only roughly. It's strategic research. Our detailed findings are confidential to our clients, an ASEAN pharmaceutical consortium with United Nations backing.'

'ASEAN?'

'Sorry. Association of South-East Asian Nations. We're analysing the self-cleansing systems of certain marine micro-organisms found in the Pacific. The aim is to provide scientists in our clients' Singapore-based biotechnical laboratories with the blueprints they need to create improved versions of these organisms for use in local marine cleansing programmes and hopefully for export.'

'Thus pipping the established multinationals to the post?'

'Right!' Otley's enthusiasm was obvious. 'Speed was of the essence, you see. If I'd backed out early it mightn't have been possible to find a suitably qualified substitute straight away.'

'But you did back out in the end. How was that?'

'Personality clash is the standard phrase, I suppose. Dr Finchley breathed down my neck rather. Requested fortnightly progress reports. Got his secretary to make copies of my data sheets with and at least once without my consent. Caught her at it.'

'Do you believe you were singled out for special treatment?'

'Sure I was, from what my friends told me. Hard to prove, though. When I tackled Finchley, he just hinted that I was being paranoid—part of my general instability. That shut me up for a bit. I was afraid he was right. Until my friend Stacey—Stacey Caldwell—came along.'

'Was she staying at Plumtrees then?'

'Yes. And researching in the History Department. Eve

Parsingham Wells found her a temporary job in the Institute to help her through a financial crisis when she chucked in her research and her grant. That's where we met. Stacey bossed me into getting myself properly diagnosed and treated. Made me see that Finchley's behaviour was paranoiac, my reactions normal. Persuaded me that I'd work better in an environment where I was treated as a sane responsible adult. That's when I started applying for other jobs.'

'Risking the success of your project?'

'Not at all. The bulk of the work's done. The deadline's nine months away, and we're ahead of schedule. Cambridge is bursting with young microbiologists who could wrap the thing up on time, with the prospect of a follow-up contract to motivate them.'

'No regrets, then?'

'Yes, but my work in Pakistan will be equally important. And there with luck I'll be treated as a mature scientist, not a neurotic schoolboy. Besides, I'm grateful to the Karachi appointments board for disregarding what must have been another bad reference from Finchley. First time I've even made the short list.'

'To get back to the letter. Would it surprise you to know that Rupert Parsingham himself photocopied it?'

'Amaze me. I've only spoken to him once or twice at the Director's parties. Grim occasions, but I went with the rest in my first year.'

To curry favour? Surely not. Why, then, did Julian look embarrassed? 'I get the impression that you didn't much like the deceased.'

A grimace. 'No, to be frank. I was disgusted by the way he kept looking at Mrs Finchley those evenings at Appletrees—must have been twice her age. Not that she would have let him lay a finger . . .'

'Did you ever see Parsingham at the Institute?'

'In passing, yes. He and his sister often rendezvoused there. He'd pick her up in his van—wait for her in Valerie's—Mrs Gates's office. She's the Director's secretary.'

'And in charge of personnel files.'

He nodded, biting his lip. 'Filing cabinet—same office. Look, I haven't a clue what's behind this, and I don't care. But if Finchley found out Mrs G. had left that cabinet open, he'd go bananas. Give her the sack, perhaps. And she's not a bad stick . . .'

Baxter smiled. 'I've no immediate intention of raising the matter with the Director.' He sipped tea. Tepid—his preferred temperature. 'You'll want to be on your way, Dr Otley. Thanks for being so frank.'

A blackbird in the sycamore contributed a timely coda. Baxter's pocket radio joined in.

CHAPTER 10

'So friend Julian's an unlikely blackmail victim—always supposing there was a blackmail victim. Agreed?' Baxter checked.

Bill Armstrong and Wendy Powers, now conferring over a second round of tea in the Chief Inspector's Cambridge cubby-hole, made affirmative noises.

'Which is not to say he mightn't have killed for some other reason,' Armstrong added. 'Jealousy, for instance. He's no proper alibi as yet, and who's to say he's one hundred per cent sane?'

'Which of us is?' Powers murmured.

Baxter nodded. '*Nobbut thee and me, and even thee's a bit daft* . . . True, Wendy. Let's keep Bill's point in mind, though. Meanwhile, what joy at the cottage?'

'Thought I'd check up on the peat, sir.'

'Peat?' Baxter asked stupidly. Information overload was setting in. Time to switch off for the day, his central nervous system was telling him. But he daren't. Not yet.

'They found traces,' Powers reminded him. 'On the rug below the window and upstairs.'

'From Parsingham's garden?'

'Seemingly not. All the bags of compost on his premises were peat-free. I didn't trouble Mrs PW, but her cousin was positive that Rupert hadn't used the stuff for twelve months or more. He was involved in a Fenland conservation campaign.'

'Lord, yes. Remember Sarah telling me, but I didn't make the connection. Any other ideas?

'The Beresfords—Rupert's Trumpington employers, assuming they weren't campaigners. Suppose Phil made a return visit?'

'Sounds like our best bet. Anything else, Wendy?'

'Don't know if it matters, but I found a TMA instruction sheet tucked inside a book.'

'Come again?'

'Tutor-marked assessment, Open University.' Bill Armstrong, whose wife was a spare-time student of long standing, provided the translation.

'Really? What subject, Wendy?'

'Third-level honours course in economics, dated July of last year. Also there were some recent texts on economics and politics stashed away behind horticultural books in the spare room. No reason why Parsingham shouldn't have taken OU courses. Plenty of old folk do. But why hush it up?'

'If you'd seen and heard as much of his sis as we have, you'd understand,' Armstrong assured her. 'Mature students need morale-boosting and Eve's hardly one to be tactful about bad grades.'

'OU enrolment may well be a cardinal sin among the

Cambridge mafiosi,' Baxter added. 'Any other finds, Wendy?'

She shook her glossy dark head. 'Sorry, sir.'

'Don't be. My fact-crunching plant is feeling the strain. What's new with you, Bill?'

'Nothing that could explain the £4,600. According to the transactions in his Natwest account, Parsingham's sole sources of income were his state pension and his salary from the Garden Centre.'

'Which was—?'

'Meagre. £7,000 or thereabouts.'

'No occupational pension from teaching?'

'I queried that. Bank manager reckons that if he'd taught outside the state sector he'd have been insured through a private scheme and could have cashed in when he set up in business.'

'Withdrawals?'

'Nothing exciting. Largest recurrent item was a monthly standing order for £150 to his sister. Token rent, presumably. Otherwise, irregular small cheque payments—to local shops, mostly. Small withdrawals from cashpoints.'

'And his will?'

'Everything to the sister, but Goronway Garbutt confirmed that he'd little to leave.'

'So Eve owns Plumtrees?'

'Not outright. In view of the trike development I raised the issue of her resources. My informants switched off—confidentiality, much as my job's worth, the usual. But when I pointed out that her daddy's will is in the public domain, Garbutt unbent a millimetre.' Armstrong paused to dunk his second ginger nut—a slow process in the cooling beverage.

Baxter chewed his Rich Tea with the thoroughness recommended by his gastro-enterological consultant and counted ten.

'Old Ralph Parsingham made a pile as a stockbroker,

but Garbutt reckons he'd a conscience about his deviation from family tradition,' Armstrong volunteered at last. 'Anyhow, he left the bulk of his estate to the University.' Armstrong consulted his notepad. 'To be used to further the scientific study of the tropics.'

'At the Parsingham Institute?'

'There was no formal stipulation, but that's where the money went. Appletrees had been leased to the University rent free for the use of directors of the Institute ever since Ralph's father's retirement. Ralph said this arrangement was to continue through his children's lifetimes, perhaps to prevent redevelopment.'

'And the family legacies?'

'Ralph's wife had predeceased him. Son Rupert got £25,000—a sum worth having twenty-three years ago—which he blued on the market-gardening venture. Eve got the contents of Plumtrees, some of which had belonged to her mother. Plus a life interest in the house, grounds and cottage. Plus the income from trust holdings valued for probate at around £50,000.'

'And subsequently multiplied by six or sevenfold under competent trusteeship?'

'The lawman clammed up on that one, and on the current value of the property. Eve's life interest, whatever it was, would have been transferred to Rupert if she'd died first. So maybe Ralph didn't trust his son's financial competence a hundred per cent either.'

'What about the grandchild . . . Eve's daughter?' Baxter checked.

'A nun—doesn't fit, does it? Grandfather Ralph left £10,000 to her convent.'

'So who gets the properties and trust capital when Eve and Rupert are dead?'

'The University. Same earmark as before. To further the scientific study of the tropics.'

'Interesting—very interesting. If Julian Otley's to be believed—'

'Big if,' Armstrong cautioned.

'Eric Finchley's got a motive for eliminating the brother and sister, hasn't he? Plumtrees is on a prime site—sale of the house and grounds should yield a handsome sum, even allowing for planning restrictions on redevelopment. Sum that could be more than doubled if Appletrees were thrown in. If Finchley's as devoted to the Institute as Julian would have us believe, the prospect of a massive injection of capital must have been very appealing.'

'True. Fund-raising must be an uphill struggle these days. And with only a couple of septuagenarian mavericks standing in his way . . .'

Baxter shivered a little.

'One of whom, according to Julian Otley, has been making passes at his wife,' Armstrong continued.

'OK, OK. We'll talk to Finchley. But not yet—I need to do some homework.'

'What next, then?'

'I want someone to mind the shop in case young Damien is located. Also, the Office Manager may need guidance on the finer points of the Super's new computer system. And seeing as Wendy was his star student on the advanced induction course . . .'

The softest of sighs as Powers brushed crumbs off her dark green dress. She knew Baxter well enough to be sure she'd get her share of the action sooner or later, so no time-wasting gripe.

Which was one of the characteristics he appreciated in his favourite detective-sergeant. That and her sharpness and trimness and humour. And how much did the Welsh lilt in her voice and her shiny black hair count for in the assessment? He worried about these things when he was making out reports. But not for too long today.

She stood up. 'Where'll you be, sir?'

'Green Street—Julian Otley's flat. With luck, he'll still be at the Institute, and we'll catch Stacey Caldwell on her own before curtain-up.'

'What would a scriptwriter be doing at a second night anyhow?' Armstrong wondered aloud.

'Ushering, prompting . . . who knows? From what Emma's told me of shoestring productions, everyone's expected to do everything.'

Five minutes later Stacey greeted them through a mouthful of pins at the door of the top-floor flat.

'OK, OK.' She cut into Baxter's introduction. 'Eve told me to expect you. But I'd appreciate it if we could get through quickly. I'm helping out with costume repairs, and you see how it is back there.' She gestured across her shoulder to the scene in the living-room behind her. One young man was at work at an ironing-board in one corner. A second stood, arms outstretched, whilst a third pinned up the sleeves of his academic gown. A girl was feeding something tartan and voluminous through a sewing machine.

Baxter nodded. 'We'll be as quick as we can. Somewhere else we can talk?'

'The bedroom. Go on through.' Stacey indicated a door, lingering a few moments to negotiate with her co-workers.

The seating options comprised a mattress laid on the floor, and two canvas director's chairs. The detectives chose the latter. A mistake, Baxter realized, when Stacey flung herself on the mattress a few seconds later, and stared up at them, hands clasped behind her curly fair head.

'You don't mind, do you? When I'm screwed up like I've been this last couple of days I think better lying down.'

'No problem,' Baxter muttered. It was, though. *Screwed*

up hadn't helped. She wasn't to know that he'd had this thing about curly-haired blondes ever since . . . oh hell.

'Funny, a woman like Emma having a fuzz for a father.' Stacey eyed him with interest, as though visited by literary inspiration.

They were all at it, dragging Emma into the case. The child with Sarah's eyes and his cheekbones who had grown up one year in London when he was too busy to notice. The woman of whom he knew almost nothing that mattered. Not even what she would like as a birthday present.

'You saw Mr Parsingham yesterday, we understand,' he began.

She nodded. 'At lunch-time. But only for a few minutes.'

'Tell us about that meeting.'

'Not much to tell. I was in and out within five minutes. Eve had asked me to collect some cutlery she was borrowing for her party.'

'What did you do after that?'

'Made paper lanterns until four-thirty, as I'd been doing for most of the morning.'

'In Mrs Parsingham Wells's company?'

'Our paths crossed now and then, yes. But I worked mostly in my room. I was edgy about the show and other things. Personal things. Didn't want company. Four-thirty, I shoved off to Eastside Community College, where *Spin City* is playing, to help with various last-minute chores. OK? Ask Emma if you want.'

Baxter addressed the air above her head. 'Let's get back to your meeting with Mr Parsingham. What was his state of mind, would you say?'

'Low. But no worse than at other times over the previous fortnight.'

'You'd been a frequent visitor?'

'Over that period, yes. To help Eve out—she was really

concerned about him. He'd had a virus infection, which pulled him down, I guess. That and the prospect of quitting his job.'

'Did he ever talk about taking his life?'

'No, but he wouldn't to me. We weren't tight.'

'Oh?'

'Look, don't get me wrong.' Stacey sat up, ran her fingers through her curls.

Baxter's gaze dropped. She was Mary Martin, damn her, washing that man right out of her hair, and he a nine-year-old in the Upper Circle at Drury Lane.

'Rupert was a nice old guy,' she was saying. 'Kind, sympathetic. A good listener—up to a point. But when I went on too long about serious issues, he'd blank off. Make a joke or dish out some Pollyanna-brand reassurance. This I couldn't relate to. And people like that can't cope when Fate plays the joker. So it crossed my mind more than once that Rupert might kill himself. Can you be sure he didn't?'

'Quite, I'm afraid.' Baxter forced himself back into his middle-aged and professional present.

Stacey's open face puckered. 'Oh hell. What could anyone get out of killing him?'

'Money?'

'Didn't have a dime. At least . . .' She frowned.

'Well?'

'Look, I don't know . . . I could be wrong.'

'Tell us all the same.'

'One Sunday—five weeks or so ago, it would be, I called to see Rupert. Left my purse behind. Guess he didn't hear my knock when I came back. Tried the handle, and the door wasn't locked. I was late for a date with Julian so I sang out and barged in. Not for the first time. Rupert had never minded before, but that day he looked quite put out. He stashed something into a drawer double quick and I could've sworn it was banknotes.'

'He offered no explanation?'

'Nope—and in tbe best English tradition I let on I hadn't noticed. But it bugged me. Rupert never came across as a miser. Generous to a fault, I'd have said.'

'And obliging?'

She stiffened. 'What's that supposed to mean, Chief Inspector?'

'In photocopying that reference, for instance. If he did so on request, that is. I take it Dr Otley's been in touch.'

She nodded. 'Julian knew nothing about that bloody reference—need never have known. Why'd you have to tell him?'

'He's clearly an interested party.'

'If Julian had wanted to copy the stuff in his file, he'd have done the job himself, wouldn't he?'

The sewing-machine buzzed in her long silence.

'That all you propose to say on the subject, Ms Caldwell?'

'I'm not clued up on British law. Do I take it that unauthorized copying would be an offence?'

'That's right.'

'And the case would go to court if I admitted to complicity?'

'I doubt it, but it'd be up to the Crown Prosecution Service. You have, of course, the right to remain silent on the matter.'

'And if I do?'

'We'd probably raise the issue with Dr Finchley. Dr Otley thought that might make trouble for his secretary.'

'Yeah, he's a soft spot for old Valerie. Can't say she showed me much sisterly solidarity during my three months with that outfit, but twelve years' exposure to Finchley has probably eaten into her soul.'

'You found him uncongenial?'

'Our paths hardly ever crossed—if he could tell one

junior secretary from another he sure as hell didn't let on. But I saw enough of the way he harried Julian to hate him. Finchley's an ecologist, two-bit ecologist—what I hear. Modern microbiology's way outside his range. And Julian's work is world class, according to his colleagues. OK, he'd a temporary psychological problem—told you, he said.'

Baxter nodded.

'But that's history. He'd really got his head together before I left the Parsingham to write full-time. About six months ago, that would be. Julian had started to believe in himself—in his ability to find a better working environment. Then Finchley applied the double-bind. Stepped up the petty interference and blocked his efforts of escape.'

'How could you be sure of that?' Armstrong asked.

'Not just from Julian. I nosed around, sounded out his contemporaries. Everyone gave me the same story. The jobs he was being turned down for in Cambridge and elsewhere were going to his inferiors. Which could only mean Finchley was badmouthing him.'

'Did Dr Otley share your view?'

'Not at first. And by the time he did he was feeling too boxed-in and depressed to take any action. When I suggested he should have a peek at his file, he was horrified. Shot me the school prefect line about sneaking. Nor was he prepared to confront Finchley and demand to see what he'd written. But I couldn't just sit on my hands and watch him cracking up. Which is why I turned to Rupert.'

'You asked him to filch Dr Otley's personnel file?' Baxter checked.

'Yeah. Last May, I asked him. Sounds crazy, I know. I'd have done the job myself, but Valerie knew I'd been glad to quit the place, and it would've looked kind of sussy if I'd started hanging around. Whereas Rupert was there at least once a week to pick up Eve and her shopping, and most often she'd be late.'

'Did he agree right away?'

'Not right away.'

'Did money change hands?'

'You just have to be joking. OK, I've a little capital from my grandmother's estate, which is why I could afford to give up the Institute job. But just enough to launch myself as a playwright, and most of it's tied up in the States. Besides which, Rupert would have been mortally offended . . .'

Baxter didn't think she was lying. 'Go on, please.'

'At first he flatly denied that a Director of the Parsingham could do the dirty on a fellow-scientist. Guess I hadn't registered up to that point how much the Institute meant to him, how proud he was of the family connection. But once I presented my evidence, he crumbled. He didn't say, but I got the impression that he'd other grounds for disliking Finchley.'

'Something to do with Mrs Finchley?' Baxter asked softly.

Stacey leapt to her feet. 'Eve dropped hints, did she? Just because Dolly's a Filipina and she was so goddamn possessive of her little brother! Emma's dad or not, you're as bad as the rest. Scratch a fuzz and uncover a frigging stereotype.' She retreated to the window.

Baxter rose rather wearily. 'Mrs Parsingham Wells dropped no hints that I was aware of, but Dr Otley seemed to think her brother was attracted—'

Stacey swung round to face him. 'As was Julian, before I came on the scene. Dolly's a very attractive person. Which doesn't mean that she has it off with every guy who propositions her.'

Wherever that speech had come from, it wasn't from the script of *South Pacific*. 'Look, Ms Caldwell, no one's saying—'

'But I bet they will, you know.'

Baxter held his peace.

Stacey slipped gear, spread apologetic hands. 'Guess I'm not helping Dolly any by going all defensive. She visited with Rupert quite often—out of kindness, I'm sure. Helped him catalogue his slides and stuff like that. My guess was, she'd let slip that her marriage was less than fulfilling, and that Rupert would have given his all for a suit of shining armour.

'Anyway, he shed his scruples pretty fast, and agreed to my plan. With the proviso that if the file contents were as libellous as I suspected, there'd be a showdown with Finchley in which Rupert would do the talking. I think he meant to force Finchley to resign.'

'When was the file copied?'

'Second and third weeks of June. Don't remember the exact dates. Rupert needed two bites of the cherry—Eve nearly caught him at it the first day.'

'And when was the showdown?'

'It wasn't.' She returned to the mattress and sat down, knees drawn up to chin. 'My doing.'

'Why so?'

'If the references had been all of a piece, I'd have had no doubts. But the last one Finchley had sent to Karachi—its file copy, I mean—was way out of line with the others. It was favourable. Glowing, even. No hint of a psychiatric history.'

'Remember the date?'

'May, but further than that, no. Julian was really keen on the Karachi post—he'd just been shortlisted. Last thing I wanted was to spoil his chances. So I begged Rupert to hold off until the appointment was made.'

'And afterwards?'

'We both sort of backed down. We began to doubt whether the evidence was strong enough to pressure Finchley into resigning. Also, I was still concerned about the impact on Julian. He wasn't finding it easy to accept the fact that I wouldn't be coming to Karachi with him.

'But mainly, I guess, other priorities took over. I'd begun to work round the clock on *Spin City*, and I got the distinct impression that Rupert was involved in some new project of his own.'

'What sort of project?'

'That I don't know. It was little things. Like, he began to take more interest in the evening paper I'd bring over next morning from Plumtrees. He'd chuckle over some item or other, and clam up when I asked him what the joke was. Then there was the episode of the banknotes. Private business venture, I guessed. It annoyed me somewhat that he didn't confide in me, but I was glad he'd something to take his mind off his retirement.' She glanced at her wristwatch. 'Oh my God! I need to eat before the show, and there's nothing more I can tell you about Rupert.'

'Mrs Parsingham Wells was sure you'd want to tell us about Damien Ronson.'

'Oh-oh.' Stacey bit her lip. 'Twenty-four hours ago I'd have shot my mouth off on the subject.'

'So what's new?'

'Your daughter, would you believe, Chief Inspector?' A giggle. 'Thought you mightn't appreciate that.'

Stay out of this, Emma! But she'd always gone her own way.

'She and Paul Sinton saw me turf Damien out of Plumtrees last night. I was so mad about him showing up again, I told them about the damage to Eve's trike. Has Emma put you in the picture?'

'Mrs Parsingham Wells.'

'No kidding? Well, your daughter reacted by accusing me of class prejudice, which didn't sit well with me at the time. But since what happened to Rupert, I've revised my position somewhat. I was wrong to badmouth Damien. He'd motive to kill Eve, sure, but I've nothing else to go on. And as far as I'm aware, he'd no grudge whatsoever against poor old Rupert. Guess somehow it'll be a long, long time before I call anyone else a murderer!'

'Glad to hear it.' All the same, Baxter hadn't the slightest intention of letting up on the hunt for Ronson.

CHAPTER 11

On his way downstairs on Thursday morning Baxter caught sight of his daughter's minivan.

'Emma back?' he asked Sarah as he joined her at the breakfast-table.

'Mm.' She licked marmaladey fingers. 'Told you last night she'd rung, didn't I, to say they'd fixed her van?'

'You did. Slipped my mind.' He helped himself to muesli. No need for Sarah to know he'd taken the van trouble as an excuse. She'd remind him fast enough that Emma had never felt the need to lie about her sleeping arrangements. That she wasn't likely to start now.

'How's the neck?' Sarah asked.

He rotated it cautiously. 'On the mend. So you noticed?'

She nodded.

'Then why the hell—'

'You know why, Richard.' He caught her quizzical eye. They'd been through this many times before, especially in their last fraught year in London. Emotional withdrawal was a weapon of last resort. Silent martyrdom would be silently ignored.

'Sorry, love.'

All in all, Wednesday evening had been less than satisfactory. Jaded after the interview with Stacey, Richard had returned to his temporary office and forced himself through two hours of tedious but necessary paperwork.

Things had improved temporarily on the drive home. His late start had delivered him from the rush hour traffic out of the city and the later incoming streams of Festival patrons. His spirits had risen at the prospect of Sarah's cooking and cosseting. A little drink perhaps, an early night . . .

Then he had read her note on the fridge. He had quite forgotten about the monthly meeting of the Holtchester Horticultural Society. No point in sulking. The contents of the casserole were fragrant if mushy. He had dined off a tray in the living-room, munching slowly and drinking moderately. Balking at the prospect of the early but empty bed, he had dozed off on the settee to the accompaniment of Mozart's C Minor piano concerto.

But Wolfgang Amadeus had let him down. Disturbed by Sarah's headlights around eleven, he had jerked into consciousness and pain. Piqued by his wife's failure to pick up his non-verbal signals, he had fended off her inquiries about his day's work and faked absorption in ground cover, the horticultural topic of the month in Holtchester.

He must, he supposed, have been dozing when his daughter came home. But he'd spent most of the night awake and rigid, ill-prepared for a 7.30 call from Police Headquarters.

'ACC Crime wants you to report to him at eight-fifteen, sir, before you leave for Cambridge. Says the jewel thefts investigation has come off the back burner . . . No, nothing else, sir.'

One murder, one aggravated criminal damage. Now this. He'd replaced the receiver, appalled.

Fifteen minutes later, crunching muesli in the sunny kitchen, he chuckled. When life becomes impossibly complicated, it becomes farcical.

'What's the joke?' Sarah asked.

He explained. They both laughed, the last barriers between them dissolving. His neck hurt again, but less sharply.

Seated now in an HQ office enlivened only by a huge map of the county, several dozen silver cups, group photographs of policemen and three fleshy-leaved pot plants, Baxter waited for the Assistant Chief Constable to clear his throat. For this was the preliminary to Littleton's every significant utterance. A nervous habit, Baxter assumed. Substitute for a pipe-tamping ritual, perhaps. The man seemed healthy enough.

'Hm-hm. I sent for you, Baxter, because I had a disturbing phone call at home at five-thirty this morning. From Mrs Thurstone.'

'Mrs Alma Thurstone?'

'Hm-hm. The same.'

Baxter braced himself. Phone calls from Alma Thurstone inevitably meant trouble.

'Hm-hm. Of the Police Committee,' the ACC added unnecessarily. 'At her urgent request I made her a personal visit.'

'I see, sir.' As stand-in, no doubt. It was no secret that Alma had wiped the Shire Hall tiles with Francis Montgomery on more than one occasion. She wouldn't have thought twice about dragging him out of bed in the wee small hours.' Anything serious?'

'Hm-hm. Theft of a brooch to which she was much attached. Emeralds and rubies. Bird design.'

Baxter's spirits sank. 'That scraggy stork thing?' Alma had worn it every time he had seen her in the ample flesh, and in the photograph the local newspaper printed above her periodic fulminations.

'Hm-hm. Liver bird, actually. Liverpool emblem, y'know. Wedding present to her mother from the family shipping firm. Insured for eight thou, great sentimental value. Mrs Thurstone is naturally most anxious for its recovery.'

'Safe broken into, sir?' The likeliest hypothesis, given the hour of the phone call.

'Hm-hm, no.'

'You mean she was wearing it at the time?'

'Not that either, hm-hm.'

Baxter brightened. 'Embarrassing for her, isn't it? I mean, when she's not lambasting the Force, she's laying into members of the public who fail to keep tabs on their goods and chattels. If she's left a valuable brooch lying around . . .'

'Hm-hm. Mrs Thurstone didn't. The brooch was stolen from her youngest daugher, who had borrowed it. Mrs T. only became aware of the incident this morning. My impression is, Angela had been afraid to break the news—'

'That figures.'

'The theft occurred on Tuesday night at a Jazz Concert in the Cambridge Corn Exchange. Angela left her jacket with the brooch in it on her seat during the interval.'

'Tuesday night! In a town overflowing with Festival visitors and other assorted tourists. My God, sir, we haven't a hope at this stage.'

'Hm-hm. Probably not, Baxter. But we must be seen to make our best efforts. I feel sure the Chief Constable would wish it.'

'No doubt, sir.' The Chief Inspector was thankful that Montgomery's wishes impinged only rarely on his decision-making processes.

Baxter's visit to the Old Rectory, Fen Holton, home of the Thurstones, yielded little of substance. In demanding the early recovery of the brooch, Alma was clearly asking the impossible. The all-stations alert initiated by the ACC had been thirty hours too late. The Liver bird had almostly certainly fled the region, if not the country. Baxter made the point politely, out of sympathy for Angela, a tear-blotched nineteen-year-old who would probably have liked to follow its example.

It was ten before Baxter reached his office in Cambridge. DI Armstrong, as requested, was sorting the contents of his in-tray.

'Wendy not back from the Parsingham?' He had asked her to obtain Dolores Finchley's London address from her husband.

'On her way.'

'Coffee, Bill?'

An affirmative grunt. It had already been brewed. Armstrong helped himself to a generous segment of shortbread, not his first to judge by the scatterings of sugar.

'Dog get your fadge this morning?'

'Maureen's passed the test, so Gran's moved on to champ.'

'Sounds revolting.' Baxter unwrapped his second soda-mint of the day.

Armstrong's square face took on a dreamy look. 'Spuds, milk, chopped shallots, all mashed up with a well for the butter. Great stuff, but filling. So I'm lucky it's not a breakfast dish. How'd it go with the Thurstones?'

Baxter gave him the gist. 'What's new that I need to know about?'

'Couple of leads on Damien Ronson. Traffic cop cautioned him for speeding Monday last. He was driving a candy-striped Ford transit—eye-catching number, wouldn't you say?'

'Which he'll have flogged pretty quick if he's anything to hide.' Baxter rubbed his stomach.

'We've also got three addresses supplied by his former

probation officer, and we know he works off and on in the roofing trade—'

'Where cowboy contractors are two a penny. Oh, great! Sorry to wet-blanket, but it's obvious that we'll get nowhere fast with the trike business unless we go public. And the ACC—pressurized by Eve—has vetoed an early media release. What else, Bill?'

'DI Mercier of the Met wants a personal word. Be in conference, he said. He'll ring you back.'

With an invitation to some Met shindig, no doubt, which like many another would have to be turned down. Baxter wouldn't miss the wining and dining bit too much—there'd be few familiar faces from his London days. But he relished the after-dinner gossips on police and antiques matters with his old friends Lou and Jo Mercier.

DS Powers arrived as Baxter was scanning the printouts in Armstrong's top priority pile. He gestured an invitation to coffee.

'How'd it go, Wendy?'

'I'm not sure, sir.' She smoothed the skirt of her pink cotton two-piece.

Nervous gesture. Not like Wendy to be nervous.

'Slight problem with Dr Finchley's secretary, to begin with.'

'Valerie whatsername?'

'Gates. She knew me by sight, unfortunately. Lives next-door but one to Keith's mother.' Keith—the estate agent and house-sharing boyfriend. Time was, a house-sharing boyfriend would have been grounds for dismissal from the Force.

'Does she know your job?'

Powers wrinkled her nose. ''Fraid so. And worse still, she twigged I was on the Parsingham case.'

'Hell.' The whole point of sending Wendy was to keep the thing discreet, low-key. To avoid embarassing Finchley.

'I didn't confirm or deny—but I'm sure she suspected. Also, I've a strong feeling she's something she wants to unburden. She followed me out into the entrance hall when I was leaving—actually grabbed my arm. Then the receptionist came after her with some query or other and I scarpered.'

'Could've been hoping to pick up some gossip,' Armstrong suggested.

'Could have, but Val struck me as a sharp lady. I'm sure she'd know better.'

'How'd you get on with Finchley?'

'Stuffy bloke—like his office. I played it as per instructions. Explained that we wanted to question everyone who had seen Rupert on Tuesday—that his wife's name was just one of three Eve had given us. That Mrs Finchley—or perhaps he himself—might be able to add other names to that list.'

'And?'

'He said he couldn't come up with any names. Volunteered a rundown on his own programme for Tuesday, by way of demonstrating how few opportunities he had to observe Rupert's cottage. But it came over as a little defensive.'

'Where was he at the times that mattered?'

'Parkside swimming-pool, he says. Five forty-five to six forty-five.'

'Mention meeting anyone he knew?'

'No. Didn't think you'd want me to ask at this juncture.'

'Quite right.'

'All the same—and, mind you, sir, this is just a hunch . . .'

'Fire away.' Wendy was canny with her hunches.

'I believe he's a fair idea of the approximate time of death, which he certainly didn't get from me.'

'Mm. Talked to Eve on Wednesday morning, didn't he?

She might have said something about the state of the body when she found it.' But that wasn't enough. 'Get a contact number for Mrs Finchley?'

'Not sure. He gave me the number of a migrants' welfare organization she'd worked for at one time, but he claimed not to know her current whereabouts.'

'Odd. Could be he's shielding her,' Baxter said. 'If she's involved with domestic workers at risk of deportation.'

'Could be, but he was really edgy. My guess is he's scared she's walked out on him.'

If so, why? Baxter asked himself. Also, why now?

'So when do I get my gold medal?' Clive Sinton emerged unhurriedly from his son's bathroom and lowered himself into the only comfortable armchair in the small Victorian flat.

'Silver.' Emma played his game for Paul's sake, and despised herself for it. 'This morning's effort was your penance for skipping the Plumtrees party.'

'Which will incidentally get you out of a visit from the cops,' Stacey put in. 'Eve's been asked to supply them with a guest-list.'

'Furthermore,' Emma continued, 'Eve was the one who softened up the Eastwave TV team and I was the one who spent yesterday morning on their producer's doorstep.'

'And finally,' said Stacey, now embarked on a stretch-relax routine on the hearthrug. 'Finally, Clive, you just loved belting out those gags about the Camford higher education system. Bet they transmit every last one, and scrap the *Spin City* footage.

'Let me guess.' Paul abandoned all pretence of studying an 1851 Census Report. 'He gave them the one about Cambridge being the only place in the world where wet feet are a status symbol. Am I right? Also the one about the light blues of the—'

'Stuff it!' Clive fired a cushion. 'I'll settle for a bronze gong. Anything is better than hearing my finely honed one-liners being done to death. God knows how I sired a son with a cloth ear for the rhythms of his native tongue. No fault of his mother's.'

'Mum rang me when you were out, Dad.' Paul addressed the space above his father's head. Oh God, Emma thought. Why did I bother? This is going to spoil everything. He's making a terrible hash of sounding casual.

'She's managed to wangle Saturday off work,' Paul went on. 'So she'll be coming to the final performance and shacking up here tonight. And I thought, if you can hang around that long, Dad, why don't we all eat together somewhere cheap and cheerful after the show? You, Emma, Mum and me. Stacey and Julian too, if they'd like to.'

'Yes, why not, Clive?' Stacey urged. 'I just love family reunions. You get a whole new slant on your friends when you see them interacting with Mom and Pop.'

Paul flinched, but Clive seemed unruffled. 'Can't think the Sinton generation games will make scintillating spectator sport. But you can chalk me up for tomorrow's team, Paul, if I can talk my way out of dinner with my agent. Where d'you keep your phone?'

'Hall. Oh—just remembered. A bloke left a message for you, Dad.' He dug in his hip pocket and handed his father a crumpled piece of paper. 'Rang about an hour ago. Didn't leave his name, just the number. Said it was rather urgent.'

Clive read the digits, wrinkling his elegant nose. 'Cambridge number, too. Chair of Drama going begging, perhaps? Honorary D.Litt.? How d'you say no in Latin?' He got up, stretched and unhurriedly left the room.

Stacey departed to the kitchen to make coffee. Emma perched on the arm of Paul's chair, and began to play with his hair. 'Pleased your dad's accepted the invite?'

'Mm. And surprised he agreed to meet Mum in Cambridge. I get the impression he holds the place responsible for their divorce. God knows why.'

'When was it they split?' Emma searched her memory for the few scraps of family history Paul had vouchsafed in their Lancaster student days.

'Seven years ago. But it was a bumpy ride for as long as I can remember . . . They stuck it because of me, I guess, but I often wished they'd get it over with. It was rough hearing him shout one minute, plead the next, seeing her try not to cry in front of me.'

'And neither remarried?'

'No. They've had other relationships—quite a few in my father's case—but nothing seems to work out. They can't live with each other or without each other, it would appear. Corny old cliché.'

'Sad old cliché.' Emma kissed the crown of his head. 'For them—and you.'

'Yeah—well.' He caught her right hand and kissed its palm. 'I wonder sometimes if I've inherited the jinx, if any marriage I make will founder. Daft, eh?'

'Utterly daft.' But Emma, who had her own reasons for giving matrimony a wide berth, disregarded the mute appeal for a reassuring cuddle.

Clive reappeared when they were drinking coffee, but refused to join them, saying he must be on his way.

'To stake your claim to the Chair or the D.Litt.?' Stacey prompted.

An instant's blankness before he switched back into facetious mode. 'Both, of course. Besides which, there's this rumour that HRH will shortly chuck in the Chancellorship.'

Stacey giggled appreciation, but Emma, sensing a new anger beneath the bonhomie, was puzzled and a little frightened.

'Spare us an hour of your precious time for lunch or

supper, sir?' Paul's heavy-handed humour didn't help.

'Not today. Sorry, folks—truly.' And perhaps he was, Emma thought. 'Something's cropped up, as they say. But I'll keep the Saturday dinner-date, so help me, and I'd like to foot the bill. Ring my hotel when you've made a booking. OK, Paul? I'll let myself out.'

'OK,' Paul said in a bleak voice and reached for his census report.

'Better shift my ass too.' Stacey drained her coffee mug. 'With any luck the sewing-party will have quit Julian's place by now, and I can get down to some work.'

She made tracks for the kitchen. 'Did I tell you, Em?' she called over her shoulder. 'I've been rerunning some tapes my grandma made for me when she was dying? About Brooklyn the way she remembers it from the 'thirties. And they've given me this fantastic idea for a new musical—'

Paul raised his eyes to the plaster ceiling-ornament.

'Tell me in the van,' Emma called back. 'I'll run you over to Green Street on my way to Brixton. Had an offer of a house-share there, which I want to reccy. See you at the show, Paul. Oops! Sorry, Stace.' The two women had collided at the door between hall and kitchen. Stacey's hand sent the telephone receiver flying and with it a scrap of paper.

As her friend bent to retrieve both, Emma saw that the paper bore the message 'Dad, please ring' and a six digit number which meant nothing to her but something, apparently, to the American.

'About this dinner-party on Saturday—I'm gonna take a raincheck,' Stacey said on the way downstairs. 'Tell Paul it's not personal.'

'OK—but why the flip-flop?'

They had reached the front door of the house before Stacey answered. 'Truth to tell, Em, I'm going off Sinton

Senior fast—on account of the company he keeps. Know whose call he was returning just now?'

Emma shook her head. None of anyone else's business, she tried to say but couldn't.

'Dr Eric Finchley's. That's the number of his direct line at the Parsingham.'

Emma followed her friend across Mawson Road in puzzled silence.

CHAPTER 12

Lou Mercier rang Baxter just after lunch.

'Drinkwater—You're sure it was Drinkwater?'

'Listen with Uncle, boy. It's all on your desk at Holtchester District, but I gather you're on the hoof. Simon Drinkwater, as ever was. Ex-Eton, ex-Balliol, ex-Pentonville. Heavier, browner, but the same eyebrows. For Chrissake, Dick, which of us could forget those eyebrows? Nine-thirty this morning I'm seeing off these customers of Jo's at King's Cross, when I rumble our old pal behind a ticket barrier.'

'Heading where?'

'Heading for the Smoke. Having stepped off a train from Cambridge, sleepyhead. So, bearing in mind your little local difficulties—'

'You brought him in? I appreciate this, Lou, I really do. If there was one brain behind those jewel thefts, it had to be a good one. And quirky. Which fits old Simon.'

'Aka Sam Dunnett nowadays. Been breeding racehorses in Argentina for over a decade now, according to our info. Squeaky clean as far as Interpol can tell us. Which is why my bosses won't bring him in without good cause.'

'For crying out loud! One session with our Alma bloody

Thurstone is good cause in anyone's book. If you'd any idea of the grief that woman's caused us . . . I've half a mind to pass her the word, Lou.'

'You wouldn't.'

'Why wouldn't I?'

'Apart from the job's worth angle, there's the old pal's worth angle. Remember the runaround friend Drinkwater gave me last time, only to stumble into Wee Willie Brougham's arms? Which happy event put our Willie into orbit. It's Commander Brougham now, would you believe?'

'Courtesy of Simon D? Come off it, Lou. You oversimplify.'

'Maybe so. All the same, Drinkwater owes me, and he's not going to make a monkey of me again. Which is why I'm backing Them Upstairs. Stands to reason he's not carrying a load of rocks on his person. So it's obbo and nothing but obbo until he leads us somewhere interesting. And if you jump in with two flat feet, Dick, we're through. I mean that.'

Lou probably did. The memory of the Lakes Bank affair hung awkwardly between them.* Not Baxter's fault that Mercier had been transferred back from the City Force to the Met without the promotion he had hoped for, but all the same . . .

'Message understood, but keep in touch, won't you?'

'Trust Uncle. By the by, Jo tells me you've never been up to see this new shop of hers.'

'Soon, Lou, so help me.' He had a sudden thought. Jo did Victorian jewellery, which fitted with a Victorian musical. Emma might fancy a piece for her birthday—or would she? Like as not, he'd end up giving her money again.

Plastic. You couldn't get away from the sight of it. Worse

* *Murder in Good Measure.*

still, the stink. In the Middlefields Garden Centre shop, the detectives' first port of call, it had mingled with flowery, earthy and fertilizer smells. Here in the store of plastic garden furniture, containers and ornaments, there was no competition apart from body odours. And Phil Beresford, who had been helping unload a lorryload of fencing, was sweating freely. At Baxter's request he opened a skylight. They sat down on three plastic chairs.

'This won't take too long, I hope? Busy time for us.' Beresford scratched his left temple. A habit born of past skin trouble? His strong brown face was faintly pock-marked.

'That will depend on you as much as us, Mr Beresford.'

A shrug. 'Tell you what I can—won't be much.'

'Let's talk about the last time you saw Rupert Parsingham.'

'Tuesday that was—day he died, poor old bugger. Two o'clock—five to, something like that.'

'You're quite sure—' Armstrong began.

Baxter frowned. 'What the Inspector means, it was an unusual time of day for a busy man like yourself to go visiting.'

'Special occasion—Rupert's retirement day. We wanted to give him a little something. My wife had intended to pop over—'

'Was Mrs Beresford close to Mr Parsingham?'

'Close? What exactly are you getting at?' Beresford's big hands fisted on his bare thighs.

'I just wondered if she was friendly with him. Friendlier than you, for example?'

Beresford opened, then laced his fingers as if to prevent a second betrayal. 'Di was softer-hearted, being a woman. Besides, her granddad was head gardener at Princes', Rupert's old college. It was different for me. Can't afford to be too palsy-walsy when you're boss, can you?'

'So why did you take your wife's place on Tuesday?'

'We'd hoped to fill a staff vacancy Monday, but things didn't work out. I decided to go head-hunting in and around Cambridge next day.'

'You can let us have names . . . addresses?'

'Sure. The wife and I can't both be off base in working hours, so it made sense for me to hand over Rupert's retirement presents.' Beresford's thumbs were playing footsies.

'Presents?'

'Yeah. Your blokes'll have turned them up, I reckon, unless the burglar got there first. Poor old Eve is really chewed up about the break-in, Di tells me. Worried that one of her pet punks might have done the job, shouldn't wonder.'

'Please describe the presents,' Baxter said coldly.

'Old print of Princes' College gardens—belonged to Di's father. Di might be able to fill you in about the artist. Plus a cheque for half a grand.'

'A print has turned up, but not a cheque.'

'Yeah, well, I suppose that figures.' Beresford's black eyes caught Baxter's and sheered away. 'Some druggy kid after cash for a quick fix. We stopped the cheque, natch, once we heard about the break-in.'

'Take us back to that visit. Notice anything special about the cottage when you arrived?'

'Special—what sort of special?' Beresford's finger-lock tightened.

'The front door, for instance?'

'A DON'T DISTURB notice, you mean? Eve told Di he'd stuck one up.'

Baxter nodded. Damn and blast Eve.

'Wasn't there when I arrived. Shouldn't have knocked if it had been.'

'Remember what Mr Parsingham was doing when you got there?'

'Let's see.' The uncertainty seemed genuine. 'Oh yes. He'd been washing dishes—lunch things, I guess. Came to the door with his hands all soapy.'

'How'd he seem?'

'Bit paler than usual—thinner. He'd been off work for a fortnight with some virus thing.'

'Did he look or sound depressed?'

'No more than usual. Di reckoned he'd been low ever since he realized he'd have to pack the job in. If so, he put a brave face on things when I was around.'

'What did you say to each other on Tuesday?'

'Word for word? Oh, come on!' Beresford's fingers were back at his hairline. 'Wasn't listening too hard. I'd plenty else on my mind—business worries. We didn't say much, come to think of it. Hardly more than hello, thank you, goodbye. He seemed embarrassed—know I was. He asked me in, but I got the impression he didn't mean it, so I made some excuse and stopped on the doorstep. Told him Di would visit at the weekend, which seemed to please him. Then I left.'

'See anyone near the cottage as you were entering or leaving?'

'Nope. Not a soul. So that's that, Chief Inspector.' Beresford got up. 'All I can do you for, I'm afraid.'

Baxter stood to confront him. 'I think not. Suppose you do what I asked you at the beginning of this interview.' Beresford's head jerked backwards. 'Tell us about the last time you saw Mr Parsingham.'

'You saying I've just given you a load of garbage?'

'We've no reason at present to doubt your account of the afternoon visit. That's not the point.'

'That was the last time I saw old Rupert, swear to God. If anyone's told you different he needs his head examining!'

Beresford looked wildly round, as if for a weapon. As

Armstrong slipped behind to block his exit, Baxter gave wry thanks for the ubiquitous plastic.

'Yes?' Baxter said softly. '£500's a generous handout from a man like yourself. Man with business worries—cashflow worries, shouldn't wonder. The little lot you've stowed here isn't earning its keep, I'd guess.'

'It will. Just what are you driving at, Chief Inspector?'

'Whoever entered Plumtrees Cottage on Tuesday night left traces of peat behind him.'

'Peat! What's that prove? Could've picked it up anywhere.'

'Not from Rupert's garden, or his sister's. And there was more—green fibre and footprints. Shoeprints, to be precise. From trainers—not sandals like those you've on you. You'd be surprised what the boffins can do with sole-marks these days. Factory of manufacture, date of manufacture, wear and tear distribution, especially if the wearer leads an active life.' Beresford made a strangled noise in his throat.

'Message received? Good, Mr Beresford. You're a busy man, we're all busy men. So if you don't feel like talking just now, suppose you just show us the shoes you were wearing on Tuesday? If you can't remember which ones, your wife may.'

'No!' Beresford staggered, then let Armstrong help him to a chair. 'Keep Di out of it. She loved the old guy. She'd never forgive me.'

'Forgive?' Armstrong echoed nasally.

The detectives sat down. Beresford stared at them dully, his eyes drifting from one face to the other.

'I didn't kill him, you know. As God's my witness, I'd nothing to do with his death.'

'No?' Armstrong challenged. 'Because whoever drove him to it made him mop the garage to cover their tracks. Which might mean they'd something mucky on their feet.'

'Swear I'd nothing to do—'

'All right, then,' Baxter cut in. 'Tell us what you did do.'

Beresford scratched his hairline, viciously this time. 'Promise me this won't get back to Di.'

Baxter shook his head. 'We can't—you know we can't. But it'll go harder with you and her and the business if you hold out on us. Think of it. Interview after interview. Police cars at your door day after day. Round-the-clock surveillance. I'm not a quitter, Mr Beresford.'

A long silence. 'All right,' he said at last. 'I went back to the bloody cottage. But not to kill, not even to steal. Oh, maybe it would count as stealing in the law books. But I went to retrieve what was mine by rights, mine and Di's. The £500 cheque she'd talked me into parting with to a man who'd no need of it.'

'No need?' Baxter's eye caught Armstrong's. 'Why'd you say that?'

'Rupert had his state pension, hadn't he? I'm prepared to bet his sister didn't charge him rent. Besides, he'd plenty of well-heeled friends. Nipped off abroad most winters for a cheapo fortnight in the villa of one old pal or another. People like that don't need handouts from the likes of me.'

'You didn't take to him?'

'Truth to tell, no. Fair do's, he taught me a lot. But there was something. I dunno . . . Partly it was the Cambridge University connection, I guess. I'm a Cockney by birth, myself. When Rupert and Di and Di's people got talking about the college gardens and college fellows, I felt pushed out, know what I mean?'

Baxter nodded. 'When did you decide to make a return visit?'

'Before the first. Early hours of Tuesday morning, when I was trying to get some shuteye.'

'And what time did you get there?'

'Twenty after midnight or thereabouts. Later than I'd intended. I'd rung Di to say I'd met a friend in a pub, which was true. Meant to do the job soon as I split with him at eleven—knew Rupert was an early-to-bedder. Hadn't reckoned with Eve's party. Heard the racket from the service road. So I beat a retreat, walked the streets for an hour or more.

'Nobody in sight when I got back. It was nearly dark, bit of a moon but cloudy. Could just about read the notice on Rupert's door when I came close. Shook me up a bit, might have put me off in my right mind. But I was woosy. Not drunk, but not reacting too fast.

'I'd no problem getting in. Sash window squeaked, but not badly. Rupert's hearing wasn't a hundred per cent. I went for the cheque first thing. Tore it into scraps, shoved the scraps in my hip wallet. That cheque was flaming well asking to be pinched, the way he'd left it on the desk beside the print.'

'Anything else out of order?'

'Not so's I noticed, but, mind, I wasn't noticing too well. Plus I'm not sure how Rupert usually kept his place. You could count the number of times I'd been there on one hand. Table in the window was laid for a meal, that I do remember. I messed things up a bit, quietly, so's not to wake him. Oh Christ. If I'd known, if I'd had any idea . . . I wasn't too keen on the old boy, but I'm not a vulture, so help me. I couldn't bear for Di to think I'd been robbing the dead.' His strong face puckered.

'You messed things up,' Baxter repeated coldly. 'How exactly?'

Beresford shook his head. 'Sorry. Can't remember any details. I was muzzy, like I said. Plus I was beginning to be scared. Plus I'd the runs. Nerves, I guess. All in all, I wasn't concentrating any too well. Scattered some books and papers on the floor, as I recall. Upended a standard lamp.'

'And then?'

'Went upstairs. Last thing I intended, but I was desperate for a loo. No sound from either of the bedrooms as I went past. It was only afterwards, when I was coming out of the bathroom, that I registered there should have been breathing.

'Then I remembered the DON'T DISTURB notice and I really got the wind up, convinced myself that the old guy had overdosed or something. The door of one of the bedrooms—the spare room, I guess—was ajar. I wriggled inside. Bed wasn't even made up.'

Beresford paused to scratch fiercely, drawing blood from his temple.

'The other bedroom door was shut. I listened again, just to make sure. I'm not a religious man, but I kept praying I wasn't going to find his body, not after what I'd done downstairs. And when I didn't, I couldn't get out of the place fast enough. The garage never entered my head until I was half way home. Too late, I reckoned. Besides, I didn't want to get involved, you see.'

'No? Who saw you leave?' Baxter asked sharply.

Beresford flared up again. 'Bastard that put you on to me, of course. All this peat business was so much crap, wasn't it?'

'On the contrary, Mr Beresford,' Baxter said wearily. '*You* put me onto *him*. "If anyone's told you different, he needs his head examining." I somehow don't think you're in the habit of hypothesizing. But if I were in your position, I'd be bloody glad of any witness I could find, sane or potty.'

'Witness? The more I think about it, the more I'm convinced that drunken sod had a hand in Rupert's death. Murderers return to the scene of crime, don't they?'

'Not if they read crime fiction,' Baxter said drily.

'No? Well, you'll not believe me, but I had it in mind to tip you off, anonymously of course.'

'Where was it you ran into this guy?' Armstrong sounded disbelieving.

'In Rupert's garden—took a header over his legs. Sticking out from behind some lavender bushes, they were. For a sec I thought he was Rupert. Hadn't been there when I entered the cottage, that's for sure.'

'What'd he look like?' Armstrong persisted.

'Oh, I don't know. Light wasn't good, remember, and I didn't see him standing. He just sat up after he'd sent me sprawling, gave me the once-over. Fiftyish, broad, around six feet tall, I'd guess. Not bad-looking for his age, but nothing special that I can remember, except for the scar on his forehead. V-shaped, it was. About here.' Beresford's forefinger hovered an inch above his right eyebrow.

'Clothes?' Armstrong prompted.

'Greenish safari suit. Shabby, but clean. Too clean for a wino.'

'Speaking voice?'

'Wouldn't know. Didn't stop for a chat. He came out with something incoherent when I made contact. When he saw me, he just laughed. And when I made off he started singing.'

'Singing what?'

'God knows. Nothing from Top of the Pops, that's for sure. Trad folk, you might class it. Bloke's voice was slurry. Only words I caught were "Stourbridge Fair".'

'Give us the tune?'

Beresford, still sweating, made an unmelodious effort to comply.

'Stou-erbridge Fai-ai-air, Stou-erbridge—'

'Like a hand with the new bumf?' Armstrong offered.

Baxter interrupted his search for a half-remembered song to contemplate the latest additions to his in-tray.

'Let's have the life and times of Drinkwater aka Dunnett. Assuming the national network did its stuff.'

Armstrong abstracted the printout, which was easily the bulkiest item in the in-tray.

Baxter skimmed its pages rapidly, then returned to the beginning. 'Want you and Wendy to read, mark and inwardly digest our Simon's criminal record, before I tackle the ACC on the subject. What I'm after more immediately is any legitimate link with the county.'

'Right.' Armstrong, mug in hand, came behind the desk to squint over his shoulder.

Baxter read aloud: 'Mm. Born 'forty-three, Bournemouth. Only kid. Father in the Parachute Regiment, killed at Arnhem. Educated Stonecrop House, Keswick, then Eton and Balliol College, Oxford. Unmarried. Not doing too well, are we?'

'Stonecrop House . . . Pure coincidence, I dare say. But, according to the piece about Rupert Parsingham's retirement in the local paper, that's the prep school he used to teach in.'

'My God. Might mean nothing as you say, Bill. But all the same, if their dates should overlap . . . Ring the school, will you, Wendy?' Whatever the outcome, Baxter felt sure that Drinkwater hadn't been the drunk in Rupert's garden. Beresford couldn't have failed to register those pointed eyebrows.

Armstrong left the office and Baxter began to read the statements so far collected from guests at Eve Parsingham Wells's party, his daughter's among them. *Stou-erbridge Fai-air, Stou-erbridge Fai-air.* The jack o'lantern phrase danced enticingly between the lines of print.

CHAPTER 13

'Stou-ourbridge Fai-air.' Baxter tried it on Sarah. As she was going on to *Spin City* they had met for an early supper in Cambridge, in a basement restaurant off King's Parade.

'Pity you can't sing in tune, love. Does it go on like this?' She hummed a slightly extended version between mouthfuls of asparagus crêpe.

'Yes, yes. What is it?'

'Something Emma's got on tape, that's all I know. Could even be in the show. Pop round with me and ask her before curtain-up if it's important.'

Emma again. Now her mother was dragging her into the case. 'Not that important. Tell me about your day.'

'Par for the course this morning. Two barneys with stroppy patients, three with hospital administrators. Odd sort of phone call this afternoon, though. From Sylvia Straker.'

'Have I met Sylvia Straker?'

'Probably not. Hon. Sec. to the Horticultural Society. She missed last night's talk and rang to check the agenda for tomorrow's committee meeting. Level-headed type, I'd have said. But she told me the oddest thing . . .' Sarah fortified herself with Liebfraumilch.

'Apparently Sylvia and her husband arrived home from holiday about three weeks ago in the early hours of the morning. Twenty-four hours early—weather had been lousy. They'd just turned into their side road—they're way out in the Fens and there are no other houses for miles—when they saw Rupert Parsingham's brown station-wagon coming towards them. At least, Sylvia was sure it was Rupert, and hooted. No reply, so she thought she might have been mistaken.

'But next morning, when she was catching up on her garden chores, she noticed that someone had fixed the windshield round their daphne bush. Neighbour's puppy had trampled it before they went on holiday. Rather sweet, don't you think?'

'Habits of immature canines?'

'Not funny. Sweet of poor Rupert to say a quiet goodbye to a garden he'd done so much for.'

'Can we be sure he did?'

'Sylvia never tackled him on the subject—so as not to embarrass him, she says. But how else would you explain it?'

Baxter shook his head. 'Sorry, love. Not up to explaining much this evening—maybe a strawberry ice will help.'

It didn't, and he was only half way through when Sarah checked her watch, shook crumbs off her swirly yellow dress and kissed him goodbye.

Ten minutes later he was back at his office desk, when his phone rang.

'Chief Inspector Baxter? Dolores Finchley.' Her voice was light and lilting, the accent faintly North American.

'Ah, good. Did you get my message?'

'Message?'

He quoted the number that her husband had provided and Wendy had rung. 'Oh no. Haven't been in touch with that Centre for weeks. They wouldn't have known where to contact me. I rang because of Rupert—when I got over the first shock. Not that I can be of much help, but I saw him the day he died. His sister will have told you?'

'Yes.'

'Poor Eve—I'd hate her to think I'd held back anything that might help you track the killer.'

'Can you come to Cambridge tonight—tomorrow?'

'I thought . . . can't we just talk on the phone?'

'I really need to see you, Mrs Finchley, and I'd like a colleague to be there. Make it London, if you prefer.'

'And if I refuse?'

'We should make every effort to find you—with the help of the Met.'

'I see. Very well.' She sounded tired. 'As Eve might say, there are better ways of spending public money.'

She gave him the address of a delicatessen near Lancaster Gate, and promised to be there between ten forty-five and eleven next morning. 'Someone's told you I'm a Filipina, I expect?'

'Yes.'

She laughed. A little bitterly, but only a little.

He pushed papers for another hour-and-a-half, breaking off every so often to breathe down the necks of the skeleton staff in the incident room. His spirits lifted as an audio-typist's screen filled with a report of a Damien Ronson sighting in the city. Then he realized it had occurred forty-eight hours before. Time to go home. He was half way there when he was radioed.

'Mr Philip Beresford—had to be you, he said, sir.' The duty sergeant sounded nervous.

'OK, OK.' Baxter turned down Mozart's Coronation Mass.

'Look, I hope you don't mind . . .' Beresford began.

Baxter heard or thought he heard accompanying scratchings. 'I'm off duty, actually. So if you want to change your statement—' More bloody paperwork?

'No, it's not that. I've just seen that bloke I told you about. Drunk I fell over in Rupert's garden.'

'Yeah? Where?' Baxter braked, eased on to the verge and prepared for a U-turn.

'On the box. Local programme called Eastwave that our girl watches. Arty-farty stuff—not my line.'

'Go on!'

'When I woke up from a kip, there was this bloke plugging some show—*Sin City*—that his son's connected with. Then he got in a few cracks about Cambridge nobs and snobs. My bread and butter, but I had to laugh. Anyway, it was the same fella. Thin lips, scar on the forehead. Same sort of voice, though he wasn't singing on the box—'

'Name? Did you get his name?' Baxter asked wearily.

'Sinton, Clive Sinton. That's S-i-n-t-o-n, I guess.'

'Sounds plausible. Keep this to yourself for the time being, will you? Thanks, Mr Beresford, and good night.' He passed back the word to the incident room and reactivated Mozart.

Clive Sinton. Clive chip-on-the-shoulder Sinton by the sound of him. Paul's father, Emma's Paul's father. And later, when Sarah and Emma came home, Baxter learnt that the song he'd been singing was indeed from the show that he thought of as his daughter's. Bloody cheek.

Not that he'd disclosed the reason for the question. Try as they might, Sinton and his like weren't going to involve Emma in a murder case.

He slept better than the night before, courtesy of Mogadon. He dreamt, as he often did in the early stages of an investigation, of eel-like creatures tangling in a murky pool. One of them was trying to swallow Alma Thurstone's Liver bird.

'DCI Baxter?' Dolores Finchley had materialized in the doorway of the Kensington delicatessen. He and Wendy Powers showed their IDs.

Dolores nodded. 'I thought we might talk in the Gardens—or a restaurant if you prefer. My friends here are pushed for space, I'm afraid.'

His brief survey of the thousand-and-one types of food-stuff crammed on to the narrow shelves inclined Baxter to believe her. 'The Gardens would be nice,' he said.

He had taken Emma to sail her toy boats on the Round Pond on occasional long-ago Sundays, but he couldn't think when he had last used this Lancaster Gate entrance.

'There's a seat down this way I often use when I'm talking to people,' Dolores said, as they skirted the fountains of Long Water. 'It's usually quiet.'

'People—clients, do you mean?' Baxter prompted.

'Just people—we're a mutual befriending network, there's no them and us. But you're here to ask about Rupert, aren't you?' Physically, she looked completely at ease in her black-and-brown cotton shift, with her black hair tied up in a hot-weather style. And mentally? She might well be a tough customer. Baxter decided to postpone serious questioning until Powers had her notebook at the ready.

They walked three abreast. As they drew level with the bronze figure of Peter Pan, Dolores halted. 'First time I saw that statue was when Rupert brought me. He'd loved it since childhood.' She spoke gently.

'And you?'

She pulled a face. 'Can't say I'm enamoured of its base. Look! All those grovelling little women and animals. Not a male rival to Peter among them. A little boy's fantasy. Rupert empathized with little boys. Not that he approved of them running wild. Eve's lodgers' kids brought out the schoolmaster in him.'

The detectives exchanged glances.

'Did Mr Parsingham ever talk of his teaching days? Mention any of his pupils by name?' Baxter asked, when they had laid claim to a bench overlooking the water.

Dolores frowned. 'Occasionally, but I doubt if I'd remember.'

'Drinkwater ring a bell—Simon Drinkwater?'

'No—oh, wait. That might have been the name of the boy he taught to conjure. Who turned to crime later on. Rupert felt responsible, I think.'

'Sounds like the one.' Baxter tried to make it casual. 'Did they have any contact after Drinkwater left school?'

Dolores shook her head. 'Not that I heard of. But Rupert could be reticent about some things—as I can. It didn't stop us being friends. I'll miss him, I'll miss him dreadfully.' She stared unseeing at the waterfowl.

'Tell us about the day he died.'

'What do you want to know?'

'What you talked about—his mood?'

'It was a short visit. Only ten minutes or so. If only . . . but that's foolish. I'd shopping to do, so I asked Rupert if he needed any errands done. He said not. I asked him how he felt—he'd had this virus. He insisted he was OK. He was rather dreading an official retirement visit from Di Beresford of the Garden Centre, he told me. Her husband came instead, I noticed later, when I was in my kitchen. We talked very briefly about me—about my work here and what else I might do. And when he said goodbye he said—' Her voice broke.

'Take your time.' Baxter touched her arm.

'He said . . . one day soon it would be our last goodbye. I said "Not yet, Rupert. Promise." And he promised. So I'm sure, you see, that he didn't kill himself. Not of his own free will.'

'But he had it in mind?'

'Oh yes. Since early May—since he realized he'd have to retire. Though I often wondered, if he hadn't known I was going away . . .'

'Going away?'

'Leaving Cambridge, leaving my husband.'

'How long had Mr Parsingham known that?'

'For nearly five years—since I started my Open University course.'

'In Political Sciences?'

'Yes. Who told you? Eve? Eric?' There was fear in her voice.

'We found an OU document among Mr Parsingham's books.'

'I see. Not that it matters now. I told my husband when I rang him last night. The graduation lists will soon be in the papers. It was just . . . if Rupert had gossiped about that, he might have gossiped about other things.'

'Your relationship, do you mean?'

'My work here, my friends,' she said in a small, cold voice.

'Did Mr Parsingham give you tuition?'

'Goodness, no. Politics were a closed book to Rupert. Didn't pay my fees either, though he offered. I raised the cash by selling patchwork, would you believe? Suitable pastime for a home-based Varsity wife, don't you think? Poor Eric had no idea I was paid for it. I registered from a London address, so that's where the correspondence went. But Rupert encouraged me, provided study cover. He'd a massive collection of botanical slides, partly his, partly inherited, which I catalogued several times over.'

'Why so much secrecy?'

'My husband was totally opposed to the idea. He'd have been quite happy for me to top up my Mod. Langs. degree from Quezon with a Master's at Lucy Cavendish. But a politically minded wife would do him no good in the University, or so he claimed. And, as far as Eric is concerned, his job comes first, second and third. You must think me dishonourable.'

'I didn't say so.'

Dolores smiled wryly. 'You don't have to. I can sympathize with that viewpoint. There should be verbal loyalty between partners even in a marriage of convenience honestly made.'

'Which yours wasn't?'

'Not quite. I met Eric when he came to Manila for a conference. I was a schoolteacher, earning just enough to keep body and soul together if I stayed healthy. There was nothing romantic about his proposal, but that didn't bother me. All I had to show for romance was a bundle of airmail letters from the States and the memory of a botched abortion.'

Wendy Powers made sympathetic noises.

'What interested me was money. My youngest sister wanted to be a doctor. My parents were also teachers, also poor. Eric promised to finance Carmel's medical education. It wasn't a great financial sacrifice. He's a private income in addition to his salary. Nevertheless, I was grateful. He said he wanted desperately to marry, he was heterosexual with no major hang-ups, but he was shy. I promised—I'm a Catholic of sorts—to make him a good wife as long as I lived.'

'But you changed your mind?'

'Yes. Nothing to do with Rupert, whatever Eve may think.'

'No?'

She sighed. 'Five years ago I found out that my husband had a pastime he hadn't told me about. Nothing illegal, nothing offensive to some women, perhaps. But to me, seeing what I've seen on the streets of Olongapo—' Her voice cracked. 'Let's just say I took my future back into my own hands.'

'And enrolled with the Open University?'

'As a means to an end. I'd met many other Filipino immigrants by then, who'd had a far rougher deal than I had, who'd been forced into emigration by poverty. And it wasn't enough for me any longer to dole out the emotional sticking-plaster. I wanted desperately to go back home, to help fight the debt problem, the social injustices, all the causes of that poverty.

'I couldn't go straight away—couldn't cut off Carmel's income while she was still training. She didn't complete her internship until last January. Besides which, I couldn't afford the fare—still can't. So I decided to study while I was waiting.'

'The BA course?'

'Yes. I'd have left Eric and moved up to Town the minute Carmel became independent, but for Rupert. I could see retirement on the horizon months before he did—his eye trouble and arthritis were so much worse. I thought if I hung on for a bit, he'd come to terms with his situation, but it didn't work out that way. I lost patience with him in the end. Started telling him to pull his socks up, count his blessings. All the usual futile platitudes. When a crisis call came for me on Tuesday, I was half glad of the excuse to go.'

'And now you don't intend to go back?'

'Only to collect some clothes some time. I've told Eric, but I don't think it's fully registered. There's a teaching job going begging in Docklands which will see me through my Master's course at Birkbeck, and leave something over for an air fare. I've friends who'll put me up free in exchange for babysitting.'

She bit her lip. 'Odd I should be offloading all this on you. Perhaps it's because my friends here have so much else to cope with. It doesn't seem fair to burden them.'

'Did Mr Parsingham tell you he was planning to kill himself?' Baxter checked.

'Oh yes. Soon after he'd told the Beresfords he was retiring. But he promised he'd work out his notice first, and say goodbye to me beforehand. I tried to raise the subject two or three times—tried to talk him out of the idea—but he was quite determined.'

'Was he often depressed these last three months?'

'Often, but not always. Sometimes he seemed rather pleased with himself, almost as though he was up to some schoolboy prank. Also, he'd taken to going out in the van at night.'

'Every night?'

'No. Two or three times some weeks—then not at all for a fortnight or more. But always in the early hours of the morning. My husband never mentioned it, probably wasn't aware. We didn't sleep together in summer. He's allergic to bee-stings, so he has nylon screens on his bedroom windows which make me claustrophobic. From the room I was using at the back of the house I could hear Rupert's comings and goings quite distinctly.'

Baxter made a hasty reappraisal of Sylvia Straker. 'Did you raise the subject with him?'

'No. I half hoped that he'd found himself a lover, someone who'd fill the emotional void when I'd gone. But it seemed a weird schedule for septuagenarian love-making.'

'Indeed. Did he ever say anything to you about a will?'

'Not as such. But he told me there was money he wanted me to have—a nest-egg to fall back on during my MA course or to pay my fare home afterwards. His savings, I suppose.' Dolores looked and sounded as though she meant what she said. 'I was embarrassed—kept telling him I didn't want it, that I'd rather he gave it to Eve to help with her roof repairs.'

'Let's go back to last Tuesday. Did Mr Parsingham have visitors other than Mr Beresford and yourself?'

Dolores frowned. 'He said Eve had been in early that morning, but I didn't actually see her. I did notice Valerie Gates, Eric's secretary at the Institute, coming out of his garden gate late in the afternoon. Four-thirty or thereabouts.'

'After the DON'T DISTURB notice went up?'

'Yes, it must have been.'

'Was she a frequent visitor?'

'No, but Eve, for all her Radical leanings, is inclined to regard the Institute staff as her personal servants. I wondered if she'd asked Valerie to run an errand for Rupert, collect a prescription perhaps.'

Or return a photocopy? 'Anyone else?'

Dolores hesitated. 'No.'

'Tell us how you spent Tuesday evening, if you will, between five and seven.'

'Me? But you can't—Of course you can. Sorry.' She fixed her eyes on the waterfowl. 'I'd been in the kitchen for at least an hour before my husband came home shortly after five. I went upstairs to bath and change while he was in his study.'

'See him again when you came down?'

Another hesitation. 'No. He'd . . . he'd said he was going for a swim before returning to the Institute.'

'I see. What next?'

'I loaded our car with the party food I'd prepared and transported it to Plumtrees. Eve had rung me in a last-minute flap about drink. Hadn't ordered nearly enough, she'd decided. Asked me to buy in extra supplies from a downtown off-licence and the Milton Tesco's.'

'*And* not *or*?' Wendy Powers checked.

'Yes. To take advantage of two special offers she'd read about. I obeyed. Crossly, but I obeyed. Left about six, at a guess. Back around a quarter to seven. Drove straight to Plumtrees. Stayed there until after the party.'

'I don't think she told us the whole truth,' Wendy Powers said when the detectives were alone. 'I reckon she was shielding someone.'

'Her husband, most likely.'

'Whom she's leaving? Why? From fear? Or guilt?'

'Or a sense of fair play? Not a British prerogative, Sergeant.'

'No, sir.' She watched him unwrap a sodamint.

CHAPTER 14

'Allow me, Chief Inspector.' The WPC whose filing system Baxter had slighted held open the main door of Cambridge District HQ. He sidled in, his arms braced beneath a carton that he steadied with his chin.

'Mr Baxter? Mr Armstrong led us to believe you'd be back rather sooner.' His path was blocked by a short middle-aged woman in a grey pinafore dress.

'Really, Ms—'

'Sister Immaculata.' In swerving to avoid her, Baxter almost dropped his burden, but achieved an emergency landing on the reception counter. 'Mrs Parsingham Wells's daughter,' the nun elaborated. 'This is Damien Ronson,' she added with a light tap on her crucifix. 'Been in the wars, as you see. Promised I'd ferry him back to keep Mother happy, but I've other errands. When will you have finished with him?'

Damien advanced, pale in the gaps between his facial tattoos. He wore a faded Grateful Dead T-shirt and parti-coloured shorts, and his left arm and leg were in plaster. 'Like I told you, Sis, there's no call for that. Not with the rafts of fancy wheels that's parked round the back here. Shan't hold out for the Merc this time round, Mr B. Ride in a posh Porshe'd do me nicely.'

Baxter unwrapped a sodamint. 'We'll take over, Sister. Find us an interviewing room, would you, Sergeant?'

Powers and he exchanged frustrated grimaces. On the way back from Town she had argued for an early assault on Eric Finchley. But Valerie Gates took precedence in Baxter's list of priorities.

He had just transferred his package to the desk in his temporary office when Bill Armstrong chucked the second spanner of the afternoon. 'Sarah's just off the phone. Like you to ring her back at the Health Centre.'

Apocalyptic scenarios flashed in fast-forward. Sarah hardly ever called him at work.

In half a minute they put him through. Her 'hi' sounded unruffled, but she'd been trained to sound unruffled.

'Hi, love. Something wrong?'

'Nothing domestic, if that's what you had in mind. It's just—oh hell, maybe I'm wasting your time.'

'Try me.'

'One sec.' As she took a reassuring farewell of a patient, he opened the carton with his free hand. The miniature chest-of-drawers gleamed darkly in its nest. 'Right,' she went on. 'I'd a Horticultural Society committee this morning—remember?'

'Mm-hm.' He'd forgotten.

'Well, over coffee everyone was talking about Rupert—he was one of our show judges.'

'Mm.'

'Sylvia Straker went through her spiel, which caused a bit of a stir, as you can imagine.'

'Easily.' Sensations were rare and prized commodities in Holtchester horticultural circles. Baxter accepted a mug of tea from Armstrong and gestured an invitation to inspect the chest-of-drawers.

'Then Barton Yarwood got in on the act. Remember old Barton? Dog-breeder, Desert Rat as was.'

'Who won the Battle of Alamein single-handed?'

'The same. But reliable in other respects, I'd have said.

Anyhow, he's troubled by insomnia, and around three on Wednesday morning he went downstairs to raid the fridge. Spotted something moving in his garden from the kitchen window. Or someone. Too big for a dog, he reckoned, but he's shortsighted. Doubled back upstairs for his specs and stick he keeps in his bedroom just in case. Heard an engine revving on his way down. His first thought was for his prize begonias, but they were all quote present and correct unquote. Only puzzle was the mulch layer around his *Eleagnus pungens*. Been meaning to top it up for weeks, he said. Looked like someone else had done the job.'

'Wednesday morning? You're sure he said Wednesday?'

'Shouldn't have rung you otherwise. Sylvia Straker's convinced it was Rupert's ghost, but that didn't wash with Barton. Some weirdo, he reckons. He's talking of keeping a night-watch in his greenhouse.'

Baxter heard distant knockings. 'Come in, please,' he called out over his shoulder.

'That's it, love. Over to you.'

'Got Yarwood's phone number on you?'

She supplied it.

'Thanks, sweetie. Thanks for everything.'

Armstrong answered the intercom. 'Wendy's got Ronson in Room D. Ready when you are.'

'Not yet. Tell her to read his palm or something.' Baxter was trying to contact the Assistant Chief Constable.

Littleton was less than enthused by his narrative and his proposal. 'Hm-hm. I don't know, I really don't know, Baxter. Suggestion's a powerful thing. One dotty old dear comes up with a cock-and-bull story, second old dear follows suit. Yarwood sounds the type who wouldn't care to be upstaged by a woman . . . No. Hm-hm no. You can't seriously expect me to make representations to the Met on his say-so.'

'No, sir. But I should like to make a suggestion.'

Several dozen throat-clearings later, the ACC gave it his grudging agreement.

Baxter joined Wendy Powers and Damien Ronson in the interview room.

'Lost quarts of the red stuff over that little lot. On my tenth life, the doc said. Two years ago, that was.' Damien, his left sleeve rolled up to display a jagged scar, had evidently been treating Wendy to his surgical history. ''Lo, mate.' He grinned at Baxter.

'Chief Inspector, Mr Baxter. Take your pick.'

'Pardon me—lost the habit. Blame it on old Eve and the Plumtrees mob. Dead against handles, they was.'

'Was?'

'Skived, ain't they? Left the old b. in the lurch.'

'As the pot might have said to the kettle.'

'You got it wrong, Mr B. Don't class me with them effing arse-lickers. Never had no intention of staying away for good. Always had a soft spot for the old doll—take more than that argy-bargy at the House Meeting to put me off her. Why else do you think I'm here?'

'Because the good sister took you in charge?'

'Come off it—rang Eve from Addenbrooke's this morning soon as I could hobble to a phone. Guy in the next bed passed me his paper to read, which was the first I knew about Rupert. Been out of touch these last few weeks, you see. Some bastard nicked my radio.'

Possible if not probable. Better let it go for now. 'Eve got Sister Maccy to pick me up when they discharged me and run me over to Plumtrees. Then she put me wise about the trike job. News to me, as God's my witness, but she kept on till I promised to tell you so in person.'

'Thanks.'

'You know who dunnit?'

'Not yet. Any ideas?'

''S 'matter of fact I do. Not hard evidence, mind. What you might call an intelligent guess.'

'I might call it time-wasting, Ronson, if you don't come to the point soonish.'

'Remember Matt Vickery? Wino that drowned hisself in the Cam a few weeks back?'

'Inspector Armstrong will.'

'Funny old prat. Didn't get on with the other bums. His first summer in Cambridge—wouldn't help, I suppose. 'Sides, he acted stand-offish. Hung out with the Milton Man mostly when he was sober.'

'Milton Man?' Powers echoed. Baxter wished she hadn't. Attention was obviously meat and drink to young Ronson. Accidental-on-purpose injury was one of his chosen baits: fantasizing might well be another.

'Geezer that spouts poetry in the Market Square—dead ringer for Jimmy Savile with this great buckled hat on.'

'Let's get back to Vickery and the tricycle, shall we?' Baxter suggested wearily.

'OK, OK, guv.' Damien's one mobile arm gestured surrender. 'Lady copper asks me a question—I answer up, that's all. When old Vickery was hitting the bottle hard, the Milton Man didn't want to know, right? Bad for trade, I guess. So Matt would make off with his booze to Midsummer Common or Jesus Green or Alexandra Gardens, if he could make it up the hill. I've seen him many a time, hanging on to the railings on Chesterton Lane or sitting on the wall outside the DHSS, bracing himself for the climb.'

Damien paused briefly, staring into the middle distance.

'Matt was outside the DHSS one day when I came out after some hassle or other. Crouching on the wall, as per usual. Taking no notice of nothing except the Johnnie Walker he was clutching like an effing hot-water bottle. Then wham! Leapt to his feet like he'd been electrocuted.

Bloody near dropped the booze. Just stood there, cursing under his breath and staring.

'So I looked where he was looking, natch. It was Eve, would you believe, riding by on the old trike.'

'Oh, come on. Bloke was drunk, you say. Even if he stared at Mrs PW, who knows what he saw? Pink elephant, like as not.'

'But that wasn't all. Day or so after—around five one evening, it'd be—he showed up in the service road back of Plumtrees. Eve wasn't there but the trike was, not for the first time. Her memory's going, you know. She'll pop into the house, meaning to take a few minutes, and get stuck into something for hours on end. Anyhow, there was the trike and there was old Matt on his hands and knees working out how many Johnnie Walkers it was good for. Or so I thought.

'Couldn't have been more than a week later that the brakes was cut, if Eve's right in what she told me this morning. But I wasn't to know anything about that at the time, was I?'

Baxter grunted non-committally.

'Bawled Vickery out—wheeled the trike into the garden—gave Eve a talking-to for leaving it around. What else could I do, Chief Inspector?'

'What you can do now, Ronson, is to fill us in on your whereabouts since you left Plumtrees.'

'Every hour of every day?' Damien traced a snake tattoo on his forehead with a ringed forefinger.

'First thirty-six hours, for starters.'

A broken-toothed smile. 'You're in luck, Chief Inspector. They was special, them days. Half my life's a closed book to me. Got this blanking-out syndrome—honest. It's all there on my record. One of the Youth Custody shrinks wrote me up in a thesis.'

'Now look here—'

'OK, OK. Don't get the knickers in a twist, guv. Left Plumtrees half an hour after that effing House Meeting. Van was low on juice, I was low on bread. So I headed for the Square and Tassel in hopes of a free jar. Which is where I met Rosa and her girlfriend.'

'Rosa what?' Powers checked.

'Corelli. Eye-tye language student—New Way College if you're interested. Rolex watch, Gucci handbag, but no current nightlife. No wonder. Ninety per cent of those language school kids is birds. Someone somewhere gets their sums wrong, wouldn't you say, Mr B.'

Baxter growled.

'OK, OK. Gist is, I spent the next couple of nights at Rosa's pad. Scruffy dump off Milton Road, not her style, but the landlady was away for a week . . .'

'Address?'

'Slipped my mind, but I could take you there easy. Better still, take the Sarge.' Tattoos twitched as he waggled his eyebrows in Wendy's direction.

'Go on,' Baxter said.

'High-class cook, that kid. Didn't need much tuition in the other thing, either. Don't suppose I'm the type Mamma Mia would go for—maybe that was an added attraction. Then Rosa's Eye-Tye boyfriend phoned to say he was flying over. Kid panicked. Gave me my petrol money and a stack of pizzas. I upped sticks for Fenport.'

'To work in the brickyard?'

'Which I did for a week. Then they started laying people off. So after a while I headed back for Cambridge.'

'The day Rupert Parsingham died?'

'Day before, actually. Ran into a bunch of folk singers I'd met at Plumtrees. They'd come early for the Cherry Hinton Folk Festival—was milking the tourist mobs downtown in the meantime. Hung out with them that day and the next—food was OK if you don't mind vegetarian.'

'You were with them all that time?'

'All the time you'll be interested in, guv. Tuesday afternoon, Tuesday evening we was stuck like limpets. Ran them over to the Fen Skaters, far side of Midsummer Common, for a Folk Club night. By eleven I'd had it up to here with *Dirty Old Town* and the rest. So I thought, why not get a breath of fresh air, why not see how old Eve is getting on?'

'Not old Rupert?'

''Course not. Never had anything against the poor bugger, but never had much to do with him, either. Headed straight for Plumtrees. Was a bit fazed by the fancy lights—Eve didn't go much for entertaining. But I thought maybe if she was in the party mood she'd be ready to let bygones be bygones.

'Which she might, if her Yankee lodger, that Stacey, hadn't muscled in. Wheeling Eve's trike, she was. All of a sudden she let it go, grabbed hold of me, called me a filthy little murderer.'

'And you ran?'

'OK, I ran. Daft, you're thinking, but I'd a few pints inside me. When I heard "murderer" and saw the trike I remembered the way Matt Vickery had looked when Eve was riding it. And I thought, Oh Christ, she's dead. Some other old soak has done for her. And they'll blame me, Stacey and the rest. Comes second nature to their sort to blame me. So I scarpered.

'Drove the van out the Holtchester Road, blew what remained of my last Social handout on a bottle of vodka at a service station, parked on some waste land I knew about. Conservation area, the notice says, but nobody does any conserving outside weekends far as I can see. Ideal location for a spot of off-the-record nookey, Sarge—'

'Ronson!' Baxter heard himself shout. Powers raised an amused eyebrow. Amused by Ronson? By him?

'That's about it, guv. Stay off the vodka as a rule, so it

works a treat when I need it. Spun it out until yesterday evening. My head hurt, of course, but I was thinking positive. Ever find a headache does that for you, guv? Focuses you, sort of?'

Baxter growled.

'I mapped it all out. First I'd line my stomach, then I'd find out what happened to Eve, then I'd go to the fuzz and tell them I hadn't done it, whatever that crazed chick Stacey had tried to put across. Veggie food's OK, but I really fancied Rosa's Bolognese and a little TLC, so, just on the offchance, I tried the Square and Tassel. There she was—on her tod, as I thought, in this grey-and-white mini dress. Nothing fancy, but it brought up her tan—'

Baxter tried counting ten backwards. Forwards wasn't working any longer.

'Sight of me shook her up too. I could tell. She mumbled something I couldn't make out. Next thing, she was staring over my shoulder and someone was grabbing me. Then she started talking Italian to this bloke—he'd been in the Gents, I guess. Started crying.

'Talk about community spirit, guv! That Eye-Tye bastard—six six with muscles to match—strong-armed me out of that bar, bloody near strangling me in the process, and nobody took a blind bit of notice. Finished off by kicking me down the steps outside, which did for my shoulder. Be there now, I dare say, if some crumblies hadn't come out of a Bingo session opposite.'

Baxter despatched Damien five minutes later by standard issue Vauxhall, not before checking Armstrong's recollections of the late Matt Vickery. It had been an accidental drowning. The coroner had had no doubts, nor had the multinational clutch of passive onlookers or the two Swedes who had attempted a rescue. Archibald Shanks, aka the Milton Man, had identified the body. Leaving Wendy Powers to extract anything else of interest from the Vickery file, and Armstrong to track down Shanks, Baxter turned his attention to his in-tray.

He couldn't settle, his resentment of time wasted on and by Damien remaining to distract him. Tea might help. No harm in a quick shuteye while the kettle was coming to the boil. It boiled. It switched itself off. Next thing he knew, Armstrong was at his elbow.

'From morn
To noon he fell, from noon to dewy eve,
A summer's day.

Old boy knew how to write, didn't he?'

'What the hell!'

'Milton. *Paradise Lost.* Didn't they make you learn hunks of it at your school? Came back to me the minute I heard Shanks. Not that he put it over the way our English teacher did—touch of the Cockney. But all the same. With an Oliver Cromwell hat and a cloak and a Jimmy Savile wig, he could make it quite creepy. Tourists were lapping it up. No wonder he wouldn't take much time out for me.'

'Enough?'

'I reckon. You're going to like this. Old Eve's going to like it.'

'Well?'

'Vickery was ex-civil service, like Shanks. Which is why Archie felt sorry for him, he says. Been on his uppers himself before he hit on the Milton thing. Father played the Northern clubs—memory man act. Taught Archie the tricks of the trade, so he knew memorizing wouldn't be a problem. Then he saw that little Irish chap who used to spout Shakespeare—'

'Vickery,' Baxter interrupted. 'For God's sake, Bill, concentrate on Vickery.'

'Getting there,' Armstrong said coldly. 'Archie nagged

him to build on his skills the way he had. Go in for woodcarving or something else in the craft line. Matt could do anything with his hands, apparently.'

'Ah!'

'Thought you'd like that one. Matt had a skill, but he also had a gripe. Variation on a popular theme. A stretch twenty-odd years ago that had sent him on the downward spiral, or so he wanted to believe. And the old lady who had dished the gravy—in Guildford. Guildford, Surrey, please note.'

'Pass.'

'Three weeks before he drowned, Matt butted in on one of Archie's performances to announce that he'd just seen the magistrate who'd done him down. Archie didn't attend to the details. He wasn't best pleased about the loss of trade. Besides, Matt was sloshed. But he's sure Archie said the old girl was riding a trike. On Chesterton Lane. Geddit?'

'Eve?'

'Supposing her to be Cousin Esther.'

'Of course. Fancy a cuppa, Bill?'

'Any chocolate digestives?'

'For those we go through channels.' Baxter rang the incident room.

CHAPTER 15

'There you are, sir. And there.' Wendy Powers's forefinger stabbed twice at the inventory of items found in the drowned man's pockets. Stashed among his box of matches, six dog-ends, sixty-seven pence, Social Security payments book, St Christopher medal, nylon pak-a-mak and *Playboy* centrefold, Vickery had carried a penknife and a length of insulating tape. 'Pretty strong evidence, wouldn't you say? Pity it's only circumstantial.'

'Thanks to Eve,' Armstrong lamented. 'If she hadn't been so damn quick to chuck the cut brakes.'

'What does it matter?' Baxter soothed. 'The late lamented can't stand trial. We've confirmation that Esther Parsingham sent him down at Guildford in 'sixty-eight. There's enough in my estimation to put our live suspects in the clear. Eve's safe. Let's break the good news to her, Wendy, before we tackle Valerie Gates. Any problems about getting Valerie's home address?'

'Not really. She sounded nervous when I rang, but she was obviously relieved that we didn't want to interview her at the Institute. I don't think somehow that she'll alert Finchley.'

'Let's hope you're right. How d'you feel about a night shift, Bill?'

'Yeah, sure.' Armstrong sounded less than eager.

'But what?'

'But nothing. It's just . . . well. It's Gran-in-law's last night, and Maureen says she's moved on to colcannon. Lovely grub, that. Cabbages, spuds, lashings of butter—'

'Take your word.' Baxter's ulcer had lodged a token protest. 'After supper would be fine. What I had in mind was a horticultural job half a mile from your place. The item I cleared with the ACC earlier on.'

'Oh right, fine. Nice tie-in, if it works.' Armstrong agreed, native caution tempering his optimism. Baxter outlined the project and its rationale for Powers's benefit.

Her response was less inhibited. 'Cripes, guv!' Then an afterthought: 'Doesn't the Chief Constable belong to the Horticultural Association? Wouldn't it be a hoot if—'

'Three hoots,' Baxter agreed. 'But Montgomery wouldn't see the joke, I fancy.'

*

'It's the money, isn't it?' Valerie Gates paused just inside the door of her living-room. 'It's all here, you know. Never touched. Four hundred.' She went to a writing bureau by the window and retrieved a sealed, stamped foolscap envelope addressed to Rupert Parsingham.

'It was a present—whatever you may think. Just a present. Mr Parsingham wanted to show his gratitude, he said. I refused at first, but he was most insistent. In the end I took it to please him.'

Baxter nodded. 'Why don't we all sit down, Mrs Gates?'

'Yes, yes, I'm sorry.' Valerie tugged at the peplum of her tight tan two-piece. The same tan as the dralon sofa cover, perhaps, before time had faded it.

'Odd sort of sum, four hundred,' Baxter said, accepting the envelope.

'He offered me five to begin with—he'd these bundles of notes in his desk drawer, but you'll know that. He kept on and on. Hadn't much longer to live, he said. Token of appreciation, he said, for all I'd done for the Institute. In the end I gave in, just to keep him happy.

'Wouldn't take the five, but there was a suite in Eaden Lilley's sale that my fiancé and I coveted. Four hundred more than we could afford, so I took that. Didn't think how it would look. Norman—my fiancé—hit the roof Tuesday evening when I told him. Especially when he heard about the other cash in the drawer. Tax evasion or worse, Norman reckoned. He's a job at the Guildhall, so he can't afford to be mixed up in anything iffy.

'I promised to post it back first thing Wednesday, and I meant to. Truly. Told Norman I had. But somehow, I couldn't bring myself. Then the news came through about the old boy's death. And I thought, well, it's not like he's going to get any good out of it. My Norman's worked hard half a lifetime, without much to show for it. I wanted to make this place nice for us, that's all. What's wrong with that, eh? Tell me what's wrong with that!'

Valerie dabbed brimming eyes with a small embroidered handkerchief. 'How'd you find out? Did he tell his sister before he copped it?'

Baxter shook his head. 'Someone saw you leaving the cottage.'

'Oh no!' Valerie's orange-tipped fingers flew to her mouth. 'So I needn't . . . you didn't know. Oh, bloody hell.' She hugged herself, rocking. 'Yes, I'd have kept the cash, spent it on this and that. Little gadgets, fuel bills, holidays. Norman would never have guessed. Is that so terrible? What happens to it now?'

'That'll depend on how Mr Parsingham came by it. Did he throw any light on the subject?'

' 'Course not. Never dreamt of asking. Old people hoard money all the time, don't they? Never entered my head there could be anything fishy, not until Norman said . . . He needn't ever know, need he? He worries.'

'No promises. But it'll help if you cooperate with our inquiries. Why did you go to the cottage in the first place?'

Valerie hesitated.

'Come on, Mrs Gates. You'd something to give Mr Parsingham, hadn't you?'

'If you already know—'

'We need to hear it from you.'

'All right. The engineer was here on Tuesday to give the photocopier in my office a routine service. When I was cleaning up afterwards I found a spoilt sheet with a thumbprint copied on to it that must have slipped down between the machine and the wall. The thumb was a funny shape. Couldn't think whose it might be, till I smelt tobacco off the paper.

'Then I thought of Mr Parsingham. He used to meet his sister in the Institute—pick her up in his car. If she wasn't on time, he'd wait in my office, smoking his smelly old pipe.'

'Of which you didn't approve?'

She wrinkled her nose. 'There's a no smoking notice, and other visitors are made to toe the line. I've complained to Dr Finchley. But he wouldn't let me say boo to a Parsingham. Anyhow one day—last May or June, can't remember which—Mr Parsingham had been in my office when I went to lunch. Not for the first or last time by a long chalk. But this day, when I came back, I had to use the photocopier. It felt warm. And there was a shred of pipe tobacco on the top cover.'

'Did you raise the matter with anyone?'

'No. I naturally assumed Mr Parsingham had been copying his own private papers. Dr Finchley wouldn't have turned a hair over that. Just another perk, like the coffee he expects me to lay on for his visitors.'

'Can you describe the photocopy you discovered on Tuesday.'

'It was taken from the file copy of a letter.'

'Go on.'

She licked orange lips. 'A letter written by Dr Finchley to a Professor Something—can't remember the name.'

'Sergeant Powers, if you please . . . This letter, Mrs Gates?' Wendy Powers handed over the document, sleeved in polythene.

Valerie skimmed its contents.

'A confidential letter, copied without authority, and written by your boss, Mrs Gates. Surely the first instinct of any loyal secretary would have been to take it back to him?'

She flushed. 'Maybe I'm not the one you should be lecturing on loyalty, Chief Inspector.'

'Oh?'

Valerie took a deep breath. 'Fancy a sherry? No? Mind if I indulge?' A quick trip to the drinks cupboard, a second tug at her peplum as she resettled on the sofa. 'If the letter had been taken from any other file, or if the copy had been made by anyone else—yes, I'd have gone to the Director straight away. There'd have been a row, I'm sure. Dr Finchley would have accused me of leaving the filing cabinet keys lying around, which I haven't. But I'd have gone all the same. You don't believe me, do you, either of you?' Her glance zigzagged between the detectives' faces.

'What was so special about Dr Otley's file?' Baxter's neutrally toned question cut through Powers's reassuring murmurs.

'I felt Julian Otley had been badly treated. OK, he's an uptight little sod, takes himself and his work very seriously. But to read the references Dr Otley gave him, all except the last, you'd think he was crazy. In the four years I've known him I've seen no sign of it.'

'You typed those references from dictation, I imagine? Did you raise the issue with Dr Finchley at the time?' Wendy Powers asked.

'The first time, yes. But no go. He said he'd seen sides of Julian I hadn't, that the Institute's reputation would suffer if he sold a goose as a swan. Then he shot the "more in sorrow than anger" line. All lies, of course. I knew it was just that he didn't want Julian to resign. That he was prepared to hang on by fair means or foul.'

'So you left it at that?' Powers followed up.

'What could I do? Warn Julian? Dr Finchley might have found out that I'd spilt the beans, might have fired me. Different for you, Sergeant. You don't chuck in jobs when you're forty-nine. Not without thinking twice. Hadn't twigged then that the job wouldn't always be there to chuck.'

'Meaning?' Baxter prompted.

'Meaning that Dr Finchley's precious Institute is for the chopper.' Valerie poured herself a second sherry.

'How'd you know?'

'"Informed sources."' She giggled, crossing plump thighs. 'That's what they say on the box, isn't it? Don't ask me for details—Secretary to the Chairman of the Board of Management handles stuff like that. But it's an open secret that a big sponsor has backed out, leaving a hole no one else is likely to plug. Chances are, the outfit will be disbanded within two years. Doesn't worry me. Made contingency plans a couple of months ago. I'll be down that gangway before the ship founders, thank God. Only reason I could risk telling you what I've told you.'

'OK,' Baxter said. 'But I'm still unclear why you returned the photocopy to Mr Parsingham.'

'I was hopping mad that he'd been so careless. Didn't want any repetitions. When I leave the Institute, I leave of my free will. I'm not giving Dr Finchley the satisfaction of showing me the door. So I told Mr Parsingham this would be the last time I covered for him and Stacey.'

'Stacey Caldwell? What made you think she was involved?'

'Likeliest person to have told him where to look for the cabinet key. I'll swear I never let anyone outside the office staff have sight of my hidey-hole. Stacey worked at the Parsingham for a time last winter. She's Julian Otley's girlfriend. American, pushy type. Mr Parsingham wouldn't admit it, but I'll bet anything you like she put him up to it.'

'Let's get back to basics. When exactly did you arrive at the cottage?'

'Four-fifteen, near as I remember. I left my office at five past—cycled over.'

'In working hours?'

'I'd flexitime owing. Besides, I knew the Director would be at a Board meeting until five or later.'

'Was there a notice on the cottage door when you arrived?'

'Yes, PLEASE DO NOT DISTURB.'

'But you did?'

'Yes. Felt I'd a right, after what Mr P. had done. I'd have given up pretty soon, I guess, in case he was laid up. But he answered the third knock.'

'Go on.'

'Don't remember every word, but I complained that he'd put me on the spot. He was very apologetic. Gave me his word that he'd destroyed all the other copies he'd made from the file. Swore the whole thing was his responsibility. Said Julian had no idea. He begged me not to tell him—not to tell anyone.'

'Who raised the subject of money?'

'He did—honestly. Like I said, he kept on and on.'

'Then you took it and went? Was that that?'

Valerie stared for several seconds at the dregs in her sherry glass. 'No—no, it wasn't.'

'Go on.'

'Easy for you to say, isn't it? I've got to go back to work tomorrow morning. "Yes, Dr Finchley, no, Dr Finchley." And after what happened to that old man, I'm scared, you see.'

'You mean Mr Parsingham may have died because he passed on something you told him?'

Valerie nodded dumbly.

'If that were so—big "if", mind you—aren't you at risk as things stand? Assuming the murderer could guess the source of Mr Parsingham's information?'

'I don't know . . .'

'You'd do better to tell us, Mrs Gates. If the need for protection arises, we're in a better position than Mr Parsingham to provide it.'

She sighed. 'Oh, very well. I'd been worrying for a long time, but there was no one I felt I could talk to, not before I knew Mr Parsingham had read that file. That's what gave me the biggest jolt, you see.'

'I don't quite.'

'Last May Dr Finchley did a complete turnaround. The last reference he wrote for Julian Otley—the one for the Karachi post—was a hundred per cent positive. Not a word about mental illness. It didn't add up. Except that he wrote it the morning after he'd had dinner with Aubrey King, and that didn't add up either.'

'Aubrey King?'

'Makes science documentaries for TV. He and his team had just spent two days shooting at the Parsingham. He'd said goodbye to Dr Finchley—heard him myself. No word of another meeting. But they had dinner together that evening. Restaurant called the Ruffled Feathers—near Royston.'

'I know it. You're sure?'

'Absolutely. Didn't see them face to face, mind. We weren't eating in the same part of the restaurant, my fiancé and I. But Norman ran into Dr Finchley in the Gents, and I spotted his car and King's in the car park. Odd, wasn't it?'

'Perhaps, but I don't see why you should have made the connection with Otley.'

'On account of the Pacific pollution research Julian is in charge of. Dr Finchley took a special interest in it. Mind you, he kept a close eye on all the strategic projects—'

'Strategic, is that what you said?' Wendy Powers checked.

'Yes. That's what they term the studies that are commissioned and paid for by governments or international bodies. As distinct from purely academic projects and commercial projects. Not that they do any private commercial work at the Parsingham—against its constitution, or something. Anyhow, funds for straight academic stuff being in short supply, Dr F. wants more strategic contracts. He's forever telling project leaders that the standard of their work is the Institute's best advertisement. Churning out memos on deadlines, quality control, client confidentiality . . .'

'"Careless talk costs contracts"?'

'That sort of thing, yes. He took it further with the Pacific pollution project. Never could understand why—don't think Julian does either. The funding isn't brilliant. But for whatever reason, Dr F. was forever demanding copies of progress reports, statistics. Quality control exercise, he called it. Filed the copies in his personal safe, he said. And at first I believed him.' Valerie paused for dramatic effect, her braceleted right wrist dangling from the arm of the settee, her fears seemingly forgotten.

'What changed your mind?' Baxter prompted.

'One afternoon last March I went into Dr Finchley's office to collect his teacup. He'd been called out to talk to the Chairman of the Board—Sir James Ogilvie-Walnutt—in the waiting area. Left his desk in a hurry, by the look of things. As I reached across for the teacup, my sleeve caught a pile of papers and scattered them. When I was putting things to rights, my eye fell on an airmail envelope. Addressed, filled, but not properly sealed.

'Shouldn't have peeked, should I?' Valerie leant forward, compressing her freckled cleavage. 'But every so often I get this funny little feeling—sixth sense, my late hubby called it. Odd enough seeing an envelope addressed to anyone in Dr F.'s writing. Odder still seeing Aubrey King's name on it. Chalk and cheese, that pair. King—seen any of his shows?'

Wendy Powers grunted affirmatively.

'Smarmy type, wouldn't you say? And Dr Finchley's a cold fish—no wonder he used to go in for underwater photography. Be that as it may, something told me this wasn't a personal letter.' Valerie wagged her right forefinger.

'The envelope opened ever so easy. As if it was meant,

you might say. I took one quick peek before I resealed it. There were two sheets of A4 inside, photostats of the last progress report on the Pacific pollution project that the Director had demanded from Julian Otley. I'd been sent to collect it as per usual. Dr F. had made the copies on his personal photocopier, I guess. The Institute letterhead and the names of the research team had been masked out, also one or two words in the report. Place names, mostly. But I'd no doubt what it was. None.'

'Remember the address on the envelope?'

'Yes. Made a special point of memorizing it. Some day, I thought, someone's going to ask me that. 113 Rue des Chouxfleurs, Lucerne, Switzerland. Got that, Sergeant?'

'Yes, thanks.'

'And you told this to no one—no one at all—except Rupert Parsingham?' Baxter checked.

Valerie nodded. 'I was out of my depth—scared. Didn't take it in at first. The way Dr F. carries on, you'd say his life was bound up with the Parsingham. I just couldn't believe he and King had something going on the side. Then I realized it might tie in with those awful references. If Julian was laying golden eggs for Dr F. as well as the Institute, he'd use fair means and foul to hang on to him.'

'So why should he change his mind?'

Valerie shrugged. 'My guess is that King backed out of the deal at that hush-hush dinner in May. Dr F.'s been different ever since—edgier. I noticed it first thing next morning, even before he dictated the reference for Julian's Karachi job. Other people have remarked on it.'

'You put all this to Mr Parsingham?'

'Yes. Didn't mean to at first. But, well . . . Someone had to be told. I've worked all my life for the University, you see. Just because I've had to look after Number One doesn't mean I don't know right from wrong, does it?'

Wendy Powers made soothing noises.

'Thought Mr Parsingham might appreciate being told, on account of the family connection.'

'And did he?'

'Oh yes. Came as a shock, of course. But he told me I'd done the right thing. Told me he'd take appropriate action next morning. Maybe he didn't wait, poor old sod. Maybe that was why . . .'

'It doesn't quite add up,' Baxter complained on the drive back to the police station.

'No, sir? Why not?'

'Mrs Finchley said her husband had inherited capital. Also, he comes over as a canny type. It doesn't make sense that he'd risk his academic career for the sake of a few dirty thou.'

'Expect you're right, sir. But you don't mind if I look into King, do you?'

'Feel free, Sergeant. I can think of more beautiful sights.'

'Such as—or shouldn't I ask?'

'Actually, I was thinking of gemstones by starlight.'

'Any gems in particular, sir?'

'Nope. Pearls, sapphires, diamonds . . . I'm easy.'

CHAPTER 16

It was in fact rubies and emeralds that winked up at Baxter at three o'clock on Saturday morning. In the light, not of stars, but of the flickering fluorescent strip that overhung the work-bench in Barton Yarwood's garage.

The ex-soldier donned his bifocals to make a detailed inspection. 'Rum sort of birdie! Half starved, by the look of it. Stork, crane, would you say?'

'Liver bird.' Baxter began to replace its earthy wrappings.

'Really? Hang on. Seen something like that before somewhere . . . Got it! Councillor woman who's always getting her pic in the paper. Alma . . . Throstle, is it? No, Thurstone!'

'Best if you forget about her for the time being, Mr Yarwood. You gave us an undertaking earlier on—'

'Which I'll honour to the letter, Chief Inspector. Mum's the word. You're talking to one of Monty's men, remember. This little episode puts me in mind—'

'Sorry, sir,' Baxter interrupted. Armstrong didn't look fit for a guided tour down Memory Lane. 'Duty calls. Thanks again for your cooperation.'

'Delighted. My *Eleagnus pungens* is a hardy specimen, thank God. If you'd wanted to ferret around the root system of a camellia, I'm not sure I could have seen my way . . .'

The half-hour at Yarwood's place had been a doddle compared with the subsequent interview with the Assistant Chief Constable. In Baxter's view, a case could now be made for a search of Simon Drinkwater's London accommodation, if not of his person. But the ACC flatly refused to rouse senior Met officers from their beds with a request for such action.

Baxter was surprised to find Emma as well as Sarah at breakfast when he came down after a short nap. Bill Armstrong's and Sarah's reassurances notwithstanding, he had become more and more convinced that the miniature chest-of-drawers, now stowed at the back of his wardrobe, would be out of place in his daughter's London home. A denial of her adult tastes, a conspicuously expensive embarrassment.

He listened gloomily as Emma negotiated the loan of her mother's car for the day. The repairs to her van had left it with a tendency to stall at awkward moments. Talk turned to *Spin City*. Sarah was enthusiastic—declaring herself more than willing for a second visit in Richard's company. The last Cambridge performance was impossible, he declared, but he promised to defy Heaven, Hell and if necessary, his Chief Constable, to make the Edinburgh Festival.

The previous night's show had, he learned, been less than perfect in the eyes of its director. Three of the cast had been incapacitated, and Paul Sinton had been among those pressed into last-minute substitution.

'He did very well, considering,' Sarah insisted. 'Splendid singing voice. Bass-baritone—ideal for a Proctor's Bulldog. Spoken sequences weren't quite as good, perhaps, but he didn't have much to say.'

'Just as well,' Emma muttered into her muesli. 'Timing, pitch, stress. Poor old Paul got everything wrong he could get wrong. Two of Stacey's best cracks went off like damp squibs. Not his fault, I grant you. His father's the actor in the family.'

'What makes you say that?' Baxter asked, suddenly very wide awake.

'Oh, lots of things. Clive's TV interview yesterday. The sober citizen image he projected at the interval on our first night. The way he looked in the Signal Box when I passed at six-thirty, I reckoned he'd never make it to the show, let alone mingle at half-time.'

'Six-thirty? You're sure that's when you saw him in the pub, Emma?'

'Sure. I was stuck in a traffic jam right outside. Remember checking my watch to find out how long Clive had to sober up. But why should the time matter? What is this, Dad? An interrogation? Working from home now?'

'Please, darling!' Sarah put in.

'Keep out of it, Mum.' Emma was on her feet, glaring down at him. 'Listen, Dad. If Clive Sinton's on your list of suspects, OK. But play by the rules. Ask me whatever you want in a police station, before a police witness. Mind you, I'm not guaranteeing I'll answer.'

'You're right, Emma. I'm sorry. Truly. It could help quite a lot, actually, if you were prepared to sign a sworn statement repeating what you've just told me. You wouldn't be doing the dirty on Sinton—quite the reverse. Think it over, will you?'

'OK, but no promises.' She didn't say another word to him before he left for Headquarters.

'Sit you down, Baxter.' The Assistant Chief Constable gestured, pen in hand, and signed the last of a batch of outgoing mail. His secretary departed.

'Any luck with the Met, sir?'

'All sewn up.' The ACC leant back in his executive chair. No throat-clearings, Baxter noted, as he returned Littleton's rare, gold-and-white smile.

'You mean, they've raided Drinkwater's London pad? Found what we're expecting?

'Not yet.' Littleton carefully replaced the top of his pen. 'Not until he goes out this morning. Things look promising, all the same. Drinkwater's phone's being tapped. He's a meeting lined up with an old acquaintance we'd all like to talk to.'

'Oh?'

'Wright Cratchitt. Name ring a bell?'

Baxter nodded, his excitement growing. The jewel fence who had gone abroad after the Norwich Museum theft. 'Thought he was in the Low Countries.'

'Crossed back to Harwich yesterday by the late ferry. Overnighted in a motel off the M11. Essex have him under obbo. Look, Baxter. I've yet to be convinced that Rupert Parsingham was involved—criminally involved—in this business. All the same, I'm happy for you to go up to Town as the Force's representative, if you've nothing more urgent to attend to.'

'Thanks, sir, but no, thanks. Couple of Cambridge interviews lined up in Cambridge I'd better not defer or delegate.'

An hour later, on the threshold of Clive Sinton's room in the University Arms hotel, Baxter half-wished he had given a different answer.

'Well, well.' The playwright returned his ID. 'I've met your daughter. Perhaps she's told you? Very good friend of my son's, as we used to say. But I hardly imagine you and your colleague are here to talk dowries?'

'Hardly.' Baxter bit back his anger, as Sinton stood aside to let the detectives enter.

'Then to what or whom do I owe the pleasure?' Sinton asked over his shoulder as he bent to log off from his word-processor.

'To a witness of your excursion into Mr Parsingham's garden on the day of his death.' Baxter had expected radical chic in the playwright's appearance, but found none. His grizzling hair was of medium length. He wore a striped Breton sweater and neatly pressed navy shorts. The scar on his forehead was too small and too old to disfigure his sallow face, which was attractive in a thin-lipped way.

'Oh Lordy. Sit down?' Sinton waved towards the rumpled bed, and commandeered the single chair. 'Beer? Whisky? No, you wouldn't, would you?'

There were no glasses or bottles on open display, and no smell of alcohol.

'If you're here to quiz me about that brief encounter, I'm afraid you're wasting your breath. As he, she or it will have told you, I was pissed at the time. When I came to God knows how many hours later I didn't recall a thing to begin with. Then I felt this bloody great bruise on my shin—' He broke off to display its multicoloured splendour. 'And I remembered this bod—male, I think, but I wouldn't swear to it—falling over me. Also, I believe I was singing.'

'Right. Let's take another tack. Why did you go to Plumtrees Cottage?'

'To see Rupert Parsingham.

'And did you see him?'

Sinton shook his head. 'There was a DON'T DISTURB notice on the door.'

'Lights inside? Noises?'

'Not that I registered. I couldn't decide whether to knock or not, and I wasn't in any great shape for deciding. Reckoned a kip might clear my brain. That was that, until this guy ran into me.'

'I see. Tell us now, what was the purpose of your visit?'

Sinton hesitated. 'To renew an old acquaintance, you might say. To set a record straight.'

'You and Mr Parsingham knew each other?'

The playwright grimaced. 'By sight only. Our last confrontation was twenty-five years ago—a somewhat traumatic occasion. I suspect he remembered my face. I certainly remembered his, although it wasn't until I saw the piece about his retirement in Tuesday's local paper that I was able to put a name to it.'

'Are you telling me you and Mr Parsingham once had a quarrel?'

Sinton shook his head. 'He saw me doing something of which he disapproved. He showed his disapproval. I resented that—I still resent it. When I saw his picture in the paper Tuesday evening, I decided to pay him a visit, have it out with him. Daft idea, but the little grey cells weren't at their sparkiest.'

'Can you fill us in on the where and why of your confrontation?'

'Can but won't. Until further notice anyhow, Chief Inspector. Not just being bloody-minded. But (a) this has nothing to do with Parsingham's death, of which I know nothing, and (b) other parties are involved, one of whom doesn't deserve to be embarrassed. OK?'

'In the short term. What I want more immediately are details of your activities last Tuesday from mid-afternoon onwards.'

'Let's see. Mooched about in the colleges for a couple of hours. King's, Princes', Trinity—the usual tourist round.'

'But you don't strike me as the usual tourist.'

A wry smile. 'Maybe not. Let's call it a sentimental journey. I was curious to see how my past labours had stood up to wind and weather.'

'Labours?'

'You disappoint me, Baxter. I assumed you came fully briefed. To save your gofers the hassle of trawling through the cuttings files, let me fill you in on my career. Started out here in Cambridge as a mason—facer mason, if you like to dot the "i's", Inspector Armstrong. Before I read *Jude the Obscure*, you understand. Chucked that for scaffolding, chucked scaffolding for playwriting. Downhill all the way, wouldn't you say, Inspector?'

'No comment,' Armstrong replied in his flattest Belfast drawl.

'How long did your sentimental journey last?' Baxter asked.

'Till fourish, at a guess. Not given to measuring out my life in coffee-spoons. One reason for my lack of progress in masonry, no doubt.'

'Where next?'

'To the pub. Hadn't done my daily stint of writing that morning, wasn't in the mood to begin. Guilt-provoking situation, also thirst-provoking. Don't pretend you understand, Baxter.'

'Which pub?'

'Signal Box, just off Mill Road. One of my nicest discoveries in Cambridge. Easy-going establishment. No students, no tourists. No Real Beer, either, but I'm not a beerdrinker.'

'Go on.'

'Not much to say. Lowered a few whiskys, chatted to the barman, watched a thriller on the box so abysmal I worked up a head of steam about overpaid scriptwriters. Lowered another whisky and asked the barman to turn down the sound so I could make up my own dialogue. Half way through the car chase I got bored with that game. Besides, it was time to sober up if I was to make the show, as promised.'

'Time—what time?' Armstrong prompted.

Sinton laughed. 'Oh, for a literal police mind. I covet it, Inspector. Kid you not. Life would be so much less disconcerting. Didn't consult my watch at that juncture because the biological early-warning system did the needful. I took head and switched to caffeine.'

'So you drank a cup of coffee?'

'Several. Also, I read the local paper, and saw the photo of the late lamented Rupert. Plus name, plus address.'

'Go on.'

'Back here to change, with a swim at Parkside Pool on the way. Don't look so sceptical, Inspector. It's a thing I do.' Quite possibly. The biceps half-exposed by the short-sleeved T-shirt were not unimpressive. 'Then straight to East-whatever school for the kiddies' show.'

'All this on foot?' Baxter checked.

'That's right. Knew the route. Someone—your daughter, come to think of it—had given me a lift to the dress rehearsal. Back here after the show for a hair of the dog. Or two. Or three. I'd time to kill, because I wanted to steer clear of the Plumtrees party. Then to Rupert's. Which is where you came in, metaphorically speaking.'

'Remember the time you arrived at Parkside?' Baxter asked.

'There you might just be in luck, would you believe?' Sinton looked and sounded amused. 'As I explained, I'm not a clock-watcher. But I'm told I was seen in Parkside at six-thirty.'

'Told? By an acquaintance?'

Sinton shook his head. 'Sorry.'

'Someone else who doesn't deserve to be embarrassed?' Baxter countered.

'On the contrary. But not just yet.'

Baxter's patience broke. 'Now, look here, Sinton. We're investigating the murder of a vulnerable old man, a man who may have wanted to die, but at a time of his own choosing. Nothing melodramatic. Nothing you could wow them in the stalls with. But we take it seriously. Last thing I want is to play damnfool games.'

'Really?' Sinton steepled his fingers. 'In that case you should seek vocational guidance, Chief Inspector. From where I sit, ninety per cent of police work is games. The power game, the intimidation game—'

'Save the rhetoric for your word-processor, Mr Sinton.' Baxter prepared to leave. 'Don't assume the matter is closed—far from it. But for the present I suggest we stop wasting each other's time.'

'Egotistical bastard! Why'd you let him off so lightly?' Armstrong demanded on the way downstairs.

'Because I take him for the type that softens if stewed in his own juice and because he's an alibi.'

'Courtesy of the anonymous friend?'

'Courtesy, I regret to say, of my daughter, who saw him in the pub at six-thirty.'

'So his anonymous friend, if he or she exists, is a liar.'

'Ten out of ten, Bill. And faintly depressing. But say not the struggle naught availeth. With luck, HQ will soon have something more from the Met.'

Instructions for Baxter to ring the ACC from his Cambridge office came through on the car radio as they were parking. Steering a swift course through the chuntering terminals and fax machines in the incident room, he hurried to comply.

'Hm-hm. First the bad news, Richard.' His heart sank. 'Essex have made a booboo.'

'WC?'

'Hm-hm. Wright Cratchitt—'fraid so. We can speak freely, by the way. I'm using the hot line.'

Which meant he was also using the Chief Constable's desk. Baxter pictured Littleton's skinny frame behind that sea of afrormosia.

'What went wrong?'

'Cratchitt spotted his tail, or one of his henchmen did. Can't be sure. Anyhow, he did a runner from the motel before daybreak. All-ports alert, but with his resources . . .'

'Point taken, sir. I can hear stable doors banging. And the good news?'

'Cratchitt didn't warn Drinkwater before he left home to meet him.'

'So they pulled him? What was he carrying?'

'What you predicted. One hand-drawn map of one garden. Crazy paving, lily-pond. Not Barton Yarwood's, by all accounts. Hm-hm. Owe you an apology, Richard. If I'd backed your hunch more strongly, made representations to Essex—'

'Oh, I don't know, sir. Cratchitt was always a slippery eel. He'd probably have scarpered however many bods were staking out that motel. Drinkwater talking?'

'Not yet.'

'Any joy with his London pad?'

'More than we'd any right to expect. Three dozen more garden maps hidden in a cistern, the linings of suitcases—all the obvious places.'

'List of addresses?'

'No, but Parsingham's ex-employers could presumably supply a list of his clients.'

'There's evidence of his involvement?'

'Botanical dictionary, with his name in the fly-leaf.'

'Careless bastards! So it's out with the metal-detectors, is it, sir? Or does X mark the spots?'

'Not quite. They found a list of numbers, you see, one to thirty-seven. And opposite thirteen of the numbers—those that were used, one assumes, were alpha-numeric codes. My thought was that the numbers in the codes might indicate distances and the letters plant names. In which case, we've a sporting chance of retrieving a substantial number of gems with or without Drinkwater's cooperation.'

'And without upsetting the local gardening fraternity.'

'My God, Baxter. It'll be like offloading an albatross. You haven't seen the confidential memos from the Home Office. You've no idea how much damage those jewel thefts were inflicting on our image—on the image of every force in the region.'

'No, sir. I'm delighted, of course.' It occurred to Baxter for the first time that Drinkwater's activities had put the ACC's job on the line.

'To be frank, Baxter, you don't sound delighted.' His senior's atypical bluster had evaporated. 'Not—hm-hm—sickening for anything, I trust?'

'Nothing like that, sir. It's just that the murder case takes priority.'

'Hm-hm, naturally. When have I ever implied otherwise? Should have thought—hm-hm—that Drinkwater deserves promotion to the top of your suspect list?'

Baxter murmured emollient nothings and rang off as soon as he decently could. The more he recalled of Drinkwater, the harder he found it to cast him in the role of killer. In the last couple of days the case against his preferred candidate had strengthened, but he felt underequipped for a confrontation none the less.

He briefed Bill Armstrong and Wendy Powers on recent developments over coffee. Then he asked his sergeant what if anything the national police network had yielded on Aubrey King.

'Just this, sir.' Reproach tinged Wendy's voice as she fished the relevant printout from his in-tray.

King's name had been referred by the Department of Inland Revenue to the Fraud Squad in connection with suspected tax offences. 'Good, but not good enough.'

'Want me to ring them, sir?'

'No, thanks.' Instead he phoned Louis Mercier.

'If this is about Drinkwater, old son, you've punched the wrong button.' His friend didn't sound like a man with a long-awaited promotion in his grasp.

'Oh? Thought you'd be dancing on your desk by now. Nothing wrong, is there? You're not telling me Drinkwater's scarpered?'

'I'm telling you our big boys have taken him over. Top brass shall speak unto top brass. Your ACC'll hear what's what a damn sight sooner than yours truly.'

'Which is not to say he'll rush the story to me,' Baxter soothed. 'Wanted something else from you, actually. Something easy. Is there anyone I know on the Fraud Squad?'

'Des Charrington, late of Star Street. Mean bastard, as you'll remember.' Lou said it with a certain sour satisfaction.

Baxter sighed. 'I remember.' No point in pursuing that line. Not yet.

Wendy Powers approached as he rang off. 'Been thinking about Finchley, sir. Mind if I make a suggestion?'

CHAPTER 17

'Go ahead,' Baxter invited.

Powers resumed her seat beside Armstrong on the far side of the Chief Inspector's desk. 'If Valerie Gates told us the truth, it's likely that King had a profitable sideline in scientific espionage. That Finchley was supplying him with data from the Pacific pollution project and who knows what else. Agreed, sir?'

Baxter nodded.

'Data which King presumably sold to a commercial client,' Powers continued.

'Cutting Finchley in on the proceeds,' Armstrong added.

Powers shook her head. 'I'm not so sure. From what his wife said, Finchley isn't on the breadline. On the other hand, he's hooked on his job. And finance for research institutions is in short supply. Suppose his price for the deal was a big donation to the Parsingham?'

'And when King backed out he turned to more desperate remedies?' Baxter put in. 'And tried, if my hunch is right, to implicate Sinton in a false alibi. But why didn't he act sooner, assuming he'd nothing to do with the tricycle business?'

'How do we know he didn't use Vickery as his agent?' Armstrong objected.

Baxter shook his head. 'That pathetic old picklebrain? Won't wear it. Ten times riskier than doing the job himself. Your ball, Wendy.'

'Suppose he explored other avenues. Tried to persuade the University to keep the Parsingham afloat until he'd tapped new private sources. Suppose it wasn't until this month's Board meeting that he got the big turndown.'

'Nice, Wendy, but too many supposes,' Baxter replied. 'Want to try for some facts? Like a list of firms making grants to the Parsingham over the last five years, plus the sums donated. Stuff like that should be in the annual reports.'

'Where do I go for those? To the Institute?'

'No—too risky. Especially if Valerie took that sick leave we suggested. Try the City Reference Library—the *University Reporter* should have what you want. Follow up every company listed in *Who Owns Whom*.'

'For an associate or subsidiary in the decontamination business?'

'That would be neat,' Baxter agreed. 'But anything pharmaceutical will do. If you strike lucky, note the directors' names. *Kompass* should provide the needful. I'll take it from there. Oh, and dig out the University address and Department of Sir James Ogilvie-Walnutt, while you're at it.'

'Ogilvie-which?' Armstrong echoed, as Powers left the office.

'Walnutt, would you believe. Chairman of the Institute Board of Management. Time for us to shuffle the backlog, Bill.' So saying, Baxter upended his overflowing in-tray.

Fifteen minutes later he received a telephone briefing from an ebullient Assistant Chief Constable, who was about to leave for a meeting on the jewel thefts to be held in Scotland Yard. A high-level Inter-Force strategy meeting, Baxter learnt with some relief, where his presence would not be required.

Drinkwater, whether from greed or fear of retribution from his former fence, had so far admitted to only thirteen of the crimes. One object of those assembled would be to discuss ways and means of persuading him to come cleaner. Baxter didn't give much for their chances.

The thefts to which Drinkwater had confessed were those for which documentary evidence had been seized. They had all been committed on and after the day of the Newmarket 2,000 Guineas, where he claimed to have met Parsingham.

The dead man, according to Drinkwater, had provided temporary hiding-places for items stolen on or after the day of their meeting. He had buried all except the last—the Liver bird brooch—in person. Drinkwater had hoped that his knowledge of his clients' habits would enable him to escape attention, or, failing that, to provide a plausible excuse for his activities.

Drinkwater had assumed that the old man's motive was financial. The sum of £5,000 had been agreed in advance for cooperation in the period before his retirement—after which he would no longer be mobile—and was paid in four instalments. Drinkwater had heard Parsingham speak of his death, but not of suicide. He had supposed he was suffering from a terminal illness.

After a brief show of amnesia, Drinkwater had revealed the alpha-numerical code in which the locations of the buried pieces of jewellery had been noted. He had parted less reluctantly with his alibi for the estimated time of the murder. A drinks party at Henley. Some names and a couple of addresses were available and would be faxed through to the incident room. Baxter might wish to liaise with Thames Valley.

Armstrong, who had been sweating in the stuffy office, agreed to give the matter his personal attention. Baxter returned to his paper-pushing.

Fifteen tedious minutes later he was buzzed by the desk officer. Sister Immaculata would appreciate a few words. She was rather concerned about her mother.

It was a nuisance, as he had by this time used all available surfaces, including the two spare chairs, for separate subspecies of paperwork. All the same, recent events had revived his own anxieties about Eve Parsingham Wells. And he was concerned that her daughter should be concerned.

'Are you any nearer to finding Uncle Rupert's murderer, Chief Inspector?' she asked, as she perched on a hastily cleared chair, clasping sunburnt hands over her plump pinafored stomach. She looked much as she had looked yesterday in the crowded lobby, Baxter supposed. Same pinny, same crucifix, same sensible sandals, same-different shirt. But here in tête-à-tête she was far more intimidating. A reincarnation of the only other nuns who had asked him frank questions at close quarters. About his bowels mostly, and in hospital.

'We live in hope, Sister.' He realized too late that the reply might strike her as blasphemous.

'I want to get Mother away for a while. Partly because of Uncle Rupert. She's bearing up, but his death's been a sad blow, all the same.'

'Of course . . .'

'She's always had a short fuse, but I've never found her so irritable. Every little thing seems to upset her. At first, I thought it was just me. I remind her of Daddy, always have.'

'Oh?' Baxter tried in vain to visualize Eva's husband.

'Poor Daddy—her political gesture, you know. It's hard on a man being someone's political gesture. She hustled him off to fight in the Spanish Civil War, before her conversion to pacifism. Daddy hated it. Not the fighting so much as the intellectual snobbery. Imagine, a garage mechanic in the International Brigade among all those poets. Took him years to get over the humiliation. I'd never quite forgiven Mother before this visit. Sorry. Not your problem, of course.'

Baxter made understanding noises.

'But it isn't just me Mother's been snapping at. She's

been dreadfully rude to everyone except Damien. Including people like Cousin Esther and Dr Finchley who've gone out of their way to offer sympathy and help. I feel quite embarrassed to remember what she's said when I'm showering at Appletrees.'

'Showering?' Baxter echoed stupidly.

'Yes. Mother's electricity's been cut off for some time, because of the roof repairs, so the Finchleys insisted she used the washing facilities at Appletrees. Uncle Rupert's gas water-heater is somewhat erratic, I understand.'

'Are you planning to take your mother away for a holiday?'

'My rule doesn't permit, and anyhow I doubt whether it'd work out. But somewhat to my surprise, she's agreed to a month at a friend's cottage in Devon, which would allow time for roof repairs.'

'By Damien Ronson and Company?'

'Goodness, no. Damien's moving out today. We're employing professionals. I've made the arrangements, and Dr Finchley has volunteered to keep an eye on progress. He's actually offered more than once, it seems, to finance the repair out of his own pocket. But there'll be no need for that, if Mother controls her generous impulses. The bank made no difficulty about an advance.'

'When is she planning to leave?'

'At eleven on Monday, if you've no objection. I'd have liked it to be sooner, but she's anxious to keep an appointment with her solicitor. I'll travel up to Town with her and see her on to the West Country train at Paddington before returning to my community in Gloucestershire. I'll be back for Uncle Rupert's funeral. Mother says she'd rather not. Funerals don't mean much to her, not being a believer.'

'No problem about this from our end, Sister, provided you can let me have your address and hers.'

'Oh, thank God! Here you are, Chief Inspector.'

Surprised by the strength of the reaction, Baxter accepted a sheet of paper on which two addresses had already been written in a neat script. 'You said your uncle's death was one reason for your wanting to get your mother away, Sister. What was the other?'

The plump fingers laced. 'I fear she's at physical risk. Oh, not just because of the hole in the roof. This business of the bicycle—'

'But Vickery's dead . . .'

'I know. But since Damien's been cleared, Mother's been chatting about it to all and sundry. And Damien's bound to talk. Sell the story to a paper, perhaps. I'm so afraid—so is Dr Finchley—that one of the other unstable youngsters Mother got involved with may attempt something similar.'

'There'll be more houseguests, I imagine?'

'No. We've had some straight talking on the subject. Genuine cooperatives are fine. You might say I live in one. But Plumtrees was never like that. When Cousin Esther and her friends told Mother the kids were exploiting her—I've heard them often—she took no notice. When I told her she'd been exploiting *them*, it seemed to make an impact.'

Sister Immaculata allowed herself a brief self-congratulatory smile. 'I suggested she should give up her rights in Plumtrees and move into a small flat. I suppose it would mean varying Grandfather's trust, but I should think the University would be delighted to get its hands on the property. Mother took to the idea quite quickly—had been thinking on similar lines herself, she said. Agreed to raise the matter with her solicitor on Monday.'

'Thus putting your mind at rest?' And Finchley's, Baxter added mentally.

Sister Immaculata shook her neatly cropped head.

'Not quite, Chief Inspector. I've another anxiety I'd like to share. I've been helping Mother sort through her belongings. Not that she's much left of value—her houseguests saw to that. But some of the junk that was moved out of the attic when the roof was damaged could fetch good prices in a charity shop.

'Yesterday I was going through an old cabin trunk when I found the holster for Grandpa's service revolver—he'd fought in the First World War, smuggled it home as a souvenir. He showed it to me when I was seven or so, and I'm ashamed to say I was quite impressed. Mother walked in on the conversation—protested loudly. She was an ardent pacifist by then. She wanted Grandfather to get rid of the thing, but he wouldn't hear of it. Hid it where he thought she wouldn't find it, I imagine.

'Yesterday, when I asked Mother if she'd thrown the gun out, she said yes. But I was surprised she hadn't got rid of the holster. And she was so flustered, so self-contradictory about the circumstances when I pressed her, that I felt sure she was lying. I was convinced it had been stolen.'

'Why should your mother lie about that?'

'For the reason that led her to hush up the trike business. To protect her little stray lambs—regardless of the suffering one of them might inflict.'

'You may well be right, Sister,' Baxter said. 'I'll ask your mother to let us have the holster—there could be identifying marks. But my guess is that the revolver, if stolen, was stolen for financial gain. Collectors will pay well for pieces of that vintage, but you'd go a long way to find suitable cartridges in usable condition.'

And yet, and yet. As he ushered out the nun, visibly reassured, the Chief Inspector was uneasy.

Twenty minutes later he and Armstrong were about to abandon paperwork for the cafeteria when Powers rejoined them.

Baxter, whose stomach made trouble without regular

relining, proposed a working lunch. The cafeteria tables being too small to accommodate Powers's notebook and photocopies as well as one lasagne, one shepherd's pie and one Cornish pasty, she reported briefly from memory.

'I've been through the last five of the Institute's annual reports as printed in the *University Reporter*. Eighteen firms are named as donors of money or kind over that period, but some of the gifts were very trivial. Prizes, small pieces of equipment and so on.'

'Ignoring the tiddlers, how many firms with pharmaceutical interests?' Baxter asked.

'Three. First, Skysey Agrochemicals, who are heavily into fertilizers and foodstuffs. They've funded a research fellowship at the Parsingham, as has Findheim Firenze.'

'Implausible name,' Armstrong objected.

'But authentic.' Powers tapped her sheath of photocopies. 'FF are a Swiss-Italian conglomerate with a finger in many pies. But their sole pharmaceutical interest, from what I've checked, is in cosmetics.'

'Number three?'

'Bryce-Benson International. Mega-multinational with a clutch of pharmaceutical associates and subsidiaries. But the offshoot that caught my eye was Detoxicon, which is based in Munich and specializes in decontamination. More especially, marine decontamination.'

'That's it. That's got to be it!' Armstrong waved a gravy-dripping forkful of shepherd's pie over Baxter's lasagne.

'Too good to be coincidental,' Baxter agreed.

'Trouble is—' Powers cut open her Cornish pasty and inspected its contents—'trouble is, Bryce-Benson's contribution wasn't as generous as the other two. Five thousand a year to the Institute's equipment fund over the last three years. Would an ambitious director risk professional disgrace for that sort of money?'

'Still less, would he risk murder?' Armstrong added.

Baxter chewed thoughtfully before replying. 'It mayn't have been quite like that.'

'What's your theory, then?' Armstrong asked.

'Later. Nice work, Wendy. Write it up after lunch. But let me have your personnel list for the Bryce-Benson conglomerate right away, will you?'

Ten minutes later he rang DCI Charrington of the Metropolitan Fraud Squad.

'Keep this short, will you.' Charrington sounded as tetchy as ever. 'I'm parched, I'm hungry, I'm overdue for a briefing session.'

'OK. You're investigating Aubrey King at the instigation of the Inland Revenue. Right?'

'So?'

'I'm interested in his sources of undeclared income. Like to give me an overview?'

'High-level inquiry, old son, international ramifications. Not a squeak without a need-to-know from your CC.'

'Oh, come on, Des—'

'Go through channels. I don't make the effing rules, remember. And I can't afford to break them.'

'You can't afford to shoot yourself in the bloody foot either, can you? Listen, Des. You're in a hurry, I'm in a hurry. I'm not after something for nothing. It's give-a-little, take-a-little time.'

'So what are you giving?'

'Industrial espionage. How does that grab you?'

'Guesswork—intelligent guesswork.' Charrington's tone had changed, though. Baxter discerned curiosity behind the cynicism.

'OK, here's a name. Lord Bryce of Bryce-Benson. Am I right in thinking he did business with King?'

A long pause. 'I'm not saying he didn't. Best I can do, mate. Your turn to give. What's in it for me?'

'Something tomorrow, with luck, Des. Apply through the usual channels.'

The reply was the Charrington growl, sonorous and catarrhal, just as Baxter remembered it from his Met days. He rang off, chuckling.

Ten minutes later, as he wove his way among slow-moving clusters of tourists on the perimeter path in the First Court of Princes' College, Baxter was visited by doubts. Would Sir James Ogilvie-Walnutt, Professorial Fellow of Princes', Rhadegund Professor of Tropical Zoology, and Chairman of the Parsingham Institute, agree to see him without an appointment? Would he talk openly to a middle-ranking police officer with a Birmingham degree? Would he report his visit to Finchley?

The staircases were labelled in alphabetical sequence, starting at the Porters' Lodge, and in order to reach Ogilvie-Walnutt's stair, K, Baxter had to cover a side and a half of the square court. Had it not been for the bowler-hatted porter on traffic duty, he would have risked a diagonal short cut over the sacred turf reserved for the feet of Fellows and their escorted guests.

And, apparently, of Parsinghams. For just as Baxter passed the door labelled H, a bald, elderly man emerged from K, with a stern-faced Eve Parsingham Wells and an impassive Sister Immaculata in tow. Signalling to the porter, the don launched his guests on to the grass turf before scuttling back to base. Eve and her daughter set off at a smart trot, casting no glances in Baxter's direction.

Under cover of a trio of large Nordic tourists, he slipped up K staircase, and knocked at the worm-eaten linenfold door of K-3, Ogilvie-Walnutt's set of rooms on the first floor. The bald man answered.

He looked rather unwell, and the multicoloured shirt worn over shrunken cricketing flannels didn't flatter his beige complexion. The sight of the detective's ID didn't help either. But Ogilvie-Walnutt's 'Oh Lord!' was more resigned than astonished.

'You'd better come in, I suppose. Mind you don't step on the bones.'

CHAPTER 18

'Duck-billed dinosaur—just a baby. Reconstructive palæontology is my vacation hobby.' Ogilvie-Walnutt explained as Baxter skirted the half-assembled skeleton that occupied most of the Professor's Turkey carpet.

'Very nice.'

'Fearfully and wonderfully made, isn't it?

Some call it Evolution
And others call it God.'

And Ogilvie-Walnutt's bedmaker might call it something else again, Baxter surmised, as he settled on the window-seat. The Professor perched on a Regency library stool which he would have liked to examine in detail.

'No idea why you're here, Mr Baxter. No idea at all.' Ogilvie-Walnutt glanced uneasily at the ancient bones as though they had been dishonestly come by.

'Would it surprise you to know my visit concerned the Parsingham Institute?'

The faintest gasp. Then: 'Yes. Of course it would. The Parsingham is a University institution. I'm not in the habit of discussing University business with police officers.'

'Nor with Mrs Parsingham Wells?'

The Professor stiffened. 'You saw Eve leave just now, I suppose? Known her all my life—we discuss all sorts of things. Her great-grandfather was a Princes' man, you know, likewise her grandfather and late brother.'

'Whose death I am investigating.'

'Ah yes. Dreadful business. Poor Rupert. Intellectually undistinguished, but a lovely man for all that. Hard to believe anyone would want to murder him. Can you be sure—can you really be sure?'

'I'm afraid we can. It's in that connection that I want to ask you some questions about the Parsingham Institute.'

Ogilvie-Walnutt nodded, twisted his signet ring, his beige complexion fading to putty.

'Can I have your word, Sir James, that you will regard this interview as strictly confidential?'

'In the ordinary way, I should wish to make the Director privy to anything concerning the Institute.'

'The situation is extraordinary. Do I have your word?'

Ogilvie-Walnutt checked on the wellbeing of his ten stubby fingers before replying. 'Very well. Fire away. Mind you, I shan't promise to answer every question you may put.'

Baxter, who had expected tougher resistance, tried not to show his surprise.

'I should like to ask you about the Institute's dealings with Lord Bryce, Chairman of Bryce-Benson International.'

Ogilvie-Walnutt flushed muddily. 'That's all on record. Bryce-Benson was one of our benefactors.'

'Was?'

'Three-and-a-half years ago the company announced its intention of donating £5000 per annum to the Institute's equipment fund for a period of three years. The final payment was made last April.'

'But there were hopes, were there not, of something considerably more substantial?'

'I decline to answer.'

'Please, Sir James.'

'To do so would be to break my word—I see no reason for that.'

Baxter eyed the skeleton and plunged, as if into a primæval marsh. 'I must tell you that Lord Bryce is under suspicion of involvement in scientific espionage. That he very probably hired an agent to secure client-confidential data from the Parsingham for the benefit of his subsidiaries.'

'Oh my God. Did Rupert find out about this?'

'A part if not the whole. Enough, perhaps, to endanger his life.'

'Dreadful.' Ogilvie-Walnutt shook his bald head. 'Quite dreadful.'

'So I'd like you to think again, Sir James. My information suggests that two or three years ago Bryce tempted his Parsingham informant with a very attractive bait, which he withdrew this summer. Why, we've yet to establish. What was that bait?'

'You're asking *me*?' Ogilvie-Walnutt boomed. 'This is my second term as Chairman of the Board of Management. A voluntary and an unpaid post, you understand.'

'But highly regarded, no doubt.'

'Status has never meant much to me, Chief Inspector. Integrity has. Are you seriously implying that, committed as I am to the Institute's welfare, I was party to a deal that would impugn its moral reputation and my own?'

'No. I assumed the strings on the offer were tucked away where you couldn't see them. But I think all the same that the offer had to be made to you and by Bryce in person if our mole was to be persuaded it wasn't his linkman's invention.'

Ogilvie-Walnutt stared. 'Can you name the linkman?'

This was more, far more than Baxter had intended to risk. He braced himself for a second plunge. 'Off the record and confidentially?'

'Yes.'

'Aubrey King, the TV producer.'

'How sad . . . So rare, so often underrated, the talent to make science come alive. Bernal had it, Bruner and Bronowski. So had King. My grandchildren are hooked on his current series. Tell me, who was his informant?'

'I can't. Not yet.'

'In that case, I'm afraid—'

'I must ask you to trust me, Sir James. And to remember that my prime concern is a murder.'

The zoologist sighed. 'Very well. I've known Bryce slightly for almost a decade, mostly from dreary, hand-wringing conferences on the interfaces between industry and higher education. Our paths crossed at one such event about eighteen months ago. It had quite slipped my mind that he was a Parsingham benefactor—fund-raising's not really my thing. Bryce went out of his way to remind me of the fact. He went on to enthuse about the flattering reports his "spies" had given him of the Institute. Actually used the hackneyed term. Bloody cheeky, when you think of it.' Ogilvie-Walnutt thought about it for several seconds.

'Then he came out with his offer, which was for a sum sufficient to guarantee the Director's salary for a period of seven years. Been twisting his acountants' arms, he said. Money was in the pipeline. A cert, in any circumstance he could foresee. But other commitments took priority, so it wouldn't be available for a couple of years yet—i.e. next spring. His accountants wouldn't allow him to put an advance statement of intent in writing. He was sure my Board and I would understand.'

'You confided in them and the Director?'

'Orally, yes. Bryce had encouraged me to do so.'

'He would,' Baxter said dourly. 'When did he back out?'

'I'd had a sabbatical last Easter Term, delegated all my Cambridge commitments. When I returned to my Department in early July, my secretary reported that Bryce had made several attempts to get in touch. When I did he told me the deteriorating economic climate had forced him to postpone his offer indefinitely.'

'You'd no cause to doubt his reason?'

'Why should I? The recession is a fact of life. Other sponsors were telling us much the same. The financial outlook for the Institute was so grim that I decided to chair the July Board meeting in person, although I was—am still—officially on leave. A traumatic occasion.'

'So Mrs Parsingham Wells's recent gesture must have come as a great relief.'

'You have me at a disadvantage, Chief Inspector.' The beige face went blank.

'Sister Immaculata has given me to understand that Mrs Parsingham Wells plans to see her solicitor on Monday morning. I presume she has just told you what she proposes to discuss with him. That she wishes to waive her interest in the property held in trust for her so that it can be handed over to the Institute.'

'No—no, Chief Inspector. Quite the contrary. Sister Immaculata's got the wrong end of the stick—was given it, perhaps. My conversation with Eve was in private. Her daughter waited in the next room.'

'Then perhaps you could put me right?'

Ogilvie-Walnutt hesitated.

'May I remind you again, Sir James, that I'm investigating a murder. Another life could be in danger.'

The zoologist shivered. 'Eve's?'

'It's not impossible.'

'Very well, then.'

'Dr Finchley's not here, I'm afraid.' It being a Saturday afternoon, Baxter and Armstrong had found the front door of the Parsingham Institute locked against casual visitors.

It surprised the Chief Inspector a little that the receptionist was present to answer it.

'You're quite sure? When I rang him at home, his housekeeper gave me to understand—'

'He *was* here,' the receptionist conceded, shifting peppermint toffee from the right side of her mouth to the left. 'Only two or three minutes since he left. Wonder you didn't pass him. But you wouldn't, I suppose, on account of the one-way system.'

'Ask him to ring me as soon as he returns. It's urgent.' Baxter scribbled the number of the incident room on a card.

The receptionist pursed iridescent mauve lips and consulted her wristwatch. 'Mightn't be back before I left, he said. I'm doing a spot of overtime to help with the typing, you see, with Mrs Gates being off.' Baxter was relieved to hear that Valerie had accepted his advice to take leave.

'Did Dr Finchley tell you where he'd gone? Leave a contact number?'

She shook her head.

'Hazard a guess?'

'Sorry. Not as though I'm his secretary, is it? Might have gone somewhere to meet Mr Sinton, I suppose?'

'Sinton?' Baxter echoed, his skin prickling.

'Last phone call I put through was from a Clive Sinton. Dr Finchley left immediately after that.'

'Just one more. How about the Romanian elevator lady? She's sixtyish and her feet hurt.'

'N-O, Stacey. Absolutely, no. Read her yourself.' Emma Baxter scowled at her friend across Julian Otley's kitchen table. 'Four New York accents I can't do properly are more than enough. I haven't a clue what West Side Romanian sounds like.'

'Forget her goddamn accent, concentrate on her feet. Oh,

come on, Em. I don't know whether I'm writing garbage or not till I hear someone else reading it.'

The phone rang. Stacey answered. 'You're off the hook for a couple of minutes. It's your mother.' She handed Emma the receiver.

'Sorry if I'm interrupting, darling. Rang Paul's flat first. No reply.'

'I've been here since after lunch and Paul's probably at Landers College. He'd a stack of books to return to the college library—told me he'd probably put in a couple of hours when he was there. Took your car, actually. You don't mind, do you?'

'Of course not. Thing is, though, Joy Butley's broken her ankle and I've had to take over her duty tonight. I've tried in vain to contact your father. So I'm sorry to be a drag, darling, but I'll have to beg back the Granada. Need it by six-thirty.'

'Sure, Mum. Want me to run it home?'

'And miss your last show? Thanks, but no need. Joy's son's got a Saturday job in Cambridge, and he normally buses. You remember Alex?'

'Scruffy little kid with a squint?'

'Scruffy six-footer with a squint. If you can get the car to Emmanuel Street by six, he'll gladly drive it here. I'll stand you your taxi fare home unless you decide to stay over. OK?'

'OK. Trust me, Mum. The National Health Service is safe in our hands.'

Emma rang Landers College Library. A whispered argument ensued before the undergraduate on weekend issue desk duty agreed to leave her post to search for Paul.

When he replied in the same library whisper, Emma passed on Sarah's message. 'Can you rendezvous with this Butley lad in Emmanuel Street?'

'I suppose.' Paul sounded unenthusiastic.

'But what?'

'It'll mean a detour home. Haven't got the car here.'

'Why the hell not—'

'Well, actually, I lent it to Dad.'

'You what?'

'OK, OK, Em. I'm sorry. Simply didn't occur—'

A background 'Shhh!'

'Where's Clive taken the car?' Emma asked coldly.

'Bet you what you like it's back in Mawson Road by now. Dad said he'd pop the keys through the letter-box when he returned it. He's been on a bookbuying spree. Wanted to shift his heavy gear from the hotel to a left-luggage locker at the station, save himself the hassle of finding a taxi first thing tomorrow morning.'

And the expense, Emma thought sourly. 'Huh!'

'Suppose you check at my flat,' Paul suggested. 'Ring you there in ten minutes.'

'Don't bother!' Emma slammed down the phone and picked up her cotton cardigan.

'Trouble?' Stacey asked.

'Clive Sinton trouble. Take-the-little-woman-for-granted trouble. Can I borrow your bike?'

'Yeah, sure. And don't say I didn't warn you. Anyone who's in cahoots with Eric Finchley—'

'We don't know that, Stacey. One phone message doesn't prove anything.'

But the notion niggled none the less as Emma cycled down Green Street.

There was no yellow Granada anywhere in Mawson Road. It would be a waste of time to wait for Paul's phone call, she decided. Instead, she cycled the short back-street route to the railway station. There was one H registration yellow Granada at the far corner of the station car park. Emma, who couldn't for the life of her remember the number of her mother's vehicle, pedalled over for a close inspection. The Ninja turtle inflatables and frisbees on the back seat didn't look like Sarah's playthings or Clive Sinton's.

Ten wasted minutes. Emma decided to make a circular tour of city pubs, but not before leaving a sharply worded note for Sinton at the reception desk of the University Arms Hotel. Accordingly, she cycled the humid length of Station Road and turned right into Hills Road and thickening rush-hour traffic. She was queuing at the traffic-lights at Gonville Place when she caught sight of a yellow Granada ten yards ahead. *The* yellow Granada. For that was without doubt the back of Clive Sinton's head. He carried no passengers.

Sinton had doubled his lead by the time the lights changed, but Emma managed to keep him in view throughout his stop-go progress down Regent Street and St Andrew's Street. A mandatory right-hand fork into Emmanuel Street freed the Granada from the preceding buses. When Emma followed suit, it was nowhere to be seen.

Casting a quick sideways glance into Drummer Street bus station, she chose Emmanuel Road as the likeliest available option. When she was circling the Seven Lamps roundabout, she saw that she'd guessed right. The Granada was making good speed between the rows of chestnut trees that overhung Victoria Avenue.

She lost it again before she made Victoria Bridge and Mitcham's Corner. Right or left, she asked herself as she pedalled up the hill. Left for Chesterton Lane and Appletrees. A possibility, if Stacey was right and Clive and Eric Finchley had some sort of association. But had they? Why should a Cambridge Establishment Man hobnob with a professional debunker?

Emma, sweating heavily now, turned left none the less. If, as seemed likely, she failed to find the Granada in the grounds of Appletrees, she could phone her mother from

Eve Parsingham Wells's house and advise her to make contingency transport plans.

Appletrees looked deserted, with its Venetian blinds shut against the sun, as Emma pushed her bike between the flowerless shrubs that lined the steep drive. But having followed the path to the back of the house she found a woman's cycle parked in a covered stand camouflaged by laurel bushes. And at a little distance a blue Volvo and a yellow Granada with a 'doctor on call' notice on its windscreen.

Emma retraced her steps to the front of the house and rang crossly. She was headachey now as well as hot and her nose was running. She honked into a tissue.

A small, pop-eyed woman carrying a feather duster answered more quickly than she had expected. 'Oh, thank God someone's come. Come in—do please come in.'

Standard greetings for her mother, Emma supposed. Drama she could at the present moment dispense with. Standing her ground beside a leonine doorscraper, she explained her mission.

'But I can't tell Mr Sinton nothing. Nor Dr Finchley. That's the point.'

'Sorry to be thick,' Emma said. 'But I'm not altogether with you. It's Emma Baxter, by the way.'

'June Oakes. Dr Finchley's housekeeper. Cleaning lady really, but the boss asked me to do a bit extra—get supper and that—while his wife's away. Wish to God she was here today. Clever lady. She'd have known what to do. Oh, dear. Perhaps, if you came inside, love . . .'

Emma followed her into the hall. It was cooler than she'd expected. Air-conditioned, she surmised from a background hum. 'Where can I find Dr Finchley?' she asked patiently.

'He's in his darkroom—he and the Sinton bloke. Locked in. Didn't want to be disturbed, the boss said.'

Emma's frustration yielded to curiosity. 'Been here before, this man Sinton?'

June deposited her feather duster on a console table. 'Not that I know of. Told me he'd an appointment, see, and the boss acted like he was expected. It was odd, though, the boss showing him into the darkroom.'

'Odd—why?'

'Never known him to let another soul in there. Mrs Finchley said he was worried about someone nicking his fancy cameras. Thought at first Sinton might be a salesman, might have photographic gear in that suitcase of his.'

'Sounds very likely,' Emma prevaricated. 'And I've no intention of interfering with any deals. So if you'll just show me—'

'No, wait.' As June Oakes fiddled with the top button of her shirt, Emma saw that she was goiterous. 'Couldn't have been more'n a minute, you see, before the lock clicked. I was dusting in the passage—couldn't help hearing. Funny, I thought. I mean, why bother locking themselves in, if they was just buying and selling? Then all the stuff they show on *Crimewatch* came back to me. Suppose this Sinton bloke is some kind of con man?'

'He is.' Emma had diagnosed hyperthyroidic emotionality. 'He's just conned someone into lending him my mother's car. She's a doctor. If I don't get it back to her quickly, her patients could be in deep trouble. Sorry to be blunt, Mrs Oakes, but you could be in deep trouble too unless you back off. Now, which is it to be? Do you show me to the darkroom or do I yell the house down?'

The housekeeper gripped Emma's arms. 'Shh. I'll show you. But please, *please* don't knock—not before you've had a little listen. Promise?'

Emma sighed and promised. June led the way along a corridor hung with oriental embroideries to the last of several mahogany doors. Emma applied her ear to the keyhole. She listened for almost a minute. Silence. Then a burst of dialogue, too muted to be comprehensible. The pattern repeated itself. She stood up.

'Doesn't sound right, does it?' June whispered.

Emma shook her head. She knew enough about the intonation patterns of English speech to be sure this was no mere business transaction. One man was very angry, the other very frightened.

June whispered again. 'Just suppose it wasn't cameras the Sinton bloke had in his suitcase. Suppose it was a gun.'

CHAPTER 19

Emma knocked. More silence, more mumblings.

Then: 'Later, June. I told you I didn't wish to be disturbed,' in a high, strained voice.

The two women backtracked along the corridor.

'Sounds scared, don't he?' June hissed. 'Like he was being threatened. Reckon we ought to phone the police?'

'Not yet,' Emma replied. She couldn't bring herself to believe that Clive Sinton was a killer. If he was putting the frighteners on Finchley, it must be his idea of a black joke. And she wanted to tell him in person how unfunny she had found his jokes these last few days. That he owed it to Paul to switch out of manic mode before tonight's family reunion. 'Is there another way into that room?' she asked. 'An open window?'

June shook her head. 'Boss won't allow it, not in summer. On account of the bees, you see.'

Emma didn't. 'Bloody hell.'

'There's the side door, of course.' June fumbled with a bunch of keys clipped to her waistband. 'Leads into a cloakroom off the darkroom. Boss lets me clean the cloakroom on Fridays.'

'Big deal. Let's have that key, then.'

June handed it over. 'No saying if you'll get any further, mind. Door between the cloakroom and lab's most probably locked.'

'Worth a try. Don't buzz the police or anyone else until I tell you.'

Would June comply? As she tiptoed among the tubs of dwarf conifers that surrounded the house, Emma didn't much care. She was in no mood to protect Sinton from a caution for harassment or whatever he was up to, always provided she'd got her own word in first.

The lock squeaked faintly as she let herself into the strip of a cloakroom, which had a boxed-off lavatory at one end. But the noise had probably been drowned out by the creaks, rustlings and conversation in the darkroom. She closed the outside door carefully and listened.

The door between cloakroom and darkroom was flimsy, badly fitting. There was a key in the lock, so she couldn't see anything. But she could hear what was said.

'Tell me about this one.' That was Sinton. But a new Sinton. No humour, no pretence of humour. Just cruelty.

'I can't . . . I swear I can't remember.'

'Try.'

'Seaside—I took it somewhere at the seaside.'

'That much is obvious, you bloody fool. There's sand, isn't there? There's sea. Whereabouts at the seaside?'

'I can't remember, I tell you.'

'Later then. What about this?'

'Dinner—Photographic Society dinner.'

'And the lady's name?'

'Mary—no, Marianne.'

'Marianne who?'

'Swear I can't remember.' Finchley was sobbing now.

'Does this help?' A dull clunk. The gun?

'No!' in a loud whimper. Praying that June would hear, would disobey her, Emma tried the handle of the darkroom door. It gave to her touch. She opened it, stepped inside.

'What the hell?' Clive Sinton was standing within a yard of her in front of a work-bench. His sallow face looked bloodless above his black cotton Polo. His right hand was twisted behind him as though holding something on the bench.

He's crazy, Emma thought. He's a full-blown psycho. This Cambridge visit has sent him over the edge. 'I've come for my mother's car keys,' she said quietly.

Sinton threw back his head and laughed. 'You look like an avenging bloody angel. All in good time, my love, but not quite yet. There's a queueing system.'

'Don't *my love* me, Clive. I want those keys and I want them now. If not, I'm going for help.'

'No!' Sinton's left hand gripped her shoulder. 'You're the one that's going to part with a key, Emma. The key of whatever door you came into this house by.'

'Why should I do that?' She stood very still, forcing a little smile as she mentally rehearsed her martial arts routine.

'Tell her why, Finchley.'

'The bees! The b-bloody bees.'

Sinton's right hand swung into Emma's field of vision. It held a string, from which dangled a jam-jar covered with some sort of metallic gauze. But the filter didn't stifle the buzzing.

'Do what he says, for Christ's sake.'

Emma looked for the first time at the man in the pink shirt who was seated on a lab stool further along the work-bench. At his slack, frightened face. At the several dozen faces of frightened women—in grey-and-white, sepia-and-white and full colour—that stared up from the bench in front of him.

Sickened, she handed Sinton the key. He backed out

through the cloakroom, jar in hand, to lock the side door.

'Tell me what all this is in aid of,' Emma said when he returned.

'Mrs Finchley for you, sir. Can you take the call? She rang earlier, she says.'

'Yes—yes. Put her through.'

'Glad I caught you this time round, Chief Inspector.'

'If you'd left a number . . .'

'I'd cold feet. Wasn't sure. I'm still not sure if what I'm going to tell you will do any good.'

'But?'

'But I rang Eve this morning. She told me what had been done to her trike. Said you knew who did it, and he was dead. Is that right?'

'Looks that way.'

'Worried me all the same, to think she was talking about it to all and sundry. That was why—' Dolores spoke very softly.

'Go on.'

'The first thing I want to say is . . . my husband has his problems. Problems I found it hard to come to terms with. But he's not a violent man. I can't believe he would have hurt Eve or Rupert. I've only ever heard him speak with loathing of one person—his stepsister. She died three years ago. In hospital. Cancer.' She paused as if to let the diagnosis sink in.

'I hear you. And the second thing?' Baxter prompted.

She sighed. 'I'm not sure I'd be prepared to testify to this in a lawcourt.'

'Like to hear it all the same.'

'Can't believe Eric was responsible for Rupert's death, but he might just know something. He visited Rupert on the evening he died.'

'When was this?'

'Shortly before six. I saw him go into the cottage, but he didn't know that. I was upstairs, rooting for my party dress in one of the spare rooms.'

'Did you see him come out again?'

'No. No, I didn't.'

The moment she rang off he keyed the number of the Parsingham Institute. No reply. The receptionist had presumably gone home. He tried Appletrees.

June Oakes answered. 'You again? Oh, thank God!'

'OK, OK, Mrs Oakes. Just tell me what's the matter. Take it easy. Take your time.'

'Time! There's no time. That Sinton's in the darkroom with the boss. He's a gun, I think. And the girl's in with them.'

'Girl?'

'Emma something. Sinton took her mother's car, she said.'

'Be with you right away.' It needn't be her, Baxter told himself as he buzzed Wendy. Mustn't.

'Enlighten her, Finchley.' Sinton had locked the side door and pocketed the key. He clasped both hands round the jam-jar, holding it against his stomach. There were six or seven honeybees inside, plus some white stuff. Syrup, Emma supposed.

Finchley shook his head.

Sinton smiled. 'Make the effort. Emma's a policeman's daughter.'

'Why should that worry me? There's nothing here to interest the police.'

Which was quite possibly true. The women in those photographs that lay within Emma's field of vision were neither nude nor indecently posed. All they had in common were expressions of fear, ranging from terror to mild alarm.

'You're the lawbreaker, Sinton. Forcing yourself in here, intimidating me—'

'Your housekeeper will have phoned the police by now,' Emma cut in.

'Then time's precious, Finchley.' Sinton closed up on him, swinging the jam-jar gently, like a censer. 'Tell Emma why I'm doing what I'm doing.'

The other man cowered, shielding his face with his bent left arm. 'Don't, for God's sake.'

Emma considered making a grab for the jar, but held back for fear of breaking it.

'Tell her why.'

'How can I, Sinton? How do I know how your crazy mind works?'

'Tell her what I told you.' Clive set the jam-jar down on the bench.

Eric Finchley lowered his guard, and stared at the photographs, his lopsided mouth quivering. 'He said . . . he said he wanted me to feel what she had felt.'

'She?'

'Anne. My wife—my ex-wife. Show her.'

Finchley handed Emma a faded and blurry snapshot. She stared, more embarrassed than frightened now, at a girl in a baby-doll nightdress with long, fair hair. She was sitting on the edge of a bunk bed in what looked to be the cabin of a boat or a caravan. Behind her were posters and a bookshelf. Her face was so badly focused that its expression was unreadable.

'I didn't hurt her. You're the one . . . Didn't touch her, even. I swear I didn't touch any of them. I never wanted . . .' Finchley was saying.

'You threatened her with a knife. Her and how many others?'

'Three—only three, I swear. Anne was the last. Threats never worked well. All the others are candid camera stills and video clips. Anne wasn't taken in. She knew I was bluffing. Ask her . . .'

'Crap.' But Finchley had hit home all the same. Emma felt sure of it.

The Director shifted in his seat. 'Listen, I need . . . I need to use the loo.'

Sinton jerked his head. 'Don't be too long or too noisy.' When he had shut the lavatory door behind him, Sinton sat down and Emma followed suit.

'You think I'm the pits, don't you?'

'I've nothing to say to you, Clive, till you set them free.' She indicated the bees.

He shrugged. 'As you like. Served their purpose.'

She watched him go through the cloakroom and side door. He deposited the jam-jar at the side of a brick path and loosened its cover. The bees rose crossly, confusedly into the humid air.

When he came back, Sinton added Anne's photograph to a wallet which already contained its negative. 'I'll give her these tonight. She's a right . . .'

'Will she want them after all these years?'

He shrugged. 'Her right to decide.'

'Will you tell her how you put the screws on Finchley?'

He flushed. 'No. Will you?'

'I'm not sure. It was horrible. Sick. And it's not enough to say it wasn't as bad as these.' Among the photographs, Emma had noticed several of Dolores in traditional costume. Clips from the video of a Filipino folk dance, perhaps. Systematically biased clips. *Then all smiles stopped together.*

'Tell me, Clive,' she said. 'What did Finchley mean when he said you were the one who hurt your wife?'

He grimaced. 'Anne did waitressing at various colleges when she was studying at the Tech. After the caravan incident I made her promise never to go back to Princes'—Finchley's college at that time. He was a Junior Research Fellow.'

'She knew it was Finchley who'd photographed her?'

'No. She'd known him only by sight at College, and he wore a mask for the break-in. But I knew when she imitated the first sentence he spoke: "Fond of reading, are we?" She got Eric's half-rolled r and his sneering emphasis on the *read* to perfection. And I couldn't tell her. I was too bloody ashamed to tell her.'

'Ashamed?'

'Explain later. Upshot was that I shot Anne some shitty line about the Princes' Clerk of Works reporting me to my foreman for timewasting. Said I'd been laid off the contract as a result. She didn't think that was good reason for her to chuck in an evening job there at time-and-a-half plus bonus.

'Heard from a third party that she was still working at Princes' now and then. There was a Parsingham occasion the evening I found out. Annual lecture or something, with a feast to follow. Old Rupert and Finchley were among those at High Table where Anne was serving. I marched into the hall and yanked her out. Hurt and humiliated her.

'I meant to talk to Rupert about it on Tuesday night, to justify myself.' Sinton passed a hand over his mouth as if unsaying the words.

'Could you have, if you'd had the chance?' Emma asked.

The lavatory door clicked. Finchley came back into the darkroom.

Sinton shook his head. 'Not then. Not without the intervention of my friend here. Which wasn't intended as therapy, I suspect. Show the lady a candid camera shot of me, old boy.'

Finchley stared. 'You're out of your mind.'

'Humour me.'

It was in black-and-white. An eight-by-ten blow-up. There was a panelled room, a wall lined with books. A boy with shaggy hair in sweatshirt and jeans who might have been a lefty student except for his hands, which were scarred and chalky. The right hand was reaching for a book.

'Geddit, Emma?' Sinton prompted.

She glanced at the boy's profile and then at Sinton's. 'Yourself when young?'

'In our friend's room at Princes'— sorry, Finchley—his *set* of rooms. Didn't bother me that the bedroom door was ajar that day. Usually was. I'd been working on his side of the court, you see. Repairing the ashlar work. Stage one in face masonry. Never made it to stage two. No matter. Gave me plenty of time to observe Academic Man. Stimulated the imagination, you might say.

'Got to know Finchley's little ways. Went to Hall for lunch from five to one till five to two regular as clockwork, didn't you? So how was I to know you'd taken to doubling back when I was in the Portakabin scoffing my sarnies?'

Emma turned to Finchley. 'You spied on him? You took those pictures?'

'As evidence for the police—I'd every right to protect my books.'

'Books your uncle bought, Eric. That to judge by the dust you'd never read.'

'If that were true, which it's not, it would be irrelevant. Tell her about your next visit, Sinton. Tell her how you cringed and crawled. Swore you'd pack in your job on the Princes' contract right away if I didn't turn you in to the police.'

'And you didn't? Why didn't you?' Emma asked Finchley. She thought she'd heard something outside the side door. Scufflings? A whisper? Neither of the men appeared to have noticed.

It was Sinton who answered. 'Like a fool, I'd told him I was desperate my wife shouldn't find out. You'd seen me around the place with Anne, hadn't you, Finchley? Fancied her? And you thought it would be safe to get back at me through her. The "Fond of reading?" reprise was deliberate, wasn't it? You knew she'd repeat it to me. Knew I'd rumble you, but that I wouldn't dare point the finger.'

'That's a lie.' Finchley's mouth twisted.

'It's the truth. The bloody truth that destroyed my marriage.'

'Really? On the evidence of your macho act in Hall, I'd have guessed that temper was the major factor.'

Emma turned back to Sinton. 'Your ex-wife paid twice over for your guilt feelings, didn't she? In the caravan and in Hall.'

Sinton nodded. 'I suppose.'

'And you never told her?'

'Never plucked up courage. Bloody stupid, that. Tonight I just might, though. Our friend here showed me how stupid I'd been when he proposed his trade-in the other day.'

'Trade-in? There was no trade-in. He's fantasizing.'

'What big words you use, Mr Wolf. Believe it or not, Emma, I'm here today because our friend promised to hand over these old pics.'

'For a price?'

'Oh yes. The price was an alibi. An alibi for Rupert Parsingham's murder.'

'My God.'

'Concentrates the mind wonderfully, murder. Forces you to revise your priorities. No, you don't, Finchley!' He lunged to wrest a matchbox from the other man's hands.

'Lies—it's all lies.'

'My son took your phone message,' Sinton said.

'Stacey Caldwell recognized your number on the note,' Emma added.

A loud knock at the side door. 'Police!'

'Sounds like your dad, Emma. Best not wind him up, eh?' Sinton dug in the hip pocket of his shorts and tossed her the house and car keys.

She hurried to the door.

CHAPTER 20

Baxter and Wendy Powers faced Finchley across one of the work-benches. Clive Sinton had left in a police car to make a revised statement at District HQ. Emma had promised to call there after delivering her mother's Granada.

'You know what Sinton's going to say, don't you?' Baxter began.

Finchley shrugged.

'I think he's going to talk about blackmail, don't you? Not a pretty word.'

'It never happened. Sinton's lying.'

'You rang him on Thursday, he said. My daughter and her friend heard his son give him your message.'

'All right—I rang him, for old time's sake. I'd seen him in the swimming-pool on Tuesday evening, half-recognized him. It wasn't until I read a piece about *Spin City* in the *News* the next day that I knew he was Paul Sinton's father. And on a trip to Cambridge. It seemed like an opportunity to heal old wounds.'

'And to reminisce about old photographs?'

'That was Sinton's doing. Ask your daughter. He forced himself in here. Threatened me—'

'With a weapon?'

'With a jam-jar full of bees. I see that amuses you, Sergeant.'

Wendy flushed. 'Sorry, I didn't—'

'Ever been poisoned, Sergeant? Badly? Ever had a serious bout of asthma or giddiness? No? Add the lot together, multiply by ten and you'll have some idea of what bees do to me before I pass out. Sinton knew. Imagination's his business, isn't it? Anne must have told him about the allergy. There were flowers in the caravan that night. Something buzzing. That's why I left in a hurry, why the picture was spoilt.'

Baxter was puzzled, but this was no time to pursue irrelevant hares. 'According to what you told DS Powers, you returned home around five last Tuesday. Spoke to your wife, changed and showered. Left on your bicycle at about five-forty, spent the hour between five forty-five and six forty-five in Parkside swimming-pool. Right?'

'Right. And what's more, Sinton knows it's right. He was in the pool when I arrived.'

'I must ask you to think again, Dr Finchley. We've evidence to the contrary from the landlord of the Signal Box and one of his customers.' No need to rely on Emma's testimony, thank God.

'I—really? I slipped in here for a bit—may have got my departure time a few minutes wrong.'

'More than that, according to our evidence.'

'Yes? Well—what does it matter, for Christ's sake?' Finchley blustered. 'I'd other things on my mind—have. Professional concerns. This nitpicking is such a waste of time, so unnecessary.'

'You've made it necessary, Dr Finchley. You talked to Mrs Parsingham Wells on Wednesday morning, didn't you? Learnt from her that her brother had had his five o'clock tea and cleared up before he died. Realized that it would be desirable to have an alibi from five-forty onwards—'

'No! It wasn't like that.' Finchley ran a finger inside his shirt-collar. 'It's bloody embarrassing, actually. Dolly was upstairs having her bath when I called out that I was leaving. To be honest, I came in here. For how long, I'm not sure. This isn't something I want to come out in court—so distressing for Dolly, so humiliating.'

'And damaging for your career prospects?'

Finchley nodded. 'I shan't deny it. I—I needed to be here, you see. It had been a rough day at work. You wouldn't understand—you don't have to understand, Chief Inspector.'

No, thank God. But Finchley was determined that he should listen. 'It started when I was twelve or so, when my stepsister Laura was bullying me, teasing me. She was fifteen then. A big girl, attractive. She could twist my stepfather round her little finger—almost. She wasn't able to stop his remarriage and she never came to terms with it. No one listened when I complained about her, so I gave up complaining. The worst sting reaction I ever had was Laura's doing. At a picnic, she . . .' His voice broke. 'Sorry. Even after all these years, I can't bear to think of it.'

'There's no need—' Baxter tried in vain to stem the flow.

'It was in hospital afterwards, looking at a picture like this in someone else's holiday brochure—' Finchley pointed to a shot of an O-mouthed, goosepimpled teenager leaping into turquoise waves. 'That's when I found my way of getting my own back. I used cuttings at first, before I went into photography. They're all her underneath, you see. They're all Laura.' Flushed now, and sweating, he shoved the prints aside, out of his sight.

But Laura had won in the long run. She'd hung in to obsess him. Poor bastard. Poor disgusting bastard. And also, very likely, a murderer. 'We're not here to plumb the depths of your fantasy life,' Baxter said crisply. 'We're investigating Rupert Parsingham's death.'

'But I've told you—'

'Not quite everything. Not why you visited Mr Parsingham on Tuesday evening.' Finchley's head jerked back briefly, then steadied. 'Or why you concealed the fact from DS Powers.'

'It's a lie . . . fabrication.'

'I must warn you . . .' Baxter administered the formal

caution. 'You were seen going into the cottage, Dr Finchley, but not coming out.'

A shake of the heavy head.

'Let me help. You'd had a rough day, you said. More specifically, I'd guess, a rough Board meeting.'

'Nothing to do with the case.'

'No? According to our information the announcement of the Bryce-Benson back-off hit the Chairman and his colleagues pretty hard. You'd seen it coming as long as last May, hadn't you? That night in the Ruffled Feathers—'

'Aubrey King.' The pale eyes widened. 'What's Aubrey been saying?'

'Lots—or he will, soon as the Fraud Squad sink their teeth in. From what I hear, King would ditch any dirt anywhere to further his interests.'

Tears gathered in Finchley's eyes. 'The glitterati circuit . . . money. I didn't need things like that. Anything I did I did for the Institute. And her.'

'Her?'

'My mother.'

His stepsister . . . his mother. Was his wife a poor third or nowhere, Baxter asked himself.

'Don't judge me by these.' Finchley gestured towards the photographs. 'Mother had no idea. She always wanted the best for me. That's why she remarried—to give me a good schooling, a good start. When my stepfather died, it was almost the way it had been. She was so proud the first time I showed her over the Institute, soon after I became Director. She died soon after, but I always think of it as her place. The place where I can be the son she wanted, where I can still talk to her. That matters to me, don't you see? That matters more than anything else in the world. I couldn't let it go without a struggle.' He blew his nose.

'Detoxicon,' Baxter said quietly. 'You passed Otley's Pacific pollution data to Detoxicon?'

The soft mouth opened and closed soundlessly.

'It's too late, Finchley. I've spoken to Sir James.'

Tears welled up in his pale eyes. 'All right. It didn't come off, but I'm not ashamed of trying. What difference will it make in the long run? What chance does a Third World scratch team stand against the multinationals?'

'Less, because of you and the likes of you,' Wendy Powers muttered.

Finchley made a despairing gesture, let the tears trickle down the furrows of his slack face.

'Rupert and his sister were your last chance, weren't they?' Baxter prompted. 'With them out of the way, the trust capital and property—'

'No. I never thought like that, never allowed myself . . . Besides, it wasn't necessary. Plumtrees is too much for those two old people to manage—has been for years. The sensible thing would be for them to relinquish their rights in favour of the University. In exchange for an inflation-proofed annuity which I'd have been glad to supplement from my own pocket. Discreetly, of course.'

Finchley allowed himself a wry self-congratulatory smile, as if denying his dealings with King and the implications of their exposure.

'Of course. But you'd put this proposal to Mrs Parsingham Wells, hadn't you, and had it rejected?'

At that time, yes.' Again, the smug smile. So Eve, that downy old bird, had fooled Finchley as she had fooled her daughter. 'It occurred to me on Tuesday evening that an approach to Rupert might yield fruit. That he might be able to persuade his sister.'

'An unlikely scenario, surely, given their respective characters?' Baxter retorted.

Finchley shrugged and sighed. 'Rupert said he would speak to her. Perhaps he did. Perhaps that accounted for her change of tune.' A joyless smile, this time. The hopelessness of his situation had struck home. Even if—as he obviously believed—the Institute's future had been secured, his own career there was finished.

'What else did Mr Parsingham say?' Baxter asked.

'Oh, I don't know. Small talk.' The words came slowly now, painfully. 'I apologized for disregarding his notice and he said it was aimed at the partygoers. I asked him if his virus trouble had cleared up. He said he still felt rather tired. Then I spoke about the Institute's financial crisis, told him a major sponsor had backed off.'

'You didn't name names?'

'No. Rupert was discreet, but Eve isn't. I was afraid he'd pass Bryce's name to her. It could have prejudiced future relationships with the corporation if the episode had been publicized outside the Institute.'

'Did he speak of suicide?'

'No. But he wouldn't, I suppose. We were never what you would call close. Dolly—Dolores—knew him much better than I.'

There was no hint of jealousy in the statement.

'How long were you in the cottage?'

'What does it matter? What does any of this matter?'

'To us it does, Dr Finchley.'

A shrug. 'Fifteen minutes, perhaps. I put my case briefly, because Rupert was yawning a bit. I thought perhaps he was ready for a nap.'

'OK. You came back here. Did you speak to your wife?'

'No. The car was gone, so I assumed Dolly had used it to transport food to Plumtrees or to do last-minute shopping. She came back later, though. She was in the house when I left for the Parkside Pool.'

'When did she return?'

'No idea.'

'But surely you must have seen or heard the car?'

Finchley shook his head. 'Wouldn't have seen it from

here with the blinds drawn. As for hearing. Well, to be frank, when my mind's on other things—' He flushed, letting his eyes stray to the photographs.

'Did you speak to your wife after she returned?'

'No.'

'Then how—?'

'Heard her start up the washing-machine in the basement. That's when I looked at my watch, decided I'd better get going soon.'

Baxter had a sudden vision of clothes rotating in a washing-machine.

Dirty clothes—oily clothes?

'What time was this?' he asked.

'Six twenty-five. I remember checking. You're not suggesting that Dolly . . .? No, I'm sure she's not capable. Unless Rupert, unless he's tried . . .' The words trailed off helplessly.

'Notice your car as you left?'

'No, but I went out by the side door. And as you saw, the turning space and garage are at the back.'

'Very well.' Baxter stood up.

'You've finished with me?' Finchley asked dully.

'Personally, yes. For the moment.' Baxter used his radio to summon the second pair of uniformed constables and to liaise with Armstrong. 'You've no objection, I take it, to providing my colleagues with a fuller account of your dealings with Mr King? There's a car waiting to run you to the police station.'

Finchley raised his large hands and let them fall. He got up awkwardly.

June Oakes had given up all pretence of dusting when Baxter and Powers joined her in the hall. 'Washing? Yes. Did a load yesterday morning.'

Baxter cursed silently.

'Anyone other than yourself been in there recently?'

'Since Mrs Finchley went to London? Only Mrs Parsingham Wells and Sister Imm—whatever she calls herself. Mrs PW has been showering and laundering here ever since the power was cut next door. Her poor old brother didn't have much in the way of mod. cons., I suppose. I bumped into her here yesterday lunch-time, as a matter of fact, on her way down to the utility room. Odd, really.'

'What was odd?'

'Oh, just that she didn't ring the doorbell. Mrs F. had given her a key so she could let herself in, but she and her daughter had always rung first, all the same, any time I was around. Didn't want me to come down with her yesterday. Bit short about it, but you make allowances, don't you, after a bereavement? I insisted on coming, of course.'

'To help carry her laundry bag?'

'Oh no. She didn't have a laundry bag. She was looking for a sock her daughter had left behind from her last load, she said. Horrible thick greyish things, Mrs PW wears. We searched all over. No joy. The old girl wasn't too put out. Said she'd have another look at home. That she'd lose her head next time round.'

Baxter edged towards the basement staircase.

'Mustn't witter, must I? Like me to show you the way?'

Baxter declined as politely as his growing excitement would allow.

'Right-oh. Straight ahead at the bottom. Can't miss it.'

Nor could they. The large utility room and two small cellars comprised the whole of the basement.

The washing-machine sparkled inside and out. So too the tumble-drier. Who'd use a tumble-drier in this heat? Unless . . . He squatted to inspect the filter. Unless they were in a hurry.

'See what I see?' He made way for Powers.

'Lint—some of it's blue.'

No sight or smell of oil, but he poked the filter out all the same. 'Wrap it up, will you, Wendy? And let's keep looking.'

'For a sock?'

'Anything but that, I fancy. Anything that looks out of place.'

Dodging between clothes-airers and an ironing-board, Baxter opened one of the roomy cupboards that lined two of the walls. Powers followed his example. The contents comprised cleaning equipment and detergents, large cooking receptacles and items of china which were presumably not in daily use.

It was in a copper fish-kettle that Powers found the revolver.

Baxter made a quick inspection. 'Webley Mark 4.'

'First World War vintage?'

'That's right.' He sniffed and squinted. 'Unloaded. No sign of recent use.'

'It's inconvenient. Tell them it's bloody inconvenient, Ginnie!' Eve Parsingham's protest resonated down the dusty front staircase of Plumtrees.

A murmured dialogue ensued. Sister Immaculata materialized, frowning, and descended. 'Could you possibly come back at another time, Chief Inspector? Mother suggests Monday at eleven, but perhaps tomorrow? She's really quite exhausted.'

'*Really?*' Baxter raised a quizzical eyebrow.

'Emotionally if not physically,' Immaculata amplified. 'It's taken its toll, sorting out Uncle Rupert's belongings.' She indicated two black polythene sacks just inside the front door.

Baxter read the labels. *Oxfam, Jumble Sale*. 'Clothes, I take it, Sister? All your uncle's?'

'Plus a few items of my mother's that she'd been meaning to dispose of.'

'All washed or drycleaned, I presume?'

'Naturally!' Immaculata bridled, clutching her crucifix. A pious alternative, perhaps, for counting ten backwards? 'What's this all about, may I ask? Why the cross-examination?'

'I've reason to believe one or both sacks may contain items relevant to our investigation. I propose to remove them for detailed examination.'

'I can't think what Mother . . . we understood from the Scenes of Crime officer that the police had no further interest—'

'Sorry, Sister. New circumstances have arisen. A careful inventory will be made. Meanwhile, there's a question I want to ask you. Have you used the washing-machine in Appletrees in the course of this visit?'

Her forehead puckered. 'Yes, I thought I'd already told you. Mother had *carte blanche*.'

'And the tumble-drier?'

'In this weather? Good gracious, no. I hung the spun clothes out for an hour or two before taking them back for ironing. But what possible interest—?'

'Sorry, Sister. Now I need to talk to your mother. Yes, now, I'm afraid. Would you ask whether she would prefer to see us upstairs or downstairs?'

Immaculata obeyed without further argument, asking them to wait in the large front room which Baxter had seen on his last visit. In her absence, he sent Powers to stow the sacks in the boot of his car. A minute or two after her return, Eve bustled in.

'I resent this, Chief Inspector. I resent it wholeheartedly.' Eve's chain-hung glasses glinted against her plaid house-coat as she threw herself into a tub-chair and fixed him with a Churchillian glare.

'I regret it, Mrs Parsingham Wells,' Baxter said soberly. 'But I've more questions to ask. You currently use the laundry facilities at Appletrees, I understand.'

Eve nodded.

'When did you last use them?'

'I—I—can't remember.' She clutched at her spectacles.

'Would it surprise you to know that you had been heard washing clothes last Tuesday? When Mrs Finchley was out shopping at the supermarket? We won't have difficulty in checking out her story, I imagine. Filipinas aren't thick on the Cambridge ground.'

'Possibly. I really can't—yes, I did a load last Tuesday.'

'In the midst of your party preparations?'

'Found out at the last minute that my caftan—only thing I had fit to wear—was grubby. Shoved in a few other garments as makeweights.'

'Did you use the tumble-drier?'

'No—yes, I believe so. Ecologically improper, but it saved me from ironing the caftan.' She made a business of polishing her glasses. 'Eric Finchley was snooping about, I take it? Reporting on the noises off? Well, if that's all—' She started to rise.

'Not quite. Why, for example, didn't you tell me about this sooner?'

'Slipped my mind. Effects of shock, I dare say. Don't they teach you people things like that?'

'Shall I tell you what I think? I think one or more of the garments you washed and dried is now bagged up for charity.'

'So what?' Eve clasped her hands tightly. To stop them shaking?

'The filter, if you please, Sergeant.'

Powers held it up, sheathed in polythene.

'I've a hunch the forensic scientists will be able to match fibres from this gunge with garments in your charity bags.

I've a hunch they'll find traces of petrol and or motor oil.'

'So what?' It came fainter this time.

'Let's talk about your sock, now.'

'Sock?' A barking laugh.

'The one you lost, remember? The one Mrs Oakes tried to help you find.' He signalled to Powers, who held up the revolver.

Eve thumped on the arm of her chair. 'Monday! Why couldn't you wait until Monday? Now you've buggered up everything.' She wept noisily, like an elderly toddler.

CHAPTER 21

'You'd hoped to defer this encounter until you were on your way to Devon, had you?' Baxter asked. 'Was it really to be Devon or somewhere farther afield?'

Eve lifted her chin. 'Neither. I agreed to the Devon scheme to shake off Ginnie—Immaculata. I'd every intention of leaving the train at Bishop's Stortford and doubling back. Seeing Harrison Garbutt is what mattered. Matters.' Her voice strengthened. 'Sorry, Chief Inspector. I've no intention of helping you further until I've spoken to Harrison.'

'Couldn't his brother Goronway serve your purpose? Or their partner?'

Eve snorted. 'That pair of twisters! Wouldn't trust either of them as far as I could throw them.'

'But presumably you've a higher opinion of Professor Ogilvie-Walnutt? I gather you showed him your hand this afternoon.'

'James passed on what I told him in confidence to you? To a policeman? I don't believe it. I refuse to believe it.'

'Correct me if he misled me, then. He told me you wished

to renounce your interest in the trust created by your father's will in favour of the University. You made a proviso, however. If your legal application succeeded, none of the capital thus released to finance tropical scientific studies was to be assigned to the Parsingham Institute.'

'James really did tell you all this? He'd no right—'

'I'd placed other facts before him. No doubt he felt grateful. He added that your wishes would be respected.'

'Oral assurances aren't enough. I confided in James as a precautionary measure—in case I was struck down by the proverbial bus. But I shan't be happy until I've conveyed my written directions to Harrison in person.'

'That could still be arranged,' Baxter said quietly.

She shot him a 'Promise?'

'I promise. Please put that on record, Sergeant.' Powers made a note.

Eve sighed. 'Very well.'

Baxter administered the caution.

She grimaced. 'Ginnie had a soft spot for her uncle. I'd rather she were miles away.'

'To learn from the media that you'd been arrested for his murder?'

'You won't let up, will you?'

'Not now.'

She grimaced. 'Better get it over quickly, then. Like brimstone and treacle. Which was before your time, I suspect?'

He nodded.

'Cure for hives, as I remember. Sulphurous taste stuck to the tongue for ages. Bear—Rupert—made a tremendous fuss about swallowing his. Made such a fuss about everything when it came to the bit. Even dying.'

'You were there?'

'You know I was there, doing what he'd asked me to do. Doing my duty. It was difficult. Bear made it so damn difficult.' Eve's brown eyes refilled with angry tears.

'You don't have to distress yourself,' Baxter said quietly. 'The facts will do.'

'No, they bloody well won't. I put them on paper on Wednesday night, actually, soon as I'd got Esther off the premises. Right-hand top drawer of my dressing-table, in case you're interested. Never intended to let anyone else take the rap, once you'd twigged it wasn't suicide. Hard to get one's motives into writing, though. So you two are going to hear them—you're damn well going to hear them.' Her eyes zigzagged between the detectives' faces.

'We'd a pact, Rupert and I, that we'd help each other end our lives if help was needed. An unlikely contingency in my case, total physical incapacity always excepted. But he was always the weaker vessel. Loathed boarding-school twice as much as I did, but I was the one who ran away. Three times,' she recalled with evident satisfaction.

'Rupert professed pacifism in nineteen-thirty-nine, which I could have respected if he'd gone to prison instead of signing up for the Ambulance Corps.'

'Let's talk about last Tuesday.' Baxter's ulcer was pricking. He helped himself to a sodamint.

Eve made no acknowledgement of the interruption. 'My brother reminded me of our pact the day he'd been warned that his driving licence wouldn't be renewed. He told me he wanted to die immediately his work at the Garden Centre ended. That he'd like to gas himself—and quickly—in his garage, where I would almost certainly be the first to find him. He added that the arthritis in his wrists was worse on some days than others, so he might need help in fixing a hose to the exhaust pipe.' Eve paused, blew her nose again.

'We argued. I was distressed. I wish you to understand that I was distressed. And angry. If he had been terminally ill . . . But giving up driving was such a little thing, which so many—myself included—have done voluntarily. From principle. But my poor dear brother was never what I would call a principled person. Mother and Father were away a great deal when he was small, you see. Grandfather was over-indulgent. Our suffragette aunt died too soon to be a major influence.'

Baxter cleared his throat.

Eve surveyed him with grim amusement. 'Patience, Chief Inspector. I am now proceeding in a forwardly direction. I was distressed, as I said, at the prospect of losing my brother for such a trivial reason. And angry when I thought of the causes crying out for supporters to which he could have put his talents. But having said my say, I gave in. We agreed that we wouldn't discuss the matter further, but that I'd honour our longstanding agreement. Do what he'd asked on the evening of his retirement.'

'Had he asked for that?' Baxter pointed to the revolver.

Eve's colour rose. 'Not in so many words—but he'd said: "Keep me to it, won't you, Pudding? Don't let me cop out." It seemed the best way. Grandfather took us duck-shooting in the Fens once or twice when we were kids. Rupert hated it—he was terrified of guns, even then.' Her voice broke.

'When I saw the notice on his door on Tuesday afternoon I took it as confirmation. Dolly Finchley was the only person who might have disregarded it, but I kept her busy with preparations for the garden-party.'

'An odd day for you to give a party.'

'I knew I'd need distraction, don't you see? I'd need it desperately. I asked Dolly to do some last-minute shopping for drink and nibbles that would entail a trip down-town and another to the Milton Tesco's and give me half an hour to play with. I felt sure she'd wait until after the rush-hour, which she did. I fiddled about in the garden, listening out for her. As soon as I heard her drive off, I took the revolver from the kitchen drawer where I'd temporarily stowed it.

'I felt worse, so much worse than I'd expected. I had to force myself to take every step. Rupert looked ghastly when he came to the door. He'd been off form for a couple of weeks, but I'd never seen him like that. Greyish.' Eve stared as if he had returned to her.

'He started to make difficulties the minute I was in the cottage. Said he still wanted to die, but he wasn't quite ready. He'd things to do—people to talk to. Couldn't we put it off for twenty-four hours?

'But I couldn't face that, don't you see?' Eve's plump hands fisted. 'Couldn't have gone through all that again, even if I believed he had good reason. Which I didn't. I thought—think—he was making excuses. So I brought out the pistol. It wasn't loaded—you'll have seen—'

'Not when we found it,' Baxter conceded.

'Not on Tuesday either. But Rupert never guessed. I told him that if he didn't keep his word I'd shoot him and then me. I asked him if he'd want Dolly to find us—that struck a chord.' There was a note of malice in the phrase.

'Didn't he attempt to disarm you?'

'Didn't dare, I imagine. I've always been fitter, though I was female and four years older. Besides, with his wrists and his eye-trouble . . . He caved in when I mentioned Dolly. Picked up a notepad for the suicide note. My suggestion. Went ahead of me into the garage.

'I'd plastic gloves on. I'd thought out beforehand what must be done to cover my tracks.'

'That was important to you?'

'Of course. As I've told you, I've views on voluntary assisted euthanasia—'

'*Voluntary*,' Powers echoed ironically.

'Which if Hardy came to Hardy, I'd have defended in court. But Deep Green takes priority, and there are limits to what one can contribute to a movement from behind bars. I'd thought everything through in detail. Rupert obeyed my suggestions silently, shakily. I told myself it was teaching him to swim all over again. Had to make light of it to myself, don't you see?'

Baxter thought of the frightened old man and grunted.

'He wrote the note from the driving-seat. I'd retreated to the door of the garage by then. Couldn't see which hand he was using, and it didn't occur to me to wonder. When he'd finished, I told him to switch on. He'd two things to ask of me first, he said. It was horrible, the way he said it. As if I were his executioner.'

'Which you were, weren't you?' Powers said so softly that Eve seemed not to hear.

'Rupert said Eric Finchley had called on him very recently. Pushed the line he'd tried on me and failed. The Institute was in desperate straits, Finchley had said. He'd found generous sponsors in the past—could find more, given time. But the University wouldn't give him time without an early and substantial cash injection. Rupert and I were his only hope.

'Rupert had agreed to raise the matter with me, but only to warn me. Finchley was unfit to be Director, he said. He should be sacked. I agreed. I'd always disliked the man. Dr Fell thing—the reason why I could not tell. Rupert was more specific—said Finchley had treated his staff abominably, that he had almost certainly used illicit methods to raise finance.'

'How'd your brother know this?'

'Through Stacey and Julian, I guessed. But Rupert wouldn't say, and I didn't ask. It didn't matter. If the Institute folded, the directorship was a non-issue. Didn't say a word to Rupert, but I'd taken soundings in the weeks since Finchley had approached me. I'd already decided the place had become an absurd anachronism, an insult to my great-grandfather's memory. He was a rebel, you know, a

Darwinian when Darwinism was a heresy. He looked to the future, as we must all look to the future!'

Baxter belched discreetly. It was an odd experience to be preached at by a murderer. 'Your brother had a second message, you said?'

'Said he'd stowed some cash savings in a desk drawer, which he'd intended to give to Dolores Finchley. He didn't mention a sum. A few hundreds, I suppose. I promised to see to it later, after the police had been. Never dreamt you people were going to turn the place upside down. Now I shan't be in a position . . . That money must go to Dolores the minute you've finished with it. I shall speak to Harrison.'

'In view of its likely origins, that may not be possible.'

'Origins? Explain yourself, Chief Inspector.'

To his surprise, he heard himself obeying. Eve's sombre face dissolved in laughter. 'The old slyboots. Might have let me in on it. Nice to think his last summer wasn't just doom and gloom, all the same.'

'You promised you'd see Mrs Finchley got the money. What then?' Baxter prompted.

Eve reverted with evident distress to the scene in the garage. 'Rupert made . . . made more difficulties. Repeated that he wanted to say goodbye to Dolores. I said better not, for both their sakes. I threatened to shoot myself. He switched on the ignition soon after that, started up the engine. I waited until the fumes were quite bad, four or five minutes, perhaps. I said: "'Night, Bear."

'Then I left, handling the lock as little as I could, so as not to spoil Rupert's prints. I listened outside for a little. Nothing but the engine. Hurried home to change, then took my bag of laundry to Appletrees. Ran it through a short cycle. Not long enough, but I didn't want Dolores to come back when I was unloading. In fact, she brought the booze straight back to Plumtrees.

'She was setting out chairs in the garden when I sneaked

back, so she didn't spot me or the laundry bag. Just told her I'd been bathing at her place. Everything would have worked out very well, you see, if it hadn't been for Inspector Armstrong. Except for the money, perhaps.'

'She might have found it an embarrassment.'

'Perhaps you're right. I've been unfair to Dolly at times, I admit. Bear had this thing about young women, ever since his young wife died. I thought Dolly was taking advantage. Didn't know about the OU course, until she told me over the phone the other day. Might do something academic myself, I suppose, in the slammer. Ecology perhaps . . . Time for us to be on the move, isn't it? But first I'll have to break the news to poor Ginnie.' She sighed.

'Unless you'd rather—'

'No, no. Buck stops here and all that. Who said that? Roosevelt? Eisenhower?'

At four o'clock next morning Baxter woke from a dream of Eve. Was she dreaming in her cell, he asked himself? As much to exorcize her image as from personal curiosity, he padded downstairs to his dining-room to consult the *Penguin Dictionary of Modern Quotations*.

So the proverbial buck had stopped with little old Harry S. Truman. Who'd have thought it? A man gone and almost forgotten. As Rupert Parsingham soon would be. But neither of them would vanish as completely as the anonymous maker of the miniature chest-of-drawers that awaited his daughter's descent.

He untied the fancy wrappings that Sarah had found for it and made a final inspection. The front curved sweetly, the crossbanding was finely wrought. The mahogany had been thoroughly waxed and buffed, as well it might. Jo Mercier's London overheads obliged her to charge her friends something approaching London prices. He lifted each drop handle in turn, and found spots of tarnish on the undersides of two of them. He went into the kitchen for brass polish. Retrieving it from a high shelf in the cleaning cupboard, he dislodged a squeegee mop with his sleeve and sent it clattering across the tiled floor.

A thump overhead. Bare feet padding on the stairs. 'OK, Sarah,' he yelled as he grabbed the mop, then remembered she was out on a call.

Emma was on the threshold in one of her oversize night-shirts, laughing. 'What's all this? Dad's Army drill?' As he stowed the squeegee, she caught sight of the tin of polish. 'Kit inspection? Got it bad, haven't you?'

'Looking for a light bulb,' Baxter fibbed. 'Bedside lamp's conked out. Sorry I woke you, love.'

'You didn't, I couldn't get over. Too much black coffee after supper, I suppose.'

'Uh-huh?' He retrieved the box of light bulbs. 'Weren't driving, were you?'

'No. Taxi at Mum's expense. Reckoned I owed it to Paul, though. Hard to say goodbye nicely if you're canned, don't you think?'

'You and he've split? Oh, I'm sorry.' Baxter absent-mindedly replaced the bulb box unopened.

'Me too, a smidgin. Well, more than a smidgin. Tough on Paul too, just when it looks like his parents might get something going again. Right decision to me, but you know how it is.'

'I know.'

'Mind if I talked about it for a bit, Dad, seeing as you're here?'

''Course not, Em. Take a pew. I'll make us—'

'Whisky and soda for me, thanks. Help myself from the sideboard. Can I tempt you?'

'Wait!'

But he was too late to intercept her dive into the dining-room.

'Oh, Dad! For me?' She was standing by the chest-of-drawers when he caught up with her.

'Happy birthday, Em.' He kissed her awkwardly. 'If you don't like it, you can have the cash. No problem.'

She opened each drawer in turn.

'Just because you wanted something as a kid doesn't mean you have to . . .' he gabbled. 'Don't think I'm trying to turn the clock back, trying to make up . . .' But half of him was, of course. He poured them both whiskys.

She hugged him when he came back. 'I love it. I want it. Truly. Only thing . . . You were going to polish it just now, weren't you?'

'Two of the handles. Little spots of verdigris underneath. There and there, see?'

'Thing is, darling. Way I'll be living in London, I'll do my best, but I can't promise to take such good care of it as you would. I can't even promise no one'll never put a beer-mug on it. OK?'

He swallowed. 'OK, love. You wanted to talk?' He handed her a glass.

'That'd be good.' She followed him back to the kitchen table. 'And afterwards, if you liked, you could tell me about that case of yours.'

That would be good too. He took his first sip of whisky.

THE END